PR

BECOMING MRS. CLAUS

"For those who've ever wondered, it turns out that Santa Claus isn't much different from you or me. Nor is the Claus family. In *Becoming Mrs. Claus*, P. Jo Anne Burgh's delightful follow-up to *State v. Claus*, she gives readers a family that, in its petty arguments, its stumblings, and its deep love for one another, we can all relate to. This is like no other Christmas story you have ever read, wonderfully imaginative, quite risqué, and, despite the elves and flying reindeer, so perfectly human. I guarantee that after you've read this book, you'll never see that jolly old elf in the same way again."

~ William Kent Krueger, award-winning author of
The River We Remember

"Burgh's characters live in the swirl of a magical existence blended with real life responsibilities. The result is a delightful concoction that's as heartwarming as best hot chocolate. *Becoming Mrs. Claus* is an everywoman treat."

~ Sophfronia Scott, author of *Wild, Beautiful and Free*

"I was swept away by this whirlwind of a tale. P. Jo Anne Burgh creates a rich world full of charming characters and magical settings that will have you turning pages late into the night. Grab a cup of cocoa and immerse yourself in this delightful story about the power of love, forgiveness, and believing in things that can only be felt with the heart."

~ Kiersten Schiffer, author of *The Playlist Diaries* series

BECOMING MRS. CLAUS

~~~~~~

P. Jo Anne Burgh

TUXEDO CAT PRESS
Glastonbury, Connecticut

Published by:
Tuxedo Cat Press
http://tuxedocatpress.com

ISBN: 978-1-7357157-3-5 (paperback)
ISBN: 978-1-7357157-4-2 (ebook)
Library of Congress Control Number 2023915522

Cover and interior design by Design for Writers
Author photograph by Christine Penney

To my mother,
who taught me to love books

CONTENTS

Book One

Choices

One

Fifteen years ago, when I was a second-year associate at the elite firm of McGooley, Rose & Swarthorn, I brought a client to this building for her deposition. Walking up its creaking stairs, I kept my expression professionally neutral, trying to disregard the stark contrast between MR&S's spacious downtown offices and this dilapidated rabbit warren of inadequate workspaces. The building's exterior was classic New England, but tired—white clapboard in need of fresh paint, chipped black shutters, lichen on the roof. Inside, worn industrial-grade carpet of indeterminate color covered the creaking stairs, and black scuff marks adorned the dingy walls. A sharp odor of old coffee emanated from the combination kitchenette/broom closet. Fluorescent lighting flickered. As the plaintiff's lawyer questioned my client about the accident, I could hear the occupant of the next office arguing with someone named Wesley who had apparently failed to pick the dog up from the groomer.

Back then, I'd have sworn I would never work in such a space. Yet here I was, because I needed a place to meet with clients, and this was the only option I could afford.

The walls of my cramped office still looked dull even though I'd repainted without telling the landlord. I covered them as best I could with framed photographs of local scenery: rolling Connecticut farmland, the Long Island Sound lapping at the shore, autumn color ablaze on Avon Mountain. My electric kettle sat atop the dented filing cabinet where I stored office supplies. The metal desk that came with the office was too bulky to move out, but I'd shoved it aside enough to make space for two client chairs in front of the desk. It was a good thing I didn't spend much time here, because a full day in the desk chair that came with the office left my back in spasms.

Today, a prospective client was coming in. Eddie Carlisle had contacted me through my new website about an employment matter. Mr. Carlisle was already seven minutes late, but I could cut him some slack. It wasn't as if I had dozens of other cases demanding my attention.

Twenty-three minutes after our scheduled appointment time, I heard a timid knock on the door. "Come in," I called, rising.

The door opened, and a short man with curly gray hair peeped in. "Um—Miss Riley?"

I held out my hand, smiling. "Come in, Mr. Carlisle. I'm Attorney Meg Riley."

He squinted at me. "I'm Eddie Carlisle," he said unnecessarily.

"Come in," I said for the third time. "Have a seat. Can I get you something to drink?"

"Um, no. Thanks," he added as if remembering his manners.

"Please sit down." I sat, and he did the same. "So, Mr. Carlisle, what can I do for you?" He was still squinting at me as if puzzling something out. "Mr. Carlisle?"

"Huh?"

"You said in your message that you needed help with an employment matter," I reminded him.

"Yeah, well, you see. . . ." His voice trailed off. He wasn't even trying to hide his curiosity now.

Shit. Not this again. I'd been through this particular scenario too many times over the past four months. "Mr. Carlisle," I said, my voice sharper now. "Do you have a legal problem I can help with?" The slight stress on *legal* seemed to get his attention at last.

"Yeah—I mean—well, my boss—she makes fun of me because I'm— well, you know—not tall." An understatement: I'm barely five-foot-four, but I could have sneezed down into Eddie Carlisle's thinning curls.

"What does she say?" Hoping against hope that this might be a real case after all. Employment discrimination, maybe. Hostile work environment. Punitive damages. Attorneys' fees.

"It's not *what* she says—it's *how* she says it."

"How she says what?"

"Well, like, for instance, I said I needed to talk to her, and she said she'd get back to me shortly. You know—*short*-ly."

Visions of a big juicy case faded like the morning mist. I'd have ended the meeting right there, but only two of my five open cases allowed me to demand a retainer and bill by the hour. The other three were personal injury contingency fee cases, which meant I wouldn't get paid until I recovered money for the client. Besides, the fact that this guy was hypersensitive about being vertically challenged didn't mean he didn't have a claim. So I pressed on.

"How tall is your boss?" I asked.

"She's, like, five-ten. She thinks she's so special just because she can reach the top shelf of the supply closet."

"Where did she go to college?"

"What's that got to do with anything?" He sounded uneasy.

"Wondering if maybe she played basketball." The University of Connecticut women's basketball team was legendary. If Mr. Carlisle's boss had played for Coach Geno Auriemma, no jury in this state would believe she could do anything wrong.

"Um, she got her associate's at one of the community colleges. Don't remember which one." His eyes were darting from side to side now.

One more try. "What else has she done to harass you? Besides how she says 'shortly.'"

"Well, like I said, it's not what she says as much as how. I mean, like. . . ." Except he had no examples. Of course he didn't.

"Mr. Carlisle, it doesn't sound as if there's anything I can do for you," I said with real regret. Another hourly billable file would have been helpful.

"Okay, well, y'know—I didn't really think you could do anything, but I figured it was worth checking."

If I'd had any questions left about why he was really here, that cemented it. Potential clients who truly believed they'd been wronged didn't give in this easily. My temper started to rise; I knew where our meeting was headed next. "Always good to check. Thank you for coming in." I rose, but now he stayed seated. "Is there something else I can do for you?"

He licked his lips. "Um—do you think I could be an elf?"

"I beg your pardon?" My tone was deliberately frosty.

"You're the Santa Claus lawyer, aren't you? So I figured you'd know how I could get a job as an elf. Doesn't have to be at the North Pole. I could work the malls around here or something."

The Santa Claus lawyer. That's how the local media christened me after I represented Ralph Claus, who claimed to be the son of Santa Claus, in a case that started as a mere breaking and entering and quickly escalated to baseless charges that included sexual assault and risk of injury to a minor. Everybody thought Ralph was crazy, including me—until I saw it all. The Pole, the sleigh, the reindeer. The elves. The family. Santa himself.

I wasn't about to explain to this poser that real elves were born, not hired. "Mr. Carlisle, if you want to get a job working at a mall, that's up to you, but I can't help you with that. Thanks for coming in. Goodbye."

Reluctantly, he stood up. I was tempted to tell him he was too tall to be an elf anyway, but I held my tongue. I remained standing until he pulled the door closed behind him and clomped down the stairs. Then, I sank into my chair.

I was debating whether to watch another free webinar from the bar association or go home when my cell rang. I glanced at it and smiled at the Vancouver number. Ralph's youngest brother, Mitch, had obtained this phone for him. I didn't ask how he'd managed it; I didn't want to know. I tapped, and my beloved's face filled the screen. "Hi, sweetheart," I said.

"How was your meeting?" Ralph asked.

"It was nothing. Guy wanted me to get him a job as an elf."

"Up here?"

"At the mall."

Ralph's distinctive laugh filled the room. "Are you running an employment agency now?"

"Might not be the worst idea." Money had been tight ever since the Lundstrom Law Firm and I had parted ways.

"Don't worry, honey. Things will pick up. You'll see." Some days, his optimism was encouraging. Other days, it was naïve bordering on annoying.

"Can you send me a few good cases for Christmas?"

"Is that what you really want?"

I'd stepped in it. Ever since Christmas, Ralph had been subtly—and sometimes not so subtly—urging me to close up shop and move to the North Pole. We didn't have to get married right away, he said. But we'd be together. Plus, I could start learning about the inner workings of the Pole so that someday when his mother retired, I could step into the role of Mrs. Claus, CEO.

"At this point, all I want is to go home," I said. "Sit out on the deck with a glass of wine and watch the sunset. Get takeout sushi. Kick back and relax." Not that I had much to relax from.

He didn't say anything. We both understood that I'd described a scene that could never be recreated at the Pole. They wouldn't have another sunset until September, and once they did, there would be no sunrise until March. The only way to get takeout was to go to the dining hall and get a tray from Annaliese, the elf in charge of the kitchen, and you were limited to whatever she was cooking. If you were in the mood for tacos and she was making venison stew, that was your hard luck.

"Any chance you could take the weekend off and sneak down here?" I ventured after a bit. Back in February, we enjoyed a romantic rendezvous at an Airbnb cottage in Vermont. We spent three days snuggling in front of a stone fireplace while outside the picture window, large, lacy snowflakes fell gently. Reading as Ralph dozed, I relished the sense that we were the only two people in the world.

Now, with spring budding, the idea of returning to our little cottage sent a thrill through me—a thrill that faded to disappointment when my beloved responded, "I'd love to, but I can't."

When he didn't offer more information, I asked, "Is everything okay? How's Julian?" Julian was Ralph's father. He was also Santa Claus Emeritus now. Ralph was Santa Claus.

"Pop's fine. It's just"—he lowered his voice—"I think I need to stay here."

"What's the matter?"

Pause. "I probably shouldn't say anything."

"Are you in trouble?" Ever since he escaped from a Connecticut prison and returned to the Pole, there had been an outstanding warrant for his arrest.

"No, no, it's nothing like that—it's Phil. Things are a little rocky." Phil was the second of the five Claus brothers. Ralph was the eldest.

"Let me guess. Isabella?" Phil's wife was supposed to be in charge of procurement, meaning that she was responsible for getting all the supplies necessary to run the North Pole operations. Recently, she'd been making a lot of mistakes. Two weeks ago, she failed to put in an order for reindeer vaccines, requiring Ralph's brother, Ted, who was in charge of the stables, to make a rush trip to Finland.

"Nobody knows what's going on," Ralph said now. "But it's kind of freaking Phil out. He's very orderly." To put it mildly; the first time I had dinner with the family, I watched in complete awe as he straightened out the strands of his spaghetti before twirling them on his fork. I couldn't imagine living with him, but he and Isabella had always seemed happy enough.

"Any chance she's pregnant?" I remembered my best friend Holly telling me about being pregnant with her son and how her hormones had wreaked havoc on her brain. "I couldn't remember the name for the big box in the kitchen that keeps the food cold," she told me later. "It took all day to come up with 'refrigerator.'"

"If she is, she hasn't said anything," said Ralph. "Pretty much all she does is stay in their apartment and play the cello." Phil and Isabella had met through an elderly Claus cousin when Isabella was in New York City to audition for the world-famous Juilliard School. Phil never struck me as a sweep-a-girl-off-her-feet kind of guy, but he apparently had that effect on Isabella. By the time the audition committee notified her that she'd been accepted, Isabella was already planning a North Pole wedding.

I'd have pursued the issue, but another call beeped. "Got to go. Talk to you later. Love you."

"Love you more." It was our standard response.

I tapped *accept* without the visual. "Attorney Riley speaking."

"Meg?" The voice was nervous and breathy.

"Yes?"

"Um—this is Isabella. Claus."

Either this was a hell of a coincidence—or not. "Hi, Isabella. How are you?"

"Well—I was wondering if we could talk."

"Sure. What's going on?"

"No, I mean—in person. Is there any chance you're coming up to see Ralph soon?"

"Is something wrong?" What hadn't he told me?

First, I heard sniffles. Moments later, she was crying in earnest. "I really need to talk to you. You're the only one—" The rest of her sentence was swallowed up by sobs.

"Let me see what I can do. I'll talk to Ralph."

"No!" She sounded panicked, and my protective mode kicked in.

"Isabella, what's going on? Are you okay? Are you safe?" Phil didn't strike me as the dangerous type, but I'd handled enough family cases to know that appearances could deceive. Buttoned-up façades sometimes hid a lot of anger.

"I'm fine, everything's fine. I just really, really need to talk to you."

"Okay, okay," I said, trying to soothe her in the same way I'd have done with the cats. "I'll come up Friday. Can you wait until then?"

She snuffled loudly. "I think so."

"All right, then. You go and rest. I'll set it up, and we'll talk when I get there."

"Okay, but—don't tell Ralph I called, okay? In fact, don't tell anybody." I mumbled something she took as reassurance, and she thanked me profusely and clicked off.

I ran through the list of things I'd need to organize, including making sure my neighbor, Rodrigo, was available to take care of the cats. Then, I picked up my cell and called Ralph back. "I have an idea," I said. "How about if I come up this weekend?"

"What prompted this?"

"I miss you." It was true. It just wasn't honest.

Two

Friday afternoon found me packing a weekend bag with long underwear, heavy socks, and turtlenecks. I'd learned the hard way that it was best to wear my parka, heavy sweater, and boots on the sleigh. The last time I'd gone up was in early March when the weather was relatively mild, so I figured I could wear the same mid-weight clothes for traveling that I'd worn all day. We ended up having to land somewhere in Canada so I could change into something that would keep me from freezing to death before we reached the Pole. Mitch, who was driving, didn't say "I told you so" aloud, but his snickers spoke volumes.

"Behave yourselves," I told the cats as I zipped my bag. All three were asleep on the rose and periwinkle duvet, but I assured them, "Rodrigo will take good care of you." Rodrigo was a retired opera singer who adored cats. His husband Samson was allergic to fur and dander, so Rodrigo contented himself with caring for my brood when I was away or fussing over them when he dropped by for a glass of wine while Samson graded freshman Western Civ exams.

Rodrigo and Samson might have been the most unlikely couple I'd ever met. Rodrigo was larger than life, sweeping into any room with effusive kisses, while Samson sat in the corner, intent on a scholarly tome about ancient Babylonia. When Rodrigo threw loud, lavish parties backed by lush operatic scores, Samson took antihistamines so he could read in my living room. I adored them both, but their vastly different personalities sometimes made me wonder if this marriage would last.

Now, as I perspired beneath my heavy sweater, at least I knew I was leaving the cats in good hands. I kissed each of them, but only Harry woke from his nap to acknowledge me through half-open eyes; David and Lulu slept on, undisturbed. I texted Rodrigo that I was leaving and tossed my bag into the car, followed by my parka, boots, and a tote bag containing hat, scarf, and gloves. The sweater and jeans weren't too heavy for early May, but I wasn't putting on the rest of the outfit until the last possible minute.

Half an hour later, I turned onto a rutted dirt road leading past horse pastures to a traditional red barn. Sandy, the owner, waved me toward a spot next to a stack of hay bales. "Hi," she called when I got out of the car with my gear.

"Hi, Sandy." I tossed her the key in case she needed to move the car before I got back.

Sandy and I had worked out our arrangement back in January: for twenty bucks, I could leave my car behind her barn for the weekend. Holly and I had been dropped off in one of Sandy's pastures after our first visit to the Pole. When I subsequently asked Sandy about parking here, I didn't explain exactly why I needed her help. All I said was that I'd need to leave my car somewhere safe and inconspicuous every so often and was willing to pay for the privilege. It probably sounded as if I were doing espionage. Sandy was so careful not to ask any questions that I sometimes wondered if that was her theory. Certainly it wasn't any more outrageous than reality.

My rendezvous with the sleigh always took place in Sandy's farthest pasture, out of anyone's sight. By the time I trudged out there, I could feel the sweat beneath my breasts. I was tempted to take off my bra, but just as I reached under my sweater to unhook it, I heard a loud swoosh. In the next instant, the sleigh was before me, and the driver was grinning.

"Let me guess. You were expecting Ralph," said Mitch. At twenty, he still exhibited a childlike delight in teasing Ralph, who was nearly twice his age—and now me, since I was Ralph's girlfriend. Watching the brothers banter, I sometimes felt a twinge of regret that I'd never had that kind of relationship with my own brother, Derek.

Now, I withdrew my hand from my sweater with as much dignity as I could muster. "How'd you draw the short straw?"

Mitch snorted. "Are you kidding? This is great. Everybody else is freezing their asses off. C'mon, hurry up." He secured my bag in the back as he talked. Speed was of the essence. I yanked on my boots and winter garb, followed by the black jumpsuit and ski mask that would keep me warm at altitudes high enough to fly over mountains. Mitch was already dressed in his black gear. Between us, we looked as if we were about to pull off a jewel heist.

Moments later, we were flying through a cloud bank. I was still uncomfortable traveling by sleigh. *Uncomfortable? Be honest, Meg.* I hated it. I didn't even like flying in those horrid small planes that seated a dozen passengers, but the sleigh made those look like luxury aircraft. I told myself it was the lack of protection from the elements: the sleigh had no roof, no windows, no windshield. But that was only part of it. Flying in a sleigh meant trusting not only the pilot, but the animals he was trying to control. On one occasion, a flock of birds had startled the reindeer. The reindeer bucked, the sleigh rocked violently, and only the seat belt kept me from being jolted out of the sleigh. Ralph's brother, Fred, who was driving, seemed completely unfazed while I spent the rest of the trip clutching the side of the sleigh and praying that we wouldn't fall to our deaths.

I tried to reassure myself that at least we were traveling in daylight. Even with night vision goggles, flying in the dark was nerve-racking, like barreling through a vast impenetrable nothingness. Unless we passed over a city low enough to see its lights, there was no way to know how close we might be to safe, solid ground.

Naturally, Ralph loved flying at night. "It's like being alone in the universe, just you and the stars," he waxed rhapsodically. I didn't tell him that was precisely the problem. I comforted myself with the thought that there would always be a Claus brother to handle the flying. I might occasionally have to travel at night, but at least I'd have someone knowledgeable to keep the sleigh from crashing into the blackness.

Now, we were suspended in fog dense enough to let me pretend the ground was only a few feet below us. Something about the anonymity of the black outfits in the featureless whiteness made me bold in the way you might tell your troubles to a stranger in a bar. So I asked, "How are things going at the Pole?"

"They're going." Mitch didn't sound particularly interested.

"Everything okay?"

This time, he glanced at me. "Sure."

"Good." I decided to pivot slightly. "Meet anybody interesting lately?"

"A few."

"Nothing serious?" As far as I knew, Mitch had never been serious about a girl—at least, not as the marriage-minded Clauses defined "serious." Mitch's version of "serious" meant two intense weeks followed by an abrupt cooling-off when he encountered his next great love.

If Mitch had been a woman, he'd have responded by asking me how things were going with Ralph. From there, we might have segued into a chat about life at the Pole and how the Claus wives had made the move, and I might even have been able to nudge the conversation in the direction of Phil and Isabella. But since Mitch was a typical male—at least, a typical Claus male—there was no easy entry into the subject.

We emerged from the cloud bank into a crisp blue sky that stretched literally forever. Seeing the sky from the security of an enclosed seat in business class was awe-inspiring, but hanging unprotected in a sunny, cheerful void made my stomach lurch.

Even so, I said nothing. I didn't want Mitch to think Ralph's girlfriend was a wuss. We flew in what Mitch probably thought was companionable silence. I patted my own hand the way I'd have petted one of the cats to calm them down: *take it easy, everything's okay, you're safe.* I cast around for small talk to redirect my thoughts. "What are you working on these days?" I asked finally.

"The usual stuff. R&D has a few ideas, but they're still working out the bugs." Mitch worked with the electronics team. His forte was programming. In another life, he'd have been a rising star at Microsoft or Apple, creating lucrative new versions of their software. As a Claus, he managed Santa's online presence and oversaw the workings of the tablets and other electronic goodies that today's kids demanded.

"Mind if I turn on some music?" I asked after another long pause. At his nod, I scrolled through my phone until I located a playlist of nostalgic summertime favorites. Within moments, we were sailing through the skies accompanied by the Beach Boys singing about fun, fun, fun.

"Seriously?" Mitch raised one eyebrow. All the Claus boys possessed that ability, courtesy of their mother.

"Would you prefer Motown?"

"I'd settle for something from my lifetime."

"Broaden your horizons, young grasshopper. And don't you dare ask me where that comes from," I added before he could open his mouth.

"One of your old movies, I'm guessing," Mitch said. My love of old movies was already well-known at the Pole. I usually brought up a few DVDs for movie night, much to the delight of the elves.

Under other circumstances, listening to my favorite oldies would have soothed me. Every time my tension eased, though, Isabella's call replayed itself in my head. Something was definitely not right. I opened my mouth to ask Mitch, but her plea for my silence stopped me. I tried again to come up with some roundabout way to inquire.

"So, how's your dad doing?" I asked finally.

"He's doing. Still using the cane as much as he can. He should be using the walker—or better still, the wheelchair—but you know him. Has to keep fighting." Julian had had a series of strokes the prior year that had left him increasingly incapacitated physically, although his mind was as sharp as ever. I sometimes struggled to understand his speech, but his piercing blue eyes made it clear that he understood everything I was saying—plus plenty I wasn't.

"How does your mom handle all this?"

"You know Mom. She handles whatever needs handling." The understatement of the year. Meredith Claus and I had butted heads plenty about Ralph's case. Eventually, I'd developed a grudging respect for her. After all, she had one hell of a job as CEO of the North Pole, and caring for a disabled husband couldn't have made things any easier. I couldn't imagine ever actually liking the woman, but for Ralph's sake, I did my best to be pleasant. If I couldn't muster warmth toward her, at least I could behave.

*****

At long last, we began the descent, which bore a disturbing resemblance to a roller coaster—that uncontrolled feeling of falling, of going down, down, down, when you promised God anything if He'd keep you from crashing at the bottom. Thickening clouds muted the sun. When we emerged beneath the clouds, the world was blue and white, open water and snow and ice. If I'd been watching the scenery from the safety of a movie theater seat, I'd have thought it glorious. As it was, soaring above icy waters at breakneck speed had only one benefit: at the end of this harrowing journey was Ralph.

Sure enough, when we touched down, Ralph was standing beside the barn. He jogged over to the sleigh and lifted me down as if I were a wisp of a girl. "Hey, you," he murmured, his gorgeous green eyes glowing.

"Hey, you," I whispered back. I locked my arms around his neck and stood on tiptoe as he bent down to kiss me. Heat rushed through my body when his lips touched mine. For an instant, I allowed myself to wonder how it would be to have such access to him every day, to be able to see him and touch him whenever I liked. In the next instant, I banished the notion. We were still in the honeymoon stage, practically speaking: although we'd known each other for over a year, the actual time we'd spent in each other's presence could be measured in days, not months.

"Are you cold?" he asked. "You're shaking."

"I'm fine. Let's get inside." Better he should think my trembling was the result of wintry temperatures than cowardice.

With his arm around my shoulders, we strolled into the barn. It reminded me of Sandy's barn with its stalls and feed bins, albeit with lower ceilings to conserve heat. Unlike Sandy's, each stall was occupied by three or four reindeer, all of whom perked up when Santa appeared.

Ralph guided me through the barn to the building entrance, and then down endless halls to his apartment. The creamy walls bore dozens of framed photographs of literally everywhere in the world, from city lights and cozy suburban neighborhoods to lush green forests and sunset over desert sands. Recessed lighting in the low ceilings created the illusion of daylight. The tight-looped red carpeting showed signs of wear in the center. Behind doors, the thrum of activity reminded me that the elves in Santa's workshop were hard at work.

The first time I'd visited Ralph at the Pole, I asked him where I'd be staying. "With me," he said as if it were obvious. "Unless you'd rather have the guest suite again." Holly and I had stayed in a lovely little guest suite when we came up after Ralph's initial arrest.

"I'd rather be with you," I said. "But—is it okay?"

Ralph laughed. "Why wouldn't it be?"

"I don't know, I just—" It was hard to imagine Meredith Claus approving of my having sex with her son under her roof. "I mean, if he sees you when you're sleeping. . . ."

Ralph threw his head back, roaring with laughter. I'd never met anyone else who thought I was so hilarious. "Talk about the last thing anybody would come up with," he wheezed finally. "Besides, I'm Santa, so even if that song weren't made up, I'm the one who'd be seeing you while you're sleeping, not Pop." He kissed me, adding, "It'll be much easier for me to see you if you're sleeping next to me. I mean, in the interests of upholding the tradition." He kissed me again, long and deep.

"Well, if it's necessary for the tradition. . . ." I pressed myself against him as we kissed. Like a pair of teenagers, we kissed and walked, walked and kissed, until we reached his apartment. The door was barely closed before we were tearing each other's clothes off.

After passionate lovemaking followed by a well-earned nap, I awoke to find Ralph gone. "Ralph?" I called, feeling suddenly lost.

"Right here," came his voice from the living room. I pulled on my clothes and joined him. "So, what do you think?" he asked.

For a second, I thought he was asking my opinion of the past two hours. Then, I realized he was referring to his home. Like all the other spaces at the Pole, Ralph's apartment was designed for maximum usage of limited square footage. Unlike most of the spaces I'd seen, however, Ralph's quarters lacked any photographs. In fact, it was the only place I'd seen at the Pole where the walls were completely bare. The palette was neutral—shades of sand, cream, eggshell. Even the quilt on his bed was unadorned tan. A person could fall asleep just looking around.

"It's . . . ." I groped for a word other than *dull.*

"Soothing," he said proudly.

"Soothing," I agreed. "Very soothing."

"A person can really relax in a room like this," he said.

"Definitely."

"Come in here, and it's like the entire world goes away."

"Absolutely." I'd seen hardware stores with livelier décor. "Give me a few minutes to unpack." I hung my clothes in the closet, tucked my undergarments in the drawer Ralph had emptied for me, and put my floral-print toiletries bag in the bathroom. With real reluctance, I tucked my green overnight bag in the closet and closed the door on the only spot of color in the apartment.

Ralph appeared in the doorway with two bone-colored mugs, holding one out to me. "I made tea."

"Thanks, honey." I accepted it, smiled, and sipped the world's weakest tea. He probably hadn't steeped it even a full minute. On the other hand, because it was so anemic, I didn't miss the sweetener I usually added. We stood awkwardly, him in the doorway and me in the bedroom, clutching our mugs. Finally, I said, "What if we go back to the living room?"

"What? Oh, sure." He turned too fast, and tea sloshed out of his mug onto his hand. "Ow!"

"You okay?" I didn't mention that he'd dripped on the beige rug. The lightness of the tea wouldn't leave a spot.

"Yeah, I'm fine."

We went into the living room. He seated himself on the loveseat. I plunked down in the room's only armchair. The loveseat might have been fine for snuggling, but it wasn't a place for two full-sized adults to spread out.

We sat in silence, sipping our tea. It was the first time I could remember feeling ill at ease with Ralph. Considering how he'd welcomed me, this was disconcerting. "Who decorated in here?" I asked finally.

"Nobody," he said. I must have looked surprised, because he added, "I moved in when I was eighteen. I'd shared a room with Phil pretty much all our lives, but Mom said eighteen was old enough for my own space. I hadn't even thought about it. I mean, it's not like I ever spent much time in my room except to sleep. Still don't." He looked around the room as if seeing it for the first time. "I guess it's kind of boring."

"No—it's soothing." I used the word before remembering it was his. "Peaceful," I added.

"It's not like your place," he said.

"Well, we have different taste." To put it mildly. In my home, neutrals were accent colors, not the entire palette. My living room walls were Wedgewood blue, complemented by cream-colored draperies, and the overstuffed sofa was festooned with throw pillows and a hand-knit afghan in shades of blue, rose, green, yellow, and cream.

"Why don't you have any pictures?" I tried not to sound as if I were criticizing. "I mean, I've seen them practically everywhere else. Didn't you want any?"

"I never really thought about it," he said. "Like I said, I'm not here very much except to sleep."

I finished my anemic tea and looked around for someplace to set my mug. The guest suite Holly and I had occupied boasted a coffee table, but there was none here. I rose and asked, "Are you done?" Ralph looked startled, but he held out his mug, and I carried them to the tiny kitchenette, which consisted of a sink and an under-counter refrigerator. I suspected the microwave on the countertop got more use than the two-burner stove. I looked around for dish soap and a sponge, but there was none, so I rinsed out the mugs and set them upside down on a beige dish towel.

"You want to look around?" Ralph asked.

I couldn't imagine what more he thought there was to see in his apartment, but I wasn't about to say so. "Sounds good." To my relief, he opened the door to the hallway and waited for me to exit before doing the same.

In subsequent visits, it became clear that Ralph wasn't kidding about using his apartment strictly as a place to sleep. He seemed oblivious to his surroundings, preferring life outside his rooms. He rarely used his kitchenette, taking all his meals in the dining hall. I'd have been just as happy to ease into the day with an egg sandwich and a cup of tea in his apartment, but he bounded into the dining hall at an absurdly early hour as I stumbled along behind him, desperate for caffeine and silence.

Three

By the time the dinner chime sounded, I was famished. Having no idea how Pole time lined up with Connecticut time, I didn't know whether it was seven in the evening or two in the morning at home. All I knew was that I was dying for something substantial, like meat or pasta. Unfortunately, the menu that evening consisted of cod which, while far superior to anything sold in a Connecticut fish market, was an indisputably light meal. Annaliese and her team had supplemented the cod with rice and a variety of vegetables—some of which I didn't recognize, and all of which had arrived at the Pole either frozen, canned, or dried. I marveled that such a meal would satisfy the men, but they seemed content with their lot.

Seating in the dining hall was traditional, according to Ralph. Each table sat ten adults. The Claus adults generally sat together at a table on the far wall. Elf families with young children routinely occupied the same tables at each meal. Older kids, Claus and elf, sat in their own clusters, much like a school cafeteria.

At first, it bothered me that the seating seemed to be so segregated as between Clauses and elves, but Ralph explained that it was how they all preferred it. "Like it or not, we're the bosses," he said. "Elves like the idea that even though we're all together, they get to have meal times to themselves. It's not like there's never any mingling, but for the most part, meals are a time for everybody to relax and spend time with their own families."

"But the kids. . . ." I gestured toward a table of adolescent elves and Clauses.

"Not the same," he said. "In a few years, they'll start to drift apart. Once everybody is old enough to be starting families, they'll stake out their own family tables."

"What about the ones who don't marry?" As a forty-year-old who had never married, I was well-acquainted with the experience of being alone in a sea of families.

Ralph gestured to a table where several older elves sat together. "One way or another, they form their own family units," he said. "Up here, a family is more than the people you share DNA with. In a way, the entire place is a family, but within that, we have—I guess you'd call them sub-families, with parents and kids and grandparents and whoever else is a part of that unit."

"Family by chance versus family by choice," I mused, remembering a line I'd once read. While I shared blood with my brother and my mother, my real family—the people to whom I was bound, whom I trusted with my life and my heart and my confidences—consisted of Holly, my former law partner Michael, and his wife Ruby—and now Ralph, to whom I hoped to be one day bound by choice, which was to say, by marriage. Once I married him, I'd be bound to his family as well—by chance or by choice, I couldn't say.

Mitch and the twins, Ted and Fred, were already at the table when we arrived. "Where are Claire and Anya?" I asked.

"Anya's with the kids," said Fred. Their daughter was nearly six, and their son was a toddler. Anya routinely skipped meals in the dining hall to eat with the kids. "Fred says she prefers it," Ralph explained later when I commented that it wasn't quite fair that she always seemed to have kid-duty while he ate in peace with the grown-ups. "She says it's easier for her that way. Even when Fred stays home to eat with the kids, she won't leave." It was a mindset I couldn't quite imagine.

"Claire's having morning sickness," said Ted. Just as their son, Justin, was turning eleven in February, Claire discovered that she was pregnant. She was due in November, Ralph had reported. "Obviously, the timing isn't optimal, but we'll make it work," my Santa said philosophically.

Julian and Meredith routinely ate in their apartment these days since it was a challenge for Julian to come to the dining hall. Ralph's aunt Tillie, who was Julian's cousin, frequently joined them. I asked Ralph if we should eat with his parents, but he said, "They like the peace and quiet. After eons of being surrounded by all of us, they're enjoying time to themselves." Which didn't mean there wasn't plenty of traffic in and out of their apartment—helpers, grandchildren, and young elves, as well as the adults. Anya had appointed herself the gatekeeper and guardian, sometimes to the irritation of the Claus men when she shooed them out "so Papa can rest."

Phil and Isabella were the last to arrive. I hadn't yet had a chance to see Isabella alone. I tried to catch her eye as she and Phil took their seats, but she smiled brightly at everybody and then focused on her meal.

Toward the end of dinner, Owen appeared. As always, the elf who served as attaché to Mrs. Claus was attired in a gray wool suit. I wondered whether he ever shed his work wardrobe in favor of comfortable clothing. "Good evening," he said with the formality he'd shown ever since the first day Holly and I appeared.

"Hello, Owen," I said as the others mumbled greetings through mouthfuls of food. "Would you like to join us?"

"No, ma'am," he said. Ralph's brothers exchanged smirks, but I ignored them. "Mrs. Claus would like to see you when you've finished dining."

"Everything okay?" asked Ralph as he tossed his rice, veggies, and fish together.

"Fine, sir." If Owen was ever off-duty, I'd never seen it. He turned to Isabella, adding, "Mrs. Claus would like for you to join the meeting, ma'am."

Isabella bit her lip. "Um—of course, Owen. I'll be there. As soon as I'm done."

"Anything I need to know about?" Phil's voice was casual, but his fingers gripped his fork so tightly that I thought it might break.

"No, sir." Owen was not about to give anything away. To me, he said, "I'll tell Mrs. Claus to expect you in—fifteen minutes?" The last was less a question than a recommendation.

"That's fine, thanks," I said. Owen left, and I looked at Ralph, his brothers, and Isabella. "Anybody have a clue what's going on?"

"Guess Mom wants to talk to you," said Ralph, not looking up from his plate.

"Don't worry," said Mitch with slightly overdone helpfulness. "You know Mom. She's never *not* at work. She probably just had a thought." The twins nodded unconvincingly. At the far end of the table, Isabella sat nearly motionless in front of her plate. Beside her, Phil sprinkled salt on his vegetables, steadfastly ignoring the conversation.

Too soon, I finished my dinner. I'd have loved more fish, but nobody else was going back for seconds. "Well, I'm off," I said as I stood and picked up my tray. "See you later," I added, kissing the top of Ralph's head.

"See you," he said, lifting his face for a proper kiss. I obliged, and he returned his attention to his food as I took my tray to the kitchen.

Four

Moments later, I was joined in the hall by Isabella. "Care to tell me what this is all about?" I said as we traversed the quiet hallway.

"I—I want—I mean, I'll tell you when we get to Mom's office." I couldn't tell whether she was more nervous about telling me or talking to Meredith.

"Tell me what? What's going on?" I never went into a meeting unprepared.

"Oh, it's no big deal," she said as we arrived at the elevator.

"Then talk to me," I said. "You got me up here for a reason. What is it?" The elevator dinged, and the door slid open, revealing the miniscule car. Neither of us spoke during its short trip to the office level. When the door opened, we stepped into the tiny hallway.

The forest green door to Meredith's office was open, but we knocked anyway. Behind the mahogany desk sat Ralph's mother, trim and elegant. As always, her silver hair was pinned into a loose knot. She had the same light-green eyes as her sons, the rays emanating from the corners suggesting a lifetime of laughter. It was impossible to know whether her makeup was so artfully applied as to appear utterly natural or whether she wasn't wearing any.

"Come in," Meredith said, beckoning as she rose. "Welcome back, Meg. Please sit down. Would you like some tea?" The antique tea set was on the desk, bone china teapot and cups at the ready next to cookies on a matching plate. I'd have bet anything that Owen had just brought up the boiling water.

"I'd love some," I said, less because I wanted it than to buy time.

"No, thanks," said Isabella at the same time.

Meredith smiled benignly at both of us. "Please sit down." Obediently, we sat in the jewel-toned paisley wingback chairs in front of the desk. Meredith poured tea into two cups and handed one to each of us. Isabella looked slightly startled, but she sipped obediently.

Meredith sat back. "Isabella, have you spoken with Meg?"

"No," I said before Isabella could answer. "What's going on?"

Meredith looked at Isabella, who was looking down at her knees. "Isabella. This is your idea." Her voice was firm, but kind.

Isabella lifted her head. Without looking at either of us, she said, "I want—I—I'm a musician. I want to try a musician's life."

The lack of surprise on Meredith's face clearly showed that this wasn't the first time she'd heard this. When Isabella said no more, Meredith said, "Meg, as you know, Isabella plays the cello. She and Phil met when she was auditioning for music school."

"Juilliard," Isabella interjected.

"Isabella chose to get married and move up here instead of attending school," Meredith continued as if Isabella had not spoken. "But now, she's—well, she's having second thoughts."

"No!" Isabella burst out. "I'm not having second thoughts. I love my husband. I love my life. I just—I wish—I mean, it's been ten years. I feel like—I need to know what I could have been. Could I really have been a musician? The real thing? I feel like I have to find out."

"So, you're having a midlife crisis." I didn't mean to sound unsympathetic, but I'd counseled dozens of divorce clients who wanted to rewind their lives and pick up where they'd been the day before they decided to tie the knot. They were always convinced that if they hadn't married when they did, they could have had brilliant careers and fascinating lives. In fact, what they almost inevitably discovered was that undoing the marriage to return to the vocation didn't work out. What they might have chosen at eighteen wasn't what their thirty-year-old self wanted. Too many things had changed.

I could recall only one instance where a couple had split and the spouse who'd wanted to pursue their premarital goals had ended up even moderately happy. Lucia McCormick and Anton Bruckweiller were a pair of physicists who met and married in college, pursuing their research and their dreams together. By the time they landed in my office, Lucia had elbowed Anton out of the spotlight, her radiant personality drawing the attention of journalists who interviewed her as her husband toiled in the lab late at night. Anton claimed that he could have pursued—well, something about physics that I never came close to understanding—except that Lucia's research had consumed not only all their energies, but much of the available funding. His only chance of doing the work he dreamed of was to cut loose from her, he said.

To her credit, Lucia didn't deny any of Anton's claims. Her position was that because they were married, they were both wedded to the sum total of the work, whatever it might be. That the work in question turned out to be hers was simply how things went, she said. She was better at public relations, and she was more skilled at preparing grant applications and wooing backers, so it was only right that they pursue her work at this time. Eventually, she said, they could circle back and work on Anton's project. For now, there was only room for one of them at center stage.

It was one of the sadder collaborative divorces I worked on, for the simple reason that I had no doubt about their love for each other. But love wasn't enough, at least not for a pair of gifted physicists. Lucia and Anton worked out an amicable and immensely fair arrangement, and they went their separate ways. Several years later, when there was buzz about whether Anton would be nominated for the Nobel Prize for whatever it was he'd wanted to work on, Lucia gave an interview in which she praised him as the most brilliant physicist she'd ever known. Someone else won that year, but a few months later, I happened upon an essay by Lucia where she talked about their relationship. "I hope he wins someday," she wrote. "It will mean that our separation has been worthwhile." Lucia had subsequently married and divorced, while Anton had a long relationship with a lab assistant who eventually left him for a pharmacist. Now, years later, I had no idea how either had fared. I hoped they were happy, whether together or separately.

I brought my thoughts back to the couple at issue. "I assume your husband knows about this," I said to Isabella. Her husband, who was still eating his dinner while his wife and his mother mapped out her career plans.

"Of course," Isabella said. "We've been talking about it for a while."

"The question, Meg, is about where Isabella can go," said Meredith, and then I knew why I was there. "We've considered several options, but the best one—if you're agreeable—is for her to stay with you in Connecticut."

"There are a lot of music groups in Connecticut, plus you're close to New York and Boston," Isabella chimed in. "So I could commute back and forth to either one, depending where I found work."

"Obviously, you wouldn't be responsible for her expenses," said Meredith. "Isabella would pay a fair rent, and she would contribute to the household costs as well—groceries, utilities, and the like." She looked at me expectantly, as if the only thing left was my signature on the dotted line.

"Plus gas, if you drive me to auditions or stuff like that," Isabella added. "Or I could drive myself if it's okay."

"Do you have a license?" I asked.

Isabella looked crestfallen for a moment; then, she brightened. "I can get one."

"How long are you planning to be there?" I had visions of Isabella, gray and tottery, making her way up the stairs, cello in one hand and cane in the other.

Meredith and Isabella looked at each other. When the younger woman didn't speak, Meredith said, "We think six months is a fair tryout period."

"'We'?"

"Yes." Meredith glanced at Isabella, whose focus was now on her teacup. "If Isabella hasn't made substantial progress toward a music career by that time, she plans to return to her work here at the Pole."

"You mean ordering supplies." The job she'd been screwing up for the past few months.

"Procurement," Meredith agreed. "Isabella handles orders for all our supplies—food, equipment, whatever we need to sustain this community and do our work. Which brings us to the other piece of this request."

"There's more?" Apparently, it wasn't enough that they intended to saddle me with a roommate.

"Since Isabella will be devoting substantial time to practice and auditions, she'll require assistance with her Pole-related duties," said Meredith. "We'd like you to assist her in these endeavors."

"You would." I probably sounded as dazed as I felt.

"You'd have to learn about it eventually," said Isabella. "I mean, if you and Ralph . . . you know." Her voice trailed off. Meredith wore a neutral expression, as if we were discussing a simple business transaction instead of her sons and the women they loved.

"What goes on with Ralph and me is between us," I said. "It has nothing to do with the rest of you."

"That's not true," said Meredith. "Any addition or change to the family affects the family. Obviously, this is especially true of anything involving Ralph since he's Santa. If you and he were to marry, you would eventually step into the position I currently hold, and I would retire."

It wasn't as though I hadn't expected this, but to hear her lay it out as a done deal was disconcerting. I held up my hand. "One thing at a time. I thought we were talking about Phil and Isabella."

"We are," she said. "But the family is a unified organism. Every part affects all the other parts. It would be naïve to assume otherwise."

"How about for today, we focus on Phil and Isabella." I tried not to sound as thrown as I felt. "So, what you want is for Isabella to leave Phil, move in with me, and try to be a cellist while I do part of her work here. Am I getting the picture?"

"In essence," said Meredith.

"And what about my own work? My legal work?" Not that there was much at the moment, but a person could hope.

"Obviously, you have your own obligations," Meredith said. "We don't mean to minimize them. If you're not able to help, we need to find another solution."

"Please, Meg," said Isabella. "I mean, it would be exactly the right thing. Phil wouldn't have to worry about me living alone, and you'd get rent payments, so that would help as long as your law stuff is slow." Apparently, everybody knew my practice wasn't thriving.

I cast about for something, anything, to put them off. "Wouldn't having Isabella around put the secret of Santa at risk? I mean, her name is Isabella Claus. That's going to get the attention of the police, especially with her connection to me. They're still looking for Ralph."

"Isabella would use her maiden name," said Meredith. Clearly, this issue had also been previously discussed.

"Duncan," Isabella supplied. "I still have all my old IDs in my maiden name. If anybody asks, I can say that I was living out of the country for a while—which is true. Even my social security number is still under Duncan." She seemed quite satisfied with her solution.

It wasn't unreasonable as plans went. Nothing would prevent Isabella from working in the United States. She had a perfectly legitimate legal identity, so there would be no issues about fraud, nothing to raise red flags with the police who still hovered around the edges of my life.

I set my cup on Meredith's desk and rose. "I'll have to give it some thought. When do you need an answer?"

The two women exchanged a look. "If you could let us know by the end of the weekend, Isabella could go back with you," Meredith said.

"What's the rush?"

"We'd like to get things moving as soon as possible," said Meredith. "There's no reason to wait."

"Except that I need to get ready for a long-term houseguest." Like most people, I routinely used my guest room for storage. More importantly, I needed to prepare myself mentally for the notion of having somebody living in my home.

"Tenant," said Meredith. "If you like, we can have a written lease. I know lawyers are fond of such things. Would you like for us to prepare one, or would you prefer to do it yourself?"

"What I'd like to do is to give the matter some thought," I said. "You're dropping a lot on me. I need to think about it." More importantly, I needed to talk to Ralph. It was inconceivable that all this had gone on without his knowledge, which raised the question of why he hadn't given me a heads-up. Without waiting for dismissal, I left Meredith's office and punched the elevator button. As I listened for the whir of its arrival, I tried to discern whether Ralph's mother and sister-in-law were whispering or whether they were merely waiting for me to leave before deciding how well things had gone.

Five

I glanced away from the Saw Mill Parkway toward Isabella, but she didn't seem to notice. Her left hand hovered near her breast, fingers moving in an intricate dance on an invisible fingerboard. Every now and then, she stopped, huffed in obvious displeasure, and began again. The only other sound in the car was the GPS telling me where to turn for the Henry Hudson Parkway on Manhattan's West Side. I itched to put on a podcast, but I didn't want to interfere with whatever internal music she was hearing.

Three weeks had passed since Isabella moved in with me. I'd be lying if I said I hadn't felt more than a few moments of irritation about having a roommate foisted on me. Luckily, she wasn't terrible to live with. In fact, there were advantages to her presence. For one thing, she was a neatnik. My guest room had never been so tidy. She even made her bed every morning, a habit I never bothered with since the cats routinely spent their days snuggling under the quilt.

On the other hand, Isabella knew nothing about meal preparation. No surprise, since she was barely out of high school when she moved to the Pole with its meal service. The first night after we'd arrived home, she appeared in the kitchen and asked brightly, "When do we eat?" Exhausted from our travels, I handed her the takeout menu from my favorite Asian bistro, texting with Holly as Isabella squealed over items that weren't available at the Pole: "OMG, beef with broccoli! And pork fried rice! This is amazing!" The next night, and the night after, she presented herself at mealtime with the same question. Wanting to be a good hostess—and to avoid negative reports getting back to the Pole—I scrambled through my freezer and pantry for easy dinner options. But by the fourth night, I was finished waiting on her. When she asked, "When do we eat?", I responded with unintended sharpness, "As soon as you fix dinner." She looked at me blankly, as if I'd spoken a different language, but she was game. Soon, I knew dinner prep was under way whenever I heard someone on a YouTube video taking my roommate through the steps of a new recipe.

Life at North Pole South continued to have its ups and downs, though. Meredith either could not or would not master the concept of time zones, which meant she called at literally all hours, sometimes seeking Isabella and sometimes me. "Would you please tell your mother that we sleep at night!" I snapped at Ralph one evening. "My phone rang at four o'clock this morning because she was worried about reindeer vaccines."

"I'm sorry, honey," he said. "Just don't answer. She can leave a message."

"She could also send a text or an email," I said. "Preferably an email so it wouldn't wake me up. And if one of us doesn't answer, she calls the other one. It's infuriating." I didn't tell him I'd changed my ring tone for his mother to the theme from *Jaws*.

The one topic Ralph and I continued to skirt was his failure to tell me about Isabella before my meeting with her and Meredith. When I'd gotten back to his apartment after listening to his mother's plans for my life, he wasn't there. Rather than traipse all over the Pole looking for him, I texted him: *Where are you?*

An instant later, he responded: *The finishing room. Where are you?*
Your room.
Brt

Sure enough, a minute later he opened the door, his smile widening as he entered. It faded slightly when he saw me fully dressed in his armchair, then dropped entirely when I said, "We need to talk."

"What's the matter?"

"Did you know what your mother wanted to discuss with me?"

He looked like an oversized kid who'd been caught stealing a cookie. "She asked me what I thought, whether you might be open to the idea."

"Why didn't you tell me?"

He bit his lip. "I didn't know—I mean, it's their marriage. I didn't know if Iz was really going to go through with it. It could all have been about nothing."

"Or it could have been something. Why didn't you tell me?"

He perched on the arm of the loveseat as if the seat were occupied by Phil, Isabella, and his mother—which, in essence, it was. "It's my brother's marriage. That's really personal stuff."

"Don't you trust me?"

He flinched. "It's not about trust. It's—it's family."

"Which I'm not."

"Come on, Meg." He sounded irritated now. "That's not fair. This is my brother."

"And it's me. It's my life. My home. I appreciate your brother's privacy, but when it starts to impact my life, I'm counting on you to keep me in the loop."

His eyes searched my face. "You're right," he said finally. "I love you. You were entitled to know. I shouldn't have kept it secret."

"It's not about secrets," I protested. "It's that I need to know what's going on."

"No, I get it. Okay, then. No more secrets." He pulled me to my feet and wrapped his arms around me. "In the interests of not keeping secrets, I need to tell you something else."

"What?"

"You're wearing way too much right now." As he kissed me, his hands reached under my sweater and began to unfasten my bra, and that was the end of that discussion, at least for the night. In the days to come, though, I found myself watching him carefully, trying to discern whether he was keeping something else from me—a feeling I hated. He'd said *no more secrets*. I needed to take him at his word.

*****

I forced my attention back to the New York traffic. It had been ages since I'd driven into the city, but it felt as if nothing had changed. The concrete barriers in the middle of the highway seemed not to have moved, reminding me of the time Holly and I had come down here in a stretch limo. I'd won a silent auction package that included two tickets to the Met and a stretch limousine. Rather than deal with the rush of an early dinner before curtain, we bought sushi, wine, and chocolates for a luxurious dinner in the back of the stretch. Our excitement grew as the limo glided down the West Side Highway, traffic tight on our right and the concrete barriers on the left. At 49th Street, we turned left to exit the highway. Just as Holly poured the last drops of wine into my plastic cup, a long, metallic screech startled us so that she nearly dropped the bottle. It took a second to realize that the side of the limo had scraped—was scraping—the barrier throughout the turn. "What the hell!" we exclaimed in unison, but the driver made no apology, much less inquiring whether we were all right. He merely continued to drive. When we reached Lincoln Center, he pulled up to the curb directly in front of the plaza. He came around to the right side of the limo, opening the door for us as if nothing untoward had occurred. I was enormously tempted to go around to the street side to see what damage the barrier had wrought, but Holly shook her head. "No point in making him feel bad," she said as we crossed the plaza.

"Somehow I don't think we're the ones who are going to make him feel bad," I replied.

Ever since that night, whenever I drove into the city, I worried that I, too, would scrape the barriers. I never had, but now, as I was delivering Isabella to the most important audition of her life, it seemed like exactly the kind of thing I'd screw up.

Somebody's guardian angel was watching over us, and I exited the highway without incident. As I navigated the narrow streets, I realized that years of driving primarily in and around Hartford—my idea of city driving—had made me soft. It wasn't that Connecticut drivers were so polite; it was that Manhattan drivers were so aggressive. Horns blared the second a traffic light changed. Pedestrians crossed the street against the light as taxis nosed into the crosswalk and honked at the jaywalkers who ignored them.

I knew there wasn't a shot in hell I'd find on-street parking anywhere near the audition site, so I dropped Isabella off at the curb and wound my way down Broadway and back up Riverside to the garage Rodrigo favored. "Tell them you know me," he'd said. Indeed, when I said Rodrigo Alegria had sent me, the attendant's face lit up. He assured me that he would take good care of my car; when I handed over my key—so antiquated in this day of fobs—he never blinked.

Exiting the garage, I realized that another thing that hadn't changed was the smell. I tried to imagine becoming so accustomed to the pungent stench of garbage and urine that I might cease to notice it. Hartford had no discernible odors, except maybe exhaust.

Whenever I walked in Manhattan, I felt as if I were wearing a sign proclaiming that I was Not a New Yorker. Maybe I looked around too much; maybe it was my attire (no black). I kept my face expressionless and held tightly to my bag, secure in the knowledge that my license, a credit card, and a fifty-dollar bill were safely ensconced in my bra. I debated taking the subway back to where I'd dropped Isabella, but I decided the walk would do me good. Certainly a suburban nervousness about NYC subways had nothing to do with this decision.

Besides, there was much more to see above ground. More people seemed to be walking dogs than I remembered. Couples of all configurations—male/female, male/male, female/female, and many whose gender identity wasn't obvious—filled the sidewalks and occupied tiny tables next to the doorways of bakeries and delis and coffee shops. As I moved downtown, the neighborhood shifted from narrow storefronts to full-blown eateries with cordoned-off outdoor dining. Patrons crowded into the tightly-packed spaces, the barriers so close to foot traffic that I could easily have filched a french fry from a plate. I'd forgotten how New Yorkers possess an amazing gift for ignoring passersby who might overhear their conversations. At one table, a group of ultra-thin young women picked at green salads as they lamented the unwillingness of men to perform oral sex. Next to them, a middle-aged woman glared at a balding man, hissing, "I don't care what your fucking lawyer says—you're not getting the parrot." Wait staff squeezed between chairs, trays held high above their heads, their expressions carefully neutral as phrases like "plea bargain," "nanny cam," and "the Knicks" drifted into the general cacophony, a distinctive type of music in its own right.

I arrived at Isabella's audition site and pushed open the heavy door. Two grandmotherly women sat at a table in the lobby, checking off the names of those auditioning. One asked me, "Are you here to audition?" When I shook my head, she gestured toward the hallway to her right. I glanced at the hallway to her left, which was packed with hopefuls of all ages, races, and genders. I saw Isabella several feet away, but she was too intent on her music to notice me.

Around the other corner stood clusters of people who were clearly waiting for their particular hopeful to finish. I made my way over to their area. One or two glanced at me, but for the most part, they were busy with their own conversations.

"Fourth time this month," a gray-haired man muttered. "And Diana keeps encouraging her." He scowled at the woman beside him.

"It's important to support them," said Diana. She wore heavier makeup to stand around on a Saturday afternoon than I'd have worn for a black-tie dinner. "Colin doesn't understand artists. He thinks that if something isn't bringing in a fortune the first day, it's not worth doing."

"I support her," said Colin. "I just think we should face facts. She's good, but she's not great. Seven years she's been doing these auditions, and she gets what? Maybe one callback for every dozen tries. Let's say she gets this one. It's not like she can live on it. Orchestras don't pay shit. She's still going to have to work a day job."

"This is her dream," said a petite woman with long red hair. "Everybody should get to go after their dream."

Colin snorted. "You sound like Diana." But still, he was here.

"Besides, not everybody gets their dream," offered a tall, thin woman. "Look at me. I wanted to be a ballet dancer, but I'm too tall. Nobody wants a six-foot ballerina. It didn't make the slightest difference that I was gifted. All those years of work and sacrifice, and in the end, my own body betrayed me."

As she spoke, a young man carrying a battered violin case paused as he crossed the lobby. For an instant, his dark eyes reflected terror. Then he squared his shoulders as if to say, *Yours, maybe. But not mine,* and he disappeared toward the hallway of hopefuls.

"What's yours auditioning for?" A man with strawberry blond hair and a well-chiseled jaw directed his question at me. He looked as if he belonged on a sailboat.

"Cello," I said. "Yours?"

"Same. My son, Jesse. Practices eight hours a day. Wants to be the next Yo-Yo Ma."

"A worthy goal. Is he that good?"

"He's only sixteen, so who knows? My ex is a musician, and she says he is. Don't ask me. I'm only a lawyer."

"Same here. Meg Riley."

"Scott Wilkinson," he said as we shook hands. "Nettis, Butler, & Gould. You from the city?"

"Hartford. You?"

"New Canaan. A fellow Nutmegger. Hey, Nutmeg, we're going to be a while here. Want to get a cup of coffee?"

"As long as it's tea."

"Deal." He led the way down the hall. One flight up, and we found ourselves in the main lobby. The box office windows were shuttered, but the gift shop was open for anyone wanting to buy music scores, CDs, or souvenirs. "They always open on audition days," Scott said. "People want something to remember this place by." Sure enough, the gift shop aisles were busy with customers whose appearance marked them as Not New Yorkers as clearly as mine did.

Next to the gift shop, the coffee kiosk was bustling. I ordered English breakfast tea and a lemon poppyseed muffin. Scott ordered a large French roast and a cinnamon scone. "It's a long drive back to Connecticut," he said as if I'd questioned his choice. "How long to Hartford?"

"About two and a half hours if there's no traffic."

Scott chuckled. "I'd have put him on a train for that."

"It's her first audition in a long time. I wanted to be here for her."

"That's nice." He raised his cup. "May one of ours win."

"Is there only one slot open for cello players?" I hadn't questioned Isabella too deeply about the mechanics of auditioning. I didn't want her to think I was being critical or implying that it was such a long shot that she should go back to her husband and order more supplies for the Pole.

"That's what they posted, but things change. Could be more, could be none."

"Wouldn't they cancel if there weren't any openings?"

"Not necessarily. If they hear somebody they think is outstanding, they might take the opportunity to juggle some things. They can't do too much since it's a union shop, but they can get pretty creative when they want to."

"You seem to know a lot about this." I took the lid off my cup and blew on the surface of my tea to cool it.

"I should hope so. I represent them."

"The union or management?"

"The employer." He broke off a piece of his scone.

Damn. "Sounds like your son has a leg up on the competition."

Scott shot me a fast look. "If they don't think he can perform, they won't take him." He glanced at his phone, and I took the opportunity to do the same. No message from Isabella. "So, Nutmeg, where's your office?" he asked.

"Right outside of Hartford. What about you?"

"Midtown. How many are in your firm?"

"Just me. How about you?"

"Small office. Thirty-two attorneys and about sixty staff. What kind of law do you practice?"

"Litigation. Trial work. You?"

"Employment, mainly. Some corporate. White collar criminal defense. What kind of litigation do you do?"

"Pretty much whatever walks in the door," I admitted. "Civil, family. Criminal defense—any color collars."

He chuckled appreciatively. "Sounds pretty busy. You like being a solo?"

"Sometimes. I haven't been on my own very long, but it's got its plusses." The main one being that I could take time off without anybody looking askance at my billables at the end of the month.

"The freedom must be nice," he said as if I'd spoken that last bit aloud. "My partners get pretty bent if the billables aren't up where they should be. Not that it's an issue, because my clients always have new problems. Frankly, I'd like to cut back in the next few years. Get out of the office, have a life."

"Do you have other children besides Jesse?"

"—He's the only one. How about you?"

"None."

He looked startled. "Then who do you have auditioning?"

"She's—a friend." Trying to explain the relationship felt far too involved. It was none of Scott Wilkinson's business who Isabella was—or Phil, or Ralph.

A *ding* signaled a new text. It was from Isabella: *Callback next week! So excited! Where are you?* I tapped a quick response that I'd be there in a minute.

"Good news?" asked Scott. I must have looked startled, because he said, "I'm sorry, I don't mean to pry."

"That's okay. It's my friend. She got a callback." I finished my tea, wrapped up the remaining half of my muffin, and rose. "It's been nice meeting you. Good luck to Jesse."

Scott stood up. "I'll walk down with you. He should be done soon."

"Really, you don't need to. I have to stop in the ladies' room anyway."

"Sure, okay. Well, it was nice meeting you. Listen, here's my card. If you ever need a consult on an employment matter, feel free to call." He reached into his pocket and held out a card.

"Thanks. Here's mine in case you ever need somebody in Hartford." I handed him a card which he perused for a second before tucking it into his jacket pocket. I headed back toward the stairs, trying to recall if I'd seen a ladies' room on the way up.

When I reached the lower level, I saw Isabella at the other end of the hallway. Her cello case sat on the floor beside her, and she was tapping madly on her phone. "Congratulations!" I called as soon as I was close enough.

"Thanks, Meg!" She finished tapping and flung her arms around me. "I can't believe I got a callback on my first audition! If it weren't for you, none of this would have happened! You're the best!" She resumed texting, presumably relaying the good news to everybody she'd ever met.

As we pushed open the heavy door, I caught a glimpse of Scott out of the corner of my eye. Part of me felt vaguely guilty, while the rational part of my brain reasoned that it was nothing more than a cup of tea with a fellow lawyer—networking, putting a Saturday to good use. Besides, I'd never hear from him again. Not that I wanted to, I hastened to assure myself.

Even so, as we drove past the New Canaan exits on the Merritt Parkway, I found myself glancing around to see if any exiting cars carried a strawberry blond man and his son.

That evening, when Ralph FaceTimed me, life felt normal again. "How did the audition go?" he asked.

"It went great. She got a callback. Didn't Phil tell you?"

"Haven't seen him since breakfast."

"Oh." I'd assumed Phil was one of the recipients of the texts that had consumed Isabella's attention most of the way home. Then again, I hadn't asked. As much to fill space as anything, I told him about driving down to the city, and I recounted the story about the stretch scraping the concrete barriers. I described the sidewalk café, the people bustling even on a Saturday, the traffic, and the experience of walking past Lincoln Center en route to the building where Isabella was auditioning. "They had all those signs up for different upcoming performances, and the fountain was turned on. It's like another world where people have all this time and money to flit off to the opera or the symphony whenever they choose."

"Sounds like you had a good time."

"I love New York as long as I can go home." I'd once dated a guy who was a freelance cameraman in the city. He lived with five roommates in a three-bedroom apartment on Columbus Avenue, mere blocks from Central Park. One night, my boyfriend mentioned casually how much it helped for him to be located in Manhattan because he could be at practically any location within an hour, which I recognized as his way of saying that if we got married, I'd need to move to the city. Just as casually, I said I loved the Hartford area, because it offered everything from city life to farms and woodlands, all within a ten-mile radius of my front door. For a while, our relationship was a competition—"see how nice it is at *my* place?"—but in the end, we acknowledged that neither of us wanted to live in the other's world. Our parting was amicable: I drove him to the Hartford train station, and on the way home, I picked up takeout at the Chinese restaurant near my condo, not even thinking about how, if I'd been in Manhattan, I could have had it delivered.

"How's everything going up there?" I asked, as much to change the subject as anything else.

"Busy. Christmas is coming."

"—I've heard."

"Was that Isabella's only audition, or does she have more stuff lined up?"

"Okay, this is weird." I settled into my recliner with a glass of wine. David climbed up into my lap, curling into a silky ball. "Is she not talking to Phil, or is Phil not talking to the rest of you?"

"I'm just asking." His eyes were wide and innocent.

"I feel like I'm being put in the middle of all this. If she doesn't want to tell her husband what she's doing, I don't think it's my place to feed him that information through you."

"So—now you think keeping secrets is okay?" The barb was almost indiscernible, but I felt it.

"It's not the same thing. I'm not keeping anything secret about me. I just don't think it's my place to be telling everybody about her life."

"He's my brother."

"And he's her husband. If she wants him to know stuff, she'll tell him. It's not my place to get in the middle of their marital crap." *Or your place*, I wanted to add. *Or your mother's.*

He regarded me for so long that if he hadn't blinked, I'd have thought the screen was frozen. Finally, he said, "Well, I've got to get back to work. Talk to you tomorrow. Love you."

"Love you more," I said, but he'd already clicked off.

I set down the phone. From upstairs, the clear, mellow tones of the cello evidenced Isabella's excitement about her callback. She'd already circled the day in red on my kitchen calendar. I knew she would practice all day, every day, until our return to the city. I sipped my chardonnay, remembering back when I was a brand-new associate. I'd been so excited about my profession that I could barely sleep on Sunday night because Monday was almost here. Those days felt like a lifetime ago.

I was about to call upstairs to see what she wanted for dinner when my cell rang. Ralph must have decided to apologize. I picked it up without looking and said, "Hi, sweetie."

"Um—hi."

It wasn't Ralph. "I'm sorry. Who is this?"

"Scott Wilkinson. We met today at the audition."

My cheeks flushed. "Oh, sure, right. Sorry, I thought you were somebody else."

"I figured as much." Pause. "Listen, I'm wondering if we can talk. You said you're practicing in the Hartford area these days. My firm has been thinking about establishing a Connecticut office, and we're throwing around some possibilities. If you're free some time, I'd like to come up and pick your brain about Hartford."

"Of course. I'd be happy to meet with you. I think Hartford is a terrific location. It's midway between New York and Boston, so a lot of people here are admitted in all three states, which gives you a lot of flexibility. I could show you the Hartford courthouse complex, or if you think you'd be more interested in branching out into governmental work, we could go over to the Capitol. Whatever works for you."

"That all sounds great, but we're only in the preliminary stages. Maybe I could come up and we could have dinner. You could tell me all about it then."

"Okay, sure. Let me get my calendar." As if I might have any conflicts. One of the many downsides of a long-distance relationship was that I rarely had anything scheduled with my boyfriend. "How's Tuesday?"

"Perfect. You pick the restaurant, and I'll meet you there. I can get there by seven. I'll work from my home office and then drive up. Text me the details."

"Sounds great. See you then." I clicked off and sat back. David adjusted himself in my lap. "Look at that, D. Mama's making lawyer connections." Isabella wasn't the only one with something to celebrate.

She also wasn't the only one who wasn't telling her man everything about her career.

To be clear: I didn't deliberately keep my dinner with Scott Wilkinson a secret from Ralph. I didn't lie or fudge or obfuscate. I merely refrained from offering information.

I mean, if Ralph had asked me directly, "Will you be having dinner on Tuesday with an attractive lawyer who may ultimately want to offer you a fantastic job?", I wouldn't have lied. I might have said, "Define 'fantastic'." Or, "Define 'attractive'." But I would not have lied.

Small comfort this turned out to be.

Six

I suppose it was an indicator of how solid Isabella thought my relationship with Ralph was that it never occurred to her to say something like,
"I don't know where she is," when Ralph called the house on Tuesday
evening. Clearly, she figured I'd already told him about the dinner.
Apparently, she thought I'd have told him about having googled Scott
to learn more about his firm. I guess she even thought I'd told Ralph
that when she peered over my shoulder and saw Scott's headshot, her
jaw dropped at how good-looking he was. You'd think that after ten
years of marriage, she'd know better than to tell a man things like this.
It didn't help that I'd put my cell on *do not disturb* so my business
dinner wouldn't be interrupted with a call from my mother about
something her husband's grandchildren had done. This would mean
missing a call from Ralph, but I routinely let his calls go to voicemail
if I was in a meeting, and neither of us thought twice about it. It never
occurred to me that Isabella had outed me.

Or maybe the problem was how much I enjoyed going out to dinner
with Scott. He'd left the details up to me, so I chose an excellent restaurant that was practically a Hartford institution. It was located on
the ground floor of a landmark office building comprised of two towers
separated by a vast lobby. On weeknights, it was the perfect place for
Hartford professionals to see and be seen as they savored osso bucco
and salmon while negotiating their next step up the ladder.

When I arrived, Scott was standing at the lobby entrance. Even
after a full day's work, his impeccably tailored suit and crisp light blue
shirt showed no sign of wrinkles. "I haven't been here in ages," he said.
"It's good to be back."

"I didn't realize you were familiar with Hartford," I said as he held the outer door for me. I held the inner door for him, and he didn't hesitate to enter, which pleased me. Once inside, I gave the maître d' my name. Moments later, we were seated in an excellent booth that afforded us a view of all the goings-on while protecting us from eavesdroppers.

We made small talk while considering the menu. I debated whether to suggest we get a bottle of wine, uncertain whether this would blur the lines between business dinner and social occasion. Before I could decide, our waiter appeared and inquired if we would like anything to drink. I gestured to Scott to go ahead. "Seltzer with lime, please," he said.

"Two," I said.

After the waiter left, he said, "Feel free to drink if you like. I have a long drive back."

"No worries. I have to work tonight." Meredith had emailed me a list of household items that needed to be ordered.

Scott donned a pair of tortoiseshell reading glasses and perused the menu. "Any recommendations?"

"I haven't had the filet, but people say it's excellent. I tend more toward seafood myself."

"So do I. I went to college in the Boston area, and then law school down in New Haven. Lots of fresh catch." A not-so-subtle way of inviting me to ask so he could tell me he'd gone to Harvard undergraduate and Yale Law School.

"Since you're a guest in these parts, we won't send you down to the river to fish for your dinner," I said instead as the waiter reappeared with our seltzers. Scott ordered the sesame-crusted ahi tuna steak, and I chose the seared diver scallops. Once the waiter left, we had no more distractions.

"So, you're interested in opening a Hartford office," I said when he didn't speak. "Mind if I ask why Hartford instead of Stamford or New Haven?"

"We're looking at those locations, too," he said. "Stamford has the obvious attraction of proximity to the city as well as the Gold Coast. The thing is, people who will go to Stamford are equally likely to go to the city, so it's arguably redundant. New Haven is a major hub, but it'll draw clients from the southern half of the state and not much farther beyond. Hartford, on the other hand, is centrally located. Not only is it convenient for the entire state, but it's also midway between New York and Boston, which means we could draw from both areas."

I couldn't tell whether he'd forgotten I'd made that very point when we spoke on Saturday or if he was deliberately quoting me. "What kind of a practice would you have in Hartford? More of the corporate work you do in the city?"

The waiter brought a basket of warm rolls and a shallow dish containing a generous swirl of butter flecked with herbs. Normally, I'd have foregone the bread, but tonight, I took a roll and broke it open, the yeasty aroma rising to fill the small space in our booth.

"Actually, our New York office includes a litigation practice," he said. "It so happens that my focus is mostly corporate. Our Connecticut office, wherever that may be, will also include a mix."

"What kind of litigation do you do?"

"The usual. Wrongful termination, discrimination claims, contract disputes. White-collar criminal. Some bankruptcy, some products liability." I nodded; my "usual" tended toward personal injury and divorce with all its added issues, like post-judgment compliance, visitation, and child support. Much less legally sophisticated, much more holding the client's hand. Scott continued, "In Connecticut, I imagine we could broaden our practice if the clientele is here. For example, if we were to land in Stamford, we might establish a high-end trusts and estates practice."

"Or a family law practice geared toward clients with complex finances," I suggested in an effort to build a bridge between our two focuses even though the truth was that I was trying to get out of divorce law.

"Exactly." He seemed impressed that I'd thought of this, which irked me slightly. "Or we could get into commercial litigation. We could develop into Hartford's leading firm in a few years' time."

"Hartford already has some very fine firms. A number of the larger ones have offices in this very building. Plus, we have quite a few superb boutique firms that specialize in particular areas of the law." All by way of reminding him that being the New Yorker who came to town didn't automatically mean he'd be at the top of the heap.

"I'm aware of that," he said, smiling. "You used to be with McGooley, Rose & Swarthorn, didn't you?"

So he'd also googled me. I wasn't certain whether to shrug it off as a lawyer doing his research or something else. Of course, if he'd found my biographical information, he'd likely also found all the press about Ralph's case, including my notoriety after his escape from prison. I was half-surprised he hadn't canceled the meeting after reading newspaper articles about how I'd testified at my disciplinary hearing that I believed in Santa Claus.

I was tempted to confront him with all this, but I'd spent years counseling clients to answer only the question they'd been asked. Volunteering information was what got them into trouble. For once, I took my own advice. "Yes," was all I said.

"And then you went to the Lundstrom Law Firm." From which I'd been unceremoniously booted in the wake of Ralph's escape from prison.

"And now I'm on my own," I said breezily, as if to suggest that I'd wanted more freedom than law firm life allowed.

"And you said you enjoy solo practice." It wasn't quite a question.

The waiter set green salads in front of us, allowing me a moment to regroup. "It's fascinating. You never know what a day will bring. Plus, it gives me time for other things." Like doing Isabella's job while she practiced in my guest room.

"Let me guess. You have a side hustle. You're writing a book? Doing community theater? Training for a marathon?"

"None of the above." My redirection of the conversation seemed to be effective. "How about you? What do your off-hours look like, or don't you get any?"

"One of the perks of being senior is that I have flexibility," he said. I must have looked startled, because he added, "I just celebrated my twenty-fifth anniversary with the firm."

So he was fifty, which used to seem a lot older before I hit forty last year. Ralph was thirty-eight, which sounded so young by comparison.

My mind wandered to the Pole and Ralph. When I pulled my thoughts back, Scott was enthusiastically describing how he and Jesse used to go out on his boat almost every weekend between early spring and late fall. "Luckily, my ex is really good about sharing his time," he said.

"You're very fortunate. I can't begin to tell you how much time I've spent in court because somebody isn't happy about the visitation schedule."

"One of the first things we decided was that we weren't going to use Jesse as a pawn. Some days, it feels like practically the only thing we agreed on, but we've held to it."

"That's definitely an achievement."

"He's an amazing kid." His blue eyes darkened then. If he'd been Ralph, I'd have urged him to speak about what was bothering him, but Scott was a stranger, and this was a business dinner.

The waiter took away our empty salad plates, and another server set down our meals. We ate in silence for several minutes. Then, Scott said, "We had a daughter. She died."

I set down my fork and listened. He told me about the little girl named Alice who was born with a defective heart, how they spent hours upon hours in doctors' offices and hospital rooms, how smart and funny and pretty and happy she was, and how, when she was six, her little heart gave out.

"I'm so sorry," I breathed.

His smile was crooked. "Thank you," he said. "Jesse was three when Alice died. He doesn't remember her, of course. But losing a child—that's the kind of thing that makes or breaks a marriage. We hung on for a long time, but by the time Jesse was ten, we knew we were done." He drained his glass and signaled for the waiter. "Can I have a Jameson neat?"

"Yes, sir. For you, miss?"

"Sauvignon blanc, please."

We didn't speak again until our glasses were in front of us. Then, Scott picked his up as if in a toast. "To better days," he said.

"Better days." Our glasses clinked, and we drank.

*****

On the drive home, I replayed our parting. "I'm sorry I dumped all my personal stuff on you," Scott said. "I had no right to do that."

"Don't worry about it," I said sincerely.

"I'd like to come up during the day at some point, maybe check out the area when offices and courthouses are open. If you have time, I'd be grateful if you'd serve as my tour guide."

"I'd be happy to." We shook hands. For a moment, I thought he might try to kiss me, but he was all business now. "Where are you parked?"

"Wherever the valet put me. You?"

"On the street around the corner." On-street parking was free after six o'clock.

"In that case, let me walk you to your car," he said.

"No need, I'm fine." He looked uncertain, but before he could pursue the notion that I required protection, I said, "Let me know when you want to see Hartford in action. Good night."

"I'll be in touch soon." He reached into his pocket and withdrew the ticket for the valet. As I turned the corner, I glanced back to see him standing at the valet station. He was looking at me. I gave him a brief wave. He waved back. Then, I headed up Church Street to my car, and I drove home without remembering to take my phone off *do not disturb*, which meant I missed Ralph's call again.

*****

Isabella was practicing in the kitchen when I came in. It was her favorite practice room; she said the sound bounced off the hard surfaces, making it more resonant. I had no idea what this meant, but as long as she wasn't bothering me, I didn't care.

"Call Ralph," she said without pausing her practice.

"What?"

Her fingers flew on the fingerboard. "He called on the landline. Said he couldn't reach you on your cell."

I yanked out my phone and turned off *do not disturb*. Instantly, the notifications showed four missed calls—two from the Pole, and two more from a certain Vancouver number—as well as two voicemails. A frisson of irritation ran through me: couldn't I have a simple dinner without a constant barrage of demands from up north?

The first voicemail was from Ralph's mother. "Good evening, Meg, this is Meredith Claus. Have you had an opportunity to review the requisition lists we sent down? As I'm certain you understand, obtaining supplies is complicated, and coordinating deliveries takes time, so we really can't wait until the last minute. Please get in touch with me. Good night."

Isabella was playing the same phrase over and over. Tamping down annoyance, I asked, "Did your mother-in-law call you?"

"Huh?" The rhythm of the notes continued without pause.

"Isabella!"

"I'm trying to work!" But she finally stopped playing.

"I said, did your mother-in-law call you?"

"Why would she?"

"Because apparently there's stuff she needs to have ordered."

If I thought this was going to get Isabella's attention, I was wrong. "The only one who called here was Ralph. He didn't say anything about supplies, just for you to call him." She resumed playing as if the cello were her only job.

Maddening, every last one of them. Apparently the Clauses were construing Isabella's sabbatical as a total vacation from Pole responsibility. Without bothering to play back the second voicemail, I called Ralph as I headed up to my room, the cats in pursuit.

"Isabella said you called," I said when he answered.

"Um, yeah." He seemed slightly taken aback by my terseness. "Everything okay?"

"Why wouldn't it be?"

"I tried your cell a couple times, and you didn't answer."

"I was—out." He said nothing. "I had dinner with a lawyer who's thinking of opening a Hartford-area practice and wanted some advice." It was the truth, if not the whole truth.

"So I heard." His voice was carefully neutral. I waited for him to ask something, anything. Finally, he said, "I wanted to make sure you'd gotten Mom's message. There's some stuff the workshop needs, and she's getting a little antsy."

"Why didn't you ask Isabella to do it?"

"She said she was practicing."

"But procurement is still her job. I'm only the helper."

"I figured—you know what, it doesn't matter. You two work it out and let Mom know who's handling it." He sounded like a mid-level manager addressing an underling, and I felt my hackles rise.

"We'll be sure to take care of it, *sir*," I snapped. "Is there anything else, *sir*?"

"What's the matter with you?" He sounded genuinely perplexed.

"Nothing," I said. "I'm going to bed. Have a good night."

"Okay. I love you," he said.

"I love you, too," I replied in the same tone I'd have used to tell him his supplies were on the way, and I hung up.

What was I so annoyed about? Okay, he hadn't asked about my evening, but did I really want him to? Which part would I tell him? That an attractive man had invited me to dinner and confided about his personal life, or that if I played my cards right, I might be able to work with—or even lead—the Hartford office of a New York law firm? Either one would get his long johns in a bunch.

Part of me wanted to call him back, to apologize and explain. Another part conceded that an apology might be appropriate but cautioned strongly against an explanation. After all, there was an excellent chance I'd never even hear from Scott Wilkinson again, or that if I did, it would be a short email thanking me for my time and explaining that they'd decided to go with Stamford, or maybe Westport, either of which would be convenient for a plethora of wealthy clients who might want to write wills, set up trusts, or get divorced. If I ever saw him, it would probably be at one of Isabella's auditions, and he'd probably have his ultra-understanding ex-wife on his arm because they'd decided to try reconciling.

My text alert dinged. Most likely Ralph making sure I was okay. I picked up my phone.

Thanks for a great evening. Looking forward to checking out Hartford with you. How's Friday afternoon?

Before I could respond, another alert dinged.

Didn't mean to harass you about Mom's stuff. I'll call you tomorrow. Maybe you can come up this weekend. Miss you and love you. Followed by a heart emoji and a Santa emoji.

This, I believe, is what's known as a dilemma.

*****

The easiest approach, I decided, was to confront Isabella. She could then talk to her mother-in-law, and that would be one demand off my list.

After that, all I had to do was decide between two men who wanted my attention.

Isabella was in the kitchen when I walked in the next morning. Her cello case lay on its side against the wall, and coffee was dripping into the pot of the coffee maker I'd purchased for my new roommate. "Listen, about last night," I began.

"No prob. Just let me know if you're going to be out so I can cover for you." She sounded like my college roommate, and it irked me.

"I don't need you to cover for me. I'm not doing anything that needs covering for." I edged past her to retrieve the electric kettle.

"Whatever." She waved her hand dismissively. I couldn't tell whether she was trying to appear uninterested or if she truly didn't care whether I might be sneaking around behind Ralph's back. "Hey, can you grab me a mug?"

I handed her one of my Tanglewood mugs and took another for myself. I filled the kettle and set it on its unit to boil. "We need to talk about something," I began again.

"Can it wait? I've got to run. There's this little string quartet that I heard about, and they might be looking for a new cellist, so I want to check them out. Mind if I borrow your car for a few hours?" She set the Tanglewood mug on the counter and took out a commuter mug.

"What? Of course I mind. I need it for work. What is this quartet doing at eight in the morning, anyway?" Already, I regretted taking her to get her license. She'd been borrowing my car ever since.

"It's kind of a meet-and-greet. A guy at the audition told me about it. They have breakfast at this bagel place in Manchester a couple times a week. I think the violinists both live near there, or they work near there, or something, and the viola player's brother runs the place. Anyway, this guy said that if I wanted, we could meet there and he could introduce me to the group and if we hit it off, maybe they'd let me audition."

Clearly, I wasn't the only one networking for a new job. "I'll get you an Uber. I need my car today." More like *I want my car today.* "Before you go, your mother-in-law needs to talk to you about some requisitions." The use of *mother-in-law* was deliberate.

"Can you handle it? I really need to get going. If I'm too late, everybody'll be gone." She filled the commuter mug and added sweetener.

"Won't they be offended if you show up with your own coffee?"

"That's okay. I'll drink it on the way up."

"You can't drink in an Uber." I actually wasn't sure, but I didn't want any extra charges because she spilled coffee in the car.

She took a quick sip. "I can't drink it now. It's too hot. Can you call for that Uber? I really need to go." She put down the commuter mug.

I tapped my phone to summon an Uber. "They'll be here in twenty minutes."

She frowned. "That's really long. I'm going to miss them."

I knew a hint when I heard one, but I was in no mood to rearrange my life to accommodate her. I scooped loose tea into the filter and poured boiling water through it into my mug. "That'll give you plenty of time to call Meredith back," I said, taking my mug and heading upstairs for a shower.

I'd just dropped my robe when I heard the garage door open. "Isabella!" I pulled on my robe and ran down the stairs, but it was too late. Her mug, her cello, and my car keys were all gone. "Isabella!" I screamed, running out the door in time to see her pause at the corner before driving away.

"I'm going to kill her," I muttered. A ping from my phone alerted me that another Uber was one minute away. "Shit!" I tapped as fast as I could to cancel it, but before I could get through the menu, a tan Civic pulled up in front of the townhouse. Still in my robe, I went out to the curb. "Sorry, mistake," I said. "They told me twenty minutes."

"No problem," the young man said cheerfully. "You want me to wait?" He could afford to be cheerful: I was going to get charged for the ride anyway, and waiting time was extra.

"No need. Thanks anyway." I waved as he left. Damn that selfish little bitch. Well, two could play this game. I went back inside and called Meredith. "Sorry I missed you last night," I said before she could say more than hello. "Isabella's the one who's going to handle the requisitions. She had to go out this morning, but you can reach her on her phone."

"I was under the impression you were helping her," Meredith said.

"Helping, not replacing," I said. "She's having breakfast with some friends this morning. She won't mind if you call her now."

I hung up and resumed my morning preparations. As was their custom, the cats watched as I got into the shower, and they were still clustered in the bathroom when I came out. "Your mama isn't a very nice person," I told them, but they didn't seem to mind.

Ten minutes later, my phone rang. Meredith again. I declined the call and returned to the kitchen to feed the cats and fix my own breakfast. Then, I took my tray to the basement office. I didn't need to deal with the Clauses this morning. Remarkable as it might have seemed, I had work of my own to do.

Seven

Adeline's Bar & Grille wasn't a typical lawyer hangout. For one thing, it was a solid thirty minutes from downtown Hartford, on a leafy road winding north toward Massachusetts. For another, it was frequented by ladies who lunch, not business professionals networking. If you were trying to make a connection, Adeline's wasn't your place.

And yet here I was with my former partner, Rick. Rick had been voted out of the Lundstrom Law Firm several years before me, after it came out that he was simultaneously representing the husband in a divorce and bedding the wife. He moved on to Carter Fitzhugh's firm, where they were building a reputation as the fiercest team in family law, never settling when there was a chance to fight. The local legal gossip sheet referred to them as the "divorce sharks." Apparently, they considered it a compliment.

I hadn't heard from Rick since I was in the midst of my own travails several months earlier. To be honest, I'd barely thought of him until he called two days earlier to suggest we meet for lunch. I accepted his invitation because—well, what else did I have to do? Besides, he might prove a fruitful source of new business. I had no interest in taking on any more family cases if I could avoid them, but surely some of his clients might have other legal problems. So the night before our lunch, I slipped my car keys into my purse and tucked my purse behind the bedroom door so I could be certain my roommate wouldn't help herself to my car for another breakfast outing.

Rick was already at a corner table out on the patio when I arrived. Red market umbrellas shielded tables from the sun, but not from the noise of vehicles whizzing past on the other side of the privacy hedge. I followed the hostess through a sea of gray-haired women nibbling salads and quaffing iced tea. "Meg!" he called loudly, rising and opening his arms as if greeting a long-lost friend. None of the lunching ladies looked up. I couldn't help wondering who he was performing for. Then again, I often had that thought about Rick.

"Sit down, sit down," he urged even though I was doing precisely that. "Would you like a drink?" Drops of condensation glistened on his martini glass.

"Iced tea, thanks," I said to the tiny blond waitress who had followed us to the table. I took a moment to spread the signature red cloth napkin in my lap. "So, how are you? I wasn't expecting to hear from you."

Something in his smile changed, as if he were forcing himself to hold it in place. "It's been too long. I missed you."

Luckily, the waitress brought my iced tea, interrupting before I could laugh out loud at the transparency of his lie. In leisurely fashion, I squeezed the lemon wedge and sprinkled sweetener into my tea. "What have you been up to?" I asked when he said nothing more.

"You know, the usual. I'm doing great! I'm telling you, Meg, everything's terrific!" The more he said it, the less I believed him.

"Glad to hear it. How's—" I couldn't remember his wife's name. You think I would have, considering that she was the reason he'd gotten kicked out of our firm.

"—Trisha," he supplied. "She's—she's great, she's been—she's really great." He sounded even less plausible than usual. Rick was not a guy you could take at face value. For the life of me, I'd never figured out why Eckert thought he was a good fit for our firm—although I understood completely why he'd decided to kick Rick to the curb. In all fairness, we'd all agreed on that. In those days, I had no problem cutting people loose who screwed up. I liked to think I was a trifle more forgiving now.

"And the kids are good?"

"They're fantastic, just—fantastic. Hey, do you like salmon? They have a terrific salmon burger here."

"Good to know." I opened the menu, less out of interest in Adeline's offerings than to buy time while I tried to sort out what was happening.

"This is my treat," he assured me. "I invited you. It's on me. What-ever you want."

I set down my menu. "What's going on, Rick?"

"What do you mean?"

"I mean, why am I here?" In all the years I'd known him, Rick had never offered to pick up the tab for so much as a takeout order from the South Pine Deli.

"For lunch! So we can catch up!" But I could see in his eyes that even he knew he wasn't selling it. "Plus, I have a great business op-portunity, and I think you're the one for it! But let's order first." He raised his hand, and the waitress nodded to let him know she'd seen him. "What are you going to have?" he asked me as she finished taking another party's order.

"Spinach salad with grilled chicken," I said. "How about you?"

"Oh, get something bigger! I told you, I'm paying."

"I'll pay for myself, thanks." I was starting to remember why I'd never missed Rick.

After the waitress had taken our orders—and I made a point of requesting separate checks—I sipped my iced tea. "So what's this great business opportunity?" I couldn't imagine it was nearly on a par with what Scott had to offer. Still, it was nice to have choices.

"Carter and I are splitting up." He finished his martini and looked around for our waitress. He caught her eye and held up his empty glass.

"That's surprising," I said honestly. "Any particular reason?"

"Carter wants to get out of family law," said Rick. "I still love it, though. New challenges every day. Like, I've got this one guy out in the Litchfield hills—old Yankee money—he's a musician, but he looks like a professor. I think the wife was his student and that's how they met. Anyway, now she's met somebody else, so she's trying to take everything. Like, he's got this huge collection of musical instruments—some of them are antiques, and most of them he buys and sells—and she wants the whole thing. The collection, the business—I mean, she's trying to ruin him. It's awful. Big old house that's been in his family for generations, and now she wants to make him sell it so she can buy a condo someplace. Protecting a guy like that—that's why I do this. He's such a good guy. We've gotten to be real friends. It's so satisfying, knowing I can help him so he'll be able to keep the things that are his—his instruments, his house, his reputation." The waitress brought him a fresh martini, and he flashed her his million-dollar smile. "What do you think, Meg? Do you want to be part of this with me?"

The man was good. Very good. Our former coworker, Michael, used to say Rick could sell sand in the desert. If I hadn't known him and his history, I'd probably have been tempted. As it was, I said, "But I don't want to do family."

"You don't have to! See, the way I was thinking, I'd have the family practice, and you could do other stuff—criminal, personal injury, maybe some wills or business litigation or something. You know, kind of the way it used to be at Lundstrom where we all had our specialties but we represented each others' clients. I mean, my clients have other problems besides their divorces. Like the guy I was talking about—his wife is trying to get him in trouble with the feds."

"What's he doing? Dealing drugs along with musical instruments?"

"Oh, no, nothing like that. She's a vindictive bitch who's out to ruin his life. But he may need a good criminal lawyer, and it would be great to have one right in the firm."

Before I could answer, the waitress brought my salad and Rick's corned beef Reuben. I waited until she was out of earshot before saying, "What are your thoughts on money?"

He gazed at me with practiced innocence. "Same deal I have with Carter. If you bring in the client, you get fifty percent of anything the client generates, plus a percentage of the fees you actually bill yourself."

"And if I'm not the one who brings in the client?"

"Forty percent of the fees you generate."

It didn't sound as if there was a lot left to run the office, but I wasn't savvy enough to know whether this was a viable business model. "What happens now that Carter's leaving? Are his clients going with him?"

"We're still working that out," Rick said smoothly. He took a large bite of his sandwich in a clear effort to avoid more questions about his ex-partner.

I waited until he swallowed. "Where is Carter going?"

"I think he's juggling a couple of options," said Rick. I made a mental note to put out some feelers to find out what was behind Carter's sudden desire to dissolve his old firm. "Listen, I don't want to pressure you. If you want some time to think about this, that's okay. Just—well, since we've got history, I'll level with you: you're not the only person I'm talking to." *But, hey, no pressure.*

"Thanks, Rick. I appreciate the information. I'll give it some thought." I drizzled more dressing on my salad, he took another bite of his sandwich, and the conversation shifted to other lawyers we knew.

*****

I pondered Rick's offer on the drive home. Teaming up with Rick wasn't something I would consider seriously, but it wasn't as if I had a ton of great choices. Life as a solo wasn't proving to be a delight; it wasn't lucrative, and frankly, I missed having coworkers. I still didn't know if Scott's firm would turn out to be a viable option. The fourth choice—closing up shop and moving to the Pole—was still under discussion. The only things I knew for certain were that I wasn't happy in my present situation and I was running up debt. I needed to make a change.

Isabella was out when I got home. Apparently, she'd figured out how to order an Uber. I made tea and took my mug downstairs to my office. Then, I called Michael, who was always the first to know what was happening. "What's going on with Carter and Rick?" I asked without preamble when he picked up.

"Pretty much what you'd expect," said Michael. "Carter dumped him because he couldn't keep his pants on."

I should have known. "You'd think he'd learn."

"It gets better," said Michael.

"Let me guess. Another client's ex?"

"If only. Moron was screwing Carter's wife."

My jaw dropped. "Holy Mother. You've got to be kidding me."

"Nope. So, three guesses who's been blackballed all over the family bar now."

"That explains a lot." Especially why he was looking for a partner whose practice was primarily civil or criminal.

"They didn't love him before. He was the kind who'd make a deal, and the next day he'd tell you his client changed her mind and wanted to go to trial—you know, trying to hold them up for better terms. Nobody trusts him anymore."

"I don't remember him being like that when he was with us."

"He wasn't. Eckert wouldn't have stood for it." The senior partner of my old firm was a stickler for ethics. My involvement with Ralph's case, especially after he escaped from prison and the grievance committee came after me, had spelled the end of my days in his firm. Although in all fairness, my sworn testimony that I'd previously lied under oath—and that I believed in Santa Claus—might also have had something to do with it.

Regardless, my offenses paled next to Rick's. "I can't believe he would be that freaking stupid. His own partner's wife. Sheesh."

"Rick is not a guy who learns from his mistakes."

"No shit. I mean, how in hell—" In all fairness, Carter should have known what he was getting. After all, it wasn't a big secret why Rick left our firm.

"Maybe Carter was keeping him on a tight leash. Or maybe he never believed that crap might land in his own backyard."

"He probably figured Rick could drum up some business if he smiled really nicely at the ladies."

"From what I've heard, he was doing exactly that." Not much fazed Michael.

"Are you joking?" How much had I missed while I was focused on my own problems?

"I wish. The idiot even got grieved again by one of his lady friends after he sent her a bill for his legal work. She claimed they had a little quid pro quo going on and he'd promised she wouldn't have to pay anything. I swear, I don't know how he still has his license."

"Well, this certainly explains a lot," I said. "Because he wasn't just looking for a lunch date. He wants me join his firm. Become his partner."

"You're kidding!"

"Hand to heart. He even offered to pay for lunch." Michael laughed. He knew our ex-partner never paid unless he thought he'd get more in return. I added, "I asked him why Carter was leaving, and he hedged."

"Maybe you're what he needs. If nothing else, you don't have a wife for him to screw."

"And he knows better than to try anything with me." Rick had made a pass at me once, when we were all young associates as MR&S. Without thinking, I'd hauled off and smacked him across the face so hard he still had the mark the next day. Before he could speak, I informed him that if he ever told a soul I'd hit him, I'd report him to the partners. "And that'll be the end of your career here," I said with far more conviction than I felt, but apparently he was convinced.

Now I mused, "You know what's sad about this?"

"What?"

"He was a decent lawyer back in the day. A little flashy, but that's the worst thing anybody ever said about him. Judges liked him. So did opposing counsel. And now look at him."

"Rick needs somebody to ride herd on him," said Michael. "Dude has no self-control. But you're right. I remember working with him on a couple of cases. His instincts were sound. When we were in court, he was good on his feet."

"Unfortunately, he's apparently also good off his feet," I said.

"Therein lies the problem," said Michael. "But enough about him. How are you doing?"

"Better than Rick."

"That's not a high standard."

"Maybe not, but what can I say? Life goes on. You figure out a way to make things work."

"How's life at the North Pole?"

"It's good. Takes some getting used to, but it has its . . . benefits." The thought of Ralph always made me smile.

"Ruby keeps asking me when you're getting married." Michael was nothing if not subtle.

"We're working on it."

"And that means . . . ?"

"It means that when it's time for you two to put on your parkas and come up for a wedding, I'll let you know."

"How exactly would we get there?" He sounded slightly skeptical, as if he still thought I was pulling his leg.

"Same as everybody else. Sleigh and reindeer." If there were any other way, I'd be the first on board.

"I don't travel by reindeer," Michael said.

"Even for me?"

"Well—maybe for you."

*****

When we hung up, I jiggled the mouse to wake up my computer. The first document I clicked was always my project list where I kept track of deadlines.

Although, in all candor, there weren't many deadlines on the list. One client, Barb Desmond, was being deposed in two weeks, but I'd already had the first prep meeting with her. I reviewed the notes she'd made after her car accident. Luckily, she'd listened when I told her to stop writing such notes because she'd have to produce them. "What about the ones I wrote in shorthand?" she asked.

"Those, too." I had a special respect for older professional women who'd spent their early careers taking dictation. They were from another era, back when being a secretary was a real career. Now, calling someone a secretary was considered an insult.

"Can the other lawyers read shorthand?" Barb asked.

"Probably not. I imagine they'll have to find someone who can. Either that, or they'll ask you to read them when they depose you. If they're smart, they'll do both."

"Why? So they can see if I'm lying?"

"Exactly." It was a relief to have a client who was smart and didn't take offense. At my old firm, the majority of my clients were either liars or entitled pains in the ass, but I was stuck with them because of their relationships with other lawyers in the firm. One of the few plusses to being on my own was the freedom to take only the cases I wanted.

Of course, this made it sound as if I was at liberty to pick and choose, which was far from the truth. Between the ones who made appointments to check out the Santa Claus lawyer and the ones who figured that a solo practitioner would be desperate enough to take any case without insisting on payment, I wasted far more time than I spent productively. The only reason I had Barb's case was that Michael had sent her my way. "It's a good case, but I'm conflicted out," he said. I was skeptical at first since it would have been typically Michael to toss a juicy case in my direction to help out, but it turned out that he'd represented the other driver's ex-wife in their divorce, which meant he'd learned all sorts of information about the guy that he couldn't ethically use. I already knew the driver had been impaired at the time of the crash, but I had a feeling this was the tip of the iceberg, and this was why Michael had elected not to test the ethical limits.

All this scampered around my brain as I skimmed Barb's notes. Truth was, while I still enjoyed practicing law, the thrill was gone. I didn't know if the whole ordeal with the Lundstrom Law Firm had left such a bad taste in my mouth that I'd never enjoy practice again or if sixteen years of doing the same stuff was enough and it was time to try something else. All I knew was that I no longer got excited when I found a piece of evidence that would drive a stake into the heart of my opponent's case. I wouldn't quite say I didn't care, but the urge to win wasn't nearly as strong as it had once been.

As if on cue, my phone rang. Meredith again. This time, I answered.

"I wasn't able to reach Isabella," she said instead of hello. "I've sent you the lists of items we need. Would you please take care of that today?"

"Isabella should be back soon. Don't you want her to do it?"

"She said she was busy. Something about an audition, and she didn't know when she'd be back."

I was ready to call Isabella myself, but considering the things I wanted to say to her, it would probably have been imprudent. I thought of calling Ralph to ask him to get his mother off my back. On the other hand, it did sound as if the task at hand was at least somewhat urgent.

"Fine," I said somewhat ungraciously. "Just give me the information. Do you have a credit card I can use?"

"We don't use a credit card for supplies. We use purchase orders." As if I should have known.

"All right, then. Send me whatever. Do I do all this online, or do I need to call people?"

"Online. You wouldn't be able to reach them by phone anyway. I don't think any of them are in your time zone. I'll forward the materials and all the contact information." She hesitated a second, then added, "Thank you, Meg. We all appreciate your help."

"No problem," I lied, but she had already hung up.

True to her word, within five minutes, a series of emails arrived. Each pertained to a requisition for a different supplier. Attached to each email were the shopping list and all relevant forms, including customs documents. I noted with some surprise that the goods would be delivered to Canada. At least I didn't have to worry about arranging to transport everything to the Pole; Meredith had assured me with typical Claus secrecy that "it was handled."

To the people who say legal documents are a puzzle, I can only say this: they're not nearly as complicated as requisitions for supplies when you don't know what in hell you're supposed to be ordering. I saw descriptions and item numbers and quantities, and I had no idea if any of it was correct. For all I knew, I was supposed to be ordering six of something, not six dozen.

Meredith had better have gotten her details right, because if I ever had to recreate it, I'd be well and truly screwed, as would everybody who was relying on me. Thank God she was relatively young; my best guess was mid-sixties, so that meant I'd have eons of time to learn from her. Julian was much older, but every day, he took at least two determined walks through the maze of hallways, usually with Anya hovering. Even at his post-stroke pace, he covered an admirable distance. "If you don't use it, you lose it," he said.

Unoriginal, perhaps, but still an excellent philosophy. The question was what I needed to use—or lose.

Eight

I was trying to decipher Meredith's purchase orders when the phone rang. "Hey, Nutmeg," said Scott. "How're you doing?"

"Crazy busy." An overstatement, but I didn't want him thinking I wasn't in demand. "How are you?"

"The same, but is it ever different? Listen, I wanted to apologize for last night. We were talking business. I'm sorry for muddying the waters like that."

"No problem. I was flattered that you felt comfortable enough to share all that with me." It seemed like the polite response.

"You're very kind. Are we still on for Friday, or have I scared you off?"

"I'd love to get together again, but I don't know if Friday's going to work. I'm going away for the weekend, and I'm not sure when I'll be leaving."

"I won't keep you out too late," he said. "You can leave bright and early Saturday morning. Would that be okay?"

"I've got to do some checking on the arrangements." I wasn't certain why I didn't want to admit that I was going to visit my boyfriend. *Privacy is good*, I told myself.

"Where are you going, or shouldn't I ask?" I couldn't tell whether I was detecting a thread of jealousy in his voice.

"Away," I said with deliberation. "Staying with friends," I added to soften my answer a bit.

"Where are they?"

Why was he pushing? Whatever his reason, it strengthened my resolve to keep my private life private. "A ways away," was all I said. When he said nothing, I chuckled to myself. Two could play at this game.

Finally, he said, "Well, I don't want to keep you. I just wanted to check on Friday. I didn't want to double-book."

It was all I could do not to laugh. As soon as he figured out that I had a boyfriend, he suddenly had plans. "No problem," I said for the second time in five minutes.

"Listen, maybe this is presumptuous, but I was wondering something. Would you be willing to take a quick look into an issue for me?"

Back on the professional track. "Assuming the conflicts check is clear. Who are the parties?" I routinely ran the names and attorneys of all new clients through my computer to see whether I was conflicted out by virtue of a prior matter.

"Well—it's my case, not the firm's." Scott hesitated before continuing. "You remember Jesse. You met him at the audition." Actually, I hadn't, but it was a small point. "His cello teacher—her name's Kimberly Austin—she told him about an audition, and he was very excited about it, but it turns out that she's also auditioning."

I could see why Jesse might be disappointed to be competing against his own teacher, but I didn't see how this was a case. When Scott didn't continue, I asked, "What is it you want me to look into?"

"Whether there's any way to keep her from auditioning," he said with what sounded like surprise.

"I don't understand. Where's the audition?"

"It's an orchestra here in Fairfield County. One of their cellists is leaving—I think her husband is being transferred. It's a good little group, and whoever gets the gig will be touring Europe next summer."

It sounded nice, but I still didn't see where there was a case, and I said as much.

"I told you." Impatience flashed in his voice. "She told him about the audition. She shouldn't be auditioning herself."

"Why not? Is there an age cutoff?"

"Not that I know of, but it's not right that she'll be competing against her own student for the job. There should be some way to keep her from auditioning."

"Does the orchestra have rules about this?"

"No, but—I'm telling you, it's a simple conflict of interests. The teacher shouldn't be putting her student up for a position she wants for herself."

"What if she hadn't told him about it? What if he'd found out on his own and he showed up and she happened to be there? Would that be okay?"

"Look, if it's too much trouble, just forget it."

I took a deep breath. "I'm not saying that. All I'm saying is that I'm not aware of any law that says a teacher is precluded from applying for a position merely because she happens to mention it to a student. I'll be happy to spend an hour poking around the law, but I'll tell you right now that I don't think the claim has any merit."

"Then don't bother. I wouldn't want to waste any more of your time." He bit off the words.

Placate the guy. He could be a source of referrals. "I can run the research. I'm happy to do it, but I want you to know that it's a long shot."

A pause. "The audition is next week. If you can come up with something—it doesn't have to be great, but enough to get her attention and maybe get her to rethink auditioning—that's all I want. Jesse is so excited about this chance, but obviously he doesn't have a shot in hell if he's going up against his teacher."

It occurred to me to wonder if Isabella knew about this audition. "Hang on a second," I said, carrying the handset with me up to the kitchen. The only item she'd written on my wall calendar was this morning's breakfast. "When is this audition?"

"Tuesday. The twenty-first."

"And what's the group?"

"Fairfield County Philharmonic. Why?"

"Just wondering. I'll poke around the law, but don't get your hopes up." We hung up, and I googled "Fairfield County Philharmonic audition." When the page came up, I messaged it to Isabella.

Perfectly legitimate, I told myself. I had no doubt Jesse's teacher was entitled to audition. As was Jesse, and as was Isabella and every other cellist in the tri-state area.

An hour later, I emailed Scott to let him know that, as discussed, I'd found no law supporting his position. Less than a minute later, my phone rang. "I need you to draft a letter," he said without preamble.

"Saying what? Are you hiring me to represent somebody?" Placating was already paying off.

"Of course. You represent Jesse. I need a cease-and-desist letter to keep the teacher from auditioning."

Another deep breath. "First of all, I don't represent Jesse. I did you a favor by doing an hour's research, but that's all. There are no grounds for a cease-and-desist. The teacher isn't violating any law by auditioning for the same job as her student. If Jesse doesn't like that, maybe the answer is to change teachers. In any case, there's no legal ground for a cease-and-desist."

A long pause. Then, with surprising sheepishness, Scott said, "You're right, of course. I knew that. I'm sorry, I shouldn't have pushed. It's just— you know how it is when your kid is upset. You want to do anything for them that you can. I hate to see him so upset." Another pause. "Please send me a bill for your time."

"No need—"

"Seriously. I was wrong to ask. I'd feel better if I could at least pay you for wasting time talking to me and doing pointless research."

"Seriously—no need. Wish Jesse luck for me. I hope he kicks ass." *Just not Isabella's ass.*

The next morning, my emails included an alert from PayPal that I'd received a payment. When I logged in, my activity page showed a payment of a thousand dollars from Scott. The note accompanying the payment read: "FPSR." *For professional services rendered.* "Please accept this. You'll make a crazy dad feel better."

I ran my fingers lightly over the keys. No question that I needed the money badly. On the other hand, would I be setting some sort of precedent by accepting it? Would he think he could call me with whatever crazy-ass entitled notions he dreamed up and then soothe his conscience by throwing money at me?

I texted him: *Got the payment. Nice, but you overpaid.*

Moments later, he responded: *You're worth it.*

I opened a new file, entered Scott's information, and set up a transfer of the payment to my bank account before I could change my mind. In my basement office, I could barely hear Isabella in the kitchen, practicing for the Fairfield County Philharmonic audition. With only the slightest hesitation, I texted Ralph: *Okay if I come up next weekend instead of this week? New client wants to meet tomorrow.*

Sure, he responded almost at once. Before I could text back, he added, *Come both weekends* followed by an eggplant, a smiling devil face, and several hearts.

A whoosh of love overwhelmed me. There was nobody, absolutely nobody, better than Ralph. I texted back, *Screw the client. I'll reschedule him.*

You sure?

Absolutely.

And I was.

Nine

"How'd your client take being rescheduled?" Ralph asked, sprawling on the bed as I tucked my clothes into my allotted drawer in his built-in bureau.

"He was fine." Which might have been overstating slightly. When I contacted Scott to confirm that I'd be away this weekend, he responded with a terse, *Fine. LMK when you're free.* I told him I'd be in touch when I returned; he didn't answer.

"What kind of case is it?" One of the many unusual things about Ralph was that he was actually interested in my work. Most lawyers who were married to non-lawyers routinely griped about how their spouses didn't want to hear about their cases. Even Michael, whose marriage I viewed as the gold standard of relationships, claimed that the real reason lawyers had partners was so somebody would listen to them talk about their work.

"It's not so much a single case," I said, not looking at him. "More like, his firm is thinking about opening an office in Hartford, and he wants to talk about maybe doing some work together."

"Is this the guy you had dinner with the other night?" His voice held a note of . . . something.

"Yes." Direct question, direct answer.

"Oh." Direct response.

"It probably won't turn into anything. But I figure it's worth checking out. You never know."

"I guess not." He got himself off the bed and went into the other room.

"What?" I demanded, following him. "What's the matter?"

He shrugged. "It doesn't sound as if you're interested in. . . ."

Moving here. The words were as clear as if he'd said them aloud. "It's not that," I said. "But it's not like—I mean, we haven't made any particular plans, and I need to earn a living."

Ralph turned to me then. "You know I want you here. As far as I'm concerned, you can move in right now."

"Really? Because you've never said anything. I mean, when you think about it, we've only been dating for a few months. Do you really think we're ready to live together?" Not to mention all the logistics involved, like uprooting my life.

He wrapped his arms around me. "I love you."

"And I love you. You know I do. But living together—that's a huge step. Have you ever lived with anybody before?"

"Once. A long time ago."

"What happened?"

He pulled me down beside him on the loveseat. "She decided this wasn't the life for her after all."

"How long was she here?" I fought the urge to get up and pace.

"A few months. I kept trying to get her to give it more time, really give this place a fair shake, but it wasn't for her. She ended up marrying a farmer."

"Seriously?" It was about as far from Pole life as I could imagine.

"She's the one who started the growing operations," he added. "She's why we have eggs and lettuce and stuff like that. She researched those special greenhouses they have at the other Pole and got all that going." I'd read about the greenhouses some scientists constructed in Antarctica. Thanks to Ralph's ex-girlfriend, the North Pole now had an entire structure with carefully controlled light and temperature where a team of elves raised chickens as well as some fragile crops like lettuce—things that couldn't be frozen, dried, or canned.

"Sounds like she made a real contribution." I tried tamp to down my insecurity. A farmer would be far more valuable to the Pole than a Connecticut lawyer. "What was her name?"

"Candace." Was it my imagination, or did his voice linger over the word? Then, he pulled himself back to the present. "What about you? Have you ever lived with anybody?"

"Once, a long time ago. I was still in law school. I had a summer job at my old law firm after my second year, and he was my assigned mentor. I moved in with him during my third year."

Ralph raised an eyebrow. "How long did you live with him?"

"A year, maybe. It's hard to remember now." What I mainly remembered was how I'd panicked when he started testing the waters about getting married. *But I was young then,* I assured myself. Barely twenty-five, just starting my career and my adult life. Far too young—and, let's face it, too immature—to make a lifetime commitment to someone.

The question was how far I'd come. I was no longer too young, but whether I'd acquired the necessary maturity to make that kind of commitment—that remained to be seen.

*****

After dinner, Ralph said, "Come with me." He held out his hand, and without need for thought, I took it.

He led me down the now-familiar series of winding halls. I thought at first he was taking me to the kitchen for either chocolate or wine, but he turned left instead of right. My senses prickled. At the end of this hallway was the stable. What possible reason could he have for going there?

And yet, this was his destination. We walked into the comparatively warm structure. The pungency of feed and manure, fur and life, were so different from other smells at the Pole, such as the aroma of cookies baking or the admitted stench of plastic in process—or the vaguely Meredith-scented office where everything important happened. I still hadn't fully identified that specific fragrance, only that it was crisp, like biting into an apple, with the same tart notes but an improbable warmth. Not cinnamon or cloves, but something different, an unexpected aroma that embraced you but was so subtle you didn't quite realize what was happening. Amber, maybe? No. It was a scent I could almost feel in the back of my mouth, but for the life of me, I couldn't put a name to it.

I'd been so preoccupied with my thoughts that I didn't notice Ralph holding out a jumpsuit and a pair of boots. "Are we going somewhere?" I asked. The only time I'd worn such garb was in the sleigh.

"Yes." But there was no sign of Ted, who always handled flight plans. Of course, there was nothing to prevent Ralph—Santa—from taking a sleigh and going off on his own, but the brothers maintained a healthy respect for each others' domains. It was difficult to imagine Ralph pulling rank without so much as a by-your-leave to the Claus who managed the stable.

I donned the suit and boots. He handed me sun goggles, and I put them on as he did the same.

"Come with me." He reached out his hand again. Again, I took it.

He walked away from the sleighs toward a door I'd never noticed before. If I'd considered it, I might have thought it led to a closet where bridles and reins were kept.

But it didn't.

Hand in hand, with slow, careful steps, we walked into an airlock and then out the back of the stable, into the never-ending sunshine of polar summer. The sun glinted across the snow and ice, as flat and uninspiring as I imagined the plains of Kansas to be. I turned back to see the building behind us, but the gentle pressure of Ralph's hand and the gesture of his chin returned my attention to what was ahead of us.

We walked for several minutes without speaking. The vast tundra was unbroken, unending. When I turned back again, the buildings were a distant speck. A shiver of fear ran up my spine. What was he doing? Where was he taking me?

"I think this is far enough." For reasons unknown, my heart was beginning to pound.

Even with goggles, the sun glared off the uninterrupted whiteness. Polar summers were relatively mild, with temperatures climbing into the twenties we considered frigid in Connecticut. But in Connecticut, we were protected from the starkness, cozily surrounded by trees and hills. Here, not so much as a bump interrupted the endless vista of ice and sky.

He shook his head. "Not yet." He held onto my hand, and we continued walking.

"I'd rather go back." My voice was trembling. Ralph himself had warned me about going out alone. *Never, ever*, he cautioned. Not only were there no landmarks, but there was wildlife. Real-life polar bears weren't cute and cuddly the way children's books depicted them. Not only were they enormous, but they ran faster than any human—and they liked fresh meat.

"Trust me," he said now. His voice was rich, soothing.

"Seriously, I want to go back. Please." I was trying hard not to panic in this tremendous expanse of ice and snow.

He stopped walking then. He rested both hands on my shoulders. "Trust me," he said again. "I promise, it's okay. Just as long as you never come out here alone."

I couldn't see his eyes behind his goggles, but somehow I knew they were every bit as warm and loving as they'd ever been. I mustered every bit of courage I'd ever known and said, "Believe me, I won't. And don't you do it, either. Promise me. We can't afford to lose Santa." *And I can't afford to lose you.*

He laughed—not a ho-ho-ho, but the kind of laugh I remembered from when we first met, back when I knew what my life was supposed to look like, when I could see what was in front of me and I wasn't afraid. "I won't," he promised, resting his arm around my shoulders. Closer now, we continued walking.

At last, we stopped. When I turned back, I could barely see the dot of the building on the horizon "Watch this," Ralph said. He made the most piercing whistle I'd ever heard. Once, twice, three times, echoing in the frigid air.

At the edge of the horizon, I saw movement. We stood still. Slowly, the figures wandered in our direction. I couldn't tell whether they were aware of our presence. The faintest sound, like a distant crowd snapping their fingers, floated in the stillness. Ralph must have sensed that I was about to ask, because he held up a finger to counsel silence.

Finally, they were close enough for me to make out their shapes. "Are those wild reindeer?" I whispered. He nodded ever so slightly, and I caught my breath.

I could see their antlers now. I was reminded of winter sunsets when I was growing up, when the bare branches of the beech tree in the back yard stood out, inky black against the brilliant colors. The highest branches were infinitely delicate, the lightest pen strokes of India ink against the watercolor sky. Once I'd held up an eyelash, trying to see which was thinner, but they were so close I couldn't work it out before darkness fell.

The reindeer took their sweet time as they ambled toward us. I wished for a handful of dried corn to toss to them, perhaps to coax them nearer. Ralph remained motionless. After what felt like an hour, when they were close—maybe ten yards away, although who could really tell?—Ralph held up his hand. As if commanded, they stopped walking. He didn't move, nor did they. I held my breath in wonder.

After a few minutes, he clicked his tongue a single time. The reindeer began walking again. As they drew near, the snapping grew louder. It seemed to come from the reindeer, but I couldn't imagine how they were making such a curious noise. Was it hooves on ice? Or something else?

The reindeer were barely five yards from us now—close enough to make me nervous. I had no idea how wild reindeer behaved. I barely felt comfortable with the ones Ted and his team had trained to do the Clauses' bidding. But Ralph stood still, his hand in mine, and it was enough for me to feel safe—at least relatively.

Ralph nickered. As one, they picked up their heads. He nickered again and squeezed my hand. We turned around, walking slowly back to the barn, a chorus of clicking letting me know we were being followed.

Going back seemed to take much longer than walking out. Gradually, the tiny dot on the horizon grew into a structure. The clicking behind us continued, but the reindeer never tried to overtake us. Once or twice, I twisted my head to look back, but they seemed uninterested in me.

When we reached the stable, Ralph said, "You can go in and get warm if you want." *No way, honey.* I wanted to see what he was going to do next. He went inside, returning with a wheelbarrow heaped high with what appeared to be some sort of grain mixture.

"What's that?" I asked, holding the door for him.

"A special feed. Ted makes it up. I don't know what he puts in it, but the reindeer love it." He pushed the wheelbarrow about twenty yards from the stable and tipped it over, spilling out the contents. For a moment, I couldn't see him for all the reindeer gathering around to feed, but then he emerged from the crowd with the empty wheelbarrow.

We stood together by the barn door, watching as the reindeer munched their treat. Slowly, one by one, they lifted their heads and began their leisurely stroll back to the far reaches of whiteness.

"Let's go in," Ralph said finally, drawing me inside and closing the door.

"That was incredible," I breathed. "Did they—do they—I mean, they're wild animals. But it almost seemed like—do they know who you are?" *Did I? Truly?*

He replaced the wheelbarrow. "I'm Santa."

"Do all the animals know? If you said something, would they understand?"

He began to shed his outer gear. "I'm Santa," he said again, as if it explained everything.

My fingers fumbled as I removed my gloves and goggles. Then I stopped and watched as he finished stripping down to his regular clothes.

"Come on," he said as he hung up his jumpsuit.

"You come on," I said.

A slow smile spread across his face. He took my face in his big, capable hands. Even though they were still chilly on my skin, a tingle of warmth ran through me. We kissed. Slowly, tantalizingly, he unzipped my jumpsuit. Inch by inch, he exposed my turtleneck and my sweater. Then, he eased the jumpsuit off my shoulders, holding it while I extracted my arms. I looped my arms around his neck, and he eased the suit down.

"Boots," he said when it could go no further. I was about to stop him when he picked me up and carried me, his hands under my armpits, to an unoccupied stall. "Wait here," he said, returning a moment later with several blankets from the sleigh. He spread them on the floor and said, "Now, let's get those boots off." I sat, and he removed my boots—and my jumpsuit, and my sweater, my turtleneck, my pants, and my underwear and socks. Then he did the same to himself with lightning speed. In the dim light of a reindeer stall, wrapped in blankets, we made love while under the midnight sun, reindeer munched treats from Santa.

Ten

Coming home from the Pole always felt like moving from one world to another—which, let's be honest, it was. At the Pole, I was with Ralph, which felt so right that leaving him was like amputating part of my essence. But at home, I settled quickly into my familiar routines. If it hadn't been for the near-constant phone calls and texts with Ralph, it might have been two years earlier, when I thought Santa Claus was a fantasy children outgrew.

Of course, now that Isabella lived with me, returning to my home no longer offered the pure privacy of earlier days. The cats had become accustomed to her, meaning they pretty much ignored her existence unless she brought home sesame chicken. The cello was a near-constant background noise that I could hear from anywhere, even my basement office. Even when she was out and I had the house to myself, I always knew it was temporary and that any minute, my solitude could be punctured.

Still, I'd be lying if I said I didn't sometimes enjoy having her there. She found delight in the smallest things, like bringing in the mail even though it was always for me. I'd suggested to Phil and the others that they send her handwritten notes so she could get some mail of her own. The first time a note from the Pole arrived, I casually flipped through the mail and said, "Oh, here's one for you," and her joyful squeal caused the cats to scurry out of the room.

She wasn't perfect, of course. After a decade of having someone else handling cooking and laundry—at the Pole, teams of elves managed such tasks—Isabella veered between being excited to do these domestic chores and expecting them to be done without her lifting a finger. Some nights, I came upstairs from the office to find the kitchen a shambles, with every pot and pan I owned stacked in the sink and greasy crumbs adorning countertops. Not infrequently, I discovered her drying lingerie draped over the shower rod in my bathroom because there wasn't enough room in hers. More than once, I opened the closet in search of a particular shirt, only to come downstairs and find her wearing it because "I didn't have anything clean!"

Still, she was a pleasant enough roommate. Certainly, the rent check helped. Nobody had said so, but presumably, these payments would continue as long as she remained in Connecticut, even if I moved to the Pole to live with Ralph. I had no present plans to sell the condo, but if I did, Isabella would need go somewhere else—either to a new apartment or back home with her husband. I wondered whether Meredith, who master-minded everyone's lives, had a plan worked out to address all these contingencies. It wouldn't have surprised me.

Today, I had errands to run. I slid behind the wheel of my car. Although Isabella used my car regularly, she never remembered to get gas. As a result, the fuel gauge needle often hovered above the red E. I pressed the button on the sun visor and listened to the familiar mechanical sounds of the garage door opening. Then, I backed out and went to town.

I couldn't believe how free I felt. I could go literally anywhere I wanted. I had a list, but if I wanted to skip things or add things, it was fine. Nobody would complain if I bought the wrong item, because this was all for me and there were no wrong items. Granted, Isabella had added a few things to the list, but she could get them herself if I didn't feel like buying them. Right now, everything was entirely my choice, and it was glorious.

I headed into the center of town, pulling into a spot in front of the library. Leaving my windows partially down, I got out of the car and ambled in the leaf-dappled sunshine. Two doors down, a lovely little shop sold coffee and tea, a Starbucks-type establishment long before Starbucks made it to the east coast. Bells jangled when I pulled the door open. I wandered in, admiring the shelves of gourmet items before purchasing an iced white peach tea. Drink in hand, I crossed to the town green where the weekly farmers market was in full swing.

I counted fifteen vendors, each of which occupied a long table covered in local products. At one table, cakes of soap tied with colorful ribbon sat next to bottles of lotion, all made from goat milk. At a neighboring table, jars of garnet-colored jam were stacked beside bottles of maple syrup which, the sign proclaimed, had been made from their own sap. Yet another table overflowed with fresh produce—large heads of leafy greens, baskets of sugar snap peas, bags of tiny new potatoes, bunches of broccoli, new carrots with long feathery tops and bits of dirt clinging to their tips. The next table boasted bouquets of colorful cut flowers in mason jars of water with ribbons tied around the neck of the jars, interspersed amid plastic-wrapped loaves of tea breads.

I wandered through the farmers market once, twice, three times. I bought something from nearly every vendor. Later, when I got home and unpacked my bags, I wondered what had possessed me to buy garlic scapes since I had no idea what they were or how you prepared them. It hadn't mattered; I'd been caught up in the luxury of farm-fresh goods. Not preserved or dried or canned, but real, fresh, immediate.

I returned to my car and placed my purchases in the back seat. Common sense said that I should go home. Instead, I closed the car door and headed toward my very favorite place in town, the library.

When I was in law school, the law library on campus was too social and too fraught for studying, so I came here to the town library. An enormous copper beech with vast outstretched branches shaded half the front lawn. The original building was more than one hundred years old. When you walked in the front door, the tranquil reading room to the left offered tall windows with drawback curtains, wing chairs, and a non-working fireplace for patrons desiring a quiet spot to read. Long glossy maple tables ran the length of the room, perfect for people like me who came to work or study. Since my student budget was tight, I'd regularly availed myself of the library's collections of books and DVDs. When I wanted a study break, I'd flip through their copies of *The New Yorker*.

Now, as I stood in the library foyer, tears prickled my eyes. How could I borrow anything when I had no idea when I'd be able to return it? The library used to be my showroom: I'd hear about a new book and check it out. If I liked the book, I'd buy it; if not, I'd return it. No harm, no foul.

I used to dream of the day when I'd live in a home where I could have a full-blown library of my very own. I'd already read and reread most of the books on my own shelves. Common sense dictated that I should get rid of them—move my absolute favorites to the Pole and donate the rest for the library book sale—but everything in me balked at this attempt at practicality. I might leave summer clothes behind, but books? Nope. The stories I'd known and cherished for so long were not negotiable.

I forced myself to leave the library without borrowing anything. Once I was home, I made a salad from some of my new treats, just for the crunch of lettuce and cucumber and radishes that a few days earlier—maybe even that morning—had been connected to plants in the ground, real and alive, growing in the sunshine, welcoming the rain.

"What are you doing?" I hadn't heard Isabella come in. She carried her cello and had a tote bag slung over her shoulder.

"Having a salad."

"At three in the afternoon?"

"I felt like it." It hadn't even occurred to me that it wasn't mealtime. I so seldom had the urge for a salad that when it hit, I went for it.

Isabella took up a fork and speared a piece of my lettuce. She made a face. "It's kind of gritty. Did you wash it?"

"Of course." Actually, I'd only given it a quick rinse. I'd forgotten that lettuce straight from the farm had a lot more dirt on it than the sanitized version sold in supermarkets. "Do you like the dressing? It's from a farm here in town. They make it themselves."

She took another piece of lettuce. "Nice. Listen, can I borrow the car? I have a rehearsal."

At least she'd asked this time. "Where?"

"We're meeting at St. Somebody's up in Manchester. Big stone church. It's right off Main Street."

Even though I'd completed my errands, I was suddenly reluctant to give up the freedom of going wherever I chose. "Tell you what. Let me finish here, and I'll drop you off. I still have some stuff to do this afternoon."

She looked disappointed, but all she said was, "Are you almost ready? I don't want to be late."

"Give me a few minutes." It wouldn't be fair to say I deliberately slowed my pace, but I did savor each remaining bite of salad before I rinsed my plate and put it in the dishwasher.

*****

In the car, I opened the sun roof and lowered the windows.

"Hey, do you mind?" Isabella put her window back up and reached for the sunroof controls. "My hair's going to be a mess."

I glanced over at her. She'd tied up her hair back with a ribbon, but little bits were escaping as the breeze blew through the windows. She looked as if she was wearing eye makeup and lipstick. Another glance, and I noticed that she was wearing a navy dress with polka dots. "What are you all dressed up for? Isn't this a rehearsal?"

"I felt like dressing up. Anything wrong with that?" A note of defensiveness crept into her voice.

I reminded myself that her personal life was not my affair. She was entitled to her privacy. Nobody expected me to be responsible for her. Besides, she and Phil were separated, at least in practical terms. Whatever arrangements they'd agreed to were none of my business. Not that Phil was likely to be seeing other people since he was at the Pole and there wasn't anybody else to see unless he wanted to take up with an elf, which I assumed Meredith would frown on since she'd likely disapprove of her son consorting with an employee. Truth be told, I'd be concerned, too. The power imbalance was extreme: if the elf didn't welcome Phil's advances, or if she later wanted to end the relationship, she might not feel free to say so, especially considering that they lived in the same place and she wouldn't have a realistic way to get away from him.

"Do Clauses ever date elves?" I asked.

"What!" Isabella's head snapped around. "What are you talking about?"

"Nothing. I just wondered. I mean, there are so many around, and the ones I've met are really nice. Considering that the only other choice is importing someone, I wondered if it was ever a thing." I wasn't about to point out that importing someone from down below wasn't working out so well for at least one of the Clauses and that he might do better with somebody who wasn't itching to get away from the Pole.

"Absolutely not. Mrs. C. would never allow it." But she twisted her wedding ring as she spoke.

So Isabella had had the same thoughts about Phil as I'd had. Interesting. Maybe she really was getting dressed up for the fun of it. If she was worrying about him, it stood to reason that she'd watch her own step.

Unless, of course, she figured that since she was here to explore the world she'd missed out on by marrying so young, the rules were different for her. She probably thought—likely correctly—that I wasn't going to run back to Ralph and tell him if she went out to dinner with a man. On the other hand, if I walked into my kitchen one morning and found some guy in his underwear making coffee, that would be an entirely different situation. Then I'd need to figure out what—if anything—I was going to say to Ralph. If the choice was between keeping quiet while she cuckolded Ralph's brother and ratting her out—thereby ensuring that everyone in the family would hate her and she'd never be able to go back—it would be a tough choice.

I pulled into the church parking lot. Two other cars were in the lot. A man and a woman stood by the church door, both holding violin cases. At least the rehearsal was real, a point I hadn't realized I questioned until the thought flashed through my mind. The man was short and chunky, with leonine features too large for his face, but his smile was arresting. The woman was taller and slender, with long gray-brown hair. The way she leaned forward, smiling and nodding as he spoke, suggested that she found the man entrancing.

"Will you need me to pick you up?" I asked as Isabella got out of the car.

"Don't worry, I'll get a ride. Some of us might go out afterward." She opened the back door to retrieve her cello. "Thanks, Meg." She slammed the door ever so slightly harder than necessary and waved to the violinists. As I pulled away from the curb, another car drove into the lot. When I got to the exit, I glanced in my rearview mirror. The new arrival was a younger man with blond hair and a reddish-blond beard and a viola case. I watched as he greeted the others. I was about to pull out into the street when I looked again. The violinists had gone inside, but Isabella and the violist were still on the sidewalk. I saw him bend down so that their faces were close. She tilted her head upward. They were far enough away that I couldn't tell if they were speaking, but then, they both turned as if to look at my unmoving car. When I didn't move, they hustled inside.

I pulled out onto the street. All at once, my blissful day felt very far away.

*****

Instead of going home, I went to the park next to one of the elementary schools. At least, the town designated it a park; in fact, it was a large patch of woods with walking trails. Luckily, I was wearing sneakers, which were adequate for these purposes.

I followed a path of hard-packed dirt, careful not to trip over the occasional tree root that interrupted the smooth surface. The path ran along a ridge; several feet below, a brook rippled, splashing around rocks. I paused to watch. As if to reward me for my attention, a fish jumped up, breaking the surface and vanishing almost immediately. I stood still for a while, but he was apparently a solo act. Maybe the others were content with their lot in life, happy to remain below the surface, while he simply couldn't be so restricted.

I wandered for a while, mainly because I could. In the shade of the woods and the lateness of the day, the air was cooler, but still quite comfortable. I could go home, pour a glass of wine, and relax on the deck, and I wouldn't even need a sweater, much less a Pole-worthy parka.

Eventually, I turned around and made my way back to the car, inhaling the scent of the woods deeply. Moist dirt and hemlocks and oaks made their own peculiar perfume, one that could never be replicated at the Pole. Most of the other vehicles were gone from the parking lot. As I unlocked my car, a mosquito buzzed near, but I got in quickly and slammed the door.

Without thinking, I drove back to the center of town. The farmers market had closed down for the day. The green looked fresh and peaceful, the fountain in the center splashing its gentle music. A sharp pang of missing Ralph struck me so hard that for an instant, tears started to well up. I'd never be able to share this with him. My beautiful town with its library and shops, its parks and trails and fountains and markets—he could never see any of it. If he ever came back to Connecticut, he'd be risking arrest. Really, he'd be taking that risk anywhere in the country, because he could be extradited. I wondered what would be involved in moving to Canada, a vast expanse noted for its pleasant people and its national healthcare. Not that I'd be able to practice law there since, among other things, I knew nothing about Canadian law. I supposed I could do other things to earn a living, but at that moment, I couldn't imagine what they might be. And Ralph . . . no matter where we went or what we did, he'd still be Santa in his heart. He might abdicate, but it wouldn't change his identity. Not that I'd want him to stop being Santa, to turn his back on the essence of his being. I'd faced that long ago. It would be like asking him to stop existing.

The only place where Ralph and I could share a life, where he could move freely and be who he was, was the Pole. Which meant that I had two choices: stay here or be with him. One or the other, but not both. I could have the man I loved, but the price would be leaving the home I loved. Or I could stay in my precious home, broken-hearted and lonely—because even if I met someone else, there was only one Ralph.

Don't be stupid, I chided myself. Plenty of people moved for their spouses. Military families did it all the time. They didn't adore it, but they did it. Two or three years at one assignment, and finally, when they felt as if they were at home, orders would come through, sending them somewhere else. Ten years ago, my friend Tina's husband was stationed at Pearl Harbor, which sounded to me like a wonderfully glamorous location. Rather than live on base, they rented a condo in a high rise on a slope below the Punch Bowl. From their lanai, you could see downtown Honolulu, Waikiki, and even Diamond Head. When I visited them, we breakfasted on the lanai every morning. "I haven't closed the sliders since November," Tina told me proudly.

Partway through my visit, we attended a sendoff for one of the families in her husband's unit. The wives clustered together while Tina and I chatted with the guys. At one point when I was getting drinks, I heard one of the wives say quietly, "They're so lucky. I can't wait to get off this stupid rock." The others nodded their acquiescence, murmuring about how they missed friends and family on the mainland. Later, when I asked Tina, she said, "They're not supposed to say things like that in front of civilians. Happy front and all that. But it's hard being out here in the middle of the ocean with nobody but your husband." Her eyes got a faraway look, as if she was remembering our college years in New England. Then she said, "Did you know we have interstate highways here?"

"That's impossible!"

"Swear to God. We have the H1, H2, and H3. Just like interstate highways on the mainland."

"Except they don't go between states, which is kind of the point of *inter*state highways."

She laughed. "There's supposedly a history behind it. Personally, I think the whole thing was dreamed up by somebody who missed living in a place where you could drive from one state to another."

Tina and her husband lived in Hawaii for three years before he was transferred to a post in upstate New York, nearly on the Canadian border, where winter began in October and continued until May. From the sublime to the ridiculous, although if she minded, she never said, because that was Tina's way. She was one of the most unfailingly cheerful and positive people I'd ever known. On a beach in the middle of the Pacific or buried under six feet of snow, Tina always seemed to find something about her situation that was charming and funny and delightful.

Now, as I pulled into my garage, it occurred to me that maybe her attitude had been a choice. Granted, my growing up years hadn't been nearly as fraught as hers—Tina's father was a raging alcoholic who died the morning of our college graduation—so maybe I'd simply never needed to cultivate a talent for seeking out the good in every situation. Maybe this was something that took practice. I'd lost touch with Tina long ago; my last Christmas card, sent a few years earlier, had been returned, marked "Moved – Unable to Forward." I wished now that I could talk with her and find out how she'd developed this a remarkably useful skill.

Because after sixteen years of practicing law, I'd become disturbingly adept at finding the negative in practically any situation. After all, with a few exceptions, people only call lawyers when something has gone wrong. Even things like home sales and purchases, or adoptions—genuinely happy situations—have their downsides, potential or actual. One of my classmates, a fluffy little redhead with a perky smile, launched her practice handling adoptions, but within a few years, she closed it down and took a job in a large firm doing insurance defense litigation. "I couldn't stand it," she admitted when we met at our five-year reunion. "Everybody thinks it's so happy, but the biological mother is usually devastated. I mean, nobody is happy to give up their child. It just got to be too much. At least with insurance companies, you already know they're going to screw whoever they can, so there's no surprise."

The Pole was the exact opposite. Not that nobody ever argued or complained, but for the most part, they seemed downright gifted at finding the positive in even the bleakest situation. Last weekend, as Ralph and I snuggled after making love, he told me the story of how one year, the icebreaker's engine died a hundred miles from the Pole. "All the supplies we needed to finish up the presents were on that ship," he said. "Icebreakers are so huge that even when Pop tried to get the whales to help push, they couldn't budge it."

"Your father tried to do what?"

He winked. "Santa magic, baby." We kissed as we always did when he said that. He continued, "But even Santa magic couldn't give those whales impossible strength."

"So what did you do?" I was never quite certain whether to believe his fantastic stories, but they were unfailingly entertaining.

"We hitched every team to every sleigh. We flew down, loaded up, flew back, and did it again. Even Mom was flying. Tillie and Claire and a team of elves took care of the on-the-ground work, like harnessing and unharnessing. Every elf who wasn't actively making toys was unloading sleighs and transporting stuff to where it needed to be. Pop went out to wrangle more reindeer for when our teams were exhausted. It took four solid days around the clock to get everything from the ship to the Pole, and then we had to finish all the work that hadn't gotten done while we were doing the transport."

"What were Anya and Isabella doing?"

"Anya wasn't at the Pole—this was about nine years ago—and Iz was brand-new. She and Phil had gotten married a couple months earlier. She was this little thing, barely old enough to be a wife, but she was as tough as anybody I've ever seen. I think she even surprised Phil. I know she surprised me. She insisted on going out to the ship to keep track of what she'd ordered so we'd know when we had everything. She went out with the first team, and she wouldn't leave the ship until the very last box of supplies was loaded." He chuckled, remembering. "The ship's captain said she was the biggest pain in the butt he'd ever met. Seems she was ordering his sailors around, making sure they had everything ready for the next sleigh so there wouldn't be even the slightest delay. He said he didn't think she even sat down for the first twenty-four hours. Finally, he told her he'd throw her in the brig if she didn't rest and eat something."

"Really? I wouldn't have pictured that." I might have expected it from Meredith, but not Isabella.

"She's really something. I know this business with her music is a little—well, it's hard on Phil, not having her here—but there's a lot more to her than that. She has a lot of good qualities. I hope they figure things out." His eyes had a faraway look.

Now, as I thought about the way Isabella had looked up at the violist, I could only hope that her good qualities took control of whatever other impulses she might have.

Eleven

"I can't believe it," I muttered. My head pounded. My stomach still churned even though I'd spent the night on the bathroom floor, retching long after everything had been upchucked.

Holly poured more tea into my mug. In her soothing mommy voice, she said, "Tell me what happened."

"I don't know." Tears threatened again. Again, I blinked them back. "It wasn't anything romantic. We'd spent two hours walking around downtown. I showed him the courthouses and some of the office buildings. But then I took him down to South Pine, where Lundstrom is, to show him some more options."

South Pine Street was lined with Victorian houses with large trees arching over them. Nearly all of the houses had been converted into office space in the 1970s. Most were occupied by small law firms because of their proximity to the courthouses. The one where the Lundstrom Law Firm practiced was typical of the block: it had been beautifully restored with enough space for half a dozen lawyers. When I was with Lundstrom, my office was on the top floor, a generous space I'd shared with my paralegal, a storage area crammed full of closed files, and sweet Lulu.

Why in hell did I take Scott down to South Pine? The firm he envisioned opening in Hartford would never have fit into a converted Victorian. Even if it did, that wasn't Scott's style. He preferred opulent high-rises with lots of glass and granite. Yet when he asked about office space near the courthouses, I took him to my old neighborhood.

As we walked along the uneven sidewalk, a wave of homesickness swept through me. I'd spent nine years here in my firm with my partners. This was my true professional home, much more so than the mega-firm where I'd started out. So many hours in my spacious attic office with its sloped ceiling and dormer windows, watching snow fall or admiring the changing leaves or cursing at the air conditioner that couldn't quite battle the summer heat rising to the top floor. It was the office where I'd celebrated victories and fumed over defeats, where I'd planned trial strategies and brainstormed with Michael about legal theories. It was where I'd first met Charles, the elf who had been with Ralph when he was arrested—and who eventually managed Ralph's escape from prison.

It was where I'd first realized I was falling in love with Ralph Claus.

I didn't realize I'd gone silent until Scott said, "Everything okay?"

"Sure." We were approaching the Lundstrom Law Firm. I was careful not to look in the direction of the building, lest I encounter one of my former colleagues.

We were almost past it when I heard a door close. Then, a familiar voice called, "Meg! Good to see you!"

I forced a smile as I turned. My erstwhile partner was striding down the front walk. "Hello, Elsa," I said. "How are you?"

Elsa and I were as different as two women could be. Practically the only thing we had in common was that we were lawyers. She was tall and svelte, with a flawless complexion the precise shade of a doe's back; I was short, chubby, and pale as a maggot. She wore designer suits tailored to fit; I dressed in off-the-rack suit separates from Macy's. She delighted in putting together complicated business transactions; I preferred cross-examining deadbeat parents about why they were behind on child support. Elsa and her companion Desirée traveled to exotic locales, while I stayed at home with my cats. Elsa would have made an excellent successor to Meredith Claus. Much better than I.

Elsa shifted her Bottega Veneta briefcase to her left hand and extended her right. I remembered when she bought that briefcase. It was after she negotiated the acquisition of a start-up that was developing artificial intelligence software, a move that ended up tripling her client's net value in less than a year. "Doing well," she said. "How are you?"

"Same." I shook her hand. Like everything else about her, Elsa's manicure was impeccable.

With Scott standing by my elbow, I had no choice but to make the introduction: "Scott, this is Elsa Delacroix. Elsa, this is Scott Wilkinson. Scott's firm is interested in opening a Hartford office."

"Pleased to meet you," they said in unison, shaking hands. Elsa cast a glance in my direction with the merest question that I pretended not to see. Then she smiled graciously at Scott and said, "I must be running. Lovely to see you again, Meg. So nice to meet you, Scott. Goodbye." She strode down the sidewalk toward the Capitol like a model on a runway, the red soles of her Christian Louboutin stiletto pumps flashing.

Scott's brow furrowed slightly as we walked on in silence. Finally, he asked, "Who was that?"

"One of my former partners." It wouldn't be fair to say I was abrupt, but I tried to make it clear that I did not desire further conversation on the subject.

"She seems very nice." Either Scott was oblivious, or he was trying to jolly me into a better mood.

I made a noise that could have been taken for assent. When I was in trouble after Ralph's escape from prison, Elsa had been—well, less than warm and supportive. I didn't know why I'd expected anything from her other than a purely businesslike assessment of the risks to the firm arising from my involvement with Ralph's case. Still, a childish part of me had never forgiven her for voting to expel me from the partnership.

I pulled myself together and gestured down the block. "There's the Capitol," I said. "It's right across the street from the Supreme Court."

"Pretty fancy neighborhood," he said in a tone clearly designed to make me smile.

"Luckily, the downtown area is compact," I continued. "And it's all a stone's throw from here, so you could easily have a corporate practice and a litigation practice, including an appellate department. You could even do some lobbying if you were so inclined, and your clients would be right across the park. It's really a question of sorting out what you want." *As were most things.*

"I want a drink," he said unexpectedly. "Take me someplace that has great Scotch."

I had no idea where to get great Scotch, especially at that hour of the day, so I steered him toward Main Street. The Peppermill was a legendary Hartford restaurant with superb food, so I took a chance that their liquors were on a par with their cuisine.

Ten minutes later, we entered the almost-empty restaurant. I glanced at my watch: it was barely four o'clock. Even on a Friday, it was early for Hartford professionals to start drinking. The host seated us at a table overlooking the bar area, and an elderly Italian waiter handed us menus. "In case you'd like appetizers," he said before I could tell him we weren't there for dinner.

Scott ordered a Macallan 18, neat. It was the most expensive liquor on the menu. I was probably supposed to be impressed, but the truth was that he could have ordered a bottle of Ripple in a brown paper bag for all I cared. I ordered a glass of pinot noir and bruschetta with tomato, mozzarella, and fresh basil, and we settled in to discuss the merits of Hartford over a larger city like New Haven.

Somehow, one drink turned into two, two into three. Then, a bottle of wine and dinner, and a second bottle, topped off by the Peppermill's famous chocolate soufflé and a cognac and then another cognac because why the hell not? Throughout the evening, lawyers I recognized kept coming and going, just like the good old days except that now, none of them seemed to notice me. I tried to concentrate on what Scott was saying, but the encounter with Elsa had stirred up something in me—a longing for days of yore, maybe, back when I was a respected member of the legal community, when my biggest problem was whether I could convince my client to agree to a plea bargain. When it never occurred to me that I might not spend the rest of my career at Lundstrom with people I cared about. People who cared about me, or so I'd believed.

By the time we stumbled out of the restaurant, it was after eleven o'clock and I was as intoxicated as I'd ever been. We were the last table. The staff was flicking on the bright lights in the apparent hope we'd recognize that it was past closing time. Scott insisted on paying; I was so distracted that my protest was perfunctory at best. On the way out, I crammed a twenty into the hand of the waiter who opened the door for us and murmured incoherent thanks.

Once outside, the fresh air revived me slightly. I blinked and tried to stand up straight, patting my side to ensure I'd remembered my purse. I inhaled deeply and lifted one foot, which nearly caused me to tumble off the step. Scott reached out and took my hand; I couldn't tell whether he was trying to help me or keep himself from falling. It didn't matter. With my hand clutching his, I maneuvered the two half-moon stone steps out of the restaurant to the sidewalk, where I transferred my death grip to one of the cast iron poles holding up the restaurant's awning.

"You can't drive home," Scott informed me, his words slurring so that I could barely understand him.

"Neither can you." He was grasping the other pole.

Nobody was on the sidewalk except us. Two cars waited at the traffic light at the end of the block. We could have staggered down Main Street without fear of anything except falling over. "If you want night life, Hartford isn't for you," I said as if we'd never stopped discussing his firm's move to the capital city.

"I don't care. And I'm not driving. I'm staying over. I have a room." Suddenly, his fuzzy words sounded soft, sensual. Dangerous.

"Good for you. I'm getting an Uber." I opened my purse to search for my phone, but he stopped me, wrapping his hand around mine.

"Stay with me," he murmured.

"I can't." I couldn't seem to figure out how to extricate my hand from his.

Then, he released my hand and pulled me close, and we kissed. And kissed. And kissed some more. His hands began to roam, one down my back and the other to my breast. "Stay with me," he whispered again, pressing his hardness against me. The world spun, and I didn't know if it was him, the booze, or the sheer terror that I could do what even my drunken brain recognized as unforgivable.

A car horn blared, jolting me to my senses. I jerked away from Scott and fell backward against the stone steps, scraping my palm. He said something—I couldn't tell what—as I groped for my friendly iron pole. Clumsily, I gained upright status and clung to the pole for dear life.

"What? What's the matter?" He reached for me again.

"Get the fuck away from me!" I let go of the pole long enough to push him away, and I nearly fell again. The world was spinning faster. My groping fingers located my phone in the bottom of my purse. "We're supposed to be talking business! Not—!" I peered at my phone to find the Uber app.

"Come back to my hotel. We can talk. Just talk." His face was out of focus, and it kept coming closer.

"Bullshit! Get away from me!" I planted my hand on his face and shoved with all my might. He stumbled backward, nearly tripping over the bottom step.

"Cut it out, Meg. You need coffee," he said, recovering his balance. He sounded pissed now. "Come back to my hotel. We'll have coffee."

"I don't drink coffee!" I snapped, turning my back to him. With enormous effort, I opened the Uber app on my phone and summoned a car. Gerald, driving a blue Honda Civic. "They'll be here in"—I squinted—"three minutes."

"Cancel it," Scott said, and it sounded like an order. "Stay with me. You're not in any shape to go home."

I opened my mouth to say I was perfectly fine. Before I could produce a word, everything I'd consumed in the past seven hours spurted out of my mouth and all over his perfectly tailored suit.

"Omigod, I'm so sorry!" I couldn't tell which of us was more horrified.

A blue Civic pulled up to the curb. "That's my ride," I managed. "Apologies. Send me the drycleaning bill."

"You're leaving?" He sounded as shocked as if I'd slapped him.

I waved my hand helplessly. "Gerald's here." Clutching my phone and my purse strap, I lurched into the back of the Civic.

"There's a fee if you puke," said Gerald in a bored tone.

"I already did." As we pulled away, the last thing I saw was Scott looking shell-shocked, his fancy suit covered in my dinner.

The trip home was interminable. I fought queasiness the entire way. When I got into the house, I stumbled into the powder room and hurled again.

"Meg? Are you okay?" Isabella called from halfway down the stairs.

"'M fine," I mumbled. "Can you feed the cats?"

"I already did. Are you sure you're okay? What's the matter? Do you have food poisoning?" She came the rest of the way down.

I shook my head and pushed past her to the stairs. "Just need to get to bed."

"Oh," she said knowingly. "Well, I hope you had fun. Let me know if you need anything." I waved an acknowledgment and made my way up to my room, where I stripped down to my underwear. The cats were curled up on the bed, but when I flopped down beside them, they all leaped to the floor. Moments later, I flung myself off the bed and into the bathroom where I spent the rest of the night boomeranging between feeling as if I might die and fearing that I wouldn't.

Dawn had broken when I finally stumbled back to my bed. The cats were already there, curled into discrete furry swirls. I wound myself between them and passed out, not waking until nearly noon. As soon as I opened my eyes a slit, the events of the prior night slammed into my consciousness. I groped for my phone and called Holly. I was barely coherent, but my best friend knew I needed her.

Half an hour later, we sat at my kitchen table. She made tea and toasted an English muffin that she spread with the tiniest bit of jam. "You need to eat," she said even though I protested that I couldn't.

I told her the entire story. All of it. "I can't believe I kissed him," I repeated over and over.

"Stop it," said Holly. "You were loaded. Sounds like you both were, for that matter. Seriously, did you even know it was Scott?"

"I knew," I said grimly. That was the worst part: I knew who I was kissing. And I did it anyway.

"At least you didn't go back to his hotel with him," she said. "That counts for something."

"Really? You really think Ralph will say that since I didn't end up sleeping with him, it's all good that I was making out with some guy who was feeling me up on Main Street?" I tried to imagine how I'd feel if the tables were turned. I didn't think I could feel any more nauseated, but picturing Ralph kissing someone else made me bolt from the room and throw up my tea and English muffin.

When I got back to the kitchen, Holly handed me a glass of water and a fresh mug of tea. I slumped at the table, my head in my hand, moaning, "I'm a terrible person. The worst."

"You were drunk," Holly said for the fifteenth time. "It's not like you went there with the idea of making out with him."

"Definitely not. Ow!" The tea scorched my tongue. "He's going to hate me." I didn't mean Scott. I didn't care what Scott thought of me.

"If you want my advice, don't tell Ralph," said Holly. "Nothing good can come of it. You'll only hurt him. It's not like you're ever going to do it again. Right?"

"Of course not." Tears welled up at the notion.

"Then do both of you a favor and keep your mouth shut." She put another English muffin in the toaster. "You want some scrambled eggs?"

I cringed. "Oh, God, no." I tried to sip my tea. It was still too hot to drink. "What about honesty and all that crap? I thought couples weren't supposed to have secrets."

"What idiot told you that one?" Holly asked. "Come here. Let me wash out your hand." My scraped palm still bore fragments of dirt.

Obediently, I joined her at the sink where she washed my hand and applied antibiotic ointment with motherly professionalism. "Everybody has secrets. This is the kind of secret you keep secret. Think of it this way. You always hear about those guys who go crazy at their bachelor parties and get drunk and have sex with the stripper. How many of them do you think tell their brides about it? None that I've ever heard of, and you know why? Because it would hurt them for no good reason. It's not like he's going to make a habit of screwing strippers after they're married. It's one stupid drunken mistake. Why should the guy hurt the woman he loves and maybe ruin both their lives, just because he feels guilty?"

I added water to cool the tea. I wasn't certain I agreed with her logic, but she did raise a good point: was it worth hurting Ralph to clear my conscience? Obviously, I was never going to kiss Scott again. Shouldn't I file this under *lessons learned* and move on? But what exactly was the lesson? Don't get drunk when you're out with other lawyers?

A noise caught my attention. A shadow fell through the doorway. It wasn't moving. My heart lurched. "Isabella," I called.

"Oh, hi, Meg!" The shadow came to life, and Isabella breezed into the room.

"How long were you standing there?" I was in no mood for bullshit.

"Um—" Her gaze flicked from me to Holly and back. "Not long. I—I wanted to make a sandwich, but I didn't want to interrupt."

"What did you hear?" asked Holly in her stern mommy voice.

"Nothing!" Her voice went up two octaves.

"Don't lie to me. I feel like shit and I'm in no mood for games. What did you hear?" I'd have yelled, but my head was pounding.

"Nothing! I didn't hear anything! Just that you kissed some guy and you shouldn't tell Ralph!"

I rested my forehead in my hand. "Listen, Iz. Don't ever tell anybody about this. Not Phil, not Claire or Anya, and definitely not Ralph. Nobody. Ralph can never know. Okay?"

"Sure, Meg. Don't worry. I've got your back." She flashed Holly a *so there* look and marched out of the kitchen.

"Don't you want your sandwich?" I called after her, but she didn't answer.

Holly sat down opposite me. "Will she keep her mouth shut?"

"No idea." Tears spilled down my hot cheeks.

"Hey, it's not that bad." Holly rested her hand on my arm. "You're doing something pretty nice by letting her stay here. Maybe she'll figure she owes you."

"I can't believe I did it. Ralph is so wonderful, and I'm so awful. I don't deserve him." I broke down in sobs. Holly slid her chair over next to mine and held me as I wept. Eventually, I cried myself out, and she plunked the box of tissues down in front of me.

"You need to get some sleep," she said, but this time her mommy voice was gentle. She shepherded me up to my room and put me to bed. As my eyes closed, I heard her whisper, "Sleep well." The door closed quietly behind her, and I fell asleep.

Twelve

By evening, I was beginning to feel marginally normal again, except that as my hangover eased, my mortification increased. Even if it had been a casual outing, getting drunk and puking on Scott would have been terrible. But this was business. My behavior was beyond unprofessional; it was inexcusable.

Clutching another mug of tea, I made my way down to my basement office. First, I found Scott's home address online. Then, I called a liquor store in New Canaan and purchased the most expensive bottle of Scotch they had in stock. Fortunately, merchants in that luxe part of the state were used to dealing with a high-maintenance clientele, and so my request that the bottle be giftwrapped and delivered to Scott's home the next day—Sunday—was met with a mere, "Certainly, madam." He inquired what I'd like to say on the card. When I said, "Write, 'With sincerest apologies, Meg'," his response of "Very good, madam," sounded as if we were in a modern-day production of *Downton Abbey*.

Having arranged for the Scotch, I now faced the more difficult task: writing the apology letter. Actually, it would be an apology email, because a letter would take days to get to him. My scraped hand still ached, but I couldn't wait. I devoted the next hour to drafting the email, typing and deleting and retyping and deleting again. By the time I deemed the four-line message ready to send, I'd probably written half a dozen pages of material about how appalling my conduct had been. Finally, I pasted the approved text into an email message, wrote "CONFIDENTIAL" in the subject line, and clicked *send*.

Within two seconds, my inbox dinged. What happened? Was the message undeliverable? Had he blocked me? I clicked on my inbox—and there was a message from Scott. The subject line read, "I'm sorry."

Before I could click to open it, my phone rang, startling me so that I dropped the mouse. My breath caught until I saw the call was from Ralph. Relieved, I snatched up the phone and tapped the video. "Hi, sweetheart," I managed.

"Hey, darlin'," he said. "What's going on?"

"Nothing much," I lied. "How are you doing?"

"Same as usual," he said. "Are you sure you're okay? You sound—I don't know, not quite yourself." Ever the diplomat, he refrained from pointing out that I looked like hell, but the picture-in-picture revealed all.

"I'm fine." I tried to sound bright. "Went out last night and got a little hammered."

"Hope you at least had fun," said my innocent boyfriend.

"Not really," I admitted. "It was a business thing, and I screwed it up."

"I'm sorry, honey." He sounded completely sincere. "Want to tell me about it?"

"I was an idiot." It was true enough.

"That doesn't sound like you. Did something happen?" Damn, he was perceptive. For an instant, I regretted the fact that it was a video call.

"I just—I ran into Elsa, and it kind of dredged up some stuff. I wasn't expecting to have that reaction. I guess—I guess I miss my old firm more than I thought."

"Your old firm? Or your old life?" Ralph suggested gently.

"I don't know. Both, maybe." For the umpteenth time that day, I fought back tears.

We were both silent for several seconds, which seems much longer when you're on the phone. "I'm sorry, honey," he said again. "I wish there was something I could do."

"Don't worry. Besides," I added, "if I had my old life, I wouldn't have you. And I'd definitely rather have you." As I said it, I knew it was true. If losing my old life was the price of having my beloved Ralph, it was worth it.

"As long as you're sure." His brow creased with concern.

"I'm sure." It was the most honest thing I'd said in forever.

"I'm glad," he responded with that smile I loved so much. We chatted about inconsequential things as I went upstairs to make more tea. I felt as if I'd been rescued from a flood and set down gently on dry land. We continued talking as I fed the cats and made myself a sandwich, propping the phone up so I could see him as I ate my supper.

Finally, he said, "You look tired. I should let you go to bed."

The clock on the microwave showed only nine-thirty, but all at once, I felt exhausted. "I think I'm going to take a shower and crash. I'm so glad you called," and I meant it with all my heart.

"So am I. I love you, sweetheart."

"Love you more." With real reluctance, I tapped *end* and dropped my phone into my pocket. "Come on, guys. Mama's going to bed early." The cats remained curled up in their various spots in the living room. "You're all lazy beasts," I said, kissing each furry head before I headed upstairs for a shower and an early night.

*****

The next morning, the doorbell rang. I heard Isabella say, "Okay, thanks," and close the door. "Hey, Meg!" she called. "You got something!"

I hauled myself out of bed, displacing Harry who always slept tight against my left side. Pulling on my robe, I made my way downstairs. "What did I get?" I called as I reached the foyer.

"Look!" Isabella gestured with the flourish of a game-show model displaying a prize.

On the coffee table stood a tall vase containing two dozen long-stemmed roses in varying pastel shades. Ah, my darling Ralph. I had no idea how he'd managed this, but it was just like him to make a grand romantic gesture to make me feel better. God, I loved him so much. The flowers were extraordinary, their scent perfuming the room.

"There's a card," said Isabella.

I opened the envelope and extracted the small pasteboard square. *So sorry about the other night. Please forgive me. Scott.*

I sat down heavily. The floral odor was suddenly overpowering, cloying. The nausea that had plagued me yesterday returned with a vengeance, and I pressed my fist to my mouth to keep from vomiting yet again.

"Meg? You okay?" Isabella looked nervous.

"Get rid of them," I managed. "Throw them in the garbage."

"What are you talking about? They're beautiful! Ralph must have spent a fortune—oh!" The light bulb went on. "They're from that guy!"

Like any good lawyer, I would neither admit nor deny. "I'm serious. Get them out of here. The vase, too. Everything. I don't want any sign of them."

"It's not like Ralph's coming over," said Isabella. "He'll never know."

I glared at her. Sometimes, the girl was a first-rate idiot. I snatched up the vase and headed to the kitchen to cram the roses into the trash can.

"Wait! If you don't want them, can I have them? I'll keep them in my room so you won't have to see them. They're too pretty to throw away."

I hesitated for a second. Then, I thrust the vase at her. "Take them upstairs now. I don't want to see them ever again. If I do, they go in the trash."

"Okay, okay." She took her prize upstairs, leaving me alone, my hands shaking.

After a shower and a mug of strong tea, I began to feel more like myself. I fed the cats and puttered around the house, dusting and vacuuming. I mopped the kitchen floor and wiped down the countertops. I even cleaned all the bathrooms, my most-hated chore since childhood. Then, as the sun was beginning to set, I pocketed my phone and keys and went out for a walk around the complex.

It was Sunday-peaceful. Nearly all the resident parking spots were full, an indicator that everyone was back from their weekend fun and gearing up for the week ahead. A few birds still chirped. In moments like this, I missed Ralph so much I could taste it. How I'd have loved strolling with him in the gentle dusk, my hand in his, hearing his warm laughter, feeling his solid presence. Maybe I should take a few days off and go up to the Pole. Being with Ralph always made things better.

As I reached for my phone, it rang. *Great minds think alike*, I chuckled as I pressed *accept*.

"Hello, Meg," came Scott's voice.

I froze on the sidewalk. *Get a grip*, I commanded myself. "Hello, Scott," I said, controlling my voice with effort.

"I'm sorry to bother you. I just wanted to thank you for that incredible bottle. You really didn't need to do it. I'm the one who was wrong." He sounded sincere.

"Not at all. Incidentally, please send me the drycleaning bill."

"No need."

"I insist."

"It's completely unnecessary. I mean it."

"So do I. Please send it."

Pause. Then he said, "Very well," in a tone I knew meant that I'd never see that bill.

"All right, then. Thank you for calling. Have a good night." I tapped *end* before he could say more, heading home in the waning light.

It had long been my habit on Sunday evenings to organize my schedule for the coming week. Planning gave me a sense of control. Of course, my plans were usually shot to hell by lunchtime on Monday, but it settled my spirit to make the attempt. When I got home, I fed the cats, poured a glass of chardonnay, and went downstairs to my office. I flicked on the desk lamp and turned on the monitor.

Then I saw it. With everything else that had been going on, I'd forgotten about Scott's email. Bracing myself, I clicked on it.

His message was as succinct as mine. He apologized for his inappropriate behavior. He could not blame the alcohol; the responsibility was entirely on him. He hoped fervently that I could forgive him for his ungentlemanly conduct. Sincerely.

I studied the few brief lines. *Ungentlemanly.* This dude was the official king of the understatement. I'd half-expected him to ask me to promise not to sue him for harassment—or assault. On the other hand, he would never put in writing what he had done; after all, he was a lawyer. His behavior was far worse than mine: I got drunk and threw up on him, but he tried to take advantage of me in my intoxicated state. Lucky for him that he wasn't my boss. I could have sued him for everything he had.

In any case, it was over. I closed the message and moved on to the rest of the new messages. Most were ads I deleted without opening them. The most recent one gave me pause, though. It was from Scott; the time was only half an hour earlier. He must have sent it after we spoke. The subject line was blank.

I was tempted to delete his message. What more could he have to say? But curiosity overcame me, and I opened it.

Dear Meg,

I hope my behavior has not discouraged you from working with our firm. You are a talented and passionate attorney, and I would very much like for you to join the firm. I am leaning toward Hartford for the new office, and having a Hartford native running that office would be of enormous benefit.

I will be in touch this week about the details of the position, including the compensation package; however, you may consider this an offer of employment.

Very truly yours,
Scott

I stared at the screen. He was offering me a job. The guy got me drunk, groped me, propositioned me—and got vomited on—and now he was offering me a job. Unbelievable.

If he'd made the offer three days earlier, would I have felt different-ly? Would I have thought it was the answer to my prayers? Because I knew the money had to be very, very good. Plus, he mentioned having me "running that office," which meant that in addition to being a mere lawyer, I'd be a partner, or maybe of counsel. Either way, I'd be in the upper echelon of the firm structure, if not *the* head honcho at Hartford. Financial security, prestige, power—everything I'd had at Lundstrom, plus more.

All I had to do was to write off Scott's behavior Friday night as that of a guy who behaved poorly on an isolated occasion. After all, he probably wasn't really hitting on me specifically. Most likely, any woman standing there would have done, especially if she'd been as drunk as he was. He'd never do it again, because I'd never again drink with him or have dinner with him. Besides, no real harm had been done. He was just a guy who was drunk.

Except that Michael and I had gotten drunk together any number of times over the years, and neither of us had ever behaved like that. Of course, Michael was married, and Scott wasn't, and that was a huge difference. Scott knew I had a boyfriend, but "boyfriend" was such a temporary-sounding word. It wasn't nearly the same as "husband" or even "fiancé." I'd had boyfriends pretty much non-stop ever since high school. There were men I'd dated whose names I couldn't even remember—I only recalled dating them because of things they'd done, like the one who left me to walk home alone in the rain after I'd laughed at his praise of Arnold Schwarzenegger's acting. So a guy couldn't really be blamed for not taking a boyfriend too seriously.

Obviously, what I needed to do was to discuss this job offer with Ralph. But first, I needed to figure out how much to tell him about what had happened Friday night.

Thirteen

"I'm confused," said Ralph, except he sounded more irked than confused. "What's the deal with this guy?" He was leaning back against his bed pillow at the Pole, and I was stretched out on my bed in Connecticut.

"I told you before. His firm wants to open a Hartford office, and he wants me to join them."

It was a week after the kiss. Neither Isabella nor Scott's son Jesse had won the coveted spot in the Fairfield County Phil; that chair had gone to Jesse's teacher, Kimberly Austin, who was now also Isabella's teacher. I held my breath when I saw the announcement, but I received no angry emails or phone calls demanding her ouster. Maybe it really had been a momentary crazy-dad moment. Or maybe Scott was afraid of me now.

In any case, as promised, Scott had extended a formal offer of employment with all the terms laid out. I would join his firm in an of-counsel capacity at an annual salary approximately four times what I'd earned in my best year at the Lundstrom Law Firm. I would be responsible for setting up and running the Hartford office, including personally handling the hiring of all lawyers and staff; my title would be "Attorney in Charge." I would oversee the office with complete authority to make whatever decisions I chose, subject to approval from Scott which, he promised, would be essentially a rubber stamp. On all matters I brought in, my cut would be sixty percent of all monies paid, whether from the client or from a judgment or settlement. And on and on, until my head was spinning.

"Are you planning to take this job?" Ralph's voice was carefully neutral.

"I don't know," I admitted. "Obviously, there are upsides and downsides." The upside being that it was essentially the job of my dreams, and the downside being that it would keep me from being with the man of my dreams. For the thousandth time, I wished my beloved had some other job—and that he could come to Connecticut without risking arrest and imprisonment.

"We were counting on your help." Christmas was barely six months away, and the pace at the Pole was picking up.

"I can still help. Just maybe not as much on site." This, I suspected, was an understatement. From what I recalled about big-firm life, I'd be lucky to get one day off per week.

"I was hoping you'd be spending more time here, not less. And not only because we're busy." His voice sounded wistful.

"I was planning to. I didn't expect this offer."

"When does he want you to start?"

"They still have to work out office space and such, but he wants me to get started as soon as I can. I'd work remotely as much as possible, but I'd probably have to go to down to Manhattan now and then."

"Sounds as if it'd take up all your time."

He didn't sound as if he was trying to put pressure on me—far from it—but I felt pressured anyway. Did he think I didn't want to be with him? This was my profession, my livelihood. It was a chance at financial security, at paying off some of the debts I'd incurred since leaving Lundstrom. It would let me come to him with money of my own so I wouldn't be living off of him and his family. I could maintain some independence even if we got married.

"I'd be busy, at least for the next few months, but you'll be busy, too," I said. "It's not as if you'll have a ton of free time."

"I guess I thought we'd be busy doing the same thing," he said.

Fury flamed up in me, unexpected and at least slightly irrational. "You knew who I was when you met me. You knew what I did. You didn't have any objection then."

"That was different." Now there was heat in his voice.

"Because you needed me to be doing that job. Now you need me to do another job, so you think I should quit this one and do that one. It's all about what you need. What about my life?" I hated the words as soon as they came out of my mouth. They sounded whiny and selfish. But it was a fair question: *what about my life?* Was this part of getting married, that you sacrificed everything you had, everything you loved, everything you *were,* to join your spouse's world?

And we weren't even engaged yet. I knew everybody at the Pole expected us to get married; to be honest, I expected it myself, and I knew Ralph did. But here we were, half a year after that fateful Christmas Eve when he'd appeared in my kitchen as Santa Claus and we decided to move forward—yet how far forward had we actually moved? How well did we even know each other? It wasn't as if we'd spent a lot of in-person time together. We talked and FaceTimed several times a day, and we sent messages back and forth in between calls, and he was the first one I wanted to talk to when anything happened, but was that enough? How did you know when you knew someone well enough to shut down your life and join theirs?

Technically, I had a third choice: I could stay right here, on my own, with my tiny solo practice. Except this wasn't a viable solution, at least not for long. I'd long since run through the funds I'd gotten as the return of my buy-in at Lundstrom. At this point, I was drawing against my home equity line of credit to meet monthly expenses. I paid for groceries with credit cards. If my practice didn't change drastically—and soon—I'd probably have to call it quits anyway.

Which brought me back to my two choices: Ralph and the Pole, or Scott and his firm.

I needed to explain all this to Ralph, and I needed to do it face to face. A video chat wouldn't do. If we were really going to be a couple, this was a decision we needed to make together. "How about if I come up this weekend so we can talk about all this?"

He was silent for so long that I thought we'd been cut off. "I'll talk to Ted and see if somebody can come and get you," he said at last.

"'If'?"

"I told you—we're busy here. It's a long trip. I want to see you—and yes, I think we need to sit down and talk about this—but to be honest, I thought that by now, you'd be here full-time. I didn't think we'd be coming into Christmas and still needing to fly you back and forth."

My temper flared. "I do apologize for being such an inconvenience. Maybe it would be better if I stayed here."

"No, no—that's not what I meant. I meant—everybody's busy up here. There are only a few of us who can drive the sleigh, and we're juggling dozens of things. Speaking of which, did you get those supplies ordered?"

"Isabella did it. Days ago." As far as I knew, Isabella was still primarily responsible for supplies. I was the assistant.

Silence. Then— "No, she didn't." Another silence. "Can you coor-
dinate with Mom and figure out what needs to be done?"

"Fine."

If he heard the irritation in my voice, he gave no indication. "Okay.
If you can get that squared away, that'll help. Maybe you can come up
in a couple weeks, and we can talk then." He sounded like a warehouse
manager organizing shipments.

"Scott's waiting for an answer," I said.

"He can't expect you to rearrange your whole life that fast, can he?
That doesn't sound very reasonable. Tell him you need more time."

"But I'm not the one who needs the time. You are." It wasn't quite true.

"Okay, then—tell him *we* need more time to discuss this." When I
didn't say anything, he said, "We do need more time to discuss this—
don't we?"

"Of course."

Pause. "Does he know—about us? I mean, does he know you're in
a serious relationship with somebody who doesn't live down there?"

"I haven't told him about my private life. I prefer not to."

"Don't you think this is something he's going to need to know?
Not that I'm Santa, but that we're together and it's long-distance and
you'll need time off to come up." Silence. "You are planning to come
up once you take this job, aren't you?"

"Of course. It's not as if you can come down."

"Just checking."

"What is that supposed to mean?"

"Only that there seem to be a lot of secrets lately. You didn't tell
me about him, and you didn't tell him about me. Kind of makes me
wonder what else you're not telling."

"What is *that* supposed to mean? Are you insinuating—are you
trying to say—?" I couldn't even get the words out.

"No, of course not. I just feel—I don't know, left out of the conversation. Like a secret part of your life."

"You are a secret part. It's not as though I can tell him you're Santa.
By definition, you're a secret."

"I suppose." But he didn't sound as if he understood. He sounded
like an illicit paramour who was tired of being hidden away. "So, is he

offering you a contract? Would you have to be there for a set period of time?"

"Meaning?"

"Would you be signing on for a year? Or two, or five, or. . . ."

"He hasn't said. But even if it was only for a year, it would be enough to dig me out of the hole my finances are in."

"There are other ways to do that, aren't there?"

"Such as?"

"If you moved up here, you wouldn't need most of the stuff you have in Connecticut. Your condo, your car, your furniture. You could sell it all."

"But. . . ." I looked around my living room. The walls were covered with artwork I'd acquired at the town's annual fine arts show. Ralph had admired the oil painting over the fireplace, an impressionistic piece set in nineteenth-century Paris where the girl in the center peered over the shoulder of a sidewalk artist. The painting was alive with colors and brush strokes depicting the bustle of the day. I'd found it at the show three weeks after moving into my condo. For months after I purchased the painting, I paused to savor it every time I walked into my living room. Even now, I'd sometimes find a detail I hadn't noticed before.

There was no way I'd either sell that painting or leave it behind. Ditto with the photographs, the sketches, the watercolors, and the acrylics I'd acquired over the years that now adorned my walls. Ralph's apartment was bare; my artwork would fit beautifully.

Except I wasn't ready to sell my condo. It had been the biggest declaration of adulthood, purchased two years into my time at Lundstrom. "I want a place of my own," I'd told Holly after my landlord raised the rent for the third time in three years. When we walked into the foyer after a year of house-hunting, I knew immediately this was what I'd been searching for. The night of the closing, Holly and I sat on my living room floor in front of the fireplace with the bottle of vintage Veuve Clicquot and two goblets she'd hidden in her bag. We toasted my new home. At that moment, I truly thought I'd be here forever.

It wasn't perfect, of course. I'd replaced the dishwasher twice, the refrigerator and the range once each. I was still paying off the boiler I'd installed when the first one failed eight months after I moved in. The central air conditioning was temperamental. On mild evenings when the windows were open, I could hear my neighbors chattering, partying, engaging in loud sex and louder arguments. Sometimes when I sat out on my deck and heard Rodrigo blasting an aria, I craved a more secluded place.

Still, it was my home, mine and nobody else's. If I sold my condo to marry Ralph and move to the Pole, I would never again have a place that was completely mine.

I didn't realize I'd gone silent until Ralph said, "Meg? Are you still there?" As if he couldn't see me on the screen.

"Sorry. My mind was wandering."

"I was saying—maybe you should come up this weekend after all. Is there any chance you can catch a flight to somewhere north so it's a shorter trip on our end?"

"Sure," I said. "I'll figure out flights."

"Thanks," he said with an intensity that brought me fully back to the conversation. We exchanged *I love yous* and *good nights*, and I settled in at the computer to try to sort out my transportation. As it turned out, anywhere north of Toronto was a challenge—expensive, infrequent, and long. By the time I quit searching, the cats were slumbering around me, having apparently given up on bedtime snacks.

"No worries," I said to them as I turned off the monitor. "You'll be with me. That's a done deal." I knew Ralph had no intention of suggesting anything else, but I felt the need to say it aloud anyway. Harry lifted his head slightly, but David and Lulu slept on, secure in my promise.

Fourteen

"I'm going to lick every inch of your body," Ralph murmured as his tongue inched up my inner thigh. I lay back in the warm, smooth sand as waves crashed on the shore and his mouth approached my—

—and the ringing phone jarred me out of sleep.

I snatched it up and barked a groggy, "Hello!"

"Hello," said the last person on earth I wanted to talk to at that moment. "We need to discuss the order you submitted last week."

Half of my brain was still on a Caribbean beach with Ralph making love to me. "Are you serious? It's—" I peered at the bedside clock. Seven-twenty-three. "—early. I was up late. Can we do this later?"

"I'm afraid not. We have a problem." Meredith's voice was cool. "When you ordered the baking supplies, how much molasses did you order?"

"I don't remember."

"Would you check, please?"

"Fine. I'll check and call you back later."

"Would you please check now? It's rather urgent."

Since when was molasses urgent? I bit back a retort as I pulled on my bathrobe, tying the sash as I pounded down the hall. Isabella's door was open slightly, but I heard nothing. In all likelihood, she was having breakfast with her musician friends, none of whom apparently had day jobs. I stomped down to the basement office and flicked on the light. I sorted through papers on my desk until I found my scribbled notes. "Are you still there?" I asked.

"Yes."

"I ordered 100 cans. That's what it says in my notes."

Silence. Then, Meredith said, "Are you looking at the order confirmation?"

"I told you—I'm looking at my notes."

"I've sent you the order confirmation. Please look at it."

I woke up the computer and clicked on an email from the Pole. The attachment showed the order placed last week. "I'm looking at it. See? Quantity is a hundred. One hundred one-gallon cans." Which had seemed like a hell of a lot of molasses to me, but apparently that was what Annaliese went through in a six-month period.

"Look at the unit column, please."

"It says *CA*. So?"

"*CA* doesn't mean 'can'," said Meredith. "Molasses isn't sold by the individual can."

"What does *CA* mean?"

"Case."

"But it says one-gallon cans." I peered at the confirmation.

"Yes, it does. You ordered one hundred cases of one-gallon cans of molasses."

"But—it doesn't say—"

"Look at the manifest."

"The what?"

"The manifest. I sent it to you."

I clicked on another email. A lengthy document that looked like an invoice listed everything I'd ordered. Halfway down the page, I saw "100 cases – 1 gal. molasses."

Okay, fine. I'd screwed up. But really, how bad could it be? How many cans could be in a case? Four? Six? "How many cans are in a case?"

"Twenty-four."

Which meant that instead of ordering one hundred gallons of molasses—which already seemed excessive—I'd ordered *twenty-four hundred gallons.*

"Wow. I'm sorry. I didn't realize—I mean, can we send it back?"

"No. It's already on the icebreaker with the other supplies. I simply wanted to check with you before refusing delivery if it was an error on their part."

"But—you mean—we're stuck with it?"

"Yes."

I was almost afraid to ask. "How much did it cost?"

"It's a U.S. product, so the wholesale price was approximately seventy-five dollars a case, excluding delivery."

I did the math and blanched. One hundred cans would have cost slightly more than three cases—probably about $250 all told. Instead, I'd spent $7,500—plus delivery—on molasses. "Is there anything we can do?"

"At this point, no. We already have elves rearranging the food storage warehouse to make room. I'll need to adjust the budget on other items to offset this unexpected charge, but that's my job, not yours. I only needed to confirm that the delivery we're receiving was what we actually ordered, and you've done that. Thank you, Meg." She hung up before I could respond.

I sat at my desk, stunned. My screw-up had cost the Pole thousands of dollars. I logged into my bank accounts. I didn't even have enough ready cash to make it right. I could pull from my home equity line of credit, but it would likely take years for me to pay it off.

Still, I had to do the right thing. I clicked on my credit line. There was plenty of available credit. I tried not to look at the interest rate. I set it up to transfer $7,500 to my working account. I was about to click "transfer" when my phone rang for a FaceTime call.

"Morning, darling," said my beloved. Even at whatever hour it was at the Pole, he looked so, so good. His dark hair was slightly mussed, but the warmth in his eyes never failed to thrill me.

"Hi." I sounded as glum as I undoubtedly looked.

He chuckled. "I heard Mom called. Don't worry about it. Everybody makes mistakes."

"But this—I have to pay for this."

"No." His voice was firm. "It's not like we'll never use it. Granted, it's more than we'd normally order, but don't worry. Molasses goes into gingerbread and lots of other things. It's fine."

"It's not fine," I protested. "You're getting twenty-four hundred gallons of molasses. That's like—I don't know, a ton of molasses." Later, when I checked online, I'd discover that it was closer to four tons. Four freaking *tons* of molasses. They'd be lucky if it didn't sink the place.

"It could be a lot worse," he said. "It could have been something like eggs or milk—stuff with a limited shelf life. At least molasses can sit in the warehouse and be fine. Seriously, don't worry about it."

"But I have to pay for it," I insisted.

"No," Ralph said again. "Not only do you not have to pay, you *can't* pay. That's not how we do things. We're a family. We deal with what happens, and we move on."

"But I'm not family," I half-whispered.

"Wanna bet?" he responded. "You are in my eyes. And you are in theirs, whether you know it or not. Can you imagine what Pop would say if you tried to give him money?" I pictured myself handing Julian a check. Even in my imagination, he smiled and shook his head, pushing my hand away. "Besides," Ralph added, "It's my call. I'm Santa. And I say you're not paying."

"I have to do something." It was far too much money to say *oops* and move on.

"What you have to do is learn from it," said Ralph. "Trust me, everybody screws up sometimes. Even me."

"Really? When did you ever screw up?"

His laugh was rich and warm. "Are you forgetting how we met?" His eyes twinkled. In that moment, I saw him again, sitting in the windowless room in the courthouse basement, his orange jumpsuit clashing with his olive-toned skin, four days' worth of whiskers dotting his face—and that smile, because. . . .

. . . it was his smile that stopped me. Full lips and strong-look-ing white teeth bespoke years of good nutrition and probably a mother who made him brush after meals. A slight dimple in his right cheek showed beneath the whiskers. And a curious familiarity, as though he was greeting a friend, not meeting a stranger.

The smile that could still stop my heart. That still made me feel as if no matter what, I was safe and loved.

"Even so. . . ." I felt like an idiot.

"This is called learning. Today, you learned something. Tomor-row, you'll learn something else. You think Mom's never messed up an order?"

"What did she do?" I couldn't imagine Meredith ever being imperfect.

"I'll let her tell you. Now, tell me something good. What else is going on?"

I smiled. "I had a very interesting dream last night. We were alone on a beach. . . ."

"I think I'm going to like this." I could hear Ralph settling in. "Tell me. In detail."

I loved this man so much. "First, you were going to lick me all over. . . ."

Fifteen

The next morning, I emailed Scott to let him know that I'd be away for a few days. "Will let you know about the offer when I get back," I added and hit *send*.

A minute later, the phone rang. "You're going away?"

"Yes."

"What's this? One last vacation before you start work?"

It was the perfect opportunity. "I need to discuss this with—someone."

"Who? Is someone making you another offer?"

"In a way." I let him stew for a minute. Then I said, "I'm going to see my boyfriend."

"Where does he live?"

I was prepared for the question. "Up north."

"Where is he? Canada? You're dating a Mountie?" He was trying to disguise his jealousy, but he wasn't doing very well.

Ralph's job was none of his business. "I need to talk with him."

"Are you seriously suggesting that you'd let some guy dictate whether you can take a job?"

"Don't be ridiculous," I said.

"But you'd be planning to stay here, right? I mean, this wouldn't be like I hire you, and six months later you dump me to move in with your Mountie. Because I'll be frank with you—if that's your plan, we should stop discussions right now. I'm looking for someone who's invested in this firm for the long haul. If that's not you, have the courtesy to tell me now, before we go any further."

"I haven't made any decisions about anything," I said, holding my temper with an effort. "When I do, it will be my decision and no one else's."

"I'm surprised you even need to think about it," he said. "It's a fantastic offer and you know it." Modesty was not one of Scott's strong suits.

"It's a very good offer," I conceded. "But I haven't made up my mind. When I do, I'll let you know."

A tense silence. "You know, not a lot of people would be making you an offer like this after all that Santa Claus stuff," he said finally. "I had to go to bat for you. You owe me," he added before he hung up.

"That son of a bitch!" Lulu raised her head and gave me a drowsy look. I reached for her, and she nestled her head into my hand. "You'd like for me to have an office, wouldn't you?" I asked. Except Scott would probably never agree to my having an office cat, which was a big strike against him, in addition to his monumental ego. "Come on, guys. Time for snikkies." At the magic word, all three of them stood, stretched, and stampeded for the stairs up to the kitchen. Rising to follow, I glanced around my little basement office. It was nothing like my attic office at Lundstrom where my windows overlooked the other Victorian houses on the street. But I was coming to like it more than I'd have expected.

With Scott, I'd have money and prestige. With Ralph, I'd have love and a mission.

Here in my own home, I had . . . myself.

I flicked the wall switch. Leaving the dark room behind, I ascended the stairs to where the cats wound around the legs of the kitchen table in eager anticipation of their snikkies.

*****

After I fed the cats, I made myself an unimaginative lunch of turkey on whole wheat with lettuce, but no tomato since Isabella had eaten the last one. I imagined how it would be if Ralph were here. Warmth flooded through me at the thought of him puttering around my kitchen, how this simple meal would be infused with a glow purely because he was here to share it.

I opened a bag of potato chips and dumped more than a single serving onto the plate. Munching, I knew again how much I missed him, how much I wanted to be with him. And not just for the sex, although his touch could make me tingle like a sixteen-year-old virgin.

In his presence, everything fit. I felt warm and safe, as if nothing could go wrong that the two of us couldn't solve. I'd never known a relationship like this. With every other man, I'd had to watch out for my own heart, my own feelings; with Ralph, I didn't have to, because he was watching out for me, which meant I was able to watch out for him and we were both taken care of.

Which was why it was so upsetting when he seemed to be less than supportive about this job with Scott. Granted, I understood why: if I stayed down here, even for a year, that was a year we wouldn't be together. On the other hand, if I took the job, I could make great strides toward financial security. Ralph had teased me about the cats being my dowry, but the truth was that I wasn't comfortable coming to him with practically nothing, as if I were some poor girl who needed to be taken care of.

I spent a fair bit of the afternoon researching efficient, affordable ways to get to the northernmost part of Canada. Turned out, there weren't any. If the sleigh didn't come down all the way to Connecticut, I'd have to add at least twenty-four hours on each end of the journey, plus a whole lot of money I couldn't afford to spend.

Finally, I shut down the computer and headed upstairs to the kitchen. As I emerged from my basement office, I heard familiar music, and not played by Isabella. This was movie music, piano and orchestra, and I knew the source.

Love Story came out long before I was born, but I'd seen the movie and read the book a dozen times. When I took piano lessons, Francis Lai's famous theme was the piece I wanted to play, more than anything by Bach or Mozart.

Isabella was curled up on the sofa, a bowl of popcorn at her side, intent on Ryan O'Neal and Ali McGraw as they flirted and bantered and fell in love. "Haven't you ever seen this?" I asked.

"Sssh!"

I took that for a "no." I poured myself a glass of wine and settled in to watch these impossibly young people make decisions about their lives, and ultimately her death.

After Jenny played in a concert and she and Oliver were walking outside, she mentioned that she had a scholarship to study with Nadia Boulanger in Paris. Isabella gasped.

"What?" I asked.

She waved helplessly at the screen. "She has a scholarship? With Nadia Boulanger? And she's giving it up to marry him?"

"Who's Nadia Boulanger?"

"Only one of the greatest music teachers ever. Jeez, if I'd ever had a chance to study with her—" She scooped up a handful of popcorn and crunched violently.

"Some people would say that about Juilliard," I pointed out.

"It's not the same!" She was so vehement—and I was so ignorant about music—that I shut up and turned my attention back to the movie.

After Oliver's dramatic falling-out with his family, the young couple got married. As they zoomed toward their seedy new apartment in his fancy roadster (which he could have sold to pay for a much nicer apartment), Oliver lamented how Jenny wouldn't be paid very much in her teaching position because her name was Mrs. Barrett. When he suggested that she could be Miss Cavilleri, she retorted that if she were Miss Cavilleri, she'd be the queen of Paris. I glanced at Isabella, but she was stone-faced.

While Iz was engrossed in the movie, I dug through my bookcase for my dog-eared copy of the novel. I flicked through the pages, trying to follow along, but the movie was different. For one thing, in the movie, once he'd graduated and they'd moved to New York, Oliver told a friend that he wanted Jenny to study at Juilliard, and she wanted to have a baby, so they were making babies. A nice thought, but the book didn't say this. Book Oliver never expressed any interest in Jenny resuming her musical studies. Quite the contrary: when he was in law school, he said she could theoretically have stayed with her music groups except that by the time she got home from teaching, she was exhausted and still had to cook dinner because they couldn't afford to eat out.

Having worked my way through law school as a single person, I knew perfectly well what was involved in balancing studies with the rest of life's obligations. Plus, I'd had a front-row seat to seeing how my friend, Beth, walked that tightrope. Beth had a supportive husband, but she also had four kids, the eldest of whom was in middle school when we started law school. During our law school career, she and I competed in moot court together, served as teaching assistants together, and even did judicial internships in the same courthouse. I didn't know how often her kids or husband prepared meals or did housework, but I knew that Beth did one hell of a lot of juggling of her roles as wife, mother, law student, legal intern, and regular person with friends and interests and life.

Contrast that with *Love Story* and the spoiled rich guy whose wife had to give up her music groups so she could fix his dinner. All I could think was, "Dude—that girl is working her ass off to pay the rent because you won't sell your fancy car or ask your mega-rich family for a few bucks, and you have the gall to sit back and wait for *her* to fix dinner?"

Maybe we were supposed to think all this poverty was romantic, a sign of true love, *La Boheme* without the bohemians. Having scraped along while I was in law school—and in recent months after leaving my former firm—I could tell anybody who asked that being poor was not even close to romantic, and being voluntarily poor was just plain stupid.

By the time I refocused on the movie, Jenny was sitting on the bleachers by a skating rink as Oliver skated. A minute later, she wanted to go to the hospital. Minutes after that, she was dying and telling Oliver to screw Paris and all that crap he thought he stole from her because she didn't care about it, and then she was dead.

As the music swelled over the final shots of Oliver walking alone in snowy New York, I realized that Isabella was sobbing. Well, no wonder: it was a cautionary tale if ever one existed. Give up your dreams at your peril, because you might not live long enough to circle back around to them.

"It's sad," I observed. "She probably could have been a great musician." Isabella lifted her head and stared at me, teary-eyed and incredulous. I tried to explain: "That Nadia Boulanger person must have thought she was something. She had a scholarship and everything."

"But she didn't want that," said Isabella. "She wanted him."

"He could have compromised," I said. "Marty Ginsburg did it for Ruth." Isabella looked blank. "Ruth Bader Ginsburg. Supreme Court justice. Women's rights advocate." She continued to look blank. "They met in college. She said he was the only boy who cared that she had a brain. They got married in 1954—about ten years *before* this movie was set. By the time they *both* started Harvard Law"—I waved my hand toward the final credits—"they already had a kid, but they both went. He did all the cooking because she was lousy at it." There was so much more to tell: how Marty was diagnosed with cancer while they were students, how Ruth went to classes and cared for their daughter and helped him through school. How they supported each other's careers as they raised their family. How he truly believed that her work was every bit as important as his.

"That was them," Isabella said. "Every couple is different."

"What about you and Phil?" I clicked off the television. "Do you want him, or do you want to be the queen of Juilliard?"

"You can want more than one thing." Isabella contemplated the ice in her glass.

"But that doesn't mean you can have it all," I said gently. "Sometimes you have to choose. Jenny could have chosen to go to Paris and trusted Oliver to wait for her—or he could have deferred law school for a year and gone with her." I didn't tell her that he'd admitted as much in the sequel to the book. "They had choices. Staying in Cambridge while he went to law school meant the end of her studies with Nadia What's-Her-Name, which sounds like a hell of a sacrifice if she really wanted to be a musician."

"But when he wanted her to go to Juilliard, she wanted to have a baby," said Isabella. "So she didn't really want a life in music."

"Maybe she wanted more than one thing." I deliberately echoed her words back to her.

"Or maybe she was afraid she couldn't make it as a musician." Isabella's voice was softer now; I couldn't tell if she was speaking to me or herself. "After the concert, she kept saying she wasn't great, she was just okay. Maybe she was being modest, or maybe she knew she'd gone as far as she could. Except if that was true, why would Nadia Boulanger accept her and give her a scholarship? She had to be really special for that. And she'd already gotten into Radcliffe, which meant she had to be exceptional, except she threw it all over for him, and then she died."

By this point, I couldn't tell whether she was arguing with me, herself, or the movie. "Bear in mind that this was all happening in the sixties," I pointed out. "It was a very different time."

"What about your friend, Ruth?"

It took me a second to realize she meant RBG. "Her husband was exceptional," I said. "That was rare then."

"It's rare now," said Isabella.

"Oh, come on." I was getting exasperated with her self-pity. "You're here, aren't you? Phil's giving you time and space to figure out what you want. He's not pushing for a divorce. He's not saying you two should see other people. He's not even coming down here and invading your space. From where I sit, he's being hugely supportive."

"So's Ralph, but you're still complaining," she shot back.

"That's different," I said. "You're already married. Ralph and I are deciding whether that's what we want." Except we weren't. I knew what Ralph wanted. I was the question mark.

"I don't see why you're trying to talk me into going back when you don't want to," Isabella said.

"What are you talking about? Who's trying to talk you into anything? And what do you mean, I don't want to?" Keeping up with her was like chasing one of the cats when I needed to give it a pill.

"You think I should be Jenny and Phil should be Oliver, and I should give up my career and go back to the Pole and be the obedient little wifey until I die!" Tears streamed down her face now.

"For crying out loud—" *Okay, bad choice of words.* "I'm not saying you *should* do anything. It's up to you. This is your life. Phil isn't Oliver Barrett, you're not Jenny Cavilleri, and Julian sure as hell isn't Oliver the Third—and by the way, those people are *fictional*. The Clauses are real, and they love you. They care about you. They want you to be happy. Seriously—you've lived with them for ten years. How do you not know this?"

"I know they love me." Her voice was quiet now. "And I love them."

"And Phil? Do you love him?"

"Of course. If I didn't, this would all be easy." The clock chimed ten. "I'm going to practice." Without waiting for a response, she left the room. Moments later, I heard the theme from *Love Story* floating down the stairs like a ghost.

Sixteen

For the next few days, I couldn't get our conversation out of my head. While Isabella was upstairs practicing, I rewatched the movie. Toward the end, right before they went to the hospital, Jenny told Oliver she'd liked it best when she supported him. He responded that she'd always supported him, and after all, what was money?

I backed up and watched that interaction again. And again.

This bit wasn't in the book. I wondered if this, like the line about Juilliard, was intended to soften the effect of Jenny giving up her career for Oliver, to show him (finally) appreciating her. I wished there were a version of *Love Story* written from Jenny's perspective so we could see how much of Oliver's telling was accurate.

But assuming she really did like it best when she supported her husband even though it cost her a career in music—what did this say about her? Was supporting him an easy out so she never had to face the question of whether she could have made it as a musician? Or was movie-Jenny, in her own way, the female version of Marty Ginsburg, the person secure enough to step *out* of the spotlight? Everybody I respected held RBG up as an icon, and many of us secretly wished for a Marty of our own, but how many of us wanted to *be* Marty? How much love and courage and strength of character did it take to lay down your own dreams and say, in essence, "You pursue your passion, and I'll be right beside you"?

Being Santa wasn't Ralph's passion; it was his identity. It was who he was, start to finish. I'd known it from the day we met.

The question was whether I could be his Marty, his Jenny. Did I have what it took to let him go first? To join his world instead of insisting that he join mine?

*****

That night, I wandered through my condo, noticing things I'd scarcely paid attention to for years. The framed watercolor of a front porch with a wide swing and lots of greenery. A small oil painting of a young woman in overalls playing the flute. A graceful gray figurine of a cat made from the ashes of the Mount Saint Helens eruption. A stack of books teetering on the edge of the coffee table because the bookcases were crammed full. The coolness of the hardwood underfoot, and the softer thickness of the braided rug. The faintest scent of ash wafting from the fireplace. The trickle of water in the cats' fountain dish. The hum of the refrigerator. The way the tendons in my legs stretched as I went up the stairs. The increasing warmth as I ascended, as welcome in autumn as it was irritating in summer. The shredded fabric on the arm of the bedroom chair the cats all preferred to the scratching post four inches away. The gray-blue sky still visible between the night-darkened leaves of the Japanese maple outside my bedroom window. My perpetually unmade bed with a sheet draped over it so the cats didn't shed on the quilt. The pot of English ivy on the bookcase beneath the window, its tendrils cascading down. The spacious en suite bathroom with the Wedgewood-blue porcelain clawfoot tub on which I had splurged after my first six-figure verdict because the fiberglass tub installed by the original builders was too cramped even for someone as short as I was.

Every corner of my home was mine, arranged for my own idiosyncratic comfort and style. What would it be like for Ralph to have someone—even someone he loved—move in and start spreading her belongings all over his place? Would he feel disrupted and invaded when I came clomping in with the cats and my books and all the things that made my home mine? What if he didn't like my artwork, my quilt, my cat figurine? What if he preferred his almost painfully neutral décor? Could I feel at home in a place with so little personality?

Because while love may conquer a lot of things, real estate isn't necessarily one of them. What about my office? Granted, I'd be working with Ralph's mother in her office, but what about a place for my own work? Would I have a desk of my own?

"Don't worry," Ralph had said when I broached the question. "There's plenty of space. The entire Pole is ours. We'll figure something out that works for you." I knew he would, because that was Ralph, the man who loved me and was willing to make miracles happen if that was what it took to make me happy.

Seventeen

"Why did you guys get married?" I asked Michael and Ruby a couple of weeks later.

The Ruggieros had invited me to dinner at their home on a lake in the northern part of the state. Ruby swam across and back—a mile each way—nearly every day unless the surface was frozen. Her wetsuit hung in the mudroom with her other swimming paraphernalia and Michael's fishing gear. Their kayaks, rowboat, and other water equipment filled a shed Michael had built several yards uphill from their private pier. Seated around the dining table next to the picture window, we enjoyed a perfect view of the sunset lighting up the treetops as the water disappeared into dusk.

Michael looked startled, but in all fairness, my question startled me, too. "Who knows? It's been so long," he shrugged. Fair point: the Ruggieros had married nineteen years ago, exactly a week after they received their respective undergraduate degrees from UConn.

Ruby shot him an exasperated look. "He proposed because I was going to move to Minneapolis after graduation and get an apartment with my cousin."

"She'd been watching reruns of *The Mary Tyler Moore Show*," Michael said. "I tried to tell her how cold it gets there, but she wouldn't listen. She never does. So I proposed to keep her from freezing to death in Lake Superior."

"Lake Superior is nowhere near Minneapolis. He just didn't want me moving to the city and having adventures."

"Hartford's a city," Michael said. "You could have had adventures right here."

"Hartford's a town. Minneapolis, St. Paul—those are cities. Very nice and clean and orderly. The whole place is orderly. Remember when we went out for Sheila's wedding? All you could talk about was how tidy everything was. Now, go heat the water for Meg's tea." Michael picked up our plates, and when I started to rise to help, both of them told me so firmly to sit down that I sat. As soon as he was out of the room, Ruby said, "I knew on our second date I was going to marry him. It took him longer to figure it out. If I hadn't told him I was moving, who knows when he'd have gotten around to popping the question?"

"How did you know—all of it? That he was the one, that getting married was the thing to do, that you wanted to spend the rest of your life with this person?"

She didn't have to think about it. "It was the summer after our junior year. We both had summer jobs in Hartford, so Michael took me to Capozzi's in the South End. Our waiter looked like he was about sixteen. First, he put down a basket of bread that was lined with a cloth napkin. The table was tiny, so when he brought our wine, he put Michael's glass on the napkin. I'm sure he didn't mean to, but you know those old Italian restaurants—they always kept the lights low. Atmosphere, I guess. Anyway, by the time the waiter brought our food, we'd finished the bread. The boy had my plate in one hand and Michael's in the other. He set down mine, and then I guess he figured there'd be more space if he got rid of the bread basket, so he picked it up. Except Michael's glass was still on the napkin, so he knocked over the glass and splashed wine all over Michael. All that red wine on Michael's white shirt! The poor waiter was mortified, of course, and when he leaned over to try to help, he tipped Michael's plate and dumped linguine with red sauce down his front and in his lap."

"And it was hot," Michael said, resuming his seat.

"What did you do?" I asked.

"Michael jumped up, and the linguine fell on the floor—"

"—and all over my shoes—"

"—and I thought the waiter was going to cry, he was so young. The host came over, yelling and waving his arms. We both thought the poor boy was going to get fired."

"Then what?" I felt like a child asking Mommy and Daddy for the rest of the story.

"I told the kid to calm down," said Michael. "Mistakes happen."

"And he told the host not to blame the waiter, that it was his own fault," said Ruby. "Then he asked if maybe they had another waiter outfit in the back that he could borrow because I shouldn't have to sit through dinner with him looking like he'd been swimming in his dinner. The host said of course, and next thing I knew, we were at another table—"

"—much bigger—"

"—and Michael was dressed like a waiter, and we were treated to the best meal I'd ever had, and it was on the house."

"That's why she married me," said Michael, laughing. "Because I know how to get free food."

"No," she said, serious now. "It was because of the way he treated that boy, and the way he handled the whole evening. Remember, it was only our second date. A lot of guys would have been so embarrassed. They'd have yelled at the waiter and demanded the host fire him or something like that, or they'd have sulked about how the evening was spoiled. But Michael didn't do any of that. He was—Michael." Ruby's eyes grew soft, remembering.

"On the way out, three people tried to get me to take their orders," Michael chimed in.

"They did not!" She slapped his arm playfully. "And the whole drive home, he laughed about it."

"I can picture that." This was the Michael I'd always known.

He grinned. "What was I going to do? You can laugh or you can cry, but you've got to admit, it was funny—here's me trying to be a big shot to impress this beautiful girl, and I end up covered in wine and red sauce. You've gotta laugh. Plus, she felt so sorry for me, she let me get lucky. So it all worked out."

"Michael!" Her smack on his arm was harder that time.

"A little discretion, Ruggiero," I said, and they both laughed.

"I didn't tell you the best part," Ruby said. "On the way out, Michael said, 'Wait a minute.' He went back and tipped the waiter—the boy who'd started everything. The host hadn't let him wait on us at our new table, and Michael didn't want him to lose out."

"It was an accident," Michael said. "I told him I knew that. That was twenty-two years ago. The kid owns the place now. Bought out Tony Capozzi a few years ago, but he kept the name. He's done okay."

"We all have," said Ruby, and she winked at Michael.

Eighteen

"Meg! Meg! I got it! I got it!"

"Down here!" I called, not looking away from my monitor. Seconds later, I heard Isabella clumping down the stairs to the lower level, still calling, "I got it!"

"Congratulations!" I said when she landed at the bottom. "What did you get?"

"The seat in Ealaíonta! I got it!" She was practically dancing around the room.

"That's great!" I saved my document and turned my full attention to her. "What's Ealaíonta? A show?"

"It's the premier string ensemble in New England! They're right here in Connecticut, and they're so incredible! Their founder was a violinist from Dublin, and that's why they've got an Irish name. They play all sorts of chamber music and other stuff. Last spring, they performed with the Connecticut Chorale when they did Clark Woodman's new piece."

"Who's Clark Woodman?" She still hadn't sat down.

"A local composer. The guy has won all sorts of awards. His music is so amazing!" She went on and on, dropping names of musicians and groups and composers.

When she finally took a breath, I said, "I think it's fantastic, Iz. What did Phil say?"

She stood still, her balloon suddenly deflated. "I—I haven't told him."

"Why not? Do you think he'll be upset?"

"Who, Phil? No way! He'll be nothing but thrilled for me." Her eyes got a wistful, faraway look.

"Then why haven't you told him?"

She snapped back to here and now. "I will. I just—you know how it is. Anything you tell one of them, you tell them all."

I was learning that. "So—you're afraid of what the others will say? Don't you think they'll be happy for you?"

"Most of them."

I knew exactly who she meant. "Look, Meredith knows why you came down here. This is you showing everybody you were right, that you really do have talent."

"She's not going to be impressed. Ealaíonta's a small group. Four violins, two violas, a bass, and two cellos. I'll be first cello."

"That's impressive." Knowing nothing about string ensembles, I assumed first cello was the best.

"She won't think so. She'll think that if I'm not with the New York Philharmonic or playing solo concerts like Yo-Yo Ma, there's no point to my being here."

"It doesn't matter what she thinks," I said firmly. "What matters is that you have a job playing first cello with a string ensemble that plays for a chorale when they do Clark Woodward."

"Woodman. Will you come and hear me play?" She was like a little girl begging for approval.

"Of course. When's your first performance?"

"September thirteenth. We're playing a private event at the Wadsworth Mansion down in Middletown. Somebody's fundraiser, I think."

"Sounds fancy. Are you sure they'll let me in?"

She laughed. Even her laughter was musical. "You can come as my guest. That, or you can carry my cello. We'll figure something out." The sparkle was returning. "I should go practice. I've only got three weeks until the Wadsworth!" She darted up the stairs.

"Are you going to call Phil?" I called after her, but moments later, I heard the deep, resonant notes of the cello floating down to my office.

*****

I didn't mention Isabella's news when Ralph called that night. Instead, after a typical conversation—what I did today, what he did, how much we loved each other—I called Beth.

"Omigod, Meg! I was just thinking about you!" Beth sounded every bit as vibrant as she had when we were sitting at my kitchen table working on our moot court argument. She sounded the tiniest bit tired, though. And Beth never sounded tired.

"How's everything? Are you all okay?" It was the closest I could come to articulating my sudden fear.

"You know how it is. Craziness all the time." To put it mildly. Beth's eldest daughter was a Marine, and that alone was enough to make a mother nervous. I vaguely recalled that Kim had married a fellow soldier several years ago, but I didn't know where they were currently stationed.

"Everything good? Everybody safe?"

"As far as I know. Mark and Kim have both been deployed, so we have the kids."

"What? How is that possible?"

"Don't ask me. Kim was sent to Bosnia a few months ago, and now Mark's been sent to Afghanistan."

"How can they both be deployed? Aren't there some sort of rules about sending both parents away at the same time?"

"It's the downside of being one of the very few people who can do what they do." Kim was some sort of expert on helicopters, and Mark was an expert on—I couldn't remember what, exactly. "They asked us to take the kids for six months."

"How many kids do they have now?"

"Just the twins, but that's enough. I can't believe I ever managed four under six. Now, a pair of toddlers is wearing me out." Her kids had arrived nearly back-to-back, starting with Kim during spring break of Beth's senior year of college. By the time she and I were starting law school, the kids were all in grammar school or middle school.

"How's Sean managing all this?" Her husband was a quiet, be-spectacled man with lank blond hair and a mischievous wink.

"He's in his glory. As soon as Mark and Kim asked us, he was drawing up schedules for which of us would handle childcare on which days. The next day, he told his boss he'd need to be working from home three days a week for the foreseeable future. When the boss hesitated, he threatened to resign. So now, he's working at home half-time and trying to figure out why he ever thought this would be a good idea."

"I wondered about that." The notion of trying to work with two toddlers underfoot was unfathomable. "What about you?"

"I'm thinking of taking a leave of absence. It's hard to concentrate on murder trials when you have little kids at home." Beth was one of the top prosecutors in the state. She'd worked so hard to get where she was. She continued, "It'll mean money's tighter, but at least we won't have to worry about babysitters. I tried to work from home, but I couldn't concentrate with the kids running around. I seriously don't know how I did it in law school."

"You were younger then," I reminded her. "What's this going to mean for your seniority?"

"The union is haggling about that now. Thank God the FMLA applies to state employees." Except the Family and Medical Leave Act only covered twelve weeks of leave. Even if she figured out childcare for the kids so she could return to work at the end of three months—halfway through Mark and Kim's deployment—the FMLA didn't guarantee Beth would be able to return to her old job. The law only said she could return to an equivalent job, "equivalent" being an extremely elastic term. In other words, this leave was quite possibly the death knell for her career.

I had to ask. "Why did you agree to take the kids in the first place?"

Slight pause. "Because they asked." She sounded as if the question was ridiculous. I tried to imagine my mother if Derek and Cindy asked her to take their kids for few days while they went away. *Can you believe they asked?* Mom would say in her typically aggrieved tone.

Maybe I came from a line of selfish people who wouldn't brook any interference with their preferences, because I couldn't imagine taking a pair of toddlers for a weekend, much less six months. Longer, possibly, if something happened to one or both parents—which was not impossible under these specific circumstances. Knowing Beth, that issue had been thoroughly discussed, and likely papers had been drawn up against any eventualities. She loved her children with all her heart and she believed in them absolutely, but Beth was still a pragmatist through and through. It was one of the traits we had in common.

Nineteen

After we hung up, I contemplated the difference between Beth's marriage and Isabella's. They'd both married frighteningly young, and yet one was apparently quite happy while the other was seeking satisfaction elsewhere. Granted, Beth had spent years pursuing her chosen career while Isabella's cello sat in a corner. Was that the difference, that Beth had had that early start and was now content to step back? Or was it inevitable that a person's priorities would change during marriage, and the real question was how you managed it? For that matter, was it even realistic to think that priorities *wouldn't* change over the course of a marriage, especially a long one? After all, people change. Was anybody—married or not—exactly the same as they were ten years ago?

David hopped up in my lap. He settled down and purred as I stroked him and thought about how my life had changed in the past decade. I hadn't even had David ten years ago—he was only five. For that matter, I hadn't had Harry or Lulu, either. In those days when I was still at MR&S, most of my waking hours were spent at the office or in court. I routinely worked until nine at night and stumbled home to a silent apartment where the only other living creature was a wilting aloe plant. Even after I decided that being a partner at MR&S wasn't my ultimate destiny, I still worked all the hours that existed, because what else did I have?

I cuddled David, recalling the dramatic shift from MR&S to Lundstrom, from a huge corporate-like operation with departments for everything to a boutique firm where I was one of five nearly-equal partners (Eckert was more equal than the rest of us). It was the proverbial night-and-day experience. Not only did I have a fulfilling practice, but for the first time since law school, I had time and energy for a life outside work. I made dinner plans with friends, hiked on weekends, attended concerts and plays. I bought my condo and decorated it. I adopted Harry and David. I met interesting men and even had some relationships. I was content personally as well as professionally.

And then, I met Ralph Claus, who turned my life upside-down.

Now, I was in love with the best person in the world, something I could never have imagined in the days when scoring good seats to a show or winning a summary judgment argument might be enough to make my day. On my law school graduation day so long ago, I'd thought I knew what my future held, but none of my fantasies included falling in love with a man who lived thousands of miles away in a place nobody believed existed. An entirely new life shone on the horizon like sunrise at the Pole—if only I had the courage to say *yes*.

So maybe the bottom line was as simple as this: there was no way to know what was coming, so why not take the leap? Besides, even if I tried to stay in one place, there was no guarantee that place would stay with me. See Exhibit A, my partners at Lundstrom voting me out of the firm. Everything around me changed constantly, with or without my consent. Why not try something new? Why not be proactive rather than reactive? Especially when taking the leap came with the infinitely wonderful bonus of being with Ralph, and all the other options meant not having him.

Besides, it wasn't as if going to the Pole meant I could never again do anything law-related. I'd still be a lawyer. As long as I continued to pay my annual fees, I would remain an active member of the bar. I could handle cases from anywhere, with emails and phone calls and remote hearings. If something came up in the course of Pole life that required legal know-how, such as reviewing purchasing contracts, I'd be better qualified than anyone in the place.

I thought of Isabella, leaving her husband behind to take the plunge back into the musical world. I still couldn't decide whether she was incredibly brave or painfully foolish. I wondered whether she had a checklist for what she wished to accomplish before she went back. I wondered whether she'd set a deadline for when time would be up.

I wondered if she really planned to go back at all.

I sipped my wine as I pondered the contrast between Isabella and Beth. I'd thought I was more like Beth, looking back on long years of professional satisfaction as she prepared for a new chapter. But was I really more like Isabella, teetering on the brink of an adventure with no idea how it might turn out or what it might cost?

I tried to picture what my life might look like in another sixteen years if I elected to stay where I was. My practice might grow. My beloved cats would age and die, and new cats would join my home. The people around me, my chosen family—Holly, Rodrigo and Samson, Michael and Ruby—they might stay here, but they might not. They could retire. They could relocate for new jobs. Illness or loss could upend their worlds, requiring them to shift their focus to other parts of their lives. Holly's son Jack had moved to Chicago after his marriage; if they had children, Holly might move to Chicago to be near them. My staying here didn't guarantee that life would remain the same. Even if I remained precisely as I was, those around me had no obligation to do likewise.

Connecticut has long been known as the Land of Steady Habits. Nutmeggers are not fond of change. But the world changes daily, whether we agree to it or not. No matter what I chose—to stay or to go—my life had already changed forever the day I met Ralph.

Whether I stayed or went, I still had no idea what was coming. All I knew was this: if I chose Ralph, I was choosing a life with a man I loved with all my heart, who loved me with all of his.

Which was, after all, a pretty wonderful choice.

"What do you think?" I asked David, whose sleepy golden eyes were mere slits. "Do you want to move to the Pole?" He nuzzled my hand a bit, and his eyes closed.

I took that as a *yes*.

Twenty

"I hope you don't mind, but we're going to have to do supplies when you come up for your birthday," Ralph said when we spoke the next evening.

"What do you mean, 'do supplies'?" I sipped my wine. David snored in my lap, Lulu nestled next to my arm, and Harry snuggled against my feet. If not for the air conditioning, I'd have been sweltering in the heat and humidity of a Connecticut summer. At the Pole, Ralph reclined on his bed in the green sweater I'd bought him because it matched his eyes.

"August is when the icebreaker comes through. That's when we take delivery on most of the year's supplies." It made sense, I supposed. The Pole still enjoyed plenty of sunlight in August, and the temperatures were comparatively warm, climbing into the twenties. I was about to make an innocuous comment when he added, "Has Mom talked to you about it?"

"About what?" I shifted slightly. Lulu lifted her head, eyes barely open but still conveying her displeasure at being disturbed.

"Doing the supplies." The *of course* was implied in his tone.

A suspicion began to wriggle in my brain. "I don't know what you're talking about."

"Oh." A single syllable that revealed much.

"Tell me."

"—I think you should talk to Mom." In that instant, I could see how he must have looked as a little boy when he'd been caught sneaking into Annaliese's kitchen, his smile bright with the effort of convincing the world of his innocence.

"And I think I should talk to my boyfriend," I said firmly. "What does 'doing the supplies' mean?"

He paused for a long drink of coffee. "It's what I said. We get the supplies for pretty much the whole year. So it's all hands on deck."

"Meaning—"

"We've got to get everything off the icebreaker and back to the Pole. Then, it all has to be inventoried as it's put away so we know what's located in which warehouse." I knew food was stored separately from materials for the workshop, but beyond that, I was clueless. "The whole thing takes about two or three days, give or take."

"What's an icebreaker?" I knew by now that it was a ship of some sort, but I'd never formed a clear picture of what type of vessel it was.

"It's a massive ship. Really impressive."

"And I assume it breaks ice?"

"That's how it gets up here. The ice is several meters thick. This ship can navigate that. You should see it coming up here, sweet as you please even when there's ice everywhere. If the ice is really thick, the icebreaker can drive its bow onto the ice and use the ship's weight to break it. It's something to see."

"And it delivers to the Pole?" Keeping his story on track was like herding cats.

"Not exactly. It comes up to the Circle—"

"The Circle?"

"The Arctic Circle." *Duh, Meg.* "It can only go so far. We come out by sleigh to meet it, and that's how we pick everything up."

"And you can do all this in two or three days?" That didn't seem like a lot of time to unload a year's worth of supplies.

"Everybody's involved. It's the only time of year when the workshops aren't running." His eyes were searching my face for a reaction.

Visions of unpacking cartons flitted through my brain. Okay, it wasn't the ideal way to celebrate my birthday, but of course I'd help. Except— "So if we're spending a few days unpacking boxes, why do I need to talk to your mother?"

"Mom wants you on the icebreaker." *Thud.*

"I don't understand," I said carefully amid a growing suspicion that I did.

"Normally, Mom and Isabella handle the ship," he said. "But with Iz down in Connecticut—"

"Shouldn't she be coming up with me so she can do her job?" Extra emphasis on the last phrase.

"That's why you need to talk to Mom," Ralph said. "She thinks this would be a good opportunity for you to learn how it's done."

"How *what's* done?" Surely they couldn't intend for me to be piloting this icebreaker, whatever it was.

"The transfers."

"What transfers?" I was getting almighty sick of his assumption that I understood his shorthand phrases.

"There are two of our people on the ship—usually, Mom and Isabella—to oversee getting all our stuff transferred off. You know, making sure we get everything we ordered and not somebody else's crates. Mom wants you to do that with her this year so you can learn how it's done."

It didn't sound difficult. Standing around for a few hours with a clipboard, checking things off—the job couldn't be that onerous. Certainly less demanding than unpacking and putting everything away.

Which went to show what I knew.

*****

Six days later, I climbed out of a sleigh onto the deck of the Morski Gigant. I didn't know anything about icebreakers, but this was the most massive ship I'd ever seen.

After my conversation with Ralph, I called Meredith, who explained how I would assist her aboard the icebreaker. Our job was to track every crate that would be transferred from the Morski Gigant into a sleigh. The ship's crew would bring the crates up to the deck, we would scan their codes and cross-check them against the order, and Claus brothers would load crates into sleighs and fly them to the Pole.

"We'll take turns sleeping," Meredith said as she explained our tasks.

"What do you mean?"

"We work around the clock," she said as calmly as if she were offering me a cup of tea. "The Morski Gigant can't stay here indefinitely. Too much chance of being sighted, especially since we take delivery before sunset so they can navigate more easily. We can't afford to lose any time."

Which was why I stood on the deck of the massive vessel, the midnight sun glaring off ice and water as I ran my scanner over the codes on countless crates and matched them against the manifest on my tablet. Twenty-degree temperatures that would have felt merely frigid at home were exacerbated by the near-constant winds sweeping across the deck. "Dress warmly," Meredith had said as if she were sending me out to build a snowman. The specially-designed gloves she gave me had the dual bonus of keeping my hands warm and affording me the dexterity to manage a scanner and a tablet. I already had the goggles I'd worn for the flight; otherwise, I'd have been blinded by the sun long before we touched down at the Pole.

The crew of the Morski Gigant was a swarm of burly men in the same icy-weather garb I wore, except theirs was dark blue and mine was red. "We got them from the same place," Ralph explained once the job was done and we were snuggling in his bed after an immensely welcome shower. "No point in reinventing the wheel. These guys are professionals. They know what's needed." On the left breast of our jackets were our names; I was surprised and touched to see a jacket labeled Riley waiting for me.

Naturally, the only way to get to the icebreaker was by sleigh. At least it wasn't as bad as the trips back and forth to Connecticut. For these relatively short hops, the sleighs flew low to conserve the energy of the reindeer. It would take fifteen minutes to get an empty sleigh to the ship, Meredith explained. Loading it, however, could be time-consuming. "The loads have to be well-balanced," she said. "The reindeer can't carry more than eight hundred pounds of cargo." In other words, considering the size of the Claus brothers and the weight of the sleigh, a team of four reindeer would carry close to a thousand pounds from the ship to the Pole. Upon landing, elves would load the crates onto a trailer attached to a snowmobile, and another elf would drive the snowmobile to the warehouse where the unloading team would get to work. Once the supplies were unloaded, another team of elves—this one overseen by Claire—would inventory the supplies, place them, and record their location for future access.

"Hello, ladies! Welcome aboard!" The captain greeted us heartily as we disembarked from the first sleigh. I couldn't identify his accent. Polish, perhaps.

"Hey, Miko!" Ralph and the stocky captain exchanged a bear hug with lots of backslapping.

"Santa! Welcome to the Morski Gigant!" Ralph was nearly a head taller than Miko, but Miko lifted him off his feet, both of them laughing.

"Hello, Miko," said Meredith. No bear hugs for the Missus: Miko grasped her hands as he welcomed her, as respectful as if she were his own mother. She indicated me: "This is Meg. She's Ralph's intended." It was the first time I'd heard her acknowledge me as such.

Miko broke into a wide smile. He held my hands with both of his, pumping so hard I thought my elbows might come loose. "Congratulations! You have very good husband! Very good!"

"Thank you." Before I was could say more, Miko whirled, snatched up a bullhorn, and began thundering what I assumed were instructions. I didn't understand the language he was speaking, but crew members came running from every opening and deck I could see.

"He's a character, but he's the best captain in the Arctic," said Ralph as the crew formed a line.

"And he knows who you are?" How many people knew Ralph's secret?

"Yeah, but it's not a problem. His family has been delivering our supplies for ages. Completely trustworthy."

"What about his crew?" The first crates were making their way along the line of crewmen. "Do they know?" One idle night, I'd research how different cultures depicted Santa Claus. Turned out, there were plenty of different beliefs about the kindly man who delivered presents on Christmas Eve. Depending where these guys were from, they might not even consider the notion that the lanky beardless fellow on their ship was the real deal.

"The guys are incredibly loyal to Miko," said Ralph. "Between us, I don't think this is the only confidential delivery they do." Startled, I looked up at him, but I couldn't see his eyes behind his goggles. A shiver ran through me that had nothing to do with the freezing winds.

"Have you scanned those crates?" Meredith appeared beside me as if from nowhere.

"Um, not yet. Just about to." I scurried off to do my job, but not before I caught my beloved's lips pressed together to suppress his smile.

Each crate bore an identifying number and shipping label with a bar code. I scanned the bar code, and a list of the contents popped up on my tablet. "No crates on the sleigh until we've confirmed the contents," Meredith instructed me. She stood back, watching as I studied a packing list. Thirty bolts of fabric, one hundred yards to the bolt, assorted colors.

"Is this everything?" I showed her the tablet.

She perused it. "Have you double-checked it against the order?" She waited as I scrolled until I found the order.

"It says thirty-five bolts. Did they short us?" I saw more crates moving along the line toward us.

She pointed to the packing list. "See this?" The list referred to box 274. "The rest of the order should be in there. Set this crate aside until 274 comes up. Then, you can load everything together."

"Problem, Missus?" Miko appeared at my elbow.

"This is a partial fulfillment," said Meredith, gesturing toward the crate. "We're waiting for 274 to complete." Miko nodded vigorously and barked an order. Two of the crew members set the crate aside and returned to their places in the line.

"Why don't we load this one now?" I asked. "It has to go eventually."

"Because if the entire order comes at once, it'll be easier for the unloading team." Meredith barely glanced at me as she spoke.

"But how do we keep track on this end?" I asked.

I couldn't see her eyes behind the sun goggles, but I could feel them. "That's our job. You'll keep track of which crates have been set aside to await the complete order."

"Where do I do that?"

I'd have sworn she was suppressing a sigh as she indicated the proper spot on the tablet. I trudged over to where the crate had been set aside to record its number, only to discover that the crew had placed it with the label side down. With my tablet in one hand, I tried to turn it over, but thirty bolts of fabric were much heavier than I expected. I set down my tablet and squatted, grunting as I tried to move it.

"Here, Missus, let me," said a crew member. As easily as he might have turned over a card, he flipped the crate over. I thanked him as he trotted away. Finally, I found the shipping label and entered it on my tablet. *What a waste of time*, I mused.

Then, a sharp whistle split the air. I looked up to see a reindeer and sleigh approaching. I couldn't tell who was driving, but as the flying sleigh drew near, the loaded sleigh on deck took off. It was as neat a maneuver as I'd ever seen. Clearly, this whole thing operated like the proverbial well-oiled machine. All I had to do was not screw it up.

I couldn't have said how many hours I was on deck, hustling between crates and sleighs, before Meredith finally said, "It's time for your break." She pointed toward the doorway on the level above the deck where we stood. Before I could ask how I was supposed to get there, she was already focused on the next crate.

I wandered down a narrow corridor until I came to a perforated metal staircase. No one was around; apparently, all hands were indeed on deck. I climbed the staircase and slogged down another corridor so narrow that it made the hallways at the Pole look vast and spacious. On both sides, gray metal doors were unlabeled and tightly closed. I tried each door, and none of them opened. Ralph's words about confidential deliveries rang in my mind. What might be behind these doors?

Finally, I came to the door that opened onto the upper deck. Below, I could see men in dark blue outfits passing crates along as if they were a conveyor belt. Since they all looked alike in their blue suits and goggles, I had no way of knowing whether they were swapping out men or if these guys simply had oceans of stamina. Meredith's red suit stood out among them; even from up here, everything about her posture and demeanor dictated that she was calm and in control. Desperate as I was for a place to lie down, I stood transfixed at the railing as she gestured to the crew to put a crate here or there.

I found a room with bunks and lay down. Too soon, my phone beeped with a message: *5 minutes*. In other words, break time was over. I trudged to the stairs down to the deck. "How you doing, Missus?" Miko asked as we passed in the corridor. I wanted to call after him to let him know I wasn't Meredith, but he'd already disappeared down a flight of stairs.

Meredith handed me her scanner and tablet and left me alone to run everything. After some undefined period of time—an hour or two, maybe, but who knew?—she returned from her break, announcing, "There's food in the mess,"

I hadn't even realized I was hungry. "Where's the mess?"

"Below deck." With that, she turned her attention back to the never-ending line of boxes making their way along the human chain.

I found another flight of stairs, this one leading to a lower level. I wound through the maze of corridors until I heard voices. I opened one of the gray metal doors to find several blue-suited men with their goggles hanging around their necks. Each held a sandwich in one hand

and a thermos in the other. I hesitated, and for an instant, we looked at each other as if each had identified a bizarre mythical figure. Then, they all stood in apparent chivalry.

"Is this where I can get something to eat?" I asked. They looked at me blankly. I pointed to the nearest man's right hand, and comprehension brightened his weather-tanned visage. He pointed, and I saw a bin filled with sandwiches wrapped in waxed paper. I unwrapped one, slightly reassured that I recognized Annaliese's signature wrapping style.

Even though I didn't understand their words any more than they understood mine, the men had fallen silent as soon as I entered the room, and they remained silent as I picked up my food and drink. I gestured to them to sit; some did, and others remained standing until I took my place on a stool near the door. I wished I understood enough of their language to ask polite questions, like where were they from and if they liked this kind of work. Instead, we all sat in a silent circle, munching and drinking.

I was still chewing my last bite when I stood up to leave. All the men stood when I did. "It's okay, you can sit down," I said, gesturing for them to sit. A couple of them caught on and said something, and the others followed suit. I smiled and waved to them before I replaced my goggles and went back outside.

While the idea of midnight sun sounds like great fun, let me set the record straight: it's not. As a person who had always relied on circadian rhythms and the realities of sunrise and sunset (and a good alarm clock) to define the beginning and end of the day, I struggled in a place where you never knew if it was day or night, whether you should be asleep or awake. I knew I was exhausted, but I didn't know if what I lacked was an afternoon nap or a good night's sleep. I couldn't tell anything from Meredith or the crew, all of whom had done this countless times and who clearly knew how to cope in this timeless expanse of vivid blue sea and stark white ice.

"How're you doing?" Ralph asked when he landed some time later—I had no idea how long, because the passage of time felt meaningless. He looked mildly tired, as if he'd just played a vigorous game of soccer, while I probably looked like something the cat would have refused to drag in.

"How much longer is this going to go on?" I allowed myself to lean against him, fighting the urge to sob from sheer fatigue.

"We're about half-done," he said. "You're doing great. Keep doing what Mom says."

"My goal in life," I muttered. My feet felt numb, not from cold, but because I'd been standing here for what felt like years.

Too soon, Ralph's sleigh was loaded. He kissed me goodbye, climbed into the driver's seat, and took off. I watched for as long as I could see the speck in the sky. When he'd vanished into the blue, I turned back. My gaze fell on the stack of crates containing partial orders. Getting all these paired up and flown to the Pole would take forever. I didn't know how long Miko and his crew intended to stay here, but all at once, the idea that they should have to spend extra time in the Arctic waters merely because Meredith wanted to make unpacking easier seemed ridiculous. Presumably, Miko charged for the amount of time the icebreaker sat here. It would be far less expensive to let them unload the ship and leave. We could deal with the unpacking and storing on the other end.

I saw a sleigh approaching and made up my mind. When Fred landed, I said, "We're taking all that stuff over now."

He looked only slightly worn out—these Claus boys had stamina— but he was startled anyway. "Aren't those the partials?"

"Yes," I said. "We're going to get as much stuff off the ship as fast as we can, and then we'll sort everything out."

He held his glove in front of his mouth to smother a yawn. "Mom said to do this?"

"*I* said to do it." I used my firmest lawyer voice.

Fred looked around for his mother, who I knew to be sleeping some-where above deck. After a minute, he waved a crew member over to help him load the sleigh from the stack of partial orders, and I allowed myself a moment to bask in my victory. By the time Meredith knew how I'd made the project more efficient, it would be finished. All she'd be able to do was congratulate me for my innovation, my efficiency, and the extent to which I'd saved the Pole money.

Fred couldn't take the entire pile of partials, but he did what he could. When Ted arrived a few minutes after Fred left, the crew loaded his sleigh as he gave me the same unsure look his twin brother had. After Fred left, Phil arrived. When the crew loaded the last of the partials on his sleigh, I gave myself a mental pat on the back. I returned to scan-ning new crates until Phil's sleigh was full and he took off for the Pole.

By the time Meredith came up to the deck, I was ready to drop. On the other hand, Miko had reported that we probably had only about twelve hours left. "Only about twelve hours," I echoed groggily. "That's great."

"Very great!" His head bobbed enthusiastically. How the man had any energy left was beyond me. "Hi, Missus!" he called as Meredith emerged from her nap.

"Hello, Miko," she said. "Meg, how are things going?"

"Very efficiently," I said, not bothering to disguise the pride in my voice.

She looked uncertain for a moment. Then, she looked over to where the partials had been stacked. "Did all the matching crates come up?"

Something in her voice made me feel like a naughty child. I straightened my shoulders as best I could in my worn-out state. "No," I said. "I sent the partials over."

Her face didn't change, but suddenly her expression seemed icy. "I told you that the partials were to await their mates before going over."

"I know, but this seemed more efficient. The sooner we can get everything off the ship, the sooner Miko and his guys can leave. I figured we could save some money."

She regarded me for a long, long minute. "I believe I explained that the reason we wait to send the partials is so everything can be unpacked at once."

"You did, but there were so many partials waiting, and it didn't make any sense for them to be sitting here. This way, we can release Miko and his crew—"

"So you said." She lifted her head to watch a sleigh approaching. "You may as well take your break." She took the scanner and tablet and approached the crew to scan the crates that had come up in the past few minutes. Dismissed, I watched for a moment. Then, I stomped up the stairs to the room Miko had set aside for us, flopping onto the cot.

When I re-emerged on deck two hours later, I saw a pile of crates where the partials had been stacked before. My temper flared. "Why are these here?" I demanded.

"Because they're only partial orders," Meredith responded coolly, barely favoring me with a glance.

"But I told you—"

"This is the correct way to do it." She was intent on scanning boxes. For all she cared, I might as well not have been there. I breathed down a few choice words and said simply, "I believe it's your turn to go on break."

This time, she actually looked at me. "Meg, I know you mean well, but we have reasons for what we do. These are things you'll learn as you spend more time at the Pole. For now, you need to trust that I know what I'm doing."

"Certainly, *ma'am*," I said. "Anything you say."

If my sarcasm fazed her, she gave no sign. Biting back a sharper retort, I wheeled as sharply as my rubber boot sole allowed and picked up a scanner, fuming at Meredith Claus's stubborn refusal to consider the possibility that she might be wrong.

*****

By the time I took my next break, I had gotten myself in hand. Like it or not, this was Ralph's mother. Unlike normal families who saw each other only on holidays and the occasional Saturday afternoon, I would have to see my mother-in-law every day of my life for many years to come. With my luck, she'd be like some of the lawyers I'd known who came into the office every day well into their dotage, long after any sane person would have retired to take up gardening or birdwatching.

Eventually, I gave up on napping and went down to the mess for a bottle of juice, slugging it down as I paced the ship's corridors and did the math. If Meredith was sixty-three—I thought that was what Ralph had said—and I was forty-one, then I'd be seventy-one when she was ninety-three. In other words, I could spend the next thirty years with her hovering over me, correcting me in that infernally Canadian-polite way, never giving me a chance to see what I might have done because she was Ralph's mother and I couldn't tell her to back the hell off. Frustrated, I headed down one corridor and up another. How had I not thought of this before? I could spend thirty years under her thumb. If I hadn't been so in love with Ralph, I'd have commandeered a sleigh and headed back to Connecticut.

The alarm on my phone alerted me that it was time to relieve Meredith. I followed one of the low-ceilinged dingy corridors to the front part of the ship and up to the deck. When I emerged, there stood

Mitch in Claus-red, a three-day growth of whiskers making him look much older than twenty.

"The last of the crates are loaded," he said. "Time to wrap up. We've got a lot of work ahead of us."

"What are you talking about?"

"Unpacking's a disaster," Mitch said. "Loads of partials came over and nobody realized. Now we have tons of supplies that need to be moved around from where they were unpacked. It's going to take hours to sort everything out." He shook his head in disgust as we approached the final sleigh.

"Let's go," Meredith said, though it wasn't clear whether she was addressing Mitch or me. "There's still a great deal of work to do."

"So I've heard," I said, climbing into the back seat of the waiting sleigh. "Don't we get to say goodbye to Miko and the crew?"

"I already did," Meredith said as she settled into the front seat beside her youngest son. He snapped the reins, and the sleigh took off for the Pole.

*****

When we reached the Pole, I went straight to the warehouse. By the time I finished moving supplies from one shelf to another, I was so exhausted that I could barely stand.

"You don't have to do it," Ralph said gently as he took a box of wrapping paper from me and placed it on a shelf I couldn't reach. "Not everybody does."

"But apparently, I'm the reason for the extra work, so it's only fair." It sounded good, anyway.

But the fact was that I hadn't spent all that time in the warehouse because I felt it was equitable or just. I did it to show Meredith that I could take responsibility for my decisions.

Not that I had responsibility to take, not really. My way was better. I knew it in my bones. Her way would have kept the icebreaker anchored and the sleighs going back and forth much longer than was actually needed, increasing not only the cost of the icebreaker, but the chances that we'd be spotted. If only she'd told Claire and the warehouse crew at the outset how many partials there were so they'd know how much room to leave, it wouldn't have been a problem.

But I wasn't Mrs. Claus—at least, not yet. These decisions weren't up to me.

I heard a couple elves grumbling while I helped with the unpacking, but nobody said anything to my face. Presumably they were so respectful of her—and of me, as her successor—that they weren't going to voice complaints publicly. Personally, I'd have preferred if they'd said everything out loud.

Eventually, the last crate was unpacked and unloaded. The empties were stored in a separate warehouse for when a need arose for either shipping crates or firewood. Barely awake, I waved my thanks to everyone and stumbled off to Ralph's apartment where I fell into a deep and dreamless sleep.

As I gradually roused on a day and time I couldn't have pinned down on a bet, Ralph came into the bedroom. "Hey, Sleeping Beauty," he said, wrapping his arms around me. "How are you doing?"

"Frustrated," I admitted. "My way was better than hers, but somehow I came out the villain in all this."

He kissed me. "She's not flexible," he admitted.

"There's 'not flexible,' and there's 'unwilling to see reality,'" I said. "Reality is that her way means much more work for everybody unloading the ship, including Miko and his crew. Isn't it going to be less expensive—and safer—if we can get everything unloaded faster and they can get on their way?"

With his arm around my shoulders, Ralph guided me into the kitchen. I made tea and he made coffee. Finally, with our respective choices of caffeine in hand, we repaired to the living room, me on the loveseat and him in the armchair.

"I know she's not easy," said Ralph. "That's her. It's how she's always been. She's strong-willed and determined, and she thinks she's always right."

"But she's not."

He took a long drink of coffee. "I know, but she's been in charge of everything for a long time. When she came up—well, let's just say that my grandmother wasn't the most organized person you ever met. She was a fantastic grandma, the total stereotypical Mrs. Claus with all the cookies and everything, and everybody loved her, but when it came to management—I'll be honest, she was flat-out terrible. It was a miracle the gifts got to the right kids. So when Mom married Dad and took over the job, everybody was thrilled. For the first time in a long time, the trains were running on time, so to speak. She knew where everything was and what needed to be done. That first year that she was in charge, Christmas Eve went so smoothly that Pop was petrified something had been overlooked." He chuckled, remembering.

"Was she the one who came up with the business about unloading the supplies?" I drank tea, wishing for a cat to cuddle.

"She was the one who came up with the icebreaker," Ralph said. "We used to pick up supplies from the northern shore of Iceland. She asked Kristofer's dad—I forget his name—if he had any suggestions, and he recommended Miko's dad. I remember hearing about that first year—talk about a crazy time." He laughed and drank more coffee. "Apparently nobody knew what to do—it was your classic goat rodeo. Finally, she stood in the middle of the deck and blew a horribly shrill whistle until everybody stood still. Then she started barking out instructions. Problem was, Miko's dad was the only one who spoke English, so she had to tell him and he told his crew. By the time Pop showed up with a sleigh for pickup, the crew was lined up and crates were coming up from the hold."

"Were you there?" I drained my tea.

"Pop let me come with him. I was a little kid—maybe six or seven—but I remember us landing and Mom directing everybody. I was so confused. I mean, this was my mom, and here she was acting like the commander of the ship. Pop told me to stay out of the way. Turns out, that's the best advice anybody ever gave me about dealing with Mom."

"Lucky you," I muttered. Staying out of Meredith's way was impossible for the person who was in training to take over her job. I vowed that I would never be as hard-nosed as my future mother-in-law.

"It's not that you can't make changes," said Ralph. "You just need to do it a step at a time. This place is steeped in tradition."

Steeped in tradition. More like mired in the mud of days gone by. But this was Ralph's mother, and I needed to show respect. So I got up and put the kettle on for a second cup, and I focused on straightening the dish towels instead of railing at my beloved about his mother.

Twenty-One

"You need to learn," Ralph said over breakfast the morning after my birthday celebration. Since my actual birthday had been spent on the icebreaker, last night after dinner, Annaliese had produced an enormous sheet cake with *Happy birthday, Meg* written in Christmas-red while the entire population of the Pole sang to me. When I asked Ralph later how that one cake had been big enough for all the Clauses and all the elves, all he would say was, "Santa magic, baby."

Now, Ralph's eyes twinkled at the prospect of teaching me to fly a sleigh. "You never know when you might have to go somewhere. Besides, it's fun."

"Fun? Compared to what? A root canal?" I'd ridden in a sleigh several times by now, but I'd never stopped being terrified of being up there in the sky, completely unprotected. The only time I'd actually driven was on my first trip to the Pole, when Mitch let me drive. I hadn't been holding the reins two minutes when the baby reindeer in the team freaked out about his harness. I had to control the others while Mitch climbed out of the sleigh and straddled the reindeer as we soared through the night. I wouldn't say the experience scarred me, but—oh, hell, it did, and everybody knew it.

"It's not that bad," Ralph said. "Haven't you ever flown one of those little planes?"

"Flown *in* one, or flown one as the pilot?"

"Either." As if flying a plane was the kind of thing anybody could do.

"I've flown in puddle-jumpers—the kind with maybe a dozen seats—but that's as little as I go. And believe me—nobody wants me to be the pilot. For one thing, I'm not qualified. For another—no." I scraped my oatmeal bowl clean. "Besides, if I need to go somewhere, there are plenty of strong, virile Claus men who can take little ol' me wherever I ask," I added with a high-pitched drawl, batting my eyelashes as if I were a southern belle instead of a New England litigator.

"Are you telling me you don't want to learn because flying is men's work?" my cagey beloved suggested.

"Not at all," I parried. "I'm sure that any woman who wants to fly a sleigh will be brilliant at it. Doesn't your mother fly?"

"Of course. My grandmother taught her. Would you rather ask Mom to teach you?"

Cagey was putting it mildly. "Oh, yeah. I'm sure we'd both have tons of fun." I loaded our empty bowls and utensils onto my tray.

"She taught Isabella," Ralph said, picking up the tray. "Iz loves flying. You should ask her about it."

"What about Claire and Anya?" I asked. "Do they fly?"

"They've done it, but between us, they've not very good. Everybody's better off if they stay on the ground." He placed the tray on the counter and laid his arm around my shoulders, leading me to the stable.

"If they don't have to fly, why should I?" Even I could hear the whine in my voice.

He stopped in the hall and rested his hands on my shoulders. "Because, my love, you are going to be the wife of Santa Claus. For us, the rules are different." He kissed my forehead. "Now, come on. The ground crew is waiting."

"Ground crew?"

"Don't tell me you've never noticed the elves who hook up the sleigh and put everything away?" I couldn't tell if he was mocking or incredulous.

"Of course," I lied. Whenever I was leaving, the sleigh was ready to go by the time I got to the barn. *Spoiled little princess,* I chided myself as we headed to the barn.

The foreman of the ground crew was a tow-headed elf named Phelan. "I've harnessed two," he informed Ralph. "Polly and Tawny. Ted said four would be too many for a beginner."

Reflexively, I was about to insist that I could handle four when Ralph said, "Perfect. Thanks, Phelan. Meg, this is the harness." When Phelan stepped back, Ralph said in a low, firm voice, "This is Ted's domain. What he says, goes."

"Even if I'm marrying Santa Claus?" I whispered back.

"Even if." In a louder voice, he said, "Phelan, where's the flight plan?"

"We need a flight plan for a lesson?" I asked.

"Of course." I wouldn't say Phelan was disrespectful, but it was clear he didn't think I knew what I was doing. Granted, I didn't, but as the future Mrs. Claus, I expected more deference.

"Which one is Polly, and which one is Tawny?" I asked instead.

"Polly's always on the right," said Phelan. "She's happier there. Tawny's on the left."

"Hey, ladies," I said, petting them. Truth was, all reindeer looked alike to me. They were no bigger than ponies, their backs not even as high as my chest, but their antlers extended well over my head. Their brown hair was thick and coarse. Tufts of white hung from their throats like misplaced beards. One reindeer turned its head slightly, and I narrowly missed being poked in the eye by an antler tip.

"You need to get dressed," Ralph reminded me. We put on our gear and goggles. Then, he said, "This is the most important part. The reindeer can get excited when they're going out, so you need to be ready. Get in the sleigh and take the reins."

"But how will I get out of the barn?" Sitting in the sleigh inside a barn seemed weird.

"The ground crew will open the door. You'll tell them when you're ready. If they're not here, there's a button on the dashboard. Whatever you do, don't open the doors until you're ready to go." I scanned the dashboard as Ralph climbed in beside me. "It's that one," he said, pointing to a blue button on the far left. "Make sure you get yourself organized first."

"Why wouldn't the ground crew be here?" It wouldn't be fair to say I was panicking, but why would I be flying with no ground crew?

"Don't worry," Ralph reassured me. "Get yourself together. Press this"—he pointed to another button—"to bring up your flight plan." I pushed the button, and a map appeared on a screen in the dashboard. At the center of the map, a bright yellow line formed a loop.

"How do I know what's what?" I asked.

"That's you." He pointed to the red dot at the bottom of the screen. "The yellow line shows where you're supposed to go. As you fly, you'll see a blue line showing where you actually are. You want to keep the two as close together as possible. You know how to steer, right?"

I nodded. Mitch had taught me that the first time I rode in a sleigh. "Pull back with the right hand to turn right and with the left hand to turn left," I recited like an obedient student.

"Exactly. Pull back with both to slow down, and pull harder to stop."

"But how do I make the reindeer go down?"

I could tell he was stifling a laugh. "They're not going to stop in mid-air and hang there. If you want them to start their descent, you can say 'Down,' but if you pull back hard, they're going to go down regardless because they have to in order to stop. Have you ever ridden a horse?"

"Not for eons." Like all my girlfriends, I was horse-crazy in middle school. By high school, our attention had turned to boys. I hadn't been on a horse since the eighth grade.

"Except for the up and down part, it's like riding a horse." He sounded every bit as nonchalant as you might expect from somebody who'd been driving a sleigh since childhood.

Except for the up and down part? That was the most important part. I wasn't worried about running the team into a tree, but I was extremely worried about crash-landing a sleigh in the middle of the ocean or missing the mark and falling off a roof. Thank God I'd never have to drive a sleigh on Christmas Eve. I already knew from Meredith that deliveries were left to the brothers. We'd be sitting safely in the Control Center, drinking tea and tracking their routes.

"Ready?" When I nodded, Ralph said, "Phelan, please open the doors."

"Yes, sir." The barn doors swung open.

I waited. Nothing happened.

"Tell them to go," said Ralph. "Or slap the reins."

"I thought you said they'd go as soon as the doors opened."

"Not this pair. They'll do what you tell them. Some of them might start on their own, but these girls will sit here all day unless you tell them to go."

I took a deep breath and slapped the reins. "Let's go!"

Obediently, the reindeer moved out—and up as soon as we'd cleared the barn. "Don't pull back!" Ralph said above the initial roar of the wind. "You can't balance yourself on the reins. Give them their heads for now. Keep an eye on your GPS." Without daring to move my head, I glanced down at the screen. My blue line was going straight, while the yellow line was curving slightly to the right. "Correct your course," he said, and I pulled back on the right rein until the blue lined up with the yellow. "Good. Now level off."

"How do I do that?" I managed.

"Say 'okay,'" Ralph said, clearly oblivious to the fact that we were about to fall out of the sky.

"Okay," I called. Sure enough, our ascent flattened in the calmer air. Hardly daring to breathe, I spared a quick look at the GPS. We were too far to the right now. I pulled back on the left reins. Too far left. I pulled the right reins, then the left, then the right again. One of the reindeer—I couldn't remember which one—tossed its head in apparent frustration, while the other one snorted its displeasure at my ineptitude. Back and forth, back and forth, until the zigzagging blue line was finally pretty much tracking the yellow one.

Just as I was about to celebrate my small victory, Ralph said, "Now start your descent."

Relieved, I called, "Down!" Immediately, the reindeer started a steep downhill trek, like a roller coaster. "No! No! Up! Okay! Stop!"

"It's okay, we're fine. Pull back on the reins a bit." Ralph's voice was calm and steady, as if we weren't about to crash. I did as he said, and our descent became gentler. "Pull harder. You're looking for a smooth landing." I yanked on the reins. Below us, the featureless white gave no hint of proximity. "Careful, the ground's coming up fast—"

And we slammed into the snowpack with a jolt that nearly bounced me out of the sleigh, knocking my goggles askew. Even Ralph seemed startled. Like a pair of defiant teens who had bested their substitute teacher, the team stood perfectly still as if nothing untoward had occurred.

"We'll work on landing next time." He leaned over and kissed me. "Good job, honey."

"Liar," I muttered, my heart still pounding as I adjusted my goggles. "Are we done?"

"We need to go inside. Walk the team into the barn."

I hit the blue button on the dash, and the barn doors swung open. Phelan and another elf waited inside. I walked the reindeer into the barn, successfully stopped them, and climbed out of the sleigh, clinging to its side in the hope that nobody would see how rubbery my legs were. Without comment, the elves unhitched the sleigh, hung up the harnesses, and led the reindeer to their stalls. I probably wasn't supposed to hear Ralph instruct them in a low voice to check the sleigh's runners.

"Thanks," I said to the elves, who waved their acknowledgement as Ralph and I left the stable.

"So? What did you think?" Ralph asked eagerly.

"I think that if I never have to do that again, I can live a full and happy life," I said with conviction.

He laughed. "You just need practice."

"Nope. I am officially hanging up my reins. From here on out, I shall be a passenger only."

"You didn't like it?" The man actually sounded surprised. "But you did well—I mean, for your first time." Even he knew there was a line between encouragement and flat-out lying.

I stopped and looked at him squarely. "This is what's known as one-and-done. Did it once, and never again. Henceforth, my love, you shall be the sleigh driver in this relationship."

Ralph peered as if gauging how serious I was. When I didn't smile or otherwise suggest that I was only kidding, he said, "It's up to you. If you really don't want to, you don't have to fly." He wrapped his arms around me. "You have other talents." He kissed me, and a relieved warmth spread through my body.

Twenty-Two

I drove into my garage as the sun rose, bleary-eyed after another nerve-racking flight through the night sky. I hadn't wanted to fly home overnight, but Mitch needed to get back to the Pole to resume work on a new tablet they were developing. You had to be as young as Mitch to fly all night and work the next day, I mused, my middle-aged mind clouded with exhaustion. No wonder people hated taking the red-eye. I'd hoped to sleep, but my nerves wouldn't allow it, especially after we hit turbulence over Toronto.

I removed my overnight bag from my back seat and stumbled into my kitchen. I'd just filled the electric tea kettle when a man appeared in the doorway wearing nothing but a towel around his waist. "What the—who the hell are you!" I demanded, brandishing the kettle.

"Um—morning." His voice was butter-smooth. "I'm Tristan."

"Tristan who? What are you doing in my kitchen?" My gut twisted because in that instant, I knew.

Lest any question remain, feet pounded down the stairs. "Hey, Meg! I didn't know you were home!" Isabella raced into the kitchen, her cheeks pink, her hair tumbling over the shoulders of an oversized T-shirt that definitely wasn't hers. "Um, this is Tristan. Tristan, this is Meg. This is her place. She's my—my landlord."

"Her landlord," I echoed dryly.

Tristan extended his hand. "I'm in Ealaíonta. I play the bass." Above and below the towel, he was more muscled than I'd have expected of a musician. Apparently he divided his time between rehearsing Bach and working out. His honey-colored hair was tousled. The slightest bit of stubble adorned his tanned chin. His fingers were long and strong-looking. I was willing to bet he could do a lot more with them than make music.

"Hello, Tristan." I ignored his outstretched hand.

"We were—I mean, we wanted some coffee." Isabella's voice was determinedly bright. She opened the refrigerator and bent over in search of the coffee jar. I turned away swiftly, before I learned much more about my future sister-in-law than I cared to know.

It clearly wasn't Tristan's first time in my home, because he knew precisely where the mugs were. As he turned to the cabinets, I saw scratch marks on his back. I looked away—straight into Isabella's eyes as she closed the refrigerator door.

If I'd been waiting for one of them to apologize for this awkward scene, I'd have been disappointed. With a quick toss of her head, Isabella made coffee. While it was brewing, Tristan halved two bagels and put them into the toaster oven. By the time the bagels had toasted, he'd pulled from the refrigerator a half-empty container of strawberry cream cheese that I knew I hadn't bought. Isabella poured the coffee into two mugs. Then, they piled the bagels, mugs, cream cheese, and a knife onto my hand-carved teak tray.

"Nice meeting you," Tristan said as he picked up the tray and left the kitchen. Isabella started to follow, but I hissed, "Wait a minute." She paused, looking for all the world like a defiant teenager. "What do you think you're doing?"

She tossed her head. "I don't think that's any of your business," she said. "I happen to be a grown woman."

"A grown *married* woman," I said. "Whose husband is about to be my brother-in-law."

"What I do is my own business," she retorted.

"Not when you're doing it in my house," I shot back. "You are not going to put me in the middle of all this. If you want to cheat on your husband, that's up to you, but I'm not running a home for wayward wives. So here's the rule: no overnight guests. In fact, no guests, period. You're here to pursue a music career, not an affair."

"Like you should talk?"

"What are you talking about?"

"You and Scott," she said as if it was obvious.

"What the—I don't—that isn't even close to the same thing! I'm not married, Scott is a business acquaintance, we were both drunk, and I never—*would* never—screw him!"

"Sure, right." She breezed out of the kitchen, leaving me in a mixed state of rage and terror.

As the happy couple headed upstairs to frolic in Isabella's boudoir, the cats tumbled into the kitchen, delighted at the prospect of an early breakfast. "Did you let her bring him here?" I asked them, setting their food dishes on their respective place mats. Then, I tried to forget about the scene undoubtedly going on upstairs by recalling my weekend with my sweet Ralph.

One evening after dinner, when we were strolling the halls—more for exercise than anything else—I noticed a light on in the finishing room. Ralph didn't seem particularly interested, but after years of representing miscreants, I wanted to make sure everything was all right.

"Hi! Is somebody here?" I called, opening the door.

"It's just us," came a crisp voice from the far end of the room. Two young elves, a man and a woman, were painting the shutters and trim on a cream-colored Victorian dollhouse.

"That's beautiful!" I exclaimed. The shutters were lavender, the window trim dove-gray, and the front door was dusty rose.

"Thanks," said the man, not looking up from the intricacy of his brushwork.

"We didn't get it finished before supper," the woman said.

"Does it have to go out early?" I asked.

"No," said the man, still painting. "We didn't want to stop." He finally glanced up at us as he touched his brush to his palette.

"It looks great," said Ralph. "Thanks so much. Some kid is going to be over the moon with this one."

The woman dimpled in pleasure. "I hope so."

"I know so," said Ralph. "Come on, Meg. Let's leave Jackson and Betsy to their work." We bade them good night and drew the door closed behind us.

"Does everybody have to work late?" I asked as we continued our stroll.

"Not yet," said Ralph. "They're doing it because they want to. The crunch won't start until late October, when most of the specific requests come in."

"What do you mean?"

"Right now, we're still producing general inventory, but as the Day gets closer, there'll be more kids requesting individual items, such as a specific type of doll rather than simply 'a doll.' Plus, there's going to be more finishing and wrapping and organizing to do. In mid-November, Fred puts out an all-call for anybody who wants to work evenings and nights."

"What if nobody wants to?"

"They will," said Ralph with certainty. "We all do. I can't tell you how many nights I've spent painting fire engines or doll houses."

"Does your mom work in the workshop, too?"

"Kind of. She's not an artistic sort, so she handles a lot of the administrative stuff. If there's a lull there, she'll dress dolls or wrap gifts—pretty much whatever somebody tells her to do."

"Somebody *tells* your mother what to do?" They probably took bids for that job.

Ralph chuckled. "Everybody has different skills. Whoever's in charge is in charge, and everybody else respects that. If she's helping out in the doll room or the wrapping department, she's a worker just like the others, and she knows this."

It was an astonishing concept. "What about your father? What does he do?"

"He used to do pretty much everything. Since his stroke, he struggles with the jobs that require dexterity—which, let's face it, is practically all of them—so his main job is morale. While everybody works, he tells stories of Christmases past. He talks about the kids he's encountered, what it's like sneaking into a house—all of it. Needless to say, everybody wants to work in the room where Pop is."

Now, as the cats licked their dishes clean, I imagined working the night shift at the Pole, wrapping presents or checking items off lists as Santa Claus Emeritus spun tales of his adventures. I leaned against the counter, eyes closed, my very soul tingling at the prospect.

"Hey, nice to meet you. Bye!"

My eyes popped open as Tristan—now fully dressed, thank God—deposited the tray on the counter. He darted out of the kitchen before I could respond. An instant later, the front door closed, leaving me caught between the bliss of my future and the aggravation of my present reality.

Twenty-Three

Even though I'd lived in Connecticut my entire life, the Wadsworth Mansion was new to me. It was a mansion in the truest sense of the word, with twenty-foot ceilings supported by graceful pillars. After a colorful history in which the property ranged from a summer home for the wealthy to a retreat center to a victim of fire and vandalism, the mansion and its lands had been rescued and rehabilitated to create a venue for weddings and similar income-producing functions.

I walked through the massive front doors, feeling distinctly under-dressed in my black wool pants with a soft black cardigan over a blue silk shell. A tall, skinny young man with frizzy blond hair and round wire glasses was selling tickets. Posters for Ealaíonta's next events graced the table. I picked one up, thinking it might be nice to show it to Ralph. I didn't know whether Phil would want to see it.

I was still trying not to judge Phil for missing Iz's first concert. She had told me quite matter-of-factly that he wouldn't be coming down; I couldn't tell whether she was putting on a brave face or whether she was truly not bothered by her husband's absence. For my part, I was surprised and dismayed that he hadn't made the effort to be here. I didn't mention it to Ralph, though, because the truth was that I was also relieved. The last thing I wanted was to witness Isabella's attempts to juggle her husband and her lover. Did Phil know she was seeing other men? Did Tristan know she was married? Was the prospect of their clash the real reason she hadn't pushed for Phil to come down to celebrate her debut?

In a large room at one end of the foyer, two sleek young people in crisp white shirts and black bowties tended bar in front of a marble fireplace. Platters of hors d'oeuvres graced high-top tables around the room. The guests laughed and chatted; other than me, no one stood alone. I accepted a glass of malbec and wandered through the modest crowd as though looking for the person I meant to meet up with.

Eventually, a svelte Black woman in a shiny teal gown shepherded us into a smaller room with rows of chairs. I ended up in the front row on the left side of another marble fireplace, next to the violins and violists. This seat meant I had a perfect view of Isabella since the cellos and Tristan, who indeed played the bass, were on the right side of the fireplace.

The founder and concert mistress of Ealaíonta welcomed us to the event and explained what they would be playing. I was familiar with Vivaldi's "Four Seasons," but the concert mistress said they'd be playing a variation on that piece by someone I'd never heard of. The rest of the audience nodded as if they recognized the composer's name.

The program included vocalists as well as Ealaíonta. What stunned me, though, was the cello solo in one of the pieces. I'd heard Isabella play it at home, of course. But here, in front of an audience, there was a fire in her that I'd never seen. She was fierce, attacking the music, bringing forth nuances I'd never heard in my kitchen. If I hadn't known better, I'd have thought she was an entirely different musician.

As the well-behaved audience applauded, a chill struck my heart. *She's a performer,* I realized. Not just a musician. Not even just an artist. Isabella needed a stage, an audience. This was where she truly came alive. Which meant she could likely never be happy playing the cello in the privacy of her apartment at the Pole. The person I saw here needed the adrenalin that only a live audience could provide.

My heart sank. How on earth could I convince her to go back to the Pole when even I could see that she was born for the stage?

As the audience dispersed, I went looking for Isabella. I assumed she'd be with Tristan, but when I spotted him, Isabella was nowhere in sight. I turned and bumped squarely into someone. "Oh, I'm sorry," I said before I looked up.

"Meg! How are you?" Rick was as effusive as ever.

"Doing well, thanks. What brings you here tonight?"

"A friend was playing. Here she is now. Cassie!" He waved to the woman who'd played the viola solo in the final piece. "Meg, this is Cassandra. Cass, this is Meg. We used to work together," he added hastily, as if to dispel any concerns that he and I had ever been romantically entangled. I wasn't certain whether to be relieved or offended.

"How do you do?" Cassandra shifted her viola case to her left hand and reached out to shake my hand.

"Pleased to meet you," I responded. Her grip was strong for someone of her slight build. "You played beautifully tonight."

"Thank you," she said simply. No false modesty here. Clearly this was a woman accustomed to accepting adulation.

"Wasn't she fantastic? I keep telling her, she should let me be her manager. I could get her gigs all over the place!"

"I didn't realize you were connected in the music world," I said.

"You know how it is—you represent somebody, and they're in a particular field, so you have to learn about it. Enough to fake it, anyway." He laughed, his capped teeth on full display. Cassandra looked away as if embarrassed.

I spotted Isabella in the foyer, holding court among a cluster of silver-haired men and women in evening garb. "I need to get going. Good to see you, Rick. Nice to meet you, Cassandra." I slipped away before they could respond.

By the time Isabella extricated herself from her admirers, most of the audience had dissipated. I'd watched from the shadows of a convenient alcove as Rick and Cassandra chatted with a tall, gray-haired man who looked like a professor. I didn't want to give Rick a chance to remember that I'd never gotten back to him about his proposal. It occurred to me to wonder whether Cassandra was Carter Fitzhugh's now-estranged wife or if Rick had already moved on.

"You were amazing," I told Isabella, hugging her. Over her shoulder, I saw Tristan holding the door for a petite redhead. As they walked toward the parking lot, he draped his arm around her shoulders.

"Thanks." Up close, Isabella looked radiant and exhausted. If she knew—or cared—that Tristan had left with someone else, she gave no sign. "Hilary says we're supposed to be chatting up the donors, but I don't see her anywhere, so let's get out of here. Come on, I've got to get my cello." I followed Iz to a small closet under the grand staircase. "I hate having to store it in an unlocked closet, but it was that or carry it around all night." She opened the door and took out the cello case. "I always worry when it's out of my hands. Phil gave it to me for our third anniversary. It's a Lawrence Wilke." I could tell I was supposed to be impressed, so I nodded as she prattled on about the instrument en route to the parking lot. "Wilke makes such amazing cellos, and everybody says he's a real sweetheart besides. He doesn't live too far from here, so I'm hoping to meet him before I go back to the Pole."

Before I go back to the Pole. I made a noncommittal noise as I unlocked the car. It was all I could do not to grab my phone and text Ralph: *she's coming home!* I could imagine how happy Phil would be to have her back. As casually as I could manage, I said, "I didn't know you'd made up your mind."

She shrugged. "I miss Phil."

Everything in me wanted to grill her, to make sure she was serious about giving up her shot at a career in music. How awful it would be if Phil thought she was coming back and then she changed her mind— which she easily could. I knew what I'd seen tonight. In performance, Isabella was luminous. Her concentration was fierce—I doubt she'd have noticed if the building had caught fire. And the sounds she produced—I was no expert, but there was a quality about her music that captured me in a way I'd never experienced. Was it because I knew her? Or was she simply that good?

And if she was that good, did she truly belong at the Pole?

Twenty-Four

"Um, Meg? Where did you get all these boxes?" Isabella tried to sound clueless, but her meaning was clear. The cardboard boxes strewn across my living room were emblazoned with logos for wine or whiskey.

"At the liquor store." Everybody knew the best place to get free boxes was the liquor store. Anything sturdy enough to hold twelve bottles of wine or six bottles of Jim Beam could easily hold whatever the average mover crammed into it.

I couldn't quite believe I was moving. When I bought my condo, I swore I'd never move again. Holly asked once what I planned to do if I met somebody and fell in love. I replied blithely, *He can move in with me.*

Except it never occurred to me that I might fall in love with Santa Claus.

Isabella was loading books into a box. "You sure have a lot of books," she commented as she taped the box shut. With a fat-tipped black marker, she scrawled, "Books—what else?" on the top and side of the box.

"I need them." The defense might have worked better if she'd been cleaning out the basement with its plethora of legal books. Up here, my collection ran mostly to novels and essays. It took a special level of moxie to try to characterize a series of Irish women's fiction as necessary.

For hours, we packed and taped boxes. The books might have been voluminous, but they were a snap to pack. Much harder were the contents of the china cabinet, with crystal glasses and handmade platters.

"Are you really taking all this stuff with you?" Isabella asked as the setting sun cast a soft orange glow on the stack of newspapers we were using for packing material.

"Sure, why not?" I taped a box containing my old sets of Twain, Dickens, and Fitzgerald novels, all acquired when I was in college and signed up for the Literary Guild. In my youth, I hadn't noticed how miniscule the print was. I probably should have replaced them with large-print versions, but I'd never quite gotten around to it. Besides, I had reading glasses.

Isabella wrapped a crystal vase in bubble wrap. "I don't mean to be a pain, but where are you going to keep all this stuff?"

"In Ralph's—I mean, in our apartment."

Isabella glanced at me. "His place isn't very big."

"It's big enough." Except I wasn't at all certain it was. Ralph had assured me we'd find a place for everything, but had he really thought we'd be trying to figure out shelf space for three sets of candlesticks?

Casually, Isabella commented, "I didn't take much of anything with me when Phil and I got married. Seriously, I think I took my clothes and my makeup and practically nothing else."

"And your cello."

"Well, of course." You'd have thought I asked whether she took her toothbrush.

Just then, Lulu trotted into the room and hopped into the box I was packing. "No, you don't, sweet girl," I said, lifting her out.

"She wants to know if she's going with you," Isabella said.

"Well, of course." I matched Isabella's tone of a moment ago when I'd asked about her cello. "They all are. What did you think?"

"Nothing, really. I mean, it's a long trip, and they're used to being here. I'll bet Rodrigo would love it if they stayed."

"Don't be ridiculous," I said more harshly than I intended. "He knows they're coming with me."

Almost on cue, the doorbell rang. When Isabella didn't move, I heaved myself to my feet and answered it.

"Hello, darling!" Rodrigo leaned down and kissed my cheek. "I brought you a little something to help get you through packing." He held out two chilled bottles of Veuve Clicquot.

"Thanks, sweetie." My voice was noticeably flat. He raised an eyebrow, and I said, "I hate packing."

"I know exactly what you mean. That's why I believe in hiring movers. Where are your glasses? Still in the kitchen?"

"Of course. Isabella needs them." I was leaving the furniture and most of the kitchenware for Isabella's use. My plan was to take personal items—which in my lexicon included books, artwork, and CDs—in addition to winter clothes, my computer, and client files. Eventually, as in *once Isabella decided whether she was coming home*, we'd address the balance of my possessions.

One of the best things about Rodrigo—besides his love of my cats—was the way he could turn practically any event into a party. He poured champagne and cued up a stream of show tunes, and we belted out the lyrics to *Hello, Dolly!* and *The Sound of Music* as we drank and wrapped and packed.

"This is so exciting!" he kept exclaiming. "Such an adventure! I adore it!" He swooped me around the room, hitting the final "dream!" of "Climb Ev'ry Mountain" with a timbre that would do any tenor proud.

By the time we'd gone through *Pippin*, *West Side Story*, and *Les Miserables*, the sun was rising and we were taping the last boxes. "One day more!" Rodrigo sang as we stacked the carefully wrapped canvases against the wall.

"Speaking of which, when is all this stuff leaving?" Isabella asked.

For an instant, I wished I'd inherited the Claus trait of being able to raise a single eyebrow. I wasn't even out of here, and she was already sounding possessive about "her" space. "It's going to require several trips. Luckily, there's no rush," I added pointedly.

"I'm not saying—I mean, you'll already be living on top of each other."

"There's nothing wrong with that," said Rodrigo with a wicked leer.

"Except that sooner or later, we're going to have to get out of bed." I slumped on the sofa. "It's been so long since I've lived with a guy." I turned to Rodrigo. "How do you two do it? I mean, you're so different."

Rodrigo winked. "Samson is a dynamo in the sack." He and Isabella broke up with laughter.

"I'm serious," I said. "How do two people who are so different make a life together?"

Rodrigo sat down and put his arm around me. "Here's the thing, darling. You have to give each other space. Otherwise, you'll smother. Samson does his reading while I'm at rehearsal, and by the time I get back, we're both ready to be together." With his free hand, he poured more champagne into our glasses. "Truth is, sometimes I wish we had a bigger place. He doesn't complain often, but I know my parties bother him." I refrained from pointing out that they bothered the neighbors, too. "In a perfect world, we'd have a great big house, and we'd be able to soundproof his study so he could curl up with his books while I rehearse or entertain."

"You're not thinking of moving, are you?" Isabella asked. "I love having you guys here."

"So do I," I said, even though my own move was imminent.

"Oh, no, my dears," Rodrigo assured us. "We adore this complex. Besides, if we bought a house, we'd have to hire somebody to handle the landscaping and the snow and all that. This way, there's none of that. Meg, darling, if you ever think of selling, I'm your first call. Don't forget!" He upended the bottle, and a few drops dripped into his glass. "Now *that* is a tragedy," he announced, and we all laughed even as I felt a pang at the imminent loss of the best neighbors I'd ever had.

Twenty-Five

"Don't get your hopes up," I warned as we made a left into Sunward Villages. I'd flown into Phoenix the previous afternoon, and after sundown, Ted had dropped Ralph off at a golf course near my hotel. "My family is nothing like yours."

"You've said that a dozen times," said Ralph. "I'm sure they'll be fine."

"Care to bet?" I pulled our rental car into the spot marked for visitors and lowered the windows to keep the interior temperature somewhat bearable.

"You're her only daughter. I'm sure she'll be thrilled that you're thinking about getting married," Ralph said.

"At last," I finished.

Everything around us seemed to be neutral desert hues. Faded reddish tile roofs topped the sand-colored buildings. Even the sidewalks looked like compacted sand. Minuscule plots of grass offered tiny bits of color between the buildings and the sidewalks, bordered with large margins of white gravel. It made sense, I supposed: here in the desert, water would be precious.

Despite the sun beating down on us, Ralph looked perfectly comfortable as we walked to my mother's condo. Odd that someone who lived in the Arctic Circle would adjust so quickly to the intense heat of the southwestern United States. Then again, I supposed he was used to diverse climates from all his travel.

In all candor, I wasn't quite certain why we were there. I already knew that my mother was not going to behave in a traditional mother-of-the-bride fashion, twittering about dresses and flowers. When she married Phil, everybody—including me—assumed that she'd ask me to be her maid of honor. Instead, she chose Phil's daughter Shelly, a former teen model who was as tall and slim as her father. I tried to tell myself that Mom made this choice as a gesture to Phil, but a corner of my mind always suspected that she chose Shelly because of how she'd look in the wedding photos. My brother Derek walked Mom down the aisle at the country club, and I sat in the front row sans guest because I'd been invited without a plus-one. ("I didn't know you were dating anyone!" my mother claimed when I asked if I could bring the man I was seeing. "I wish I'd known before—we've already given the caterer the headcount.") Derek, his wife Cindy, and I sat at a table near the front while Mom and Phil sat at the head table with Shelly and her husband, Phil's son Roger and his wife, and Mom's friend Mavis and her date. The photographer took oodles of photos, but when I saw the ones Mom and Phil chose for their album, the shots of Derek, Cindy, Mom, Phil, and me were not among them. In what the photographer called the "blended family" photos, I couldn't help noticing how short and stocky Derek, Cindy, and I looked in comparison to Phil's willowy family.

And yet, while I knew better than to expect hearts and flowers from my mother, I still cherished the secret hope that she would welcome Ralph into the Riley family, assuming such a thing still existed. I'd even tolerate some talk about dresses if that miracle happened.

I rang the bell. After several seconds, the door opened, and my stepfather said, "Meg! So good to see you! And you must be Ralph!" he added in a display of stellar deductive reasoning.

Phil was tall and rangy, with a prominent jaw, a hawk-like nose, and a fringe of white hair. His scalp was spotted with scars from where he'd had skin cancers removed. Since retiring from his practice ten years earlier, he'd devoted his days to golf, his weekday evenings to bridge, and his weekends to socializing at the club. He and I had nothing in common except my mother, but we were capable of making small talk for half an hour or so when I visited every other year. If he answered the phone when I called, the small talk lasted about fifteen seconds before I'd hear him calling for Mom. The best word I could use to describe him was "pleasant."

My stepfather was a lifelong Arizona resident whom Mom had met several years ago when she and a few friends came to visit another friend, Mavis, who'd moved to Phoenix to pursue a post-divorce career as a realtor. Phil lived in the unit two doors down from Mavis. According to Mom, as soon as the Connecticut contingent arrived, Mavis hustled them over to meet Phil. "His wife died a few months ago," Mavis hissed. "He's a retired anesthesiologist. Had a very successful practice. Trust me, around here, he's not going to stay on the market long." Mavis's prediction was correct: six months later, I flew to Arizona for my mother's wedding to Phil.

"Come in, come in," my stepfather said now, stepping back. His aqua golf shirt nearly matched his eyes. His khaki shorts were slightly baggy, stopping at the tops of his knobby knees. He wore black socks with his tan sandals. "Your mother should be back soon. She's playing tennis."

We entered the condo Phil had bought from Mavis. It looked as if he'd never redecorated after the realtor staged it with standard impersonal furnishings and artwork. I found it especially disconcerting that in my mother's home, I recognized nearly nothing. Not that I should have been surprised: before she married Phil, Mom demanded that Derek and I come to our family home and claim anything we wanted. The rest, she announced, was going to be sold. "I'm ready for a fresh start," she said as if her life with us was over. Now, I recognized a mirror in the front hallway and a vase in the living room, but the rest of the décor was unfamiliar. A few framed photos sat on the mantel; when I got closer, I saw that they were Phil's grandchildren. I looked for a photo of Derek's kids, but there wasn't one.

We sat on the off-white sofa while Phil settled into what was clearly his usual off-white chair. "Would you like something to drink?" he asked, showing no signs of getting up.

"We'd love some iced tea," I said without looking at Ralph.

Phil's face fell slightly. "Oh, I'm sorry. We don't drink tea anymore. Too acidic." I waited for him to list what they did have, but he added nothing.

"Water's fine," said Ralph.

"I'll get it," I said when Phil made no effort to move. I went out to the spacious kitchen and opened the Sub-Zero. It was nearly empty. According to Mom, they ate at the club almost every night. "It's so nice not to have to cook anymore," she exulted. Luckily, several plastic bottles of water sat on the glass shelves. The last time I visited, my mother had served tap water that bore such a strong chlorine taste that it might have been pool water.

I placed three bottles and three glasses on a small acrylic tray and brought it to the living room. "Oh, no, thank you," said Phil when I placed the tray on the glass coffee table where we could all reach it. I opened one bottle, poured its contents into a glass, and handed it to Ralph, who thanked me. I poured another for myself. The third I left precisely where it was. Phil didn't seem to notice or care.

Conversation limped along for nearly half an hour before my mother breezed into the room. Her once-pale skin was golden-brown and leathery. When I was growing up, she had long dark hair that my father adored; now, her short hair was feathered and frosted. She wore a white tennis dress, pink knit wristbands, and an elastic brace around her right knee.

"Hello, darling!" she said as she entered. It was unclear who she meant, but I stood up to hug her. Ralph, who had been raised properly, also rose. She held up her hands, protesting, "Don't touch me, I'm a sweaty mess." She didn't look sweaty, but I drew back anyway.

"How was your match?" asked Phil.

"We absolutely killed them! Is that for me?" She reached for the remaining bottle of water. "Ugh, it's warm. Let me get another." She disappeared, returning a moment later with a fresh bottle.

"Mom, this is Ralph," I said as soon as she returned. My beloved reached out his hand, and she shook it as if meeting one of Phil's colleagues at the club.

The night before, Ralph had asked me what he should say if she inquired what he did for a living. "She won't ask," I assured him. "She barely knows what I do."

"Do you want me to tell her I'm Santa Claus?"

"It's up to you. They'll think you're kidding."

"But—this is your family. Don't you want to be honest with them?"

I couldn't help smiling. Ralph could be so naïve. "They'll never know the difference. It's not as if they're interested."

He stroked my hair. "I'm sure you're exaggerating."

"I'm sure I'm not. We're not a close group. We just share some genetic material."

Now, as I waited for my mother to show even minimal interest in the man I'd brought to her home—the first time in a decade I'd done so—she burbled on about her tennis match. She'd played casually when Derek and I were kids, but usually she sniffed at the women who traipsed around the local market in tennis whites and the little socks with pompoms on the back. "So pretentious," she'd said. Even in my teens, I'd recognized her disdain as envy. Now, she was one of them. I'd never seen her happier.

When she finally paused for breath, I jumped in. "Ralph and I are getting married." Beside me, Ralph startled slightly.

"That's wonderful," said Phil. "Congratulations." He didn't budge from his chair to hug us or even shake Ralph's hand.

Neither did my mother, though she did say, "My baby's getting married!" On the drive from the hotel, Ralph asked whether she'd expect him to ask for my hand, and I burst out laughing. "Not hardly," I managed finally. "Besides, I'm forty-one. It's not as if she's going to give me away."

Now, she skipped straight over inconsequential details like who my betrothed was, going straight for the truly important issues. "We can do it at the club. When the Beekmans' daughter got married, they brought in someone to do the ceremony right there. They arranged the chairs so they faced that big picture window overlooking the course, and then we all went out to the patio for cocktail hour while they rearranged everything for dinner."

"We're not getting married here," I said.

It was the first thing I'd said that truly seemed to get her attention. "Why not? This is where the bride's family lives."

"It isn't where the bride lives," I said. "Besides, Ralph has a big family, and they can't all come down here."

"Why not? We can get a block of rooms at the Marriott downtown. It'll be fine."

"There are a lot of us, Mrs.—um—" In the same moment, Ralph and I realized I'd never told him Phil's last name.

"Greenwood," I supplied.

"Call me Marge," Mom said. "How big is your family?"

Ralph counted on his fingers. "My parents, four brothers, three sisters-in-law, and my aunt. So, ten, not counting my nieces and nephews."

"That's not bad at all," said Phil. "I'm sure they can manage."

"That doesn't count any of our friends," I said. "Holly's going to be my matron of honor, and she and Michael and Ruby and plenty of other people would have to travel from Connecticut. Not to mention Derek and Cindy and the kids." Said kids had not been invited when Mom married Phil.

"You could have Shelly as your matron of honor. We'll do it at the holidays, when everyone wants to get away from cold weather," said my mother.

"And the airfares to go anywhere warm are through the roof," I pointed out.

"The holidays are our busy time at work," said Ralph.

"Surely you can get some time off," said Phil. "My practice was always busy at the holidays, but I always managed to get a couple weeks off to play golf. Relaxing is so important."

"We don't want to get married in Arizona," I said firmly. I could feel Ralph ready to break in to negotiate something, and I placed my hand on his in the universal attorney signal to keep quiet. "There's no way to do it. We both have to work, and everybody we'd want to invite would have to travel thousands of miles to get here. It's impossible."

"I don't see why. I'd plan everything. We could get an excellent price for the club. The Beekmans' daughter's wedding was beautiful. Phil, do we have any photos from that wedding?" Phil obligingly pulled out his phone and began to scroll through it.

"No." I was trying to hold my temper. This time, Ralph laid his hand on mine. "Listen to me. It's not happening. Our wedding is going to be up north, with Ralph's family."

"How far up north? Colorado?"

"Farther," I said, not looking at Ralph. "Way, way up north."

"You don't mean Canada," said Phil as if there were something particularly distressing about our neighbor to the north.

"Up that way," I said.

"Well, there's no way we could go, then," said my mother. "We can't travel that far."

"What's the matter? Is something wrong?" They both appeared to be in perfect health.

"It's too hard for us to travel," Mom said. "Managing all those electronic passes is too confusing. Not to mention squeezing into airplane seats. I know people think first-class is so spacious, but the last time we flew, I was stiff for *hours* after we got off. The lumbar support in those seats is completely inadequate. And my knee gives me so much trouble." This from the woman who had just spent the morning running around a tennis court. "Not to mention, poor Phil had a terrible time dealing with all our luggage."

"Aren't there any bellhops or porters anymore?"

"Of course, dear, but you still have to keep an eye on them. Do you know that one time, the young man tried to put somebody else's bags on *our* cart? He tried to move our bags and somebody else's at the same time! He wanted *two* tips for making *one* trip from the baggage claim to the pickup area. Can you imagine?"

"I didn't let him get away with it," Phil chimed in. "I told him we'd hired him first, and we expected his full attention. He tried some nonsense about how there was plenty of room on the cart for everything, but I made him take the other bags off. It affected his tip, I might add."

"Ralph's father can't travel," I said. "He's older than you, and he's had a couple of strokes."

"I'm sure the weather here would be good for him," said Phil.

"We have a number of people in the complex who've had strokes. They use golf carts to get around. We could arrange to have one of those for him."

"For the last time, I said no." I started to get up, and this time, Ralph restrained me.

"Mrs. Greenwood—" he began.

"—Marge—"

"Marge—it isn't that we don't appreciate the thought. What you're offering is very kind and generous. But apart from the two of you, Meg and I have no connection to Arizona. We understand how important it is for you to be a part of our wedding, but everyone else we'd like to include lives thousands of miles away. But we'd love to meet your friends sometime. Maybe later, we could plan a party at your club, and you could relax without having all the worry of throwing a wedding."

"You think we should go to the trouble and expense of hosting a party for you when you're not even willing to include us in your wedding?" my mother huffed.

"He didn't say that," I cut in before Ralph could dig himself a deeper hole. "All he said was that if you want to do something to celebrate our marriage, there are options other than the wedding itself."

"So, we're getting the sloppy seconds, is that it?" It was the first time I'd ever heard that tone from Phil. "His family gets the real wedding, and then you'll come down here at your convenience so everyone can see that we weren't important enough to be part of it."

"That's not what I meant, Mr. Greenwood—" Ralph began.

"—*Doctor* Greenwood," my mother and Phil interrupted in unison.

"Mom. Phil. Listen to us. We appreciate your offer—" I could feel Ralph's approval at my acknowledgement "—but we're not getting married here. That's it. Now, let's talk about something else. Phil, how are your grandkids doing?"

"They're great," he said.

But my mother wasn't letting go that easily. "I can't believe you're doing this to me. My only daughter's wedding, and I'm not wanted." She reached for a tissue even though I saw no tears.

Ralph started to speak, but I interrupted. "Don't be ridiculous. Just because you can't have my wedding your way doesn't mean you're not wanted. All it means is that you don't get to make the decisions."

"Don't call your mother ridiculous," said Phil.

"She's my mother, and I've known her a lot longer than you have, and she's being ridiculous on purpose," I snapped. "This is what she does when she doesn't get her own way. It's what she's always done—she turns herself into a victim, and she expects everybody to fall all over themselves to make poor Marge happy. Well, you can forget that. We're not getting married in Arizona. Period. Mom, I'm sorry you're not happy with my choice, but let's face it—when have you ever been happy with my choices?"

"If that's how you're going to treat your mother, then you can leave my house." I'd never heard Phil raise his voice before.

"Let's all calm down—" Ralph began.

"You don't want me at your wedding!" my mother shrieked, still tearless.

"Oh, cut it out!" I snapped.

"Meg, maybe we can—"

"No! We're not getting married here! I wouldn't get married here if it were the last place on earth!"

"See what you've done to your mother? Marge, honey, don't cry. They're not worth it," Phil said, his tone more bitter than comforting.

That one stopped me cold. "Who the hell are you to say something like that to us?"

"Come on, Meg. It's time for us to leave." I'd never heard that tight, barely controlled tone from Ralph. To my mother and stepfather, he said simply, "Goodbye." He laid his arm around my shoulders and shepherded me out of the house, my mother's wailing still audible after he closed the door behind us.

Twenty-Six

Ralph was silent the entire way back to the hotel, most likely because he couldn't get a word in edgewise as I ranted. When we pulled into the parking lot, he said, "I need to walk. I'll be back in a while." He kissed me and headed away from the door leading into the hotel.

I was lying under an umbrella by the hotel pool when he returned two hours later. The aqua water mirrored the cloudless sky. "I'm sorry," he said without preamble.

"About what?" I sat up, reaching for his hand.

"I shouldn't have spoken that way to your parents."

"Sit down, honey." He sat on the chaise next to mine. "First of all, you said nothing wrong. You tried to work something out, and I love you for that even though I could have told you it wouldn't work. Second, I'm sorry I put you through that. I don't know why I thought there was a shot in hell that she'd behave like a normal parent—you know, actually being happy for me, much less wanting to know anything about the man I'm marrying. That was my father's job. If he were still alive, we'd have been at their house for hours, and he'd be asking you all kinds of questions—not to pry or interrogate, but because he was always so interested in people." Unexpected tears welled up. "That's the hardest part—having to tell her husband, instead of my father, that I'm getting married. My dad was so great. You'd have loved him. He was always the buffer between Mom and me. But we weren't rich, and Dad wasn't a fancy doctor—he was middle management at an insurance company. A good steady job, but not something you brag about at the country club that we could never afford to join, not that he'd have wanted to anyway. And now, her country club is her life.

Sounds weird, but I think Phil is a much better fit for her. He's giving her what she really wanted all along."

Ralph shifted over to sit beside me on my chaise. He put his arm around me, and I leaned against him, closing my eyes. "Family can be hard," he said. "Even mine, as you know."

"Yours is different. They give you a hard time because they love you." And Meredith gave me a hard time to ensure I was properly prepared to step into the role of Santa's helpmate one day. Not that recognizing this made our day-to-day relationship any easier.

"Your mother loves you," Ralph said with forced conviction.

"Even assuming that's true, it's not the same. If you told your family we really wanted to get married here, I'll bet your mother and at least a couple of your brothers would make the trip. Then, they'd figure out some other way to celebrate our marriage back at the Pole—and they'd make it a real celebration. They wouldn't drive us away."

"They couldn't drive us away if they wanted to. I run the place." He kissed the top of my head.

"You know what I mean." I lifted my face to him, and we kissed, and it was like coming home—only to a real home, one that fit perfectly. "I love you so much," I murmured.

"Love you more," he murmured back with a smile in his voice.

"We'll see about that." I snuggled against him. One of the best things about Ralph was how safe I felt in his arms. Safe, and loved.

"You know what we could do?" Ralph said after a few minutes.

"What?"

"Elope."

I sat up straight. "What?"

"Think about it. Your parents won't come to the Pole. My family can't come to Arizona. Your friends will have to travel thousands of miles whichever way we do it. If we elope, nobody has to worry about anything."

It made peculiar sense. It wasn't as if my childhood dreams of walking down a church aisle in a white gown on my father's arm would ever be a reality—I had no father and no church, and the virginal white dress would be a joke. More importantly, Ralph couldn't come to Connecticut to get married, and that was where my friends—my true family—were. If we got married at the Pole, I was sure his mother and the elves would make everything beautiful, but at most I'd have Holly and Michael and Ruby, and maybe Derek and his clan if I was very lucky. Eloping somewhere neutral would let us get married without all the family fuss.

Except— "How can you get married anywhere but the Pole? No matter where we go, we'll need a marriage license. You'll have to show ID, like a passport or driver's license." I'd rented our car and hotel room under my name, because unlike Ralph, I enjoyed legal existence in the United States.

"Don't worry about it." He spoke with such conviction that I wondered whether he had a fake license in his back pocket. "I'm going to put on my trunks. Let's relax for a while before dinner."

"Sounds good." I kissed his hand and lay back on my chaise, eyes closed, to consider his idea. Eloping definitely had its pros, but would we wish later that we'd been married with more pomp and ceremony? No matter what he said about his family, would they be hurt that we got married without them? Or was it true that ultimately, all they wanted was whatever we wanted?

In old movies, eloping involved the boy climbing a ladder to the girl's bedroom window and the two of them escaping into the night to marry before the irate father caught up with them. For adults like us who didn't have to sneak away, it wasn't so much eloping as making our own decisions about where, when, and how to get married.

An enormous splash interrupted my musings. I sat up just as Ralph surfaced, shaking water from his hair and grinning widely. "I love swimming!" he announced. "One of the best things about being down this way." He dove back under the water, emerging half a minute later at the other end of the pool. "Come on in!" he called.

I couldn't resist. I started to walk to the shallow end where the steps were, but Ralph said, "Just jump!" I laughed, backed up a few steps, and took a running leap to cannonball into the water like a little kid. When I surfaced, Ralph was applauding and whooping, "That's my bride!" A couple down at the far end looked up. "Race you to the end!" he called out, already on his way.

We laughed and splashed and cavorted in the pool like a couple of kids. I floated, and he swam underneath me, and then he floated and I went beneath him, tickling his butt as I passed. We played Marco Polo, except I called out, "Santa!" and he called back, "Claus!" as I groped toward him. He scrambled out of the pool and commandeered two of the floats stashed by the wire fence, and when he tossed them into the pool, we laughed and splashed some more as we maneuvered ourselves onto them. Finally, blissfully tired, we floated hand in hand, the sun warming our wet skin. I looked over at him, this amazing man with shaggy dark wet hair and intense green eyes and an irresistible smile. "Hey, Santa. You wanna get married?"

His smile widened. "Yes, ma'am!"

"Me, too." I flicked water at him. "You know we're only a few hours from Vegas, right?"

"You mean today?" I couldn't tell whether he was surprised or stalling.

"More like tomorrow. We'll still need a marriage license. What do you think?"

"I think the thing I want most in this world is to be your husband. Wherever, whenever, however you want to do it is fine with me."

"I love you so much," I said.

"Love you more," he responded. He lifted my hand to his lips. "Now, let's get this honeymoon started!" He rolled off his float, I did the same, and we climbed out of the pool, dripping all the way to our room where we paused only to put the *Do Not Disturb* sign on the door before locking it behind us.

*****

The next morning, I awoke alone in bed. Ralph was sitting on a canvas chair on our tiny balcony. "Hey, there," I said.

"Morning, sleepyhead. Want some breakfast?" On the little round table between the two chairs sat a tray bearing a metal teapot with a tag hanging out, as well as two cups and a plate of pastries.

I wrapped the white terrycloth robe around me and joined him. "Just tea for now. Where did you get this?"

"Continental breakfast. Don't know if you'll have time to get anything else. They stop serving at ten."

"Ten? What time is it?"

He checked his watch. "Five after."

"Why did you let me sleep so late?"

"I figured you were tired."

"Whose fault is that?" I kissed him, and he grinned. "Still, if we're going to try to get to Vegas today, we'd better get on the road. Let me grab a shower first." I reached past him for the teapot and poured a cup. "You want some more?"

"I had coffee already. I'm good."

Something in his voice sounded . . . different. "You okay?"

"Oh, sure."

My heart started to pound. "Have you changed your mind about eloping?"

"No, not that."

"Then what?"

"I hate leaving here with things the way they are between you and your mom."

"You're sweet, but don't worry. Things between us have never been terrific. This is just one more chapter in a long, long story. You heard her. She's not willing to fly anywhere. Her knee is fine for running around a tennis court, but God forbid she should bear the inconvenience of first-class." I squeezed his hand. "I told you before—my family isn't like yours. I've made my peace with that. I have my own family now, remember? Holly, and Michael and Ruby, and my other friends. And now you and your family. Family by choice, not family by chance. That's how it is for some of us."

He shook his head. "I'm having a hard time believing you're okay leaving things like this."

"Believe it. It's not the first time. She pitched a major fit when I told her I wanted to go to law school. She went on and on about how we couldn't afford it, how it was a waste of money since I was going to get married and stop working—all sorts of crap like that. I told them I'd get financial aid and work part-time and pay for everything myself. And that was what I did. It helped that I went to UConn, so I got in-state tuition." For a moment, I was lost in the memories. "When I graduated, my mother bragged like she'd actually had anything to do with it. Fact is, I spent three years in law school, and she never once asked about my classes. I wish my father had lived to see me graduate. He'd have been so proud." Tears prickled, and I sniffed them back. Then, I straightened. "So, don't worry about my mother. She'll figure out a way to spin us not getting married here. She'll probably say we had a destination wedding somewhere."

"We are, kind of. It's just that the destination is a Vegas wedding chapel. Unless you'd rather go somewhere nicer. Maybe Tahoe. We could still elope, but it would be a lot more picturesque." He pulled out his phone and tapped. "Here," he said, passing it to me.

"Lake Tahoe Elopement Packages," I read. "Guess we're not the only ones to have had this idea." I scrolled down. "Hair and makeup? Videographer? Flowers? How are these elopements different from regular weddings?"

"I don't know," Ralph said. "Maybe that we can do them quicker."

"These aren't cheap," I said, still reading. "This one costs almost five grand. Pretty steep for something that's not a real wedding." I scrolled down. "They offer relationship counseling if we need it. These must be some fancy-ass elopements."

"It would be nice to make it special," said Ralph. "I'm not saying we need some stranger to counsel us, but I don't even have anything fancier than this." He gestured at his polo shirt and khaki shorts.

"Neither do I," I said. "I brought a dress in case we ended up going out to dinner with Mom and Phil, but it's definitely not fancy."

"Do you want to shop before we drive up to Tahoe?"

"Did we decide on Tahoe?"

"Would you rather go to Vegas?"

I poured the last of the tea into my cup. "I don't know. This feels like it's getting kind of complicated." I flipped through the elopement website to the photo gallery. "Some of these people bring a lot of friends to an elopement. Isn't it supposed to be just us and whoever's marrying us?"

"I think there has to be a witness," said Ralph. "But they probably have people who do that."

I handed him back his phone. "I don't know," I said again. "If we're going to go to the trouble of planning everything, maybe we want to have a regular wedding instead of eloping. What do you think?"

"I think that whatever you want is fine with me," he said.

"No. No, no, no. We're not doing that."

"Doing what?" His brow furrowed.

"I want this to be *our* wedding. The one we decide on together. I don't want to pick something and have you go along. I want to know that whatever we do is what you and I chose because it's what both of us want."

"But I already told you—I want to be married to you. The details don't matter."

"Our wedding isn't a detail. It's how we're starting our life together. It's important that we decide together." Ralph stood up and went back into the room. "What? What's the matter now?" I followed him inside.

"I don't want to screw this up for you." He started rifling through his bag.

"What are you talking about?" I took his arm. "Ralph. Look at me." Unwillingly, he did so. "Tell me honestly. If we could get married literally anywhere, any way in the world, what would you want?"

He bit his bottom lip. He met my eyes, and I knew. "Tell me your number one choice," he said, stalling.

I shook my head. "My number one choice is impossible."

"Anything's possible."

I shook my head. "My dream was to get married in the church we went to when I was a kid, in Connecticut, with my father walking me down the aisle. But my father's gone, and we can't get married in Connecticut because you'll end up back in prison before we finish our vows. So: impossible." His eyes looked so sad for me. "What's your number one?"

"I want us to get married at the Pole," he admitted. "I want my father to perform the ceremony. He can, you know. I want Holly to be your matron of honor. I want Michael to give you away. I want him and Ruby to sit with my family. I want your brother and his family to be there if you want them. I know your mother won't come, but I want to invite her anyway. I want anybody else you want to be there. I want Annaliese and her team to make the best wedding feast anybody's ever seen. I want everything to be exactly the way you want it, as much as it can be, because I don't want you ever to regret doing it there." His eyes glistened. I threw my arms around his neck, and he wrapped his arms around my waist.

"Then we'll get married at the Pole." We kissed to seal the deal. "Your father can perform weddings? The real deal? Legally binding and everything?"

"Of course," said Ralph. "For that matter, so can I. It goes with being Santa."

"I don't remember anything about that in the poem."

"I hate to break it to you, but Clement Moore made all that stuff up."

"Now you sound like Mitch." I kissed him again. "Is he going to be your best man?"

"Maybe. Let me think. I was Phil's, and Ted and Fred were each other's, so—yeah. It's Mitch's turn. Besides, I think he's got a soft spot for you."

"Just as long as he knows which brother I'm marrying."

Ralph laughed. "I'll make good and sure of it." His eyes glowed with such love that I could feel tears starting. He wrapped his long arms around me and whispered, "Do we have time for one thing?"

"Sorry, pal. Checkout is at eleven." It was ten of.

"Not that." He went back to his bag and pulled something out. Then, he got down on one knee. "I never formally proposed to you." He took my hand. "Megan Elizabeth Riley, love of my life, will you do me the honor of becoming my wife?"

My hand flew to my mouth as he opened the box in his hand. An oval diamond solitaire flashed fire against the black velvet. I nodded, my throat closing up. "Yes," I managed at last. He slid the ring on my finger, and all thoughts of checkout times vanished as we celebrated our engagement.

Book Two

New Life

Twenty-Seven

The morning after I officially moved to the Pole, I awoke with the oddest feeling. It was so unfamiliar that at first, I didn't recognize it. Then, I understood: I felt completely, stupidly happy. At long last, I was with my beloved. Instead of FaceTime and texts, we could talk face to face. I no longer had to fantasize about his touch, because he was right here. We could even have stupid fights, the kind we'd maneuvered around because we didn't want to waste what precious time we had arguing, and afterward we could have crazy-good makeup sex. At last, we could be like everybody else.

And yet, just as I recognized that feeling, it shifted into something else—almost like a sense of loss, but not exactly. I cast about for a name, a label. The closest I could come was recalling the days after my father's funeral, when the event was done but the reality of a changed life stretched before me like an endless highway. Kindly friends and coworkers and professors stood aside, allowing me to get through the days between his death and the service, but once the urn was in the ground, the break was over. The experience of getting used to my new world had to be done on my own time, in the evenings and weekends and middles of the night when sleep eluded me.

Ralph was usually an early riser, but this morning he slept on as I got out of bed to put the brand-new tea kettle on to boil, set up the coffee maker for him, and feed the cats. At the edge of my vision, light bounced off my engagement ring. Joy rushed in as I filled the cat dishes and set them down for my furry trio, all of whom were taking turns circling around my legs. I petted each one as I put down their dishes, and they tucked into their meals, oblivious to my moods. Because in the next instant, I felt lost again. For the rest of our lives, this was where we would go through our familiar ritual, here in this tiny kitchenette. Never again would they galumph down the stairs ahead of me in the morning. Never again would they pace and meow around the kitchen that had seemed merely adequate before, but now felt vast.

Stop it, I told myself. I'd made a choice. This was the price of being with the man I loved. If it wasn't my ideal home, I couldn't deny that living here with him beat all hell out of living there without him. I tried to recapture the goofy, happy feeling I'd had moments before, but it had slipped away, just out of reach.

I poured boiling water through the filter into my mug. As Ralph's coffee dripped and my tea steeped, I found myself thinking about the virgin couples of yore for whom the wedding night was the First Time. I didn't envy them, not at all. My first time had been with Tom Motten when I was sixteen. I hadn't had a clue what I was doing, but even though Tom was my first, I wasn't his, so at least we weren't both fumbling. Never underestimate a guy who knows how to put on a condom without making a big deal of it.

The best I could say about my relationship with Tom was that it was educational. In movies, the couple usually had missionary-style intercourse, with both of them climaxing about fifteen seconds later. I figured out pretty quickly how unrealistic this was. Luckily, Tom was game for practically anything. Armed with our research materials—a ragged copy of the *Kama Sutra* we'd found in a used bookstore and several issues of *Cosmopolitan*—we experimented and explored well into our senior year, when we reluctantly came to the realization that our only shared interest was sex. With our clothes on, neither of us found the other particularly interesting.

Ralph's first-time story was much more romantic than mine. He was eighteen and learning the world's geography by traveling on his own. In a smallish town near Tuscany, he met a young woman with long dark hair and big brown eyes—a classic Italian beauty, he said. Her name was Francesca, and she worked in her parents' restaurant. The first night he went there, they made heavy eye contact; the second, they talked; the third, he met her when she got off work, and they went for a walk in the Tuscan moonlight until they found a secluded spot on a hillside outside town. It sounded so ideal that I wondered if he was making it all up until he added, "It probably would have been perfect if it hadn't been for the stinging nettles." I cringed reflexively, and he laughed. "Guess we should have taken a blanket."

"At least you have Santa magic," I pointed out. "You could cure yours with a wave of your hand. That poor girl had to tolerate her stings."

"Sadly, Santa magic doesn't include healing powers," he said. "Luckily, there was a *farmacia* in the village. The *farmacista* had a cream that worked wonders. Apparently, we weren't the first couple to encounter the stinging nettles at an inopportune moment." He shook his head, laughing at the memory.

One of my favorite things about Ralph was how easily he laughed at himself. So many men I knew would have left the nettles out of the story for fear it might detract from their machismo, but not Ralph. He loved to tell comical stories, especially when he was the one to whom the funny thing happened or whose screw-up caused the hilarious result. It was a level of self-confidence I'd never known in anyone else, this willingness to show himself being silly or inept. I'd thought it might be a family trait, but it turned out that while the brothers were happy to poke fun at each other, only Ralph was likely to tell on himself. My beloved had no reason to build himself up or tear anyone else down; he was completely comfortable in his own skin.

"Hey, Mrs. Claus, you around?" came a drowsy voice from the bedroom.

"Out here, Mr. Riley," I called back instead of pointing out that I wasn't yet Mrs. Claus. At most, I was Mrs. Claus-elect.

As we'd driven from our Phoenix hotel to where Ralph would meet the sleigh, the question arose whether I would take Ralph's name when we got married. My knee-jerk reaction was *no way!* I was who I was, Megan Elizabeth Riley. Attorney Riley. Matthew Riley's daughter.

"We could do what one of my law school classmates did," I suggested. Both she and her husband took the hyphenated versions of their names, so that they were Jillian and Adam Hayes-Eisenberg.

"So I'd be Santa Claus-Riley?" Ralph raised an eyebrow.

"Okay, good point," I laughed, and we let the subject drop.

I knew Ralph would accept it if I chose to remain Riley, but I also knew that he really, really wanted me to be Mrs. Claus. For him, it was part of the tradition of who Santa's wife was. Granted, his mother had never been the storybook Mrs. Claus, but she was Santa's helpmate in accomplishing the central task of making and

delivering toys. Being Mrs. Claus wasn't so much a name as an identity. As far as I knew, Claire and Anya had accepted this identity
without hesitation. On the other hand, so had Isabella, for all that
was proving to be worth.

Even now that we were engaged and I officially lived at the Pole,
we hadn't settled the name issue. Our current plan was that after
our marriage, I would go by Claus when I was up here and Riley
when dealing with non-Pole folks. It seemed safer, since going back
to Connecticut as Meg Claus would obviously raise questions about
the whereabouts of my fugitive husband.

"You could take my name and leave it at that," I said now, climbing
back into bed with my fiancé. "No hyphenating. Just Riley. Ralph
Riley. A nice, average guy who isn't wanted for breaking out of prison."

"You don't think 'Ralph' might trigger somebody's memory?"

"Then go by your middle name. R. Henry Riley. R. Henry." The
more I said it, the more I liked it.

"Sounds like a writer," he mused.

"Or a lawyer," I said.

"You be the lawyer," said R. Henry. "I'll be the storyteller. I could
be R. H. Riley." He leaned back against the headboard, tasting the
name. "R. H. Riley. I like it. 'Pleased to meet you, old chap—I'm R. H.'
Sounds like I should have a handlebar mustache and a silver-topped
walking stick. And a—what do they call those eyeglasses that perch on
your nose? The ones rich guys used to wear back in the early 1900s?"

"Pince-nez," I said. "I can't believe I remembered that."

"You're amazing." He leaned over and kissed me.

"Do you need one of those bicycles with the huge front tire, too?" I
reached for my phone and tapped to find the term. "A penny-farthing.
Think R. H. would ride one of those?"

"Not very practical. I don't think the ceilings at the Pole are high
enough for me to sit on that, especially if I'm wearing a top hat." We
both laughed at the image of lanky Ralph on his penny-farthing, riding
through the halls of the Pole and holding onto the brim of his top hat
as he hunched over to avoid knocking it against the ceiling.

"But would we call you R. H.? Or R. Henry? Or plain Henry?"

"I could be Hank. Hank Riley. Nobody'd ever have a clue who I
was. Hank Riley sounds like a farmer. Farmer Riley, with his herd of
Holsteins."

"Or maybe Hank is the mechanic at the garage," I suggested. "You could fix everybody's cars with your magic, and nobody would ever know how you did it. You could be famous."

"Honey, I'm already famous," he reminded me. "I'm Santa Claus. If you were Mrs. Claus, you'd be famous, too."

"Except I'd be famous as somebody else," I pointed out. "They wouldn't know me as me. They'd only know the storybook version of me, with the red cheeks and my hair all white and in a bun." My voice faded as I contemplated the role of the fictional Mrs. Claus, wearing an apron and wire-rimmed glasses as she took a pan of cookies out of the oven. It was so completely not me. On the other hand, it wasn't any of the Claus women, and most especially not Meredith Claus.

He fingered my curls. "I think you'd look cute with a bun. Even if your hair isn't completely white."

"'Completely'? Would this be the pot calling the kettle gray?" My hair had been gradually silvering for the past few years, but it was still predominantly dark. Ralph's whiskers were already more gray than dark, but the hair on top of his head was still nearly all dark.

He ran his hand over his chin. "I think I need to shave." He kissed me; his whiskers were at the prickly stage. "You want to put the coffee on?"

"Already done." It really was a regular morning. I started to get off the bed.

"You're the best," he said, pulling me back and kissing me more deeply. By the time we got to the dining hall an hour later, Annaliese had long since stopped serving, and we had to make do with leftover muffins.

Twenty-Eight

Meredith was already in her office when I walked in the next morning. *Gee, what a surprise.* I could have arrived at five o'clock, and she'd still have gotten there first.

"Good morning, Meg," she said. I waited for something more, like *welcome to your new job,* but instead she said, "First thing each day is gift requests. Here, take a look." She beckoned for me to come around her desk to view her monitor. The email inbox showed seven hundred forty-six new messages. "You'll need to read each one and assign it to a category. That way, the workshop will know what's been requested and by whom."

She clicked on the top request. A child named Lee wanted a doll.

"That doesn't sound too hard," I said.

Meredith glanced at me. "Actually, these are the most difficult ones precisely because they're so vague. We need to figure out what kind of doll."

"How do we do that?"

"That's where Santa comes in. He has abilities we don't. He can determine the type of doll this little one wants, whether it's a baby doll, a fashion doll, or some other type."

"Not to mention whether this Lee is a boy or a girl," I commented.

"Gender isn't always determinative of the type of toy a child wants," she said. "We've had plenty of requests by boys for baby dolls or fashion dolls. Our policy is to give the child the toy they actually want, not what tradition says they should want."

"Or their parents?"

"Santa gives the gift the child wants. Now, with a request like this, since it's so imprecise, you file it under 'SC – doll'." She opened a spreadsheet and dragged the request to that heading. "He's a little bit behind, but I'm certain he'll catch up shortly." She didn't come right out and blame the lag on Ralph having taken time off to get engaged and arrange for my relocation, but I felt vaguely accused anyway.

The next request read simply, *Dear Santa, Please bring me a pony. Your friend, Amber.* "Does she mean a real one or a toy one?" I asked.

"If she's like most little girls, she wants a real pony." She highlighted the email address and clicked an icon in the tool bar. A window popped up displaying Amber's full name, address, and date of birth, as well as a photo and short bio. Amber was a six-year-old Black girl with jaunty braids and a captivating smile that was missing one front tooth. She lived with her grandmother and three-year-old brother in a high-rise condominium in Miami. Her mother was serving overseas in the Army, and her father had died of cancer two years earlier.

"What do we do? She doesn't have any place to keep a pony even if Grandma's on board with it."

"Live animal requests also go to Santa," said Meredith, moving the request to "SC – live animal." "He needs to find out whether the family joins in the request, or at least will permit it. If not, the child will get a toy of whatever the animal is with a note from Santa."

"What does the note say?"

"It contains the toy's name and other information, such as where it's from and how happy it is to be loved by such a wonderful child. Fred has a few elves who write superb notes to go with such toys. They have to be special, because if the child wants the real animal, they're going to be disappointed not to receive it, and we need to overcome that."

"Does it work?" If I'd asked for a pony and gotten a toy, I doubted a note would have helped.

"More often than you might think." Before I could ask anything else, such as where they got real animals, she clicked the next request, which was written in French. She clicked another icon on the tool bar, and the message was translated into English. "Jean-Paul wants a pink princess dress. At least that one's easy." She dragged it over to "Play clothes."

"How many requests do you get in a day?" The list was growing as we sat there.

"It depends on the time of year. In the early part of the year, we can have days with only a couple dozen requests. Now that we're into

October, we get several hundred or more per day. That's why it's so important to stay on top of the requests, even early in the year. We can't afford to get backed up, or we'll be inundated when the busy season hits." As she spoke, she continued to open requests and move them into various categories.

An exquisite emerald ring I hadn't noticed before graced her right hand, catching the light as she typed. "Your ring is beautiful," I said.

"Thank you. It's a Claus family heirloom." As was the tea set on the credenza, I recalled. I suspected that many of items that decorated her office were heirlooms, though she was so focused on her monitor that it was difficult to know whether she even noticed her surroundings.

"Are you ever completely caught up?" I asked when she said nothing more about the ring.

"Only on Christmas Eve, and that's only because we need to load the sleighs. We usually get a few last-minute requests, and we do our best to accommodate those, but it's a challenge."

"Have you ever not been able to fulfill a request simply because it's too late?"

"Once the sleighs are loaded, all requests are slated for the following Christmas. The children understand how Santa works, sometimes better than their parents. We once received an email on the twenty-sixth from an irate mother who claimed her daughter had sent a message months earlier, asking for a particular doll, and she hadn't bought the doll because she assumed Santa would take care of it. We combed through the computer looking for the request. Phil even went through the spam filter looking for it, and he turned up nothing. Finally, Mitch located it on a fake Santa site." I glanced at her, uncertain what she knew about Mitch's hacking skills, and she said with a small smile, "I don't ask."

"Did you tell the woman she screwed up?"

"We merely pointed out that she had sent her request to a bogus site and so we had not received it in time for Christmas. But since we didn't feel the child should suffer for her parent's error, we arranged to deliver the doll anyway."

"How did you do that?"

"We sent it to Kristofer to be forwarded. His mailing supplies look very official. It's clear the package is coming from Iceland rather than the Pole, but he includes a standard form letter stating that the reindeer are resting after their busy Christmas travels, and so the postal service has graciously agreed to assist. Something like that, anyway." She continued to sort requests as she talked.

Finally, she said, "Would you like to take over for a while?"

"Sure. What are the categories?"

"Click the blue icon on the upper right." I did, and a lengthy list appeared. The ones labeled "SC" were in red, and the others were in green. Meredith rose, and I sat down in her chair and began to open emails.

*****

By midmorning, I could barely keep my eyes open. Meredith looked every bit as fresh as when I'd walked in the door, but suddenly she said, "Let's take a walk."

I didn't know where she wanted to walk to, and I didn't care as long as it meant I could stand up. We took the elevator to the main level, where she strode through the halls at a brisk pace. I had to work to keep up.

"Where are we going?" I asked, more than slightly out of breath.

"Eventually, the kitchen to pick up a tea tray, but I like to take the long way around. It's too easy to stay cooped up all day. I like to take periodic breaks for exercise and fresh air." She turned and headed down a corridor I didn't recall although it was decorated with the same type of framed photographs that graced the main routes. Without pausing to allow me time to peruse these new photos, she continued, "Plus, you'll need to learn the entire facility, so we can explore some places you might not have seen before. Are you familiar with the gift warehouse?"

I couldn't remember if I'd ever seen it, but my response barely seemed to matter. She pressed a button, and a door slid open. As it slid closed behind us, another door opened, and a blast of freezing air greeted us even though we were still inside.

"Where are we?" The new hallway was frigid compared to the rest of the building.

"The passage to the warehouse." If Meredith was experiencing any discomfort from the dramatic change of temperature, she was keeping it to herself. We walked for a minute or so before she pressed a button to open an enormous door—the biggest I'd seen so far.

"This is the gift warehouse," she said unnecessarily.

The building was massive with seemingly countless subdivisions. On closer inspection, I saw that each subdivision bore the name of a country; within the country subdivisions were further dividers labeled with states, provinces, or other geographical identifiers. Shelves within the sections provided further breakdowns: New York City, Paris, London, and other major cities had their own shelves. The lower shelves were already packed with wrapped packages, while the empty upper ones bore witness to the myriad of gifts yet to be created.

A horn beeped behind us, echoing in the vast space. Meredith pulled me out of the aisle, and a forklift bearing a pallet of wrapped gifts rolled past. I watched, fascinated, as it came to a halt and two elves hopped off the back. One jumped up onto the shelf for Alberta, Canada, and the other handed up gifts to be stored there. In less time than I'd have imagined, they unloaded the pallet, hopped onto the back of the forklift, and waved as they sped away.

"Organization is key," Meredith said. "Sleigh assignments are based on region. If a gift is misfiled, someone will need to make a special trip, and that can be very challenging."

"Who manages the warehouse?" I asked.

"We do," she replied. "When we get back to the office, we'll have an updated manifest of what's here and where it's been filed."

"I thought Fred was in charge of the warehouse. Can we go somewhere warmer?" I'd forgotten how cold I was while watching the elves, but now, the chill was permeating my sweater.

"Fred is in charge of manufacturing. He's responsible from the time a request lands in his inbox until the gift is wrapped and on the forklift. At that point, he forwards the completed list to us. We'll match it against the manifest from the warehouse to ensure it comports with the original request and nothing's gotten lost or mislaid. Once the gift is filed in the warehouse, it's placed in suspended mode until it's delivered." She pressed the button to open the door to the airlock, which felt comparatively warm.

"How do you know if a gift has been delivered?"

She pressed the button on the door that allowed us entry back into the main building. The hallway now felt positively toasty. "The second on the sleigh has a scanner. Each time a gift is taken from the sleigh for delivery, it gets scanned, and the request is automatically updated as complete." She glanced at me as we walked. "You're aware of the seconds, correct?"

"Yes." Ralph had long ago told me how every sleigh carried a Claus and a second who was usually a young Claus or an elf. The night Ralph was arrested in West Hartford—it felt like eons ago—his second was an elf named Charles, who had traveled as Santa's second for decades. On that fateful night, it was Charles who got the sleigh out of sight and secured it until another Claus could be dispatched to finish the deliveries. Charles was also the one who had returned for Ralph eight months later when he escaped from prison after his conviction. It was no exaggeration to say that I owed Charles everything.

An idea occurred to me. "Am I supposed to be a second?" Not that I wanted to since it would obviously involve a lot of night-flying, but I wouldn't have anyone saying I didn't do my job properly.

"You won't be available," Meredith said to my relief. "You'll be with Phil in the Control Center. If anything goes wrong and requires attention, you'll be responsible to fix it."

"How will I do that?" Visions of missing gifts, malfunctioning scanners, and countless other glitches raced through my already-nervous brain.

"Don't worry. I'll be with you." She steered me toward the familiar corridor leading to the kitchen.

"What about Phil?"

"Phil will be handling everything else. Since all the other boys are out for delivery, he's responsible for implementing the flight plans Ted draws up. That can include watching for weather issues, dealing with breakdowns, software interfaces, and dozens of other issues." She held the door for me to enter the kitchen as she called out, "Good morning!"

"Good morning, ma'am," said Annaliese. Petite though she was, this gray-haired elf had an air of authority rivaling that of Mrs. Claus herself. She handed Meredith a tray bearing a thermal carafe and a plate of bite-sized pastries. "Oolong today."

"Lovely. Thank you so much, Annaliese." She turned to go.

"Thank you," I echoed as I trailed her out the door. Once we were safely out of earshot, I asked, "Does she do this every day?" It seemed like a lot of unnecessary work.

"Yes," Meredith said. "When I first took over the job, I wanted to get an electric kettle for the office. It would have been simpler and more efficient, but Julian explained that making up a tea tray for Mrs. Claus was a longstanding tradition, and the head chef—it wasn't yet Annaliese—would have been deeply hurt if I had discontinued it. The Pole is a curious place that way. Sometimes, a practice can be upgraded and everyone will cheer for the increased efficiency, while other times it's actually a tradition that can only be changed by the tiniest and most sensitive of baby steps. Our coming down here was a compromise, because it used to be that the kitchen staff would deliver the tray. I begged Julian to convince them I wanted to come down and get it myself. He had to cloak it in practical terms—I needed to check the warehouse or something—but the truth was that I simply didn't want to spend so much time alone in my office. I wanted to get out and move and see people. Yes, it takes longer for me to come down to the kitchen, but now it is an accepted practice. That's how things are done here. Tiny, sensitive baby steps." I wondered whether this was a reference to my attempt to alter the practice of transporting partial orders from the icebreaker to the Pole, but it seemed prudent to adhere more closely to the stated topic.

"What if you were busy and you wanted them to bring it up?" After sixteen years spent measuring my life in billable hours, I was uncomfortably aware of how long it had been since we'd left the office. By the time we got back, we'd have lost at least forty-five minutes of productive time—I had to restrain myself from thinking of it as billable time.

"If I asked, Annaliese would send someone up. But there's value in getting out of the office and being with everyone else."

"You could do that at meals," I pointed out, although she and Julian took most of their meals in their apartment with Tillie.

"It's not the same," said Meredith. "To be out among everyone working for a common goal—I find it energizing. Alone in my office, it's far too easy to lose sight of the overarching purpose for our being here, to get bogged down in numbers and contracts and details. I need to be reminded why we're doing what we're doing." She pressed the elevator button; I hadn't even realized we'd walked back that far.

"If that's your feeling, why don't you move your office down here so you're near everyone else?" I asked as we stepped into the elevator.

She smiled as one might at a foolish child. "When the boys were young, this office was my refuge. It was practically the only place where

I could get away and have the quiet I needed in order to concentrate. Remember, I was the eldest of eight children. Long before I met Julian, I knew the importance of carving out a private space. Also, this office has historically been the office of Mrs. Claus. I thought about moving it once the boys were older, but the truth is that I like it." We emerged from the elevator, and she opened the door. "It has a serenity that can be difficult to find elsewhere. Don't you agree?"

She was right. The plush beige carpet—much softer underfoot than the tight-looped red carpet in the main corridors downstairs—muffled our steps. The massive desk seemed to have been in place forever, its surface gleaming. I recalled my third-floor office at Lundstrom, how I reveled in the quietude as partners, staff, and clients bustled about on lower floors. True, Mrs. Claus's office was much smaller than my office at Lundstrom, and it lacked the windows that had allowed me to watch the seasons change and the sun setting, but it shared that sense of being set apart from the busyness of the outside world. In fact, Mrs. Claus's office felt almost cloistered, as though only a select few would be permitted to grace its doorway.

"Where does Owen sit?" I asked suddenly. There was nowhere in the office for Mrs. Claus's right-hand elf.

"Owen is downstairs with the administrative team. It's simpler for him to work with them and come to me as needed rather than the other way around."

"I don't remember an administrative team." I'd seen everything from workshops to warehouses, but if there was a typing pool somewhere, I'd missed it.

"Tillie runs that team. They're not a large group, but their functions are vital. They process orders, prepare payments for approval, and the like. Otherwise, you and I would be doing all that on top of everything else." Now it made sense: back when I was first representing Ralph, I periodically received emails from the Pole that were signed *Matilda J. Hansen*, also known as Julian's cousin, Tillie.

The Pole certainly seemed to run like a well-oiled machine. As far as I could tell, if something needed to be done, there was a Claus or an elf or a department to handle it. I began to relax. Maybe this job wouldn't be so hard after all.

Which went to show how little I knew.

Twenty-Nine

In musical theater, there's always a song early in the show known as the "I want" song. Its purpose is to define who the main character is and what they want. Sometimes both main characters sing "I want" songs, as in *My Fair Lady*: Eliza Doolittle wants a warm room with an enormous chair and lots of chocolates, while Henry Higgins wants English people to speak properly. Ralph's "I want" was easy: right from the start, he wanted me and he wanted to be Santa. Mine was more complicated: I wanted Ralph, and I wanted the rest of my life be as close as possible to what I'd left behind.

It didn't take a genius to figure out that only one of us was going to get our "I want."

Even factoring in Claus magic, the size of the sleigh limited what I'd been able to bring from home. The cats came, of course, traveling in special carriers that kept them warm; Ted assured me that these were the carriers they used whenever a child was receiving a live animal for Christmas. By the time we loaded the cats and their supplies, there wasn't much room left for my belongings. In the end, I packed as if Ralph and I were returning to our Vermont Airbnb, with warm casual clothes and necessary toiletries and not much else.

After I'd been here for a week, Ralph dispatched a second sleigh to bring my most cherished possessions. Most of my furniture and housewares were staying in Connecticut while Isabella lived at my condo, but my artwork and numerous boxes of books, DVDs, and CDs made the trip north. Where these items would reside was one of the many, many things that remained to be seen. "For now, we can store them in the library," Ralph suggested. I'd seen the closet-sized room he charitably referred to as a library; it was barely big enough to hold all my unopened boxes.

The second sleigh also contained files and materials from my office, including my laptop, my good desktop computer, and an external hard drive. The old computer I'd used at my former rented office would suffice in the basement office in case I needed it when I went back to Connecticut. Ralph had suggested that I could use Meredith's computer when I was at the Pole, but I was adamant that I required a separate one for purposes of client confidentiality. The idea of using her computer for my legal work felt like an invasion of both our privacy. So Ralph procured a small table and desk chair to tuck into a corner of our living room, and I stacked the boxes of files next to it.

Now, I crammed my underwear drawer shut. Ralph said we could use other parts of the facility for storage. My out-of-season clothes could be stored in a cedar-lined room where the other Clauses stored whatever clothing they couldn't fit in their apartments. In essence, the entire Pole was my house.

Of course, the cats lived in our apartment. One night at dinner, Ted had suggested that they could hang out in the stable with the other animals, but I said, "Absolutely not," in a voice that made it clear the subject was closed. The others glanced at each other, but I made no effort to apologize for my tone. I might be living in a commune, but some parts of my life were still mine.

Anya knocked on the apartment door. "How's the unpacking going?"

She bore a tray with a teapot, cups, and cookies. I'd never seen so many tea trays in my life as I had at the Pole. "Come on in," I said, moving discarded bubble wrap off the loveseat so she could sit down. Fortunately, Ralph had found a spare coffee table in a storage area; otherwise, I'd be balancing the tray on my lap. "Where's—the little one?" I'd never been good at remembering names. Now, learning the name and role of every occupant of the Pole was part of my job description.

"In the nursery." The Pole had a daycare so Claus and elf parents could work or otherwise get a break from their little ones. "How're you doing?"

"I'm figuring everything out." I tried to sound upbeat, but even I could hear the notes of fatigue and stress in my voice.

She poured golden tea into the cups and handed me one as if I were her guest instead of the other way around. "It's hard. I came from my

parents' house, and there were seven of us, but compared to all this—"
she waved her hand "—it was positively intimate."

I reached forward and took a cookie. "I had my entire home to
myself, at least until Isabella came along. All these people—it's—well,
it's fine, but it's different." I tried to sound convincing.

"Fine," she echoed with a knowing smile. "You'll get used to it.
You'll find your private places. Like here, with Ralph."

"Ralph thrives on being around people. Put him in the middle of a
crowd, and he's in heaven." I'd never articulated this to myself or anyone else,
but as I said it, I knew it was true. Everything in my solitary gut clenched.

"It's not easy to be with somebody like Ralph." Clearly, Anya understood. "Don't get me wrong—he's one of the best people I know.
Everybody loves him. But—"

"Everybody loves him, everybody wants him—where do I fit in?
When everybody's pulling at his sleeve—and he's perfectly happy to go
wherever they want—how do I get his attention?" I hated how whiny
I suddenly sounded. "I'm not complaining," I added even though I
obviously was. "We're just different that way."

"I wouldn't worry," Anya reassured me. "He loves you. No question
about it. Do you have any idea how much we've had to listen to him
singing your praises? Meg this, Meg that, Meg something else—we
all thought you walked on water."

"And now you've figured out how wrong he was." I tried to sound
as if I was joking.

"Don't be silly. All I mean is, don't ever doubt that he loves you.
Remember, he was willing to go back to prison to protect you. He was
even willing to give up being Santa."

"In theory. When the moment came, though. . . ." The note of
bitterness in my voice surprised me.

"He had a responsibility," Anya said gently. "Still, it was the first
time since I've known him that the question even came up. That says
a lot." She looked around at the boxes and the bubble wrap. "You know,
if you don't need all this stuff, the packing department would love to
take it off your hands. It'd make some more space in here."

"We could use more space." The facility might be huge, but the
living quarters were compact.

"Like I said, it takes getting used to. On the other hand, it's not
every place that comes with meals and housekeeping if you want them."

"What if I want to cook? I mean, really cook, not—" I gestured toward the kitchenette with its two burners and a microwave.

Anya looked thoughtful. "I probably shouldn't mention this, but before you guys got engaged, Meredith was talking about gutting this and enlarging it to make a real kitchen, and Ralph said not to bother."

"Without asking me?"

"To be honest, I didn't know you were a cook, or I'd have said something."

It wasn't that I was a cook; I just wanted choices. But I couldn't think how to say this without sounding like an idiot. "Is there anything else I should know?"

"Well—Ralph had that done for you." She gestured toward the alcove. I knew it had been added at some point after the first time I stayed here, but in all the busyness, I'd never asked why. Now, Anya answered my unspoken question: "So your cats would have a place of their own for their litter boxes and dishes. That's why there's a separate sink and cabinets in there—so you can wash their dishes and store their food and litter. He figured you'd want their beds in your room, so he said they didn't need to worry about making room for them in there." Her eyes grew soft. "He loves you, Meg. And he knows this is going to be an adjustment for both of you, but especially for you. He wants you to be happy here." She drained her cup and rose. "When you need to vent about the whole thing—moving here, settling in, and all the rest—remember that Claire and I did it, too. You can talk to us."

"Isabella did it, too," I pointed out. "And now look."

"Don't jump to conclusions." Anya set my cup back on her tray. "I know things are rocky right now, but she'll be back."

A memory of Tristan flashed through my mind. As I bade farewell to Anya, I couldn't help wondering if Isabella would ever come back. Maybe some people weren't cut out for this kind of life.

I could only hope I was.

Thirty

In those first weeks, I began to understand aspects of Pole life that I hadn't appreciated as a visitor. For example, as Anya had said, tasks like laundry and cooking were no longer my responsibility. The housekeeping team saw to the laundry, and Annaliese and her crew handled the meals.

"Sounds like heaven," Holly said when I described it to her. "Do the laundry people fold everything and put it away for you?"

"Putting it away is still our job," I said. "We leave whatever needs to be laundered in a basket outside our door, and the next day there it is, all clean and folded."

"And you don't have to cook, or go food shopping, or do dishes, or anything?"

"None of it. It's like dorm life. You show up at the dining hall, and there's whatever the food elves have prepared, as well as staples like bread and peanut butter."

"What if you want to make something different?"

"You mean, in our kitchenette? Assuming it's something I can microwave or fix on two burners, I can do it. Of course, that presupposes that I thought ahead enough to bring up whatever I want to make."

"Can't you get stuff out of the kitchen?"

"Not unless I want to get my hand chopped off with a butcher knife. Annaliese keeps a very tight rein on that kitchen."

"But you're practically married to Santa. Doesn't that mean that everything there belongs to you?"

"It's not about who owns it. There are some pretty deeply ingrained practices here, and one of them is that everybody kowtows to Annaliese. Even Ralph's mother doesn't cross her."

"Wow." Holly remembered meeting Meredith Claus when we traveled to the Pole together right after I met Ralph. It felt like eons ago. "Is she, like, the head elf or something?"

"No, but she's the head of food, and everybody here likes to eat."

"Where do you even get food?"

"A lot of it is brought in. There's an area we didn't see when we were here that's like an indoor farm, with a few chickens and a couple cows so we can have milk and eggs."

"They have grass?"

"The cows eat a special feed Ted gets someplace in South America. It's supposed to make up for not having grass. Plus, there's a team of elves who go out periodically to hunt and fish."

"What's up there that you can hunt?"

"Tons of stuff. Bear, walrus, seal, caribou. All sorts of seafood—"

"Wait—did you say walrus?" I could almost hear her cringing.

"Yep. Not my favorite by a long shot, but some people really like it. The ones who've grown up with it, mainly."

"What does it taste like?"

"It's weird. It looks like meat, but it tastes fishy. Some people think it's similar to horse meat, but I've never had horse, so I don't know."

"Don't the French eat horses?"

"I think they used to. I think the Italians were big on horse meat, too. But like anywhere else, you eat what's around you. Here, it's walrus. There's all sorts of stuff the indigenous people do with it, like fermenting the flippers or freezing rotten walrus meat for future consumption."

"Freezing rotten wal—oh, no. Now you're just making stuff up," said my friend in her comfortable Connecticut home with her freezer full of Lean Cuisine.

"I wish. Turns out, fermented walrus is a delicacy." The first time I was presented with fermented walrus was on my second visit to the Pole after Ralph and I became an official couple. At dinner, Annaliese brought out a large platter; I could smell it from across the room. Everyone else looked excited, and I tried my best to be enthusiastic. *You eat sushi all the time,* I reminded myself as she proudly presented me with the first plateful. The pungent odor nearly made my eyes water, but I forced a smile.

"That's the meat, and that's the blubber," said Ralph, pointing to the darker and lighter chunks on my plate.

"Blubber?" My stomach turned. I routinely trimmed even the tiniest morsel of fat from any meat. "So—kind of like the fat on bacon?" I asked in a desperate attempt to find familiarity.

"Except it's raw," said Mitch with a mischievous glint in his eyes.

"It's fermented," Claire corrected him.

"But it's not cooked," Fred pointed out.

"You're all eating some, too, right?" I looked from one empty plate to another.

"I can't," said Claire. "The baby." Never before had I wished I were pregnant.

"Go ahead, honey," Ralph urged me.

With everyone watching, I took up my knife and fork to cut one of the darker pieces into smaller bits. I took a morsel into my mouth, hoping to swallow without chewing, but it was too big. My molars closed on the soft, spongy meat. The sharp odor nearly overpowered me as I chewed. The flavor was gamey and tangy, nearly acidic. I forced myself to swallow, tensing my stomach muscles to keep from spewing it back onto the plate.

"How is it?" asked Annaliese as if I'd know good walrus from bad.

"It's—unbelievable. Like nothing I've ever had." I tried to make this sound like a good thing. "How do you flavor it?"

"There's no need to flavor it," said Annaliese. "Everything you taste is pure walrus."

"Really? You don't have to do anything else to it?" I could feel my stomach rebelling against the piece I'd swallowed.

"Nothing at all. The people we get it from are down in Nunavut. They dig a hole in the ground and bury the walrus. Fermenting develops the flavor. Try some blubber. The flavor is a bit lighter." When I took up my knife, she said, "Don't try to cut it. Eat it whole."

I glanced at Ralph, hoping he'd rescue me, but he didn't seem to think anything unusual was happening. I took a deep breath and popped a chunk of fermented blubber into my mouth. I began to chew. *Don't think, don't think.* It was at once squishy and tough. I tried to manufacture a smile, but my breathing was becoming rough. I nodded vigorously and gave Annaliese a thumbs-up, and she beamed with pride. She set the platter on the table before us and bustled away. Tears sprang to my eyes as I tried to manage the sodden mess sliding around in my mouth.

"Is something wrong?" Ralph sounded genuinely surprised.

I started to shake my head, but my stomach reached the end of its tolerance. I bolted from the table and out into the hall where the door barely closed before everything I'd tried to eat splashed onto the carpet. Before I caught my breath, Claire and Anya emerged to shepherd me back to the apartment.

"They forget we didn't grow up with this," Claire said as she made tea and I curled up on the loveseat.

"You did really well," Anya said. "The first time I tried it, I almost passed out."

"It's definitely an acquired taste," Claire said.

"I have no intention of ever acquiring that taste," I said firmly. With a blanket wrapped around my shoulders, I reached out for the mug Claire offered. "I mean, sushi is one thing, but that. . . ." I shuddered as I tried to cleanse my nasal passages by inhaling the infinitely preferable aroma of the tea.

"It's a delicacy," said Anya. "Annaliese loves to serve it for special occasions, like Christmas week."

"There's no occasion special enough for that—that—" The tea was still too hot to drink, but I tried the barest sip to banish the gamey taste lingering in my mouth.

"If you play your cards right, she might serve it when you get married," Clare offered with a twinkle in her eye.

The door opened. "Hey, babe, everything okay?" asked Ralph. He stroked my hair and kissed the top of my head.

"For the record: we will not have fermented walrus at our wedding." I blew on my tea. "The only fermented thing we will have is the juice of grapes. In other words, wine."

"Didn't you like the walrus?" He actually seemed to be serious.

Claire and Anya burst out laughing. "Didn't you see it on the carpet?" Claire managed.

"Is that what that was?" Incredibly, the man was surprised.

"I'll get somebody to clean that up. Feel better, Meg." Claire headed for the door, still laughing.

"Thanks," I called after her.

"You okay?" asked Anya, poised for departure. At my reassurance, she left.

"I'm sorry," said Ralph. "Annaliese wanted to do something special for you as kind of a welcome. I figured since you love sushi, you'd like walrus."

"Fermented walrus is nothing like sushi," I declared, sipping my tea.

"They're not that different. I mean, they're both raw."

"Don't remind me." He still looked perplexed, and I sighed. We'd led such very different lives. How could we ever hope to weave them together?

Thirty-One

The barn contained a number of large pens, each containing three or four reindeer. A card on each pen identified the name, age, and gender of each occupant. I paused before one pen. The card identified the occupants as Lucky (f), 16; Tawny (f), 17; and Polly (f), 15.

"Polly," I said, reaching my hand out to see if she'd come. When I spoke her name, she lifted her head and ambled to the rail. Her dark eyes glinted in the low light.

"Give her this." I turned to see Tillie holding out a carrot. "Put it on your flat palm so she doesn't accidentally get your fingers." I obeyed, and Polly took the treat with regal deftness. The other two reindeer promptly joined her at the rail, grunting for treats, and Tillie produced more carrots.

"All right, ladies, that's enough," Tillie said when they'd eaten everything. She held up her hands, fingers splayed wide, to let them know the food was gone. Lucky lifted her nose as if in disdain, promptly heading back to the far corner, but Tawny and Polly remained at the rail as we rubbed their noses and told them what good girls they were.

After a bit, Tillie said, "Feel like joining me for a hot chocolate?"

"Sure." We gave the reindeer a final pet and headed back into the relative warmth of the building. Once the door was closed, we traded our boots for slippers and hung up our outdoor gear. Then, we headed to the kitchen.

One of the things I liked best about Tillie was that, like me, she was an outsider. Granted, she was Julian's cousin and therefore a Claus, but her parents had moved away when she was a child. She and her husband, a Parisian schoolteacher, had lived for nearly thirty years in a small apartment on the Left Bank. When he died in a car accident, Julian brought Tillie to the Pole for a respite, and she never left. Instead, she provided the Claus boys with the kind of maternal warmth that seemed to be outside Meredith's purview.

We settled in with our cocoa. "I should probably have tea," I commented. My jeans were already snug.

"You look beautiful just as you are," Tillie reassured me.

We drank in companionable silence. Relaxing, I asked, "Where did you grow up?"

"In the States. Virginia. My mother hated the cold."

"But Virginia gets snow sometimes, don't they?"

"Not often enough. Dad loved snow. He'd have been happy to live up here."

"Is that how you and Julian are related? Through your dad?"

Tillie shook her head. "My mom was Julian's mother's sister. She grew up here, but she couldn't wait to get away."

"Why?"

"Some people just aren't cut out for this kind of life." She spoke casually, as if she had no idea her words might have deeper meaning.

"Because she didn't like snow?"

"Not just that. Mom wasn't a people person, not the way you kind of have to be at the Pole. She was always happiest going out by herself to explore a new neighborhood, a new city, whatever. When she was growing up, the closest she came to that was being a second on her father's sleigh, but for her, even that wasn't enough. She got to see all these amazing places, but only from the sleigh. When she was fourteen, she was the second on Grandpa Kurt's sleigh, and she followed him when he got out at a little house on the outskirts of Chiang Mai—that's in Thailand," she added. "Mom loved to tell that story, how the house was so tiny and everybody slept on mats in one room. One of the kids woke up and saw her, and he started to wake up his sister. Mom shushed him, but it was too late—Grandpa Kurt turned around and saw her. She said an instant later, they were both back outside with the sleigh, and Grandpa Kurt was furious. She said she'd never seen him lose his temper before." Tillie sipped her cocoa, remembering. "It wasn't until years later that Mom figured out that why he was so mad. If they'd been caught, Grandpa Kurt could have arranged his own escape, but he couldn't have done anything for her. If the people had called the police, Mom could have ended up in a Thai prison. At the time, though, she thought Grandpa Kurt was being unfair, and she pouted the rest of the night."

"Hard to imagine someone pouting on Santa's sleigh," I mused.

"Delivering toys is joyful, but it's also incredibly serious business with a lot of risks—well, you know," she added, acknowledging how Ralph and I had met. Deftly, she redirected the conversation: "How's the settling in going?"

"It's going. Want more?" I rose to refill my mug.

"No, thank you." She favored me with a warm smile. I couldn't help smiling back, because finally I recognized it: she and Ralph had the same wonderful smile. "I probably shouldn't say this, but—I love all the boys, but Ralph has always been my favorite."

"Mine, too," I said.

Her smile widened. "I'll tell you a secret: we were starting to wonder whether he'd ever find someone to settle down with."

"Because he's nearly forty?"

"Frankly, yes. On the other hand, Julian was in his thirties when he met Meredith. He kept telling us all to relax. Of course, he also reminded us that not everyone who's held the job has been married."

"Really?" I hadn't realized that was an option.

"It hasn't happened often, but there have been two or three Santas through the generations who never married. One of them, Great Uncle Frederich—maybe he was great-great—anyway, he never married, but he had a companion."

"He was living with a woman outside of marriage?" Clearly, the Pole was a much more progressive place than I'd given it credit for being.

"Not a woman. Rupert. They met when Frederich was delivering gifts in Australia. Rupert was staying with his sister's family for the holidays, and he was looking for a midnight snack when he ran into Frederich. From what I heard, it was love at first sight."

"Nobody up here had a problem with a gay Santa?" Multiply that progressiveness by ten, especially considering how long ago this apparently was.

Tillie laughed. "Rupert made Frederich happy. That was all anyone cared about. Also, Rupert was an enormous help to Frederich. Rupert was the one who reviewed the requests and the lists to ensure everything was correct. Frederich always had great difficulty reading—now, he'd probably be diagnosed as dyslexic—so Rupert took over the organizational end of things."

"So I'm Ralph's Rupert?"

"Basically, yes. Up to then, Santa did the administrative tasks, assisted by a couple of elves. Rupert did a great deal to organize and streamline. This freed up Frederich to handle other matters. From what my grandmother said, they were a wonderful team."

"But who took over when Frederich retired?"

"His eldest nephew, Kurt. He was only seventeen when Frederich passed away, but he had Rupert to help him."

"And that was your Grandpa Kurt who got upset when your mother snuck into a house?"

"One and the same." She rested her hand on mine. "I know the family seems complicated, but don't worry. You'll sort it out." She patted my hand and rose. "I'm going to go and say goodnight to Julian and Meredith. Thank you for keeping an old lady company."

I stood up and hugged her. "Thank you for a lovely chat." Beaming, Tillie bustled out of the room. As I watched, I couldn't help thinking that someone like Tillie would have been a much better Mrs. Claus than Meredith.

Or me.

Thirty-Two

I sipped split-pea soup—sans ham, since we had no pigs—as I studied yet another spreadsheet. This time, it was the food budget, which included farms located in several different places. "This is where we get much of our food," Meredith said the first time she showed it to me. She pointed to each line, saying, "These folks grow our tomatoes, and this is where we get different types of beans, and this one"—she pointed to an Italian-sounding name—"provides us with olive oil. And here is where we get feed for the reindeer." She indicated a farm with a five-figure budgeted amount.

I stared at the number. "This is just for the reindeer?" I thought it was the budget to feed everyone at the Pole.

"Reindeer eat a lot. There's only so much they can forage up here, and importing greens is expensive. So we need to supplement their diet. Luckily, there's a farm in Finland that has developed a shelf-stable reindeer feed in pellet form. It's pricey, but it's worth the cost."

"How does it get here?"

"It gets transported to Iceland. We used to have it taken from there by cargo ship to Alert, but now we have the icebreaker."

"What's a lert?" At least I knew what an icebreaker was now. Maybe a lert was some other type of boat.

"It's down in Canada, not terribly far from here. There are other places farther north, but Alert is actually populated."

So it was a town, not a mode of transportation. But— "*Down* in Canada?" I'd never heard anyone use that phrase.

"From here, everywhere is south," she reminded me.

I could feel my cheeks reddening. "But why would you go to a place that's populated? Wouldn't you rather have a place with no people?"

I'd have expected they wouldn't want anyone to see Pole residents picking up supplies.

"We use Hans Island sometimes, but only if there are no alternatives."

"And that's—" An island, obviously.

"Right above Greenland. For a long time, Canada and Denmark were fighting over who owned it. I'm not certain whether they've ever resolved the issue, but they both used to send military there for training exercises. In any case, the advantage is that it's land and we can make easy transfers, but the disadvantage is that if anything happens, there's no one there to assist."

"What do you mean, if anything happens?"

"Anything. Weather, accident, injury, illness. It's quite a remote area. Not long after I came up here, one of our suppliers sailed into a polar low. They lost three men."

"What's a polar low?"

"A type of cyclone. Fortunately, they're generally over water, so they're not such an issue for us here. Still, they happen, and we need to be ready. Alert has military personnel."

"Does it have an airport? Can't we get things delivered by plane?" I remembered reading that it took a full week for the QE2 to cross the Atlantic, as compared to a few hours by air.

"Alert's airport is strictly for military aircraft. They've been known to allow charter aircraft, but that's rare. If our suppliers wanted to deliver by air, they'd have to fly into Nunavut."

"And that's—?"

Meredith cast me a look that said as clearly as words that this American was ridiculously ignorant about anything outside her own country. Sadly, it was true. When I was in grade school, Canada was nothing more than a strip at the top of the map of the United States. It took years before I understood how much more there was to that vast country than Toronto and Montreal—and how tiny the U.S. was by comparison.

"It's a fairly recent Canadian territory. It used to be part of the Northwest Territories." She glanced at me to see if I knew what the Northwest Territories were. I nodded as if I did. In fact, I knew practically nothing about them beyond their name and the fact that they were obviously in a northern part of Canada. "It has a growing tourist trade, which means it's more accessible than it used to be. Alert is in Nunavut although, as I said, civilians can't fly in and out there." I made a mental note to google some information about northern Canada. I'd thought knowing world geography was Ralph's job, but apparently, I needed to know more than how to get around the Pole complex.

*****

That night, I intended to hunker down in Meredith's office and search the internet for information about the Arctic. "I can tell you whatever you need to know," Ralph said as I headed for the door with my carafe of tea.

"What's a polar low?" I asked.

"A cyclone over water. Why are you doing this?"

"Because your mother thinks I'm ignorant, and she's right. There are enormous chunks of the world I know nothing about because they never bothered teaching us that stuff in school and it never occurred to me to care. Like, practically the only thing I know about Thailand is that *The King and I* is set there and what pad thai is. I need to do better."

"You don't need to know about Thailand," said Ralph. "I can take you some time if you like, but your ability to function here isn't going to depend on whether you know to say *'sawadee khrap'* or *'sawadee kha'.*"

"You see? I don't even know what you're talking about." I opened the door to leave.

"It's how men or women say hello in Thai—"

"You're missing the point. I need to know things. There's too much I don't know, and I hate that. I hate being the only person who doesn't know." At least when I was in practice, I knew as much as the next lawyer, and often more since I not only had the best paralegal in the world, but also Russ Carsten, a kick-ass investigator.

"Nobody knows everything," Ralph said. "I've been all over the world, and there's plenty I don't know."

"But you know more than I do."

"About some things. But you know more than I do about other things, like the law."

"Big deal that's going to make here," I muttered.

"It will if Phil and Isabella can't work things out and they end up getting divorced," Ralph said.

I closed the door, my internet education forgotten. "Are you spit-balling here, or is this a real possibility?"

"You'd know better than me. She's been down there for six months now, and I haven't heard anything about her wanting to come back."

"What does Phil say?"

He shrugged. "Phil plays his cards pretty close to his vest. I've asked him a couple times how everything's going, and he just says, 'It's going.'"

"Does he want her to come home?"

"I assume so. She's his wife. He loves her." His eyes searched my face. "Does she still love him?"

"I assume so," I parroted back. With any luck, Tristan was in the past, a one-time mistake. Not that I'd had much opportunity to ask about her plans to return. I'd only been back to Connecticut once since my move, and Isabella had been rehearsing for a concert, so she was frequently out. When she was at home, she practiced constantly.

Except now that I thought about it, she was out much more than I'd have expected based on the rehearsal schedule taped to the re-frigerator. Of course, it would have been silly to expect her to behave like a hermit. She was meeting other musicians, making new friends. Certainly there was nothing wrong with her having a social life.

Still, I found myself wondering if there was more going on than merely music talk. She was an attractive and talented young woman who had been barely more than a child when she married Phil and he whisked her away to this remote location. She'd never had the freedom of even one year of college. A sudden dread clutched at me as I real-ized how naïve I'd been. For all I knew, she was experimenting with drugs or going to wild parties—in addition to sleeping with strange men—while her husband waited patiently for her to get this whole music thing out of her system and come home.

"I shouldn't have left her alone."

I hadn't realized I said it aloud until I saw the startled expression on Ralph's face. "What is she doing?" he asked slowly.

"No idea. Behaving like a college student, probably." An image of Tristan in his towel flashed through my brain.

"But she's almost thirty. She's an adult. A married adult."

"And a clueless one. Haven't you ever heard of Rumspringa?" At his blank look, I explained, "It's when Amish teens go out into the world and experiment with non-Amish life. I had a case once where my client was a fifteen-year-old girl who got pregnant by a seventeen-year-old Amish boy who was doing his Rumspringa thing. They were obviously way too young to get married, but the boy's parents wanted her to have the baby and then let them take it back to the Amish community to be raised Amish."

"What was supposed to happen to the girl?"

"She wasn't invited. As I recall, his father's comment was something like, 'She's no better than she should be.' In other words, they figured that since she'd had sex outside of marriage, she was a slut who deserved whatever happened to her."

"Their son had sex outside of marriage, too," Ralph said, echoing the very argument I'd made to the boy's parents.

"Ah, but that was different, because he was a boy. Plus, he'd decided to go home to his community and get baptized, so that made everything he'd done okay. Of course, he didn't have this convenient revelation about going home until the girl told him she was pregnant."

"What ended up happening?"

"Her parents were great. She was able to talk to them about what she wanted to do and what her choices were. She was still in her first trimester, and she ended up terminating the pregnancy. That sent the boy's parents over the edge. They actually tried to sue her for murdering their grandchild. That was when she came to me."

"And you worked everything out." The pride in his voice warmed my heart.

"Are you kidding? I kicked their Amish asses. Connecticut's hard-line on a woman's right to make her own decisions about her body. Plus, she was only fifteen, and nobody in their right mind would force a high school sophomore to become a mother. Since the boy was only two years older than she was when they had sex, it wasn't statutory rape, so we didn't have that threat, but I let their lawyer figure that one out for himself." In a stroke of luck for the boy, their one sexual encounter had occurred two days before his eighteenth birthday. "We got the case knocked out on a pretrial motion, so at least the girl didn't have to take the stand and get grilled about her sexual history."

"And you think Isabella's doing her own Rumspringa?"

"I don't know. I hope not." If she was, it was anybody's guess what would happen. I could only imagine the fireworks if Isabella showed up pregnant with another man's child. Even the normally loving, accepting Clauses would have a hard time with that.

Thirty-Three

A day with Meredith was always long, and this one was no exception. I craved the privacy of my apartment, my fiancé, my cats. Maybe I'd talk Ralph into getting trays from the dining hall and eating in.

I opened the apartment door and stopped. When I left that morning, my beautiful painting—my Paris girl—had hung over the loveseat. Now, the wall was an uninterrupted expanse of beige.

"Ralph?"

The cats were asleep in their beds. I touched each gently, and they stirred. Good. They were fine. But where was Ralph? And where was my painting?

I texted him: *we've been burglarized.*

What???

My painting is gone!!!

No response for a minute. Then: *I moved it to the library.*

WTF????

I stormed through the labyrinth of hallways until I reached the minuscule room Ralph insisted on calling the library. Sure enough, there was my painting, propped against a pile of boxed books. I snatched it up and marched back to our apartment. "Son of a bitch," I muttered.

Eventually, the painting once again hung in its proper place, giving life and color to the bland room. Fuming, I set out for the other storage area where my as-yet-unpacked boxes resided. I pulled out my blue-striped fleece throw, the candlesticks I'd kept on the mantelpiece, the Mount Saint Helens cat figurine, the painting of the overall-clad woman playing the flute. I took all this and more back to Ralph's apartment—*our* apartment—and I placed my cherished possessions around until it looked less like a hotel room and more like a dwelling where people actually lived.

I was on the loveseat with my blue throw over me, rereading *Pride and Prejudice*, when Ralph opened the door. "Hi, honey," I said brightly. "Want some tea?" The teapot with the vivid red poppies had been a gift from a British client. It now sat on the coffee table next to a matching cup and saucer. The rest of the set adorned the bookcase two elves had helped me bring over from storage. I'd also retrieved some of my favorite books from the so-called library. "Welcome home," I murmured as I placed them on the shelves.

Ralph stood in the doorway, taking in the scene. I waited for him to comment, but he said nothing. He simply walked into the bedroom and closed the door. I listened for a reaction to the new throw pillows, the oval mirror on the wall, the dried flower arrangement I'd purchased last year at the town arts fair.

Silence.

The silence continued through the night and into the next day. I didn't know if he was talking to anybody else, but he never said a word to me. I was damned if I'd break first, so the next morning, I took my tea and Holly's watercolor of beach chairs—the one that used to hang in my office at Lundstrom—and headed up to Meredith's office.

She was already behind the desk when I arrived. "Would it be okay if I hung this here?" Asking seemed appropriate since it was her office. "My best friend, Holly—you remember her—she painted it. She said it was to remind me that there's more to life than work."

Meredith regarded the painting briefly. It wasn't at all clear that she agreed with Holly's sentiment, but she merely said, "It's very nice. Where do you want to hang it?"

"I thought over here." I gestured to the wall perpendicular to the desk. "That way we can see it when we're working."

"Fine." She buzzed Owen and asked him to send up someone to hang a painting. Within minutes, an elf appeared with hanging hardware, a hammer, and a small stepstool. A few taps, and Holly's beach scene hung at the North Pole. I wanted to take a photo to send to her, but I felt odd doing so with Meredith in the office. *Later*, I decided.

That evening, I returned to the apartment to find no sign of Ralph. The cats were meowing for their supper. It occurred to me that I hadn't heard from him all day, which was unusual. I fed the cats as I waited for his return. Finally, I texted him: *Are you going to supper?*

A few seconds later, he responded, *I already ate.*

Anger flared up. *How long are you going to sulk?*

I have things to do in the workshop.

Which workshop?

No response.

Which workshop? I repeated.

I'll be back later.

Unbelievable. *This is supposed to be my home. Am I not allowed to have personal items in my own home? Or is it just YOUR home and I'm only a guest?*

No answer.

Forget it. I'm going to supper. Maybe I'll be here when you decide to come home.

Completely freaking incredible.

*****

I was half-asleep when I heard him come in. By the light of the night light I'd plugged in, I watched him enter the bedroom. He startled, presumably at the light in the heretofore pitch-dark room. I heard him sigh. He went into the bathroom and closed the door. A few minutes later, he emerged and got into bed, not touching me.

"Are we going to talk about this?" I asked.

"I'm tired."

"Bullshit. You're avoiding talking. You're avoiding me."

He sat up. "What do you want me to say?"

I sat up, too. "I want to know why you're mad."

"I'm not mad," said the King of Passive Aggression.

"Then you're doing a damned good impression."

We sat in the dim glow of the night light. Finally, he said, "I don't want a night light. I like the dark."

"That's because you know where everything is, so you don't keep banging into every—"

"Fine! Keep the stupid light! Keep everything you're cramming in here!" He threw back the covers, grabbed his robe, and stormed out of the bedroom.

I grabbed my own robe and hastened to keep up. "Wait a—dammit!" Unlike the bedroom, there was no light in the living room, and once again I'd run squarely into the armchair. I flicked on the light, and the brightness nearly blinded me. "What are you so pissed about? Why can't I have a few things of my own here?"

"A *few* things?" Ralph waved his arm. "Look at this place!"

"I've seen it, and you know what? *Now* it looks like people actually live here instead of being The Land of the Bland."

"*I* liked it the way it was!" He was shouting now. I'd never heard Ralph shout. "It was peaceful. It was quiet, and calm, and peaceful! And after a day of being surrounded by noise and people and activity, it was a relief to come in here and have nothing but peace!"

"Well, I'm sorry I'm disturbing your peaceful peace. Maybe you'd rather I didn't live here. Maybe you'd rather I went back to Connecticut so you could have your frigging peace!"

He stopped then, his eyes round with horror. "No," he whispered. "I want you here."

But I wasn't ready to concede. "You want me. You don't want anything that comes with me."

"What about the cats?"

"That's not the same. You always knew we were a package deal. I'm talking about anything that makes this place look like I'm more than a weekend visitor." To my consternation, I could feel tears welling. "Are you trying to tell me I don't really belong here?" Here, in this place where I already felt like the proverbial fish out of water, where every day was an education in how I was a newcomer and I didn't know what I was doing, much less how "we" did things, and how I didn't dare change anything. . . . I turned away so he couldn't see the tears spilling down my cheeks.

I felt his hands on my shoulders. I tried to shrug them off, but he didn't let go. "I'm sorry," he said, nuzzling my hair. "I love you. You absolutely belong here." He turned me around and held me close. "I'm sorry. Maybe I overreacted a little."

I looked up at him. "A little?"

His smile was sheepish. "Maybe a little more than a little." He kissed my forehead and hugged me tighter, and I wrapped my arms around him.

"I'm sorry, too," I said. "I shouldn't have just brought all this stuff in without talking to you."

I felt his chest heave with a sigh. "Like you said, it *is* your home. I'm new to this whole living-together thing."

"So am I," I reminded him.

"So neither one of us knows how to do this." The idea seemed to amuse him.

"Nope. A pair of clueless wonders. So, what do you want to do?"

"Now? I want to go to bed. With you. In our bed. In our bedroom. In our apartment. And maybe tomorrow, when we've had some sleep, we can figure out this—" He waved his hand.

"—décor," I supplied. "But just one thing."

"You want to keep the night light." It wasn't a groan, but it was close.

"Yes, but that's not what I meant." I reached up and ran my fingers through his hair. "I was wondering why you thought we were going to get any sleep."

His smile widened. "I told you: I'm new to this." We both laughed, and I let out the breath it felt like I'd been holding forever.

Thirty-Four

I was deep in Christmas requests when my personal phone rang. Ralph and I had agreed that I needed to keep my Connecticut number even though it could theoretically expose my whereabouts if someone knew how to ping off towers and satellites and however else calls might be triangulated.

I glanced at the screen. It was Rick. I was tempted to send him to voicemail, but instead, I tapped the icon to put him on speaker. "Hi, Rick, how are you?" I asked as I continued to click through emailed gift requests.

"Well—to tell you the truth, not so great." It was such an unexpected response that I picked up the phone.

"I'm sorry to hear that. What's going on?" I didn't know why I was asking. It wasn't as though I could do anything to help, especially if he wanted money. According to the grapevine, i.e., Michael, Rick was still practicing as a solo.

"I need your help with something." Long pause. Finally, he said, "Trisha and I are splitting up."

"I'm sorry to hear to that." A sense of foreboding began to loom.

"Yeah, well, it turns out, she really liked our lifestyle when I was successful, and now that things are a little tougher, she's not happy. Truth is, she's already filed. Wants three grand a week in unallocated alimony and child support." I did quick math: *one hundred fifty-six thousand dollars a year.* Yikes. "I could represent myself, but well—I guess I've burned a few bridges. You know how it is when you play rough with somebody—they remember. There's a lot of guys in the bar who would be happy to see somebody take me to the cleaners.

I'm not really sure it would be in my best interests to go it alone. So, I thought maybe you could represent me, and I could do some work for you to pay the bill. What do you think?"

"Rick, I already told you—I don't do family anymore." At least, I was trying not to. Regardless, I didn't take on cases for free. If Rick was asking for what was essentially a barter arrangement, it meant he didn't have two nickels to rub together.

"But you're so good at it. I remember you doing that collaborative divorce stuff—or maybe it was mediation—you know, where you'd get people to sit down and work everything out. Maybe you could do that for us."

"Is Trisha open to that?" From what he'd said, it sounded highly unlikely that she'd be willing to engage in such a peaceful enterprise. More likely, her goal was to take him for everything he had.

"Um—right now she's just pissed off that—well, I'm doing what I can to fight this whole alimony thing since I can't afford that kind of money, and she's pissed about that, but I'm sure that once she cools down, we can figure something out."

There were a lot of questions I wanted to ask, but first things first. "Who represents her?"

"Louie Pasternak." Louie was well-known among the family bar as an aggressive little fireball who never hesitated to file motions for contempt at the slightest hint of a late alimony or child support payment. More often than not, Louie not only got the late payments, but an award of attorneys' fees for his trouble. I knew Rick was familiar with such tactics, having utilized them himself on many occasions.

"I'm going to have to think about this," I said finally. I didn't want to give my former partner a flat *no*, but neither did I want to take on what would likely be a messy and time-consuming divorce—especially one that wasn't going to pay. "I'll get back to you by the end of the week. If you find someone in the meantime, by all means, don't wait for me—go with them. Just text me to let me know you're all set."

"I won't be looking for anyone else. You're the best." How like Rick to think he was going to flatter me into taking his case.

"You should keep looking," I countered. "There are plenty of people out there who do a lot more family than I do. I recommend that you consider one of them." No names came to mind, but I wouldn't have given him one anyway. I never sent a potential client to a lawyer I knew unless I also knew the client could and would pay. Once, in my early days, I'd made that mistake: I referred someone to my friend, Frank, who took the case solely on the basis of the client's statement that I'd told her to call him. Not until later did Frank find out that the client not only couldn't pay her bill, but she was willing to offer "services" in exchange and was quite offended when he turned her down. I ended up spending more time extricating Frank from this delicate dilemma than I would have if I'd taken the case in the first place.

"You're my first choice," Rick insisted. "There's nobody else I want."

As the old song said, you can't always get what you want. "Best I can tell you is that I'll think about it, but I'll be honest: I'm leaning heavily toward *no*." Leaning, as in I'd pretty much made up my mind. The only reason I didn't just hang up was that I felt a certain bizarre sense of loyalty to my former partner.

"I hope you don't," said Rick. "If there's anything I can do to change your mind, let me know."

"I'll do that. Now, I really need to go." A little more begging from Rick, and I finally clicked off.

*****

"You should have seen her," I said over dinner a couple nights later. "She was amazing. Did you guys know how good she is?"

Phil's smile held a tinge of sadness. "Of course, I know. I've always known."

I hadn't meant to bring up the subject of Isabella's concert from back in September, but Rick's call reminded me of how I'd run into him at the Wadsworth Mansion. I wondered whether he was still with his violist or whether he'd moved on.

"I've heard her play," said Claire. "I don't know much about music, but her playing is gorgeous." The others nodded.

"But—have you seen her in front of an audience?" I wasn't certain whether Phil understood what I was saying.

"Of course," he said again. "When we were first dating, I went down to the States to hear her play in a recital. I'd heard her play at her house, but on that little stage, she was a whole different person. She was just a kid, but she was magnificent. People were on their feet, cheering. She looked so—lit up, I guess. Like there was a fire inside her. Like if you turned out the lights in the auditorium, she'd still be shining." His smile faded. "Maybe I never should have taken her away from all that."

I rested my hand on his arm. "She made her choice. She chose love."

He forced a smile. "But at what cost?"

What cost, indeed?

Thirty-Five

"So? How was Christmas?" Holly asked. Behind her in the FaceTime window, the lights of her Christmas tree twinkled.

I sat back at Meredith's desk, smiling. She was downstairs with Julian. For once, I had the place to myself. "Not bad," I said, trying to sound blasé. "All the gifts were delivered, and that's what matters."

"Oh, give me a break," Holly snorted. "Tell me everything. What did you do? Did you go out on a sleigh? Did you deliver presents?"

"Hell, no!" I laughed. "The boys do that—well, except for Phil. He was in the Control Center with us."

"What's the Control Center?"

I sipped my tea. "It's the nerve center of the Pole. All the sleighs are in constant contact. If anything goes wrong, it's up to us take care of it."

"'Us'?"

"Us—Phil, Meredith, and me. You should have seen it—these enormous screens with a map of the world, and every sleigh has a different color trail, so it looked like really skinny multicolored snakes slithering and winding all across the globe."

"Yuck," said Holly.

"I know, but it's weirdly elegant. Almost like they're dancing. At one point, Mitch's sleigh had to go down in the middle of Australia—something with one of the reindeer—and we were trying to figure out who we could reroute if he couldn't get back in the air in time. It was insane!"

"Sounds like you had fun," my best friend observed knowingly.

"It was a blast!" I chortled. "I mean, not at the time, but afterward when he was back up and everything was okay—I'll tell you, Meredith had that icy calm going, but you could tell she was freaking out about her little boy in the middle of the outback."

"Was he alone?"

"Oh, no. There's always a second on every sleigh. Charles was with him—you remember Charles, don't you?"

"I know you've talked about him, but I don't think I ever met him."

"I'll introduce you when you come for the wedding. Charles is the elf who was with Ralph when he got arrested the first time." It felt like eons ago, that evening when I'd been at my desk at Lundstrom with Ralph, and three-foot-tall Charles had clomped up the stairs to my office with an air of being in charge of everything. Charles was also the one who had helped Ralph escape from prison. "Charles is usually on Ralph's sleigh, but this year, he went with Mitch—and it was a good thing he did. Meredith knew that if anybody could take care of things, it was Charles, but still—Mitch is her baby. Not that I'd ever say that in front of him."

"You don't have to. They know. Jack knows he's my baby even though he's six-three. How did Ralph do? Was this his first year as Santa?"

"That was last year." Last year, when my life changed forever. I'd never forget standing in my living room with Mitch on Christmas Eve night, and turning around to see him there in the red coat Santa uses for the "specials." I knew then that Ralph was always meant to be Santa. It was who he was.

And now, I was going to be Mrs. Claus.

And I was scared shitless.

Thank God I'd have Meredith to guide me.

*****

Now that Christmas was over, wedding preparations were thrown into high gear. Suddenly, being a bride was my full-time job. "You're not just getting married," Meredith said as we walked back to her office after a mid-morning trip to get the tea tray turned into a two-hour tasting extravaganza. "You're becoming Mrs. Claus. It's much more than a wedding. This ceremony will be akin to a coronation."

"I have no idea what you're talking about." I pushed the elevator button. For the thousandth time, I regretted not eloping.

Isabella had already called to inform me that she would not only return to the Pole for the wedding, but she would handle all the music for the ceremony as well as the reception. "Rodrigo says we can borrow any of his CDs we want. Did you know he used to DJ at weddings before he made it as a singer?"

"I didn't know." I hesitated, then asked, "Phil knows you're coming, right?" She hadn't come back for Christmas due to several holiday concert obligations and a Christmas Eve service. If her absence bothered Phil, he kept it to himself.

"Of course," she said as casually as if she'd merely run out to the supermarket. "Now, what song do you want for your first dance? Since you love all those old songs, I was thinking of 'The Way You Look Tonight,' but if you'd rather, we could use 'Unchained Melody.' What do you think?"

"I'll have to talk to Ralph," I said, feeling slightly faint at the prospect of Isabella's return.

But with my own nuptials fast approaching, I didn't have time to dwell on the state of Phil and Isabella's marriage. For one thing, I had to figure out what to wear. I felt strongly that, at my age, the traditional frothy wedding dress with veil and train would be ridiculous. Since I wasn't the high-fashion type, no sleek designer dress would have done even if I weren't short and solid. Also, while Ralph insisted I should feel free to buy whatever dress I wanted regardless of cost, I wasn't willing to use my fiancé's money to buy my wedding outfit.

As with so many things, in the end it was simpler than I'd anticipated. One evening four days after Christmas, I was summoned to the workshop. Anya ushered me to the section where the elves with sewing skills created everything from doll clothes to stuffed toys. There, Tillie stood in the doorway with Claire and an elf named Chester, while half a dozen elves giggled and whispered.

"Right this way," said Chester. He took my hand and led me over to a something—a dress form?—draped with a sheet. Two of the elves removed the sheet with a flourish.

It was indeed a dress form, so close to my size and shape that I'd have thought someone took my measurements. The dress on the form was cream-colored satin, without a button or zipper to be seen. It was the epitome of simple elegance, with a sweetheart neckline, princess seams, and a skirt so voluminous that it looked as though it would stand straight out if I twirled.

"It's beautiful." I didn't want to say that it was almost too plain. I could wear a necklace or something.

"Try it on," said Chester. "I want to be sure it fits correctly." A sheet was tacked up to transform a corner of the room into a tiny makeshift dressing room. I went behind it and stripped to my underwear. Two female elves bubbled with excitement as first, they zipped me into a petticoat, and then they held up the dress for me to step into. One reached up to smooth it on my shoulders as the other darted around to zip up the back. Then, they pulled the sheet aside, and I emerged in my wedding gown.

As far as I could tell, it fit perfectly, but Chester frowned as he examined every inch. "Where are her shoes?" he asked. Another elf came forward with a pair of pumps covered in cream satin and matching lace. I slipped into them. "Step up," said Chester, and two elves helped me to ascend until I stood on a work table. Chester moved slowly around the table, periodically reminding me to stand up straight, and an elf followed him with a ruler to measure the distance between the hem and the table.

Once he was satisfied, Chester called for a mirror. It took Claire and two elves to maneuver it so I could see without getting off the table. "It's exquisite," I said honestly. "I can't thank you enough."

"We're not done," said Tillie. Anya and another elf carried over a large box. When they opened it, I stared.

"What's that?"

"That, my dear, is your cape," said Chester. "Just as Santa has a dress uniform, so also does his wife. This has been handed down for at least six generations of Mrs. Clauses." I moved to get down, but he barked, "Stay there!" Claire climbed up on the table, and the elves handed up the box. She took out the cape, draping it around me and tying it at my throat. The heavy red velvet was edged with creamy white fur, just as on Ralph's dress uniform. Claire arranged it to drape gracefully around me. Then she asked, "Where's the headpiece?"

"There's a headpiece?" I couldn't picture a veil that would work with this cape.

"Not so much a headpiece," said Tillie. "More like a tiara."

"A *what*?"

Another elf came forward with another box, smaller than the first. Tillie opened it, and I stared in disbelief. It was indeed a tiara. Meredith's words about a coronation echoed in my mind. "Can I touch it?" I asked, and the elves giggled.

Gingerly, I lifted the tiara from the black velvet cushion on which it rested. It was lighter than it looked. From the ends to the center, swirls of platinum sparkled with diamonds and rubies. "How are you going to wear your hair?" Anya asked.

"I haven't thought about it," I confessed. Somehow, I'd expected that with all the work that needed to be done at the Pole, our wedding would be a simple, straightforward affair.

"For now, we'll assume you're wearing it down," Anya said. "You may want to put it up. We can play with that later." Tillie held the box up, and Claire removed the tiara, placing it on my head. Then, she stepped aside so that I could see the full view.

If I'd had a lifetime to imagine how I should look to marry the love of my life, I could never have come up with something more perfect. I didn't look dumpy or lawyerly. I looked regal. I *felt* regal.

Chester reached up to take my hand, and I stepped to the floor. "Walk around," he said. "We need to know if the shoes fit properly." I walked around the room once, twice, three times. "Try dancing," he said. Before I could protest, a redheaded elf bowed in front of me and held out his hands. As another elf la-la-la'ed a waltz tune that sounded vaguely familiar, the redheaded elf waltzed me around the room, my dress swishing.

"Hold your head up!" Chester barked from the sidelines. I straightened, and he said, "Better. You need to work on your posture." I was about to point out that the top of the elf's head only came up to my breasts, but he added, "Remember how tall Ralph is. You need to pretend this is him." More elves joined in the la-la-la-ing as I imagined waltzing with Ralph.

When the waltz ended, Chester asked, "How are the shoes?"

"I'm not used to wearing heels," I hedged, but he saw through my attempt at diplomacy.

"Don't worry, we'll adjust them. Get back on the table before you take them off. We don't want your hem to get dirty." Anya helped me back up on the table, holding my arm as I slipped the shoes off. Claire reached up to retrieve the tiara, and Anya unzipped the dress. I went behind the curtain to changed back into my regular clothes, feeling like Cinderella the day after the ball.

As I emerged from the changing area, I turned to them all. "I can't thank you enough. This is all so beautiful." My eyes grew moist, and I fished in my pocket for a tissue. "You're so talented, so generous—I don't know what to say."

"Just don't gain weight between now and the wedding," said Chester. "I didn't leave much room to let out the dress."

I couldn't help laughing. "I'll do my best."

*****

"You should see it," I exulted as Ralph and I got ready for bed. "I felt like a queen." I'd been rhapsodizing about my wedding outfit ever since I got back to the apartment.

"In a way, you are." He stepped out of his work pants and folded them before setting them in the laundry basket. "You're going to be Mrs. Claus. It's the closest we get to royalty around here." He sat on the side of the bed, pulled off his socks, and laid them on top of his pants.

"So, our wedding isn't just a wedding? It really is like a coronation like your mother said? I thought she was kidding."

He pulled his sweater over his head, folded it, and set it on the bureau. "She never kids. I thought you knew that."

"But how would I know what a North Pole wedding is like? You're the one who's lived up here forever."

"A regular North Pole wedding is different from Santa's wedding. And remember, I wasn't around when my parents got married," he pointed out reasonably as he laid his shirt in the laundry basket. "This is my first rodeo, too."

"At least you know how things roll. Damn, it's cold in here." I'd already pulled on my bed socks and flannel pajamas. I tossed my shirt toward the basket, but it fell short. I climbed into bed. "Get in here. I need a bed warmer."

He stood by the basket. "Would you mind putting your dirty clothes in the basket first?"

"It's freezing out there. I'll do it in the morning." It wasn't as though anybody was going to see them.

"You say that every night."

"That's because every night, you tell me to do it."

"That's because every night, you throw your dirty clothes on the floor, and I have to pick them up."

"No, you don't. I'll get them in the morning." I was starting to feel irked.

"Why is it so hard to just do it now?"

"Why does it matter? You can't see them from there."

"Because it matters! Because it looks like a mess."

"Who cares? Nobody's going to see it."

"I'll see it. I'll know it's there. Isn't that enough?"

I sat up in bed. "If you want to get on the subject of things that need to be cleaned up, how about the dishes on the counter?"

"What dishes? My mug?"

"And your plate, and your spoon. It's all sitting on the counter, but do you hear me saying anything about it?"

"You don't have to, because for your information, I already washed them and dried them and put them away. Everything's cleaned up in this place except your dirty laundry."

"Oh, for crying out loud. It's one lousy shirt. I can't believe that bothers you."

"And I can't believe you won't just pick it up. You could have done it fifty times by now."

"FINE!" I threw back the covers, stomped over to the basket, and dropped in my shirt. Then I stomped back to bed and got in, pulling the covers around me as I lay with my back to him.

So much for life as a queen.

Thirty-Six

One week until the wedding. I was doing my best to focus on work, both Pole and law. Meredith had gone to her apartment. "I'm going to lie down for a bit. I have a headache," she said. I offered her some of the ibuprofen I'd brought, but she declined, saying. "All I need is some rest." Considering that we'd been juggling the post-Christmas cleanup and wedding plans, I wasn't surprised she needed a break. I could have used one myself, and she was twenty-two years my senior.

Alone, I shifted my focus from Pole work to managing my practice. My email inbox showed fifty-seven new messages. Most were sales pitches, but two were from the court in Connecticut, and one was from a law firm I immediately recognized. I opened the communications from the court first. Both reflected dates my two remaining cases had been set down for hearings. Once I finished these, I'd be done with my practice. I allowed myself a moment to feel something about this—regret, nostalgia, sadness, relief—but the truth was that it felt no different than when I received a message from Kristofer about a shipment landing in Iceland. It was just business. Besides, I had more important things to think about.

I clicked on the third email. As I read, my eyes widened:

Dear Colleague,

Nettis, Butler, & Gould is proud to announce the opening of its new office in Hartford, Connecticut.

Nettis, Butler, & Gould. Scott's firm. In Hartford.

Apparently I'd done a fine job selling my hometown.

I studied the first line, trying to pinpoint what I felt. Not regret, I decided. The Hartford office of Nettis, Butler, & Gould could have been mine, but I didn't question my decision to refuse it. Maybe I was a trifle wistful, though. Sort of like a glimpse into what might have been if things had been different. I'd have been running that office. Plus, I'd have been raking in more money than I'd ever earned in my life.

But I wouldn't have had Ralph, which meant I wouldn't have had anything.

Definitely a good decision, turning Scott down.

I scrolled down for details. The address was a downtown high-rise, naturally. Phone numbers, website, email address. Then I scrolled down further—and my jaw fell open:

Nettis, Butler, & Gould is proud to announce that the following attorneys will be joining the firm in its new Hartford location:

Lara Marinos, associate
Gregory D. Finn, associate
Richard McGee, of counsel

Wait—*Rick???*

In his headshot, my erstwhile partner looked proper and dignified. His dark hair waved naturally rather than reflecting its usual gel-imposed gloss. His reassuring smile invited prospective clients to trust him. You'd never know this respectable-looking lawyer had been kicked out of one firm and dumped by his partner at another, both due to ethical violations.

Did Scott know about Rick's past? He must have. No way he'd have hired Rick without vetting him. But what could have prompted Scott to hire a guy who was at the last mile with the ethics committee?

You know, not a lot of people would be making you an offer like this after all that Santa Claus stuff. I had to go to bat for you. You owe me.

Scott's comment echoed in my head. Was that why he'd wanted me? So I'd owe him? Was it why he'd hired Rick?

Talk about dodging a bullet.

I turned my attention back to the announcement. Rick would practice in the areas of family law and criminal defense. Odd. As far as I knew, Rick had never done criminal work.

Well, it had nothing to do with me. I was safely ensconced in my office at the Pole. Two more hearings, and I was finished with active practice. The thought gave me a pang, but I pushed it aside and clicked the *forward* arrow to send the announcement to Michael, remembering my last conversation with Scott.

To say Scott hadn't taken it well when I turned down his offer was an understatement. To be honest, I was surprised by his reaction. From an Ivy League lawyer I'd expected something better, something classier. Maybe *sorry to lose you, but good luck.*

Instead, he sneered, "I can't believe you're turning down a world-class offer to run after some guy. I thought you were a professional."

His words stung, and not just because I'd had similar thoughts late at night as I packed. I took a deep breath and squashed my instinctive highly-unprofessional retort about what he could do to himself. I merely said, "I appreciate your good wishes. Take care."

"Wait!" There was an odd, pleading note in his voice. I waited, my finger hovering over the *end* button. Finally he said, "I don't mean to be—I'm just disappointed. I really wanted to work with you. I thought—you and I—we understand each other." His voice softened. "I feel comfortable with you." When I didn't speak, he continued, "I've told you things I don't normally tell people."

I could feel myself being drawn in. He wanted me. He was disappointed to lose me. He had confided in me. . . .

But rational thought reared up. This was the guy who tried to charm me, to seduce me, to bully me into—what? A job? A relationship? It didn't matter. Head high, I bade him farewell and hung up. He might be a fancy New York lawyer, and the offer might have been impressive, but Scott wasn't someone to trust. He was a manipulator. And a sore loser. How fortunate that I was now as far away from Scott and his firm as a person could get.

I refocused on the screen before me and clicked on the next gift request. Turning down Scott Wilkinson was definitely one of the smartest decisions I'd ever made.

My only smarter one was falling in love with Ralph Claus.

Thirty-Seven

Michael and I stood in the hallway outside the dining hall, he in his tuxedo and me in my cream-colored dream of a dress. Holly stood by the door, one hand on the handle. Everyone else—Ralph, his family, my brother, the elves—were in the dining hall, waiting for us.

I clutched Michael's arm. "Tell me again why people do this."

"You mean, besides sex? Probably so there's somebody who's legally obligated to laugh at their lousy jokes." I must have looked startled because he said, "Love, Riley. They do it for love."

"Oh, yeah. I forgot."

He chuckled and kissed my cheek. "Come on, kiddo. Let's go." Michael put his hand on mine, and we approached Holly.

"It's show time," said my best friend, opening the door to my new life.

Tillie, Claire, and Anya had transformed the dining hall into a bower of deep green holly, red berries, and red and white roses—all beautifully crafted by artists in the workshop. Banks of white candles bathed the room in soft light. At the front, a chorus of elves sang an ethereal wordless rendering of Pachelbel's Canon in D, with Isabella playing the low, rhythmic notes that grounded the piece. A runner of red carpet defined the aisle, at the end of which stood Julian, supported by an ebony cane. He was dressed in Claus-black, his attire accented with a white collar like a priest. An intricately embroidered jewel-toned stole was draped around his neck. Behind him to his right stood Meredith, attired in the red velvet cape trimmed with white fur. The tiara that perched on her silver hair sparkled in the candlelight.

Ralph stood before his parents, resplendent in his dress uniform. The red velvet gleamed; the white fur accented his dark curls with those few threads of silver. He was flanked by his brothers and mine, while Tillie, Claire, and Anya stood on the other side of Julian. Ralph had explained to me earlier that this wasn't about them being attendants; rather, it was to get the taller people out of the way so all the elves would be able to see. Yet another of the thousand tiny ways my beloved was constantly aware of the happiness of others.

A team of elves manned the video cameras and sound board. I'd already been wired with an inconspicuous microphone linked by a wire to a box at the back of my waist. Originally, I balked, but Mitch explained that it was necessary. Otherwise, my mother and stepfather, who were watching the live feed from their living room in Phoenix, would be unable to hear anything we said. "They could have heard fine if they'd come," I muttered to Holly, who agreed. But it was apparently the nature of weddings that there would be bumps in the road. It was only because of Ralph that they were even tuned in; unbeknownst to me, he'd returned to Arizona to try to persuade them to come to the wedding after my phone calls to my mother failed to get the job done. Secretly, I suspected he'd used a bit of Santa magic to win them over.

Fred's little girl walked down the aisle, scattering white silk rose petals on the red runner. Holly followed, her pine-green satin gown shimmering in the candlelight. Chester and the elves had insisted on dressing her. "It wouldn't be right for you to have a bespoke gown while hers comes off the rack somewhere," Chester said. I watched as his team did Holly's fitting just as they had done mine, my heart swelling at her awe when she looked in the mirror and saw for herself how splendidly perfect the dress was.

As Holly reached the front, the chorus sang the final notes of the Canon. My fingers dug into Michael's arm. Then, for a moment, Isabella held up her bow hand. When she nodded the downbeat, she and the chorus began the traditional bridal march, and we started our procession down the aisle toward my beloved and my new life.

Afterward, I was glad for the video team, because they captured so much that I didn't notice: the beaming elves who watched us, the tears glistening in Holly's eyes, Meredith's quiet smile of approval as I approached her son. It sounds corny, but my only actual memories were of Ralph. From the moment I saw him looking for me at the back of the dining hall, my heart began to pound, and I had to restrain myself from running down the aisle. (Michael told me afterward that he had to hustle to keep up with me. "I thought we were going for stately," he said in his toast, to the laughter of everyone present.)

When we reached the front, Michael kissed my cheek and stepped aside. Ralph and I faced each other, hands joined. Julian intoned the familiar words from the Book of Common Prayer: "Dearly beloved: We have come together in the presence of God to witness and bless the joining together of this man and this woman in Holy Matrimony." A shiver ran down my spine. My life was about to change forever. I looked up at this man, my man, and tears welled up.

"Repeat after me," Julian instructed me. "I, Megan Elizabeth Riley—"

"I, Megan Eliz—" My voice broke. I tried again: "I, Meg—" I, who had spoken with strength and confidence before juries and judges, was unable to say my own name. The third time, I barely creaked "I" before my voice broke and tears began to run down my face.

Ralph was watching me. *Dear God, don't let him think I don't want to do this.* I opened my mouth again, determined now. No sound. His brow crinkled. Panicked, I mouthed, "I love you."

He released my hands. He wrapped his arms around me. He held me close and whispered, "I love you."

For a moment, I rested my head against his chest, the only place in the world I wanted to be. Then I took a deep breath and straightened. I looked up at him, and he kissed my brow. His eyes were questioning, though. I nodded and whispered, "Let's get married."

Barely letting himself smile, Julian slipped a handkerchief into my hand, and I dabbed my face. From behind me, Holly touched my wrist, a signal to let her take the handkerchief. Then, I took Ralph's hands in mine. In the clear, steady voice that once rang through courtrooms across Connecticut, I proclaimed, "I, Megan Elizabeth Riley, do take you, Ralph Henry Claus, to be my beloved husband, to have and to hold from this day forward. . . ."

I took Ralph, and Ralph took me. We belonged to each other, now and forever. A rush of pure joy flowed through me.

"I now pronounce you husband and wife," announced Julian, and the entire assemblage burst into applause. Julian might have been about to tell us we could kiss, but we were ahead of him. As I felt Ralph's lips on mine, a blaze of happiness surged through my soul.

But we weren't done yet. As we stood before Julian, hand in hand, husband and wife, Meredith came forward. A pair of elves approached her. She released the tie at her neck, and they reached up to lift the splendid cape from her shoulders. She took it from them and said to me, "Turn around." I obeyed, and she placed the cape around my shoulders. I turned to face her, motionless as she fastened the tie at my throat. Then, she took the tiara from her own head, and she placed it on mine. It was indeed a coronation as well as a wedding.

"You will do well," she said. It sounded at once like a prediction and a command. She looked a trifle pale. Perhaps this surrender of her official position affected her more than I'd realized.

For a moment, we stood, her hands on my shoulders, her emerald ring catching the candlelight. Then, my mother-in-law kissed my cheek. Ralph bent down to kiss his mother. Meredith returned to her place, still regal.

"Beloved ones, it is my great honor to present to you for the first time, Santa Claus and Mrs. Claus!" Julian sounded as jubilant as I felt. Isabella led the choir in a rousing a cappella rendition of the Hallelujah Chorus. Everyone stood, cheering and applauding, as my husband and I walked down the aisle and into our new life.

*****

In less time than I'd have thought possible, Annaliese's team rearranged the chairs to form seating groups, leaving space for dancing and mingling. Along one wall, tables draped with deep red cloths bore platters laden with meats and cheeses. Delicacies of all sorts sat amid candlesticks with slim white tapers and arrangements of holly and golden ornaments. Two elves were pouring champagne into an array of glasses—quite possibly every glass at the Pole. A small round table with a golden cloth boasted an ivory-frosted wedding cake festooned with deep red roses.

We toasted, we kissed, we ate, we drank, we danced. The cape was a trifle heavy, but I shook my head when Ralph whispered that I could take it off. If Meredith could wear it, so could I.

The festivities were at their height when Ted slipped into the room and whispered to Ralph. Ralph looked perplexed for a second, as if Ted's words couldn't possibly make sense. Then, his face settled into a grim sort of panic. "Come on," he whispered to me, taking my hand.

"What's the matter?" I asked as he shepherded me out of the room. "It's Mom."

To tell the truth, I hadn't noticed when she'd left the reception. Now that I thought about it, Julian had left, too. "I don't understand. What's going on?" I said as we hustled down the hall behind Ted.

Ralph shook his head, and we all picked up the pace. When we arrived at the senior Clauses' apartment, a cold fear clutched me. Ted opened the door, and there stood Tillie, Ralph's brothers—my brothers-in-law—and their wives. All their faces were streaked with tears. We pushed past them into the bedroom .

Meredith lay on the bed, motionless. Beside her, Julian held her hand. Her other hand rested on her chest, the emerald ring luminous even in the low light.

"She's gone." Julian's voice broke with grief.

Sudden, selfish fear gripped me. *Dear God, no. No. She can't be.* Breathless before her stillness, my mind and heart began at last to grasp just how much this formidable, infuriating woman had meant to me. *Don't be dead. Please, don't be dead. I can't do this without you.*

"What happened?" I could feel Ralph trembling beside me.

"She said she had a headache," said Fred from behind us. "She came back here to lie down. And that was that."

Later, the cause of her death would be identified as an aneurysm. At the moment, standing by her bed in our wedding finery—which now felt like a mockery—it didn't matter. In the midst of my panic, I tasted the bitter ash of grief, a fraction of what my husband must be experiencing, the tiniest sliver of what Julian must be feeling. Her jeweled tiara felt so heavy on my head.

In the dining hall, the elves were laughing, eating, celebrating, innocent of the knowledge that their queen had died. Someone needed to tell them.

As if reading my mind, Ralph said, "I've got to tell the others." His voice cracked only slightly. While the others wept, his control held. It had to. He wasn't just the eldest son. He was Santa Claus.

I touched the fur on the cape she had tied around my shoulder mere hours earlier. Then, I took my husband's hand. "We'll tell them," I said. For the rest of my life, I'll remember the gratitude in his eyes.

We kissed Julian, who barely seemed to notice us. Then, we went back to our wedding reception to do our duty.

Book Three

Becoming Mrs. Claus

Thirty-Eight

The first days after Meredith's passing—I couldn't bring myself to say *death*—were so busy that I couldn't have broken down even if I'd been so inclined. It felt as if everyone was holding themselves together for everyone else, but at the same time. we were all on the edge of something dire. Somehow it fell to me to manage everything, from notifying her relatives to the logistics of her memorial service. Maybe because I was the newest member of the family, the one with the briefest connection to her. Or maybe because Ralph—Santa—was everyone's emotional support, and as his wife, it was my job to make his job easier—or at least, less heartbreaking. *Function, don't feel* had been my mantra after my father's death. Without thinking, I fell back into that manner of coping now.

Finally, the official rituals of death had been completed. Nothing remained to consume my attention. It was time to return to work.

I made tea in our apartment and poured it into one of my old commuter mugs. My husband had left before I woke up. Part of me wanted to go in search of him; the other part wanted to respect his privacy. For all I knew, he was sitting with his father, the two of them trying to come to grips with this new gaping hole in their lives.

Lulu was watching me. I'd planned to ease Meredith into the idea of having my sweet girl in the office with us the way she'd been with me at Lundstrom so long ago, but we hadn't gotten that far. I could have done it now. No one would have stopped me. Still. . . . "Not today, sweetheart," I said, stepping into the hall and closing the door.

I pushed the button for the elevator. It came as it always had, a mechanical device that neither knew nor cared that the woman who had ridden in it every day for decades would never do so again. The elevator didn't know it was taking me to a new world. It merely closed its doors and rose, opening them again as if nothing had changed.

I stepped out and looked at the two closed doors, Meredith's office and Santa's. I wondered suddenly if someone would have locked her office to keep things secure. Then I remembered my first visit, so long ago. Holly and I had asked about a key for our room, and Anya assured us that we didn't need one because nothing locked here. At the time, it seemed incredible.

I opened the door and flicked on the light. The room was cooler than usual for being closed off, but other than that, you'd never have known anything was different. Someone had turned off the computer and neatened the papers on her desk, but these were the only clues that Meredith hadn't momentarily stepped away. Her chair was tucked up against the desk; mine was in the corner. The wingback chairs, spaced properly in front of the desk, awaited visitors.

"Excuse me, Mrs. Claus."

I whirled as if I'd been caught doing something unseemly. Owen stood in the doorway. I knew without asking that it was he who had put everything in order. Bless him. The Clauses weren't the only ones grieving in a special way.

It was the first time anybody had called me Mrs. Claus. It didn't fit. At least, not today. "Please, call me Meg."

Owen's dark brown eyes were steadfast, almost as if they weren't rimmed by lids reddened ever so slightly by recent tears. "Ma'am," he said in compromise. "Is there anything I can do for you?"

I set my commuter cup on the desk. *Tell me how to be her,* I nearly said. For all that the woman had driven me batshit crazy, I was nowhere near ready to let her go. I'd assumed we would work side by side for years as I learned every detail about Pole operations, about icebreaker shipments and elf management and procuring reindeer vaccines and dealing with her sons and their wives, her husband and mine—

"I just—I have to figure out what to do." We stood only a few feet apart, but my voice was so low that it was a wonder he heard me.

"Since there aren't any gift requests yet, perhaps you'd like to begin with work assignments," Owen said. "—It's customary." The hesitation gave him away: he'd been about to say that Mrs. Claus customarily did this. I felt like the narrator in *Rebecca*, when she went into the parlor on her first morning at Manderley, but everything was waiting for her in the morning room because that was the established routine and she was the only one who had no idea what to do.

We'd done the work assignments before, of course. I tried to remember where Meredith kept them, but my mind was a blank. It might as well have been the very first day I walked into this office. Fortunately, Owen knew. Almost as if he was grateful for something to do, he edged past me and flicked on her computer. It took a few minutes to get going. Finally, he clicked the mouse a few times before he stepped back, handing it off to me as graciously as if he were inviting me into his private office.

Somewhat hesitantly, I slid into her chair. I always used my left hand for the mouse, and Meredith had, too. I tried to remember if she was left-handed or if, like me, she preferred to mouse with her left hand while she made handwritten notes with her right. Not that it mattered, but suddenly I needed to know everything about my predecessor, the real Mrs. Claus. Before I could ask, Owen slid a pad of paper and a pen onto the desk, next to my right arm.

I looked up then. "Thank you, Owen."

"Do you need anything else, ma'am?"

I started to shake my head, but honesty compelled me. "I feel like—like I don't know what she does." I'd spent months working with her, and yet my mind was a blank.

An odd look spread over Owen's face. It took a moment for me to recognize it: gratitude. By this admission, I'd given him the best gift possible—the chance to serve his mistress by helping me. It would be almost like recreating her presence.

Except I didn't want to recreate Meredith. I needed to forge my own trail. As much as I required her wisdom and experience and knowledge, I needed to carve out my own way of being Mrs. Claus.

I only wished I knew what in hell that might be.

I decided that I didn't need to change up any of the work assignments today. The ones on the list looked perfectly fine. I scanned the list of elves in the workshop, the finishing rooms, the wrapping rooms, the warehouses, research and development, and the stables. The list of elves working the kitchen was static since Meredith had long acceded to Annaliese's request that only trained staff work in the kitchen. Even Meredith recognized that nobody wanted a bunch of amateurs preparing meals. It was similar with the stables, but Ted was willing to allow inexperienced elves to help with cleanup so long as they stayed outside of the stalls themselves.

"Why do I need to review these lists?" I asked at last. "Don't Fred and Ted know a whole lot better than I do who should be on their teams?"

"Of course," said Owen. "But Mrs. C. liked to review the lists periodically, just so she knew who was doing what. She didn't like to be ignorant about what was happening in other parts of the Pole."

I understood her logic. It was the same reason that when we were growing up, my father had made Derek and me mow the lawn and help him clean out the gutters. "Otherwise, you won't know what's on your own property," he said, gesturing toward a cracked shingle two rows above a leaf-filled gutter.

As I peered at the list, I noted that Meredith had left blanks for other periodic jobs, including cleaning mirrors. Since there were no windows, mirrors mimicked their function, creating the illusion of daylight by bouncing the artificial light around. "Who gets assigned to these?" I pointed to the list.

"Whoever Claire decides." Claire, the North Pole's housewife. It was she who ensured that the laundry was done and the photographs in the hall were dusted and all the other things nobody ever thought about were handled.

"Then why are they blank?"

Owen hesitated. "Claire sometimes needs to be reminded to let us know about work assignments. With everything she does, she tends to forget." But there was something in his tone that made me wonder if she truly forgot or if she resisted the idea that she needed to report in. Regardless, she was dealing with a newborn right now. As far as I was concerned, that entitled her to a pass.

I scrolled through the remainder of the list. "How do I know if the right person is doing the job?"

"What do you mean?"

I pointed to the screen. "It says here that Homer is in the workshop, but what if he's really in wrapping or something? Isn't that Fred's problem?"

Owen considered me. "This is how Mrs. C. handled staffing. You may wish to do it differently." He started to walk away, and then he stopped. "If I may make a suggestion, though. Don't change too much right away. Wait until you have a feel for the place and the people have more of a feel for you. Don't shake things up just for the sake of it."

"Of course not," I said with a hint of defensiveness. I waited until I heard the elevator doors close. Then, I surveyed the office, considering different options, until I settled on the perfect spot for Lulu's bed.

Thirty-Nine

When I saw Claire and Anya in the hall a few days later, their heads bent together, I had a feeling I knew what they were whispering about so furiously, but I played dumb. "Hey, ladies," I called as I approached, leaving them plenty of time to break off their conversation. "Haven't seen you all day."

Their heads snapped up as if they'd been caught doing something shameful. "Hey, Meg," said Claire, her voice tight.

"Hi," echoed Anya in precisely the same tone.

"What's going on?" I tried to sound merely friendly, like the kid on the playground who wanted to be part of the group. Instead, I sounded to my own ears like the teacher who walks into the girls' bathroom as the smoke lingers in the air.

They glanced at each other. "I'm so mad," said Anya.

"Can you believe she left?" Claire chimed in.

"Who, Iz? She has a rehearsal." They both sniffed, and I added, "Her concert is in two weeks."

"She should have stayed." Claire's pale blue eyes flashed.

"Her husband's mother just died. He needs her." Anya's smooth brow wrinkled with disgust.

"What makes you think that?" For me, Phil was the hardest Claus to read.

"What are you talking about? He's her husband." Claire sounded downright indignant. "She belongs with him now. She should be at his side, not going to rehearsals."

"Are you sure he even wants her here right now?" I had no idea what conversations they'd had when she came up for the wedding.

The original six-month deadline for Isabella's experiment had come and gone, but neither spouse had said anything to me about how long she planned to remain in Connecticut.

"Of course," Anya snapped. "I can't believe how selfish she's being." She huffed, and Claire nodded vigorously.

"She has to work," I reminded them. They looked unconvinced, as someone might who had never needed to earn a living. "Did Phil say he wanted her to stay?"

They both looked at me as if I was a contender for Stupidest Person on Earth. "He shouldn't have to ask," said Anya. "She should know."

"How? Is she supposed to be a mind reader?" I wasn't being facetious; I really wanted to know. Did being married mean that you were supposed to know what your husband thought and felt without him saying a word? If so, poor Ralph was in for a huge disappointment.

Their faces said as clearly as words that I was an idiot. Then, Claire's expression softened. "You don't understand—you're newlyweds. You'll see when you've been together longer."

A blaze of anger flared at her condescension. With enormous effort, I said merely, "I'm sure that's true for some people. All I know is that in all my years of dealing with divorcing couples, one of the biggest issues was communication. The ones who used their words tended to fare much better." I started to walk away, and then I turned back. "Another thing I learned is that every couple's relationship is different. Just because something works for one couple doesn't mean it works for another." I strode away, fully aware that I'd eventually need to apologize—and equally aware that Isabella might face new challenges if she ever decided to come home for good.

Forty

"Meg?"

My husband's voice was tentative, with good reason. It took all my self-restraint not to snap, "Don't you knock?", but I knew he saw it on my face in that first instant, before I smoothed out my features the way I saw Meredith do so many times.

"What?"

Ralph came all the way in. He bore a tray with a covered plate, a smaller plate with a round golden-brown roll, and a glass of garnet-colored wine. "You missed dinner." He didn't say "again," but he could have and he'd have been right.

I hadn't noticed. I no longer had the innate sense of time that had served me so well in the practice of law, a million years ago when I billed my life in six-minute increments. Back then, I knew without looking how long I'd spent on a phone call or drafting a letter. Here, time was merely a theoretical construct. It didn't so much pass as evaporate.

"You didn't have to do that. I could have gotten something later." He scanned the cluttered desktop for a place to set the tray. Before he could move something I didn't want moved, I said, "Here, I'll take it." I took the tray and placed it on the credenza, next to the antique tea set.

I looked up to see Ralph's eyes on his mother's tea set. "What do you think we ought to do with it?" I asked.

"What do you mean?"

"Does your pop want it in his apartment? Or maybe Tillie. Or Claire. It seems like her kind of thing."

"Don't you want it?"

"It's not a matter of want. It's—it's not mine. It belongs to Julian. All her stuff does."

"It goes with the office."

I shook my head. "The desk may go with the office, but that tea set—no. That's like saying I should get her shoes because she wore them in here. The set belongs to Julian. It's up to him who gets it."

"You get it."

"Is that what he said?"

"The office is yours. The tea set is part of the office."

"No. The computer is part of the office. The chair is part of the office. Even those wing chairs. But that tea set—that's an heirloom. It shouldn't go to me. I've been in the family for, like, forty-five minutes. Give it to somebody deserving, somebody who knew her better." *Somebody she loved.*

I thought he was going to argue; I half-hoped he would. Instead he said, "Don't work too late," and he was out of the room before I could catch my breath.

After the door clicked shut, I stood for a minute, watching it as if he might come back. I heard the faint ding of the elevator, and the hum of the doors opening, then closing. I crept to the door and opened it: he was gone. I was alone. I turned back and moved a stack of papers to one of the wing chairs, the one festooned with Lulu's black fur. Then, I set the tray on the desk and took the cover off the plate. The garlicky aroma of fettucine with red sauce filled the air. Three little meatballs—I knew now that they were indeed reindeer—adorned the dollop of sauce atop ribbons of pasta. It was the same meal I'd had on my very first dinner at the Pole, a lifetime ago, save for the wine. Ralph had taken to bringing back a case of wine from wherever his travels took him even though I was practically the only one who ever drank it.

I resumed my seat in her chair. I still couldn't think of it as mine, any more than I could think of the office as mine. Everything here screamed her name.

I forced myself to eat, not because I was hungry, but so Ralph's kindness wouldn't be wasted. If I took the tray back without having eaten enough, his champions in the kitchen would be upset that I'd rejected his lovely gesture. I wished there were a way to dispose of the food without anyone knowing.

I also wished he'd brought the entire bottle of wine.

*****

I couldn't have said how much time had passed when my concentration was interrupted by the faint ding. An irrational fury rose up in me. "Oh, for God's sake, what now?" I shouted as the door opened.

"I'm sorry," said Julian quietly.

Horrified, I hastened to him. "No, I'm sorry, I didn't know it was you. I'm so sorry. Please, come in."

He shook his head. "I didn't mean to disturb you. I didn't realize you were working."

"Please, sit down." His hand held the cane; I rested mine on top of his. My nose prickled, a sure sign of impending tears. I rubbed it with my other hand to fend them off. After a few moments, he nodded, and I led the way into his wife's office.

Ralph's father settled himself into one of the wing chairs. "How are you doing?"

"How are *you* doing?" I sat in the other wing chair. "I wish I could offer you some tea. I don't have any water up here."

"No worries, my girl." Only Julian could have gotten away with calling a middle-aged woman "my girl."

"What can I do for you?" I asked when it became clear he wasn't going to offer the information.

"Nothing," he said.

"Were you looking for something?"

"No," he said. "I'm just visiting."

"You didn't have to come up here. I could have come to your apartment."

He smiled with sadness. "I'm not visiting you. I'm visiting her."

"Oh—shall I leave?" I had no experience with this.

"You don't need to," he said. "Just go about your business."

"I was just wrapping up," I lied.

"You're a terrible liar," he said with gentle amusement.

"I don't want to intrude—"

"You're not intruding," he said, but he was just as terrible a liar as I. I hustled to collect what I needed to deal with in the morning, but he didn't appear to be watching me.

"Do you visit often?" I asked as casually as I could, tucking documents into folders so I wouldn't have to meet his eyes.

"Every so often."

That explained the days when I came in to find things out of order—a chair moved, a pen knocked to the rug. But I couldn't begrudge him. There was no gravesite he could visit. And no matter what her son said, it was her office.

Julian didn't seem interested in talking. I thought of leaving him alone, but something in me couldn't walk away. I told myself it was because he was an old man with a cane and I was worried for his safety, but that wasn't it, not even close. Something in me needed to understand how to grieve losing the love of your life, as if understanding the grief would teach me the rest.

They'd been married forty-four years, living in this hermetically sealed environment where they were responsible for everyone and everything. She had family back in Vancouver, but for practical purposes, he was all she had, he and the children she had with him. They were each other's everything—friend, lover, companion, coworker, partner.

As Mrs. Claus, Meredith had known her Santa's role as intimately as it was possible to: the highs and lows, the joys and frustrations, all the things that never made it into the stories of Santa Claus or Father Christmas or Sinterklaas. She knew when he was cold and tired, when he was irked by bad weather or someone's error. She was the one Julian turned to when one of the specials tore at his heart, such as a dying girl to whom he'd brought a soft pink blanket, speaking softly to her and holding her hand as she died. Meredith was the one he vented to when the job felt overwhelming—because after all, who doesn't have that feeling at least occasionally? He was a man, not a saint. Human, no more.

Granted, Julian had had magic and a deep devotion to his calling, but even as Santa, he wasn't perfect. I knew this, because now Ralph was Santa and he definitely wasn't perfect, any more than I was. We were a couple of imperfect people fumbling our way through each day, trying to find our way through the thicket of obligations and responsibilities when sometimes it was all we could do to remember why we'd started the journey in the first place.

Because you love each other.

I startled. Had Julian spoken? But he was sitting in the wing chair, his eyes closed, his hands resting atop his cane, as peaceful as if he were on a park bench on a warm spring day. An unexpected small smile graced his weathered face. Was he sleeping? Dreaming of her? Communing with her in some mystical way? I peered at him, trying to divine what he was doing and how I could learn to do it.

A tap on the door interrupted my thoughts. Julian's eyes opened serenely. "Come in," I called.

Anya came in. "There you are," she said to Julian. "Come on, Papa, it's time for bed."

He glanced at me. I said, "We were just visiting. Don't worry, I'll help him when we're done."

Anya hesitated, her hand on his arm. "But. . . ."

I waited for him to protest, to say that he'd go to bed when he was good and ready. Instead, I saw something in his face shift. With the assistance of his cane, he rose. "Thank you, my dear," he said, and I wasn't certain which of us he was speaking to. Anya took his arm—was it protectiveness or possessiveness?—and ushered him out of the office. Later, when I asked Ralph about this, he said, "He knows it's important to her to look out for him."

*****

After Julian left, the office felt strangely silent even though he'd made so little noise. I pondered the idea that he visited with Meredith here. Was her spirit lingering? Could I visit with her, too?

"Hello?" I ventured. I waited for some sort of response—a sound, a feeling, the supernatural movement of something in the room—but if she was here, she gave no sign. "Are you here?" I asked after a few minutes. Still nothing. "If you're here, I need to talk with you. I don't know if you've noticed, but I could use a little help. So could your son." If she wasn't inclined to show up for me, maybe she'd make an effort for Ralph.

Apparently, she didn't feel like talking about my husband, either, because the room remained still. "Fine," I snapped. "Ignore us. Do what you want." I swiveled to face the computer and clicked the mouse.

At once, the simple text on the screen turned into a jagged blaze of color. "What the—?" I clicked the mouse a few times to no avail. Tapping keys was equally ineffective. I knew the tricks when my own computer acted up, but I was hesitant to mess with an unfamiliar machine.

I thought briefly of calling Ralph, but he was no more tech-savvy than I was. The tech whizzes were Phil and Mitch. I opted for Mitch. "Hey, have you got a minute?" I asked when he picked up. "I think I did something to your mom's computer."

"I'll be right there."

A few minutes later, the elevator dinged, and Mitch opened the office door. "Why do you have the door closed?"

"Your pop and Anya closed it when they left."

He grunted; I couldn't tell whether he was acknowledging my explanation or doubting it. I stepped away from the desk chair, and Mitch seated himself. I reminded myself that he was barely more than a kid, and he'd just lost his mother. A little compassion was in order.

He pressed the power button on the tower. A few seconds later, the monitor went dark. He waited a minute, then turned it on. The computer started up as usual, going through its paces until it came to the home screen. He checked a few more things, then said, "Looks like you're all set."

"Thanks. Sorry to bother you. I didn't know what was happening." I wasn't about to tell him I'd been trying to talk to his dead mother when the computer went wacko.

"If it happens again, have Phil take a look at it. He knows more about the system than I do." He didn't look at me as he said it.

"Okay. I—I didn't want to bother him." Mitch raised an eyebrow, and I decided to take the chance. "Does he blame me? Phil, I mean. About Isabella."

Mitch's brow furrowed. "Why would he?"

"Because—I don't know. Because she's staying in my house." *Because I'm the reason she was able to leave after the funeral. Because I know she's been screwing around and I didn't kick her out. Because I haven't told anyone what's going on.*

"It's not your fault." His words were neither kind nor unkind. "Looks like you're all set here. Have a good night." He left, and I sank into the chair.

"Sorry," I said to the computer. The screen remained blank. After a minute, I turned off the monitor and picked up the tray. At the door, I paused, but if Meredith was sending messages, they were not directed to me, so I flipped off the light and pushed the button for the elevator.

Forty-One

It turns out that life really does go on. Weddings, births, deaths—no matter what does or doesn't happen, daily life still requires attention.

For the first three months after Meredith's death, everybody struggled. Julian had it hardest, of course, although you wouldn't have known it unless you happened to catch one of those moments where he looked wistful, as if he was seeing a place far away, somewhere beautiful that he'd never visit again. The boys tried to be very stiff-upper-lip, the way their mother would have been if it had been Julian who died, but they weren't nearly as good at it. Especially within the family, tempers were short in a way I'd never known at the Pole. More than once, I had to intervene to prevent the brothers from coming to blows. I didn't know whether it was that I was still an outsider for all practical purposes and so I didn't inspire painful connections, or whether I'd had enough experience defusing hostile exchanges in my divorce practice, but for some reason, when I stepped into the fray, I could get the boys to back off enough to eliminate the present danger.

It wasn't just the family, of course. The entire community grieved. Meredith's hand had steadied the Pole. I'd never quite realized how much comfort can be found in organization, in having all the logistics in place, knowing the details are being handled properly.

As much as possible, I made a point of getting out of the office and walking through the various workplaces. Not everyone was happy with my presence, because my being there meant Meredith wasn't. I suggested that the elves call me Meg instead of Mrs. Claus, but far from making the transition easier, the idea of abandoning this cherished way of addressing Santa's wife caused the elves more distress.

Recalling Owen's advice about not shaking things up, I backed off, steadfastly smiling and greeting everyone who said, "Good morning, Mrs. Claus." And slowly, as I kept showing up, the atmosphere became less fraught, more normal.

The one who worried me the most was Ralph, because he was doing the same thing I was, namely, making sure everybody else was okay. The difference was that I'd lost a relatively recent presence in my life, while he'd lost his mother. Still, he poured himself into the family and the community, chatting and telling jokes at some times and letting them grieve at other times. He was especially vigilant about his father, going daily to Julian's apartment for meals or just to sit with him.

That was the public Ralph, and I expected no less. But in private, when it was just the two of us, he seemed reluctant to let me see anything different. We'd canceled our honeymoon even though Tillie urged me privately to take Ralph and get away for a while. "He's had two of the biggest life changes anybody can," she said. "He needs a break."

"I know," I said. "But he won't leave. It's like he's afraid to take his hands off the reins."

"He probably is. I know Julian's told him you two should take a vacation, but Ralph said there was too much to do."

"There's always too much to do. That's just how it is up here. Even I know that." Although if Meredith had still been here to run the Pole, Ralph and I could easily have slipped away for a couple of weeks in the Caribbean.

"Well, do what you can. I'll try to get his brothers to talk to him." She gathered up her organizational binder, petted Lulu who was curled up in the other wing chair, and slipped out of the office.

*****

A few days later, when I went back to the apartment to change my sweater, I found Ralph in the kitchenette. My stomach clutched. Ralph never came back to the apartment during the day. Half-afraid of the answer, I asked, "Are you okay?"

Because even though Ralph still remained aggressively cheerful even in the privacy of our home, something about his posture seemed . . . different. As if the load he'd been carrying for so long was finally overwhelming him.

"Sure, I'm fine." Except I'd never seen him so focused on adding sugar to his coffee.

"Hey." I rested my hand on his arm. He didn't look at me. I waited.

His hands stilled. Then, he snapped, "What do you *want* from me!" He shook my hand loose, splashing coffee all over the counter. He gripped the counter edge, his knuckles white.

I placed a tentative hand on his back. Beneath my touch, he was rigid, trembling. Slowly, lightly, I began to move my hand, stroking his back in large circles. His shoulders began to shake. He clenched his jaw. Tears began to spill over.

Gently, I turned him to face me. Nothing was hidden now. He released the counter and grabbed me, sobs breaking out. For the first time since Meredith's death, my husband wept.

Finally, his sobs stilled. He lifted his face, smeared with tears and snot, from my shoulder. "I'm sorry," he began, but I put my finger on his lips. He kissed it. Then, his lips met mine, and passion and grief combined in a storm.

Eventually, we lay quietly, arms intertwined. Tears slipped down his face. I kissed his damp cheek.

"What time is it?" he asked.

I craned my neck. "Five-thirty."

"We should get up. We're going to miss supper."

"Annaliese will save us something." I rolled over to get my phone.

"No. We should show up." He kissed my forehead and got out of bed.

I wanted to stay where we were, alone in our private world, but I knew my job. More importantly, I knew Ralph's job: to be the strong one, the leader, the one everyone else leaned on. My job was to stand with him, to be his right hand, to comfort those who might not want to appear weak to Santa.

So, I got out of bed and put on my clothes. I was about to open the door when Ralph stopped me. Once more, I saw the pain in his eyes. I laid my hand on his cheek. We kissed, straightened our shoulders, and headed out to resume our roles as everyone else's comfort.

Forty-Two

The next morning, an idea occurred to me. After breakfast, I went to Tillie's apartment and outlined my thoughts. She beamed as she produced a diagram of all the interior spaces at the Pole. We pored over the diagram for nearly an hour, debating, before we set out for an in-person evaluation of a medium-sized room located near the elevator.

"This could work," Tillie said. "This could definitely work."

"Don't tell anybody," I cautioned. "I want it to be a surprise."

The elves we recruited were sworn to secrecy. It took some fancy maneuvering to sneak supplies out of the workshops. "I'll make it up to Fred," I promised when Tillie looked concerned.

"Where were you last night?" Ralph asked two weeks later. "I couldn't find you."

"Just . . . doing something." I busied myself washing leftover food scraps out of the cat dishes. "Hey, guys, it's time to feed the cats!"

I could feel Ralph's eyes on me as I made a huge show of putting down cat food and stroking my babies. I pretended not to notice, putting on the electric kettle for tea and slipping past him to the bathroom. As I showered, I wondered whether I should tell him what I was doing. Part of me wanted to tell him, to share my excitement, but the other part wanted to surprise him. When I emerged from the bathroom, he was already gone, and so the part that wanted to keep my secret won.

Over dinner, Ted said casually, "Has anybody seen the lumber that was in the supply warehouse? I need to fix a couple of stalls, but it's not there."

"I haven't been in the supply warehouse in ages," I said honestly.

A pair of elves had procured the necessary lumber four days earlier.

"Weirdest thing," said Fred. "I was going to storage yesterday, and I'd have sworn I smelled paint."

"The hallways needed painting," I said. "Haven't you noticed? They're looking pretty dingy."

"Claire hasn't mentioned anything about that," said Ted.

"She probably just forgot," I said, rising. "After all, she's got her hands full with the baby."

"Where are you going?" asked Ralph.

"I've got some stuff to do," I said as innocently as possible. "I'll be home later. Bye!" I kissed him and whisked my tray over to the drop-off spot. We had a lot to finish before my team could return to the workshop.

When I reached the room, the elves were hard at work and the door was open. "Paint fumes," explained Regina, one of our most talented artists. Normally, she did delicate work on doll faces. Now, she was painting the sign for the room.

"Is that okay? Should we close the door?" Thomas was barely fourteen. He'd only been working under Fred for a few months, and practically any minor change in routine could rattle him.

"Leave it open," I assured him. "Are the shelves dry?"

"Perfect," pronounced Tyler, Thomas's twin brother. I ran my hand over the glossy red shelves. I turned to see Tyler watching me. I smiled and nodded, and a wide grin crossed his face.

"Let's get to work!" Tyler said, but Thomas was already opening boxes.

The next morning at breakfast, I stood up. "I have an announcement." The brothers exchanged glances. The elves appeared curious. "I would like for all of you to come to the elevator at noon."

"For what?" an older elf asked.

"It's a surprise," said Tyler. Beside him, Thomas fidgeted with excitement. Across the room, Regina caught my eye and smiled.

I'd forgotten how many people were actually at the Pole. At five minutes to noon, I disembarked from the elevator into a hallway that was crowded as far I could see. Smiling, I made my way through a crowd of people whose heads were barely as high as my breasts.

Along the edges of the hallway, the Clauses stood, waiting. The slightest crinkle between Ralph's eyes evidenced his curiosity. "Hi, everybody! Thanks for coming!" I gestured to my team to come to the front. "I know you all have a lot to do, so I won't waste time. Allow me to introduce you to the official Meredith Claus Memorial Library!" On cue, Tillie opened the door from inside, and those at the front pushed to get inside.

The room formerly used as storage was now bright and welcoming. In addition to the new bookshelves, the library contained two tables with chairs as well as two floor lamps and a cluster of armchairs we'd found in the storage warehouse. Practically nothing matched, but somehow, it all worked together. Not that it seemed to matter to the elves, who chattered excitedly as they examined the books on the long shelves and the DVDs and CDs on the narrower shelves at the far end. Next to the check-out desk, rows of lower shelves contained not only my childhood books, but children's books Holly had donated.

"Check out your materials at the desk where Tillie is!" I called out over the hubbub. Above the desk, Regina's beautifully-painted sign proclaimed, "CHECK OUT HERE". My heart swelled as I watched elves clutching the books and movies and music I'd brought up from home. Tillie logged each borrower's name and what they'd borrowed into the laptop I once used to take notes at depositions and off-site meetings, and library patrons bubbled with glee as they emerged into the hall, showing each other their new treasures.

"Pretty nice, Meg," said Fred. The other brothers murmured their assent.

Mitch leaned over, his mouth close to my ear. "Any chance you brought up any adult movies? Let's face it—you owe me." Ralph's youngest brother had kept my secret, making a fast trip to Connecticut to collect from Holly the boxes of children's books left over from when her kids were young.

I smacked the back of his head lightly. "Shame on you, young man. This is the North Pole. Go check out the collection. I think *Mary Poppins* may still be on the shelf."

From behind me, Ralph wrapped his arms around me. "You're amazing," he said. "What made you think of this?"

"I always loved my library at home," I began. Then I turned around as the truth dawned. "You knew what was going on the whole time, didn't you?"

His eyes were round and innocent. "What makes you think that?"

"You're Santa. You know everything that goes on here." I felt my excitement deflate. Of course, he knew. I hadn't surprised him at all.

Without regard to the people still milling about, Ralph kissed me. "It doesn't matter," he said. "What matters is that you did this. You organized it, and you donated your own books and movies so everyone could enjoy them." He kissed me again. "You're incredible, Mrs. Claus," he whispered, his breath warm against my ear.

Forty-Three

When I walked into the dining room the next morning, the tension was palpable. Ralph was already at the Claus table, his countenance grim. All he had before him was a mug of coffee.

"What's going on?" I asked. "I woke up and you were gone."

He shook his head slightly. I understood: whatever it was, he didn't want to talk about it here or now. Except considering the way the elves were whispering and glancing in our direction, it appeared that whatever the mystery was, they'd already gotten wind of it.

"Where's everybody else?" Normally at this hour, the brothers were gathered around the table.

Again, he shook his head.

My heart began to pound. "Is everything okay? Is Julian okay?" Except he must be, because otherwise, Ralph would be firmly rooted at his bedside.

"Later," was all he said.

I looked around the room. Everyone who was looking in our direction immediately turned away. "Are you okay?"

He rose abruptly. "Come with me." I thought of protesting that I hadn't yet had anything to eat, but it was clear that the situation—whatever it was—was dire.

I followed Ralph out of the dining room. He spoke not a word the entire way back to our apartment. Only after I closed the door behind us did he turn around, his eyes dark with misery.

"Isabella's having an affair," he said.

Visions of Tristan in my kitchen in a towel flooded my mind's eye. "Are you sure?"

"She told Phil."

Damn. "When?" I managed.

"Last night. Late. You were already asleep when he came down. Poor guy's devastated."

I cast about for something neutral to say. "Does everybody know?"

"The family does. The others know something's up."

I sank into the armchair. "What's he going to do?"

"No idea. Last night, he was talking about going down to Connecticut. I don't know if that's still the plan. The girls were trying to talk him out of it."

Interesting that Claire and Anya didn't want him to go to her. "Why?"

"Who knows? Maybe they think he'd look pathetic."

Or maybe they hadn't still forgiven her for going back after Meredith's death, and the affair was adding fuel to that fire. I said, "That's stupid. If he wants to talk to her in person, he should go," even as I realized that if he went to Connecticut, it would likely take about two minutes before he figured out that I'd known about Tristan since last summer.

"That's what I said. I think he's just so stunned he doesn't know what to do. Can't blame him for that. I can't imagine what I'd do if. . . ." His voice trailed off.

Lacking anything useful to say, I went to the kitchenette to make tea. I filled the electric kettle and clicked it on. Then, I busied myself choosing a mug, selecting a tea, getting out the filter and sweetener and a spoon. Anything to avoid where this conversation felt as if it was headed. I watched the kettle until it boiled, then poured water over the tea in the filter, splashing a bit on the counter. "You want some tea? Coffee? Anything?"

"Huh-uh." He paced as I leaned against the counter. "I just can't believe it," he said over and over. "She was supposed to be trying to be a musician. I mean, what the hell happened?" It didn't sound as if he was talking to me, so I held my tongue as he continued, "Doesn't she care anything about her husband? Her marriage? Their life?" His last words were practically a roar.

"What did she say about—the guy? Does she want a divorce?"

"I don't think she knows what she wants. According to Phil, she had to tell him because she felt so guilty."

I recalled Holly's advice after the drunken incident with Scott. This was what she meant when she said to keep it to myself. Hurting the person you loved just to assuage your own conscience was cruel, I realized. "Did she say if the affair is over?"

"I don't know. She should be more worried about whether her marriage is over." He turned and peered at me. For a second, I thought he could see into my guilty heart. "Hey, can you help him out? Maybe talk to him about what getting a divorce involves?"

"Me?"

"You know more than anybody else about that stuff."

"I know Connecticut divorce law. I don't know how you do it up here."

"That's because we never have. Around here, marriage vows mean something. I don't know. I just—he's my brother. I don't want to see him hurt any more."

"I understand." I put my arms around Ralph. "I'll talk to him if he wants, but I don't think this is the time. He's had a huge shock. I can't imagine he's in any shape to be making any major decisions." I kissed his neck. "Besides, people get through infidelity. I've had cases where the couple's been at each others' throats for a year and both of them are with other people, and then I get a call one day that they want to withdraw the divorce action because they're reconciling." I caressed his cheek. "People forgive all sorts of things. Phil's gotten hit by a train. It's not the time to do anything."

Ralph kissed me. "You're right, I know. I just want to fix something for him. If you'd heard him last night—he said she kept talking about how they're separated, and he was like, 'Well, yeah, you're there and I'm here,' and she kept saying, 'Not that kind of separated,' and he had no idea what she was talking about."

I turned back to the counter to remove the tea filter from the mug and add the sweetener. Unlike Phil, I knew what she meant. Legal separation is often the prelude to divorce. I could say honestly that I'd never counseled her about separation or divorce, but I couldn't imagine that would be much comfort to Phil.

A thought jolted my brain enough that my hand shook and tea spilled. What if Isabella told Phil that I knew about Tristan? I knew, and I didn't say anything to anybody—not Phil, not Ralph. Although for all I knew, she'd been sneaking men in and out of my condo every time I was up at the Pole, and Tristan was merely the first one I'd caught.

Ralph continued, "She says she didn't mean to fall for this Simon idiot, things just happened."

"Simon?" Who the hell was Simon? What happened to Tristan? Or was she seeing both of them?

"That's what she said. You know him?"

"Never heard of him," I said honestly.

Just then, my phone rang. I grabbed it before Ralph could ask who was calling. "Hello?"

"Meg? It's me." Isabella sounded as if she were sobbing.

I glanced at Ralph. The question in his eyes was clear, and I nodded. His jaw clenched; so did his fists. I put my hand over the speaker. "Go to Phil. I'll talk to her." He hesitated, and I waved him off. "Go." I waited until the door had closed behind him before speaking. "What the hell did you do?"

"I—I—" She dissolved into tears. "I didn't mean to—I thought—"

"No. You didn't think. Who the hell is Simon?"

"He plays the oboe—"

"I don't give a shit what he plays. WHO THE FUCKING HELL IS SIMON?" So much for keeping my cool.

"I'm telling you—he's an oboist, and I met him at a rehearsal for—"

"Jesus, Mary, and Joseph! I'm asking, who is Simon *to you*? Are you in love with him? Who is he that you suddenly felt the need to call your husband and rip his world apart?"

"I figured you of all people would understand!"

"What? Why would you think that?"

"Because of that Scott guy."

Ice ran through my veins. "That was entirely different."

"Oh, really?"

"Ralph and I weren't married. More importantly, I never slept with Scott. I haven't had sex with anybody except Ralph ever since we got together."

"But you went out with him, and you made out with him," Isabella pointed out.

"You really think a drunken kiss is the same thing as having an affair? Or should I say, *affairs*. Because Simon makes—how many now?"

"You don't know what you're talking about!"

"Don't I? Let's see. There was Tristan, and now there's Simon. How many others have there been, Iz? What have you been doing since I've been up here?"

"My private life is none of your business!" Her voice was shrill.

"It is when it's parading naked through my kitchen," I snapped. "And it is when it's ripping apart my family."

"They're my family, too!"

"Really? Because you're sure as hell not acting like it!" I took a deep breath to try to calm down. "Listen to me, Iz. You went down there because you wanted to be a musician—"

"—I *am* being a musician!"

"You're a married woman living in my home. I told you before: you do not have permission to bring overnight guests in. You do it again, and I'll kick your ass out. Let Simon take care of you." Not that I'd ever know. Rodrigo and Samson wouldn't snitch even if I asked them to, and I wouldn't anyway. Still, she didn't have to know that. Let her sweat.

"I thought you of all people would understand," she snapped. "Looks like I was wrong." She clicked off before I could answer.

Forty-Four

A few days later, as I made coffee and tea, I said, "I think I should go to Connecticut." When Ralph raised an eyebrow, I said, "Maybe I can talk to Isabella." I hadn't heard from her since our phone conversation. If Phil had been in touch with her, Ralph hadn't mentioned it.

"When?" He set mugs on the counter and picked up the cat dishes.

"Some time next week, maybe. I've got stuff to do before I go. Hang on, guys, your food's coming." As the water heated and the coffee perked, I opened a can of cat food and distributed it among the dishes. "How long does it take Ted to do a flight plan?"

"Not long. Just tell him when you want to go and he'll get it ready." Ralph set the dishes on the floor, and the cats dug into their breakfast. I poured coffee into one of my old commuter mugs and handed it to him, and he gave me a thank-you kiss, adding, "I've got to get to work. Let me know when you've got a plan."

"Will do." We kissed again, and he petted the cats before heading out the door.

I went to the dining hall, got my breakfast, and joined the brothers. Phil wasn't there. The other three grunted drowsy greetings and continued eating. "Ted, I need to go down to Connecticut," I said. "Some time next week. Thursday, maybe. Can somebody run me down there?"

He didn't look surprised, but then, Ted never did. He was the most unflappable person I'd ever met. If I'd said I needed to go to Peru to check out the rainforests, I'd likely have gotten exactly the same reaction. He just looked from one brother to another. "Either of you got time?"

"I can go," said Mitch. "Friday instead of Thursday okay?"

"Works for me," I said. "Thanks." Another grunt, and the brothers returned their full attention to their oatmeal.

When I was finished, I returned my tray and dishes with every intention of heading to the office for a few hours. Instead, I headed to the computer room.

Phil's lair was unquestionably the warmest place at the Pole, courtesy of all the electronics generating heat. When I opened the door, I didn't even notice him at first. His setup included three enormous monitors, all of which bore what appeared to be documents with lines and lines of numbers. Whether they were equations, calculations, records, or something else entirely, I had no idea. He was facing the monitors, his back to me. "Hey," I said.

"Hey," Phil responded without turning around.

"Can we talk?"

He swiveled in his chair. Behind his dark-rimmed glasses, his green eyes were impossible to read. "Go ahead."

"Just wanted to see how you're doing," I said.

"I feel like somebody reached down my throat and ripped my guts out." His voice was toneless. His neutral expression didn't change. Only the tense set of his shoulders gave the slightest hint of his feelings. Watching him, I was reminded of Meredith's tight self-control.

"I was thinking I could go down to Connecticut next week. I could talk to Isabella. See if I can make her see reason." Part of me wanted to ask what he thought of the plan, but I sensed it would be fruitless. He might confide in his father or big brother, but not me. Not the newcomer who sat at his mother's desk, doing his mother's work.

Sure enough, all he said was, "Do what you want. It won't help." He turned back to his monitors.

I stood helplessly, but I'd been dismissed. After a minute, I left, closing the door quietly behind me.

*****

On the following Friday morning, I was in my office when the desk phone rang. "Can you be ready to go at one?" asked Ted.

"Sure. Mitch is driving?"

"No. Me."

A surprising answer, but it wasn't my call. "Okay, I'll be ready." I hung up, logged out of my document, and went back to the apartment to pack.

I'd traveled with Ted before, and I knew he wasn't a talker, so I tucked a book and earbuds into my bag. Sure enough, we were well over Canada before he spoke. "I could wring her neck," he said.

Surprising words from Ted, the mildest of the brothers. I'd long wondered if he was so easygoing because he had to speak to the animals in such soothing, calming tones or if he worked with the animals because he was naturally soothing and calming.

"Killing people isn't good," I said. "Especially if you think about it in advance, because then it's premeditated. As your legal counsel, I advise against it."

My attempted joke fell flat. "I knew this wasn't going to work," he muttered.

"What wasn't?"

"Her going down below for the cello thing. I knew all that fancy living would turn her head."

"It's not so much fancy as different. She needs to try stuff so she can make an informed decision."

"She doesn't need to screw every guy she meets. She's a married woman."

I couldn't argue with that. "Maybe they should have laid down some ground rules before she left."

"They did. They're called marriage vows. Forsaking all others, that kind of thing."

Again, I couldn't argue. "Maybe this is something she needs to get out of her system. She was what, eighteen when she moved to the Pole? That's ridiculously young to get married. If my kid came to me at eighteen and said she wanted to get married, I'd lock her in a closet until it passed."

"If any of my kids try to get married before they're twenty-five, they'll be mucking out stalls twenty-four/seven for a year."

"To be honest, I'm not even certain twenty-five is old enough. So much of it depends on the person."

"I was twenty-five," he said as if that settled the matter.

"I don't think the issue is age. I've done plenty of divorces with people who married in their late twenties, thirties, or even later. I think it's about maturity. She was a child when she got married. It's no wonder she's going a little crazy with all this freedom."

"Don't make excuses for her." It was the closest I'd ever heard Ted come to snapping.

"I'm not making excuses. I'm trying to figure out how this happened so we can try to undo it."

"What makes you think you can get her to come home? Assuming Phil even wants her back."

"I think he does." I thought of Phil in his lair, pain radiating from him like heat radiating from his electronics. "But he's a proud man. He's not going to beg."

Ted shot me a look. I couldn't tell whether he was surprised that I'd nailed his brother's personality so quickly or if he was wondering how Ralph ended up with such a ditz. "He'll be fine without her."

"Does he want to be?"

Another sidewise look. "Dunno."

"I'll see what I can do to talk some sense into her. Then, the two of them can make their own decisions about what they want."

"How do you plan to do that?"

"I've worked with a lot of divorcing couples. Trust me, I've learned a thing or two about what people care about when they're splitting up."

Three hours later, Ted brought the sleigh down in Sandy's pasture in Marlborough. "How're you going to get home?"

"I'll call Holly. If she's not available, I'll get an Uber."

"Why not call Isabella? Make her do some of the work."

"I'm not sure I want to let her know I'm here." I checked my phone, which had reverted to Eastern Daylight Saving Time. It was 4:47 p.m. I texted Holly. Moments later, I got a reply: *Just leaving the office. Will be there in half an hour.* "Holly's coming. You can head back."

"No," said Ted. "I want to talk to her."

"Holly?"

"Isabella."

"I'm not sure that's a good idea. At least, not now. If she thinks we're ganging up on her, she's liable to get defensive."

"He's my brother. If she's going to dump him for some pretty boy, she can tell me in person."

"What are you going to do with the sleigh?"

He glanced over to the barn. "Can your friend store it overnight? Maybe give the reindeer some grain?"

It was my turn to hesitate. "Let me ask." I trudged up the dirt road to the barn, praying Sandy would be out somewhere. Unfortunately, she was mucking out stalls when I entered the cool semi-dusk of the barn.

"Hey, Meg," she said. "You need to park?"

"Not quite that easy. Any chance you have an empty pasture I can rent for the night?"

"An empty pasture?"

"I've got a couple of—livestock. They'll need some water and grain, too."

"They don't graze?"

I had no idea. "I was told grain, but maybe."

She set down her shovel. "Come on." She hoisted a wheelbarrow full of manure, and I followed her out to where she dumped it at the base of an enormous pile. "See over there?" She pointed to a white fence bordering the pasture from which we routinely came and went. "You can pasture them there. Water trough should be full, but you'll want to check. Grain's in the barn. You'll want the cart." The farm had a little motorized two-seat cart, like a golf cart except not nearly as fancy. On more than one occasion, I'd seen one of her teenage children driving it across a pasture.

"Great. How much?"

"How many?"

"Just two. As I said, overnight. Out of here tomorrow. And there's a—conveyance."

She regarded me. "Put it in the far corner. I'll give you a tarp to cover it."

"Thanks. What do I owe you?"

"Fifty. Covers everything."

"I'll get my purse. It's in the—conveyance."

"I'll be in the barn." She wheeled the wheelbarrow back, and I jogged back to the field to let Ted know about the arrangements.

By the time Holly arrived, Ted and I were seated on the bench next to the barn. The reindeer were enjoying their dinner in the far pasture, and we had maneuvered the sleigh to the farthest corner and covered it with a brown tarp. "Tell me something," I said as Holly's car approached. "Does Sandy know who you guys are?"

"I don't know. Why?"

"Just wondering. She never asks any questions, but I'm sure she's going to take a look at who's in her pasture tonight."

Ted shrugged. "It's her pasture. I'm sure she's seen us coming and going over the years, but she's never breathed a word that I know of."

I contemplated this as Holly pulled in. Maybe Sandy subscribed to the philosophy of live and let live. Maybe she was a big fan of privacy.

Or maybe she knew more than she was letting on.

*****

"So, what brings you guys down here?" asked Holly as we sped up Route 2.

"Family stuff," I said. She glanced in the rearview mirror at me. I casually placed my index finger against my lips for a second. "Speaking of, how are the kids?"

"Amy has a new boyfriend," said Holly. "Seems like a nice guy. He's applying to pharmacy school, so a lot could change. She could end up being the breadwinner for a couple years."

"They're living together?"

"I know, it was fast. I tried to tell her to wait, but they're madly in loooove." She drew out the word to underscore its ridiculousness. A few minutes later, she exited the highway and maneuvered through the streets to my complex. As we approached my condo, she asked, "Whose car is that?"

A shiny silver BMW sat in my driveway. Playing the oboe must pay well. I resisted the urge to mutter a string of obscenities directed at the rich son of a bitch who was screwing with the lives of my brother-in-law, his wife, and my family.

We pulled up to the curb. "Do you want to come in?" I asked.

"You tell me," Holly said.

"I don't think so," said Ted before I could speak.

I raised my eyebrows. "This is my home. I make the decisions here. And this is my best friend. You will be polite. Are we clear?"

"It's my brother," he retorted.

"And it's my home. Come on in," I added to Holly. I led the way to the front door, and we all went inside. "Hey!" I shouted. "Iz! Are you here?" I heard no cello. Mentally crossing my fingers, I said, "She may be at rehearsal."

"Stop covering for her," Ted muttered. Definitely not the forgiving type.

I texted Isabella: *Where are you? We need to talk. I'm at the house.* "Anybody want anything to drink?" I opened my refrigerator, but it contained only three eggs, an opened container of half-and-half, and a nearly-empty bottle of chardonnay. On top of everything else, this Simon was a freeloader.

Ted peered over my shoulder. "Do you have anything else?"

I opened the freezer. Two pints of ice cream and a bottle of vodka. "Nope."

"We could go out to dinner," Holly said in her sunny mommy-voice.

Thank you, I mouthed. I was eternally grateful to her for not leaving me alone with Ted. I'd always liked the guy, but he was not a fun date tonight.

A thought flashed through my mind. "I'll be right back," I said. I darted down the hall and opened the door to the garage.

The Beamer was in my driveway, but my own car was gone. In other words, Simon didn't want anybody to see him with Isabella in his car. Slimier and slimier, to paraphrase Alice in her Wonderland.

My phone dinged. It was a text from Isabella. *Hey Meg, didn't know you were coming tonight, we need to talk.* Exactly what I had said to her. I couldn't tell if she'd ignored the content of my text or if she was trying to get ahead of the conversation.

Agreed, I texted back. *What time will you and my car be home?* I wasn't about to let her feel comfortable with the current state of affairs.

"Is that her?" called Ted, who'd clearly heard the text ping.

Without answering, I strolled back into the kitchen where Holly was rummaging in my cabinets. Ted looked pissed off and started tapping something into his phone. I suggested, "You might do well to wait until you actually know something." He glanced up briefly to glare at me before he continued tapping.

My text pinged again. "Is that her?" he demanded. He reached for my phone, and I held it away.

"This is my phone, not yours. Hands off." I turned my back to him to read the text. It was from Ralph: *Everything okay?*

Okay is a relative concept, I texted back. *Will advise when I know what's going on. Love you.* He responded with three hearts, the emoji version of *love you more.*

I watched Ted pace the way his big brother did. Clearly, it was a Claus thing. I thought about Phil back at the Pole. And I thought about Ralph, who was trusting me to do what was necessary. How incredibly fortunate I was to have a husband who believed in me and my judgment. I closed my eyes for a moment, giving thanks to the universe for someone who might not know what I was doing, but who would stand beside me regardless.

Still no Isabella. Finally, I said, "I don't know when we'll see her. Let's get something to eat. Maybe she'll be here when we get back."

"Does she know I'm here?" Clearly—and not unreasonably—Ted suspected that his presence might discourage her from returning.

"I don't know how she would," I said. "Unless Phil's been in touch with her."

"I doubt that," Ted snorted.

Holly looked puzzled. "They may be splitting up," I said before Ted could say anything.

"Crap, I'm sorry," said Holly.

"Holly is divorced," I said before Ted could complain about my revealing Phil's secret.

"So I've been down that road," said Holly. "Anything your brother wants to know, tell him to give me a shout."

"That's very kind of you," Ted said through clenched teeth.

"Whose idea is it? Isabella's?" Holly asked. Ted nodded. "Sorry, but I can't say I'm shocked. Getting married young is *so* not a good idea."

"My mother was nineteen when she and my father got married," Ted said stiffly.

"Your mother was a very unusual woman," I said. "Marriage requires a level of maturity that most eighteen-year-olds lack."

"If Isabella wasn't mature enough to get married, she shouldn't have gotten married," said Ted.

"Sheesh, judge much?" Holly said. "I mean, correct me if I'm wrong, but wasn't it your brother who did the proposing? He must have thought she was mature enough for marriage."

"Enough," I said before the argument could escalate further. I checked my phone. Still no response about what time she'd be home. "I vote we get something to eat. It doesn't look as if she'll be back before dinner, and I for one am hungry."

"With you on that," said Holly before Ted could vote it down. "Chinese?"

"Perfect." Without a glance at Ted, I picked up my purse and headed for the door.

Forty-Five

Two hours later, we returned to find the silver BMW gone. Another strike against Simon: he was a coward. A guy who was going to leave Isabella to face the music alone was one she should dump immediately.

I unlocked the door. Cello music drifted down from upstairs. "We're back!"

The cello stopped. Moments later, footsteps descended the stairs. "Hey, Meg, I'm gl—" She broke off as she saw Ted and Holly. "Hey," she said, her voice fading.

"We need to talk," said Ted.

"*We* need to talk," I corrected him in my firmest lawyer voice. "You two need to go out for a while." It was not a request.

Ted looked uncertain. Holly took advantage of the moment to grab his arm. "Come on, let's go." She half-dragged him out the door as he stammered, "But—but—"

I ushered Isabella into the living room. "Sit down." With uncharacteristic obedience, she sat. "So, what's going on? Are you and Phil splitting up?"

"I'm—I don't know. Maybe."

"I thought you wanted to come home."

"I know, but—I don't know, Meg, I'm so mixed up. I thought I was ready to go back to the Pole, but then I met this guy, and he's so amazing—he's smart and funny and so good-looking, and he wants to be with me—"

"Your husband wants to be with you."

"I know, and I want to be with him, but it's not that easy. I mean, I really *want* to want to go back, to pick up where we left off, but I don't know if I can."

"I'll save you some time: you can't. You aren't the same person you were when you left. You've had all these experiences, all this time to think about things you never thought about before. You and Phil need to figure out a new way to be together."

"That's one of the things that scares me. What if I can't be what he wants me to be anymore? I mean, he wanted me to be a wife and to work for the family business and play my cello by myself in my spare time, but the world is bigger than that. I know that now."

"Have you been in touch with your family since you've been down here? I mean your parents. That family."

"I've talked to my mom a couple times. She's not much help. She always thought I was too young to get married. Plus, she thought I was crazy to marry a guy who lived at the North Pole. She was even trying to talk me out of it on my wedding day."

"Was she that devoted to your becoming a musician?"

"Not really. I mean, she liked the idea, but she hated listening to me practice all the time. When I lived at home, she had the basement finished and soundproofed so I could play whenever I wanted without bothering her. I think the main reason she was happy about Juilliard was because she wanted me to play somewhere else."

"What about your dad?"

"He left when I was seven. He has a whole new family now. They send me birthday cards a month late." Bitterness tinged her voice. "When I met Phil's family, I couldn't believe how different they were from mine. They really seemed to love me, right from the start. Even his mom, and you know she wasn't a real warm, fuzzy type." The understatement of the year. "Sometimes I wonder if I fell in love with Phil or with his family, with their whole way of being together. I mean, sure, they fight and all, but they really seem to like each other. You could picture them all hanging out and being friends even if they weren't related."

I knew exactly what she meant. The Clauses were unusual. I'd met very few families who were that cohesive. Divorcing Phil would mean leaving all that harmony. "Sounds like something you need to figure out," I said gently. "It's not fair to Phil for you to come back to him if what you really want is his family. He's a good guy. He deserves better than that."

"He's a great guy," Isabella corrected me. "He's the best. So sweet and kind and smart. He's the kind who'll take such good care of me."

"Do you love him?"

To her credit, she thought about the question. "I do," she said finally. "But I don't know if that's enough. I mean, look at you. You had a whole life before you went north. You had a career and boyfriends and everything, so you knew what you were giving up. I'm just starting to find that out. I'm afraid that if I go back now, some part of me will resent him—or maybe all of them—for keeping me from finding out what life would have been like in the real world."

It was a variation on a theme I'd heard hundreds of times from divorcing clients: FOMO. Fear of Missing Out. The fear that by choosing one thing, they were foreclosing another: *If I stay married, I won't get to do A or B or C. I won't get to have kids, or I'll have to have kids, or I'll never go back to college, or I'll never see Paris, or. . . .* Sometimes they were right. Some things, like wanting (or not wanting) children were generally dealbreakers. Other fears might arise from the parties' differing expectations of what marriage was supposed to look like. If the husband didn't want the wife to work outside the home, there could be a dozen reasons. Maybe his mother never held a job and the idea of his wife doing so was uncomfortable simply because it was different. Or maybe he held deeply-rooted beliefs about traditional gender roles, or he was insecure about his public image as the family breadwinner. It could be that he was proud of being able to provide for his wife, but it could also be that he felt threatened by her career and wanted to keep her in her place. The details changed, but part of my job—especially in a collaborative divorce—was to encourage the parties to listen carefully to each other's statements about what they wanted and why.

Of course, not having Phil here made it complicated. I knew—or at least, I assumed I knew—what he wanted: for Isabella to come home and life to go on as it had before. It was the same thing pretty much all the spouses on the receiving end of "I want a divorce" wanted. Even if the marriage wasn't perfect, they weren't ready for the seismic shift that came with becoming single again. I understood, and I sympathized. What could possibly be more devastating than having the person who promised to love and cherish you forever say, "Sorry, I changed my mind, I don't actually love you anymore"?

Except Isabella said she loved Phil. According to Ralph, Phil loved her. So?

"If what you want is to try to make your marriage work, the first thing you need to do is to stop seeing other men. As long as you're with Simon, your marriage doesn't have a chance."

Isabella bit her lip. "It's not Simon," she said in a voice so low I could barely hear her.

"Jesus, Mary, and Joseph! Who is it this time?" It hadn't even been two weeks since she'd upended Phil's life with her announcement about Simon. How many men was she dating?

"He's just a guy. We met last fall at a concert. After, actually—he was there with the violist, but it wasn't anything serious. He used to show up after rehearsal to pick her up, but that stopped a while back. Then the other night we were rehearsing and he came in to listen, and we all went out for drinks afterward, and he was so nice to everybody—one of the violinists was looking to upgrade their instrument, and he knows a guy who deals in strings and he said he'd hook her up. I think he said they'd worked together, or he knew him through work, or something—it doesn't matter. As we were leaving, he asked for my number."

"So you dumped Simon for this guy?"

"Simon and I were never really serious—"

"You were serious enough that you told your husband about him. That was less than two weeks ago. What the hell happened between then and now?" I could have choked her. Crime of passion. Not premeditated at all.

"I shouldn't have told him—I just felt so guilty—" Tears dripped down her cheeks.

"What you shouldn't have done was cheat on your husband." As if she didn't know.

"But I really like this guy. You should meet him. He's great. And he's so supportive. Did I tell you he's getting divorced? His ex has dragged him through the mud every way she can. It breaks my heart to hear him talk about it. She won't even let him see his kids except one night a week and every other weekend. Can you imagine?"

"Actually, that's pretty standard," I said. "He can call them between visits, can't he?"

"He could, but sometimes they won't even come to the phone! He says she's turning them against him, telling them they might have to move out of their house because he's not paying alimony and child support."

"Is he?"

"When he can! But he has a lot of expenses, and she even got part of his retirement account, so he can't draw against it."

"How old is he?" I had a sudden vision of Isabella with a septuagenarian.

"He's in his forties, so even if he did take money out of retirement, there'd be a huge penalty. He just got totally screwed." She sighed dramatically.

Nothing she'd described sounded at all atypical in a divorce. Clearly, this loser wanted somebody to whine to, and naïve Isabella had proven to be a perfect audience. In any case, his divorce wasn't the issue here.

Something occurred to me. "You're not expecting—are you thinking that if you and Phil split up, you'll get alimony?"

"Well, sure. I'm the wife. Besides, I gave up my career for him. So I should get alimony to help make up for that."

Mr. Divorce had been filling her head full of garbage. "News flash, sweetie. You left him, and you cheated on him—with at least three guys." She winced. I plowed on: "Most likely, you wouldn't get a dime. At most, you might get rehabilitative alimony for a year or two, tops." I wasn't being entirely candid with her. While she was definitely at fault, that wouldn't preclude a court from awarding her alimony since by getting married, she'd given up the opportunity to pursue her career. On the other hand, she hadn't even started school when they married, and a reasonable argument could be made that most musicians never made any kind of appreciable money. Any decent lawyer could argue that in coming to the Pole, she'd enjoyed a secure and comfortable lifestyle she'd never have realized if she'd gone into music.

Isabella frowned. I couldn't tell whether she was questioning her lover's advice or mine. I pressed on: "Since there's no question about adultery"—she flinched—"it's highly unlikely that you'd get much. Even if you could convince a court that it had jurisdiction over a guy who resides at the North Pole—and by the way, good luck with that—you'd need evidence that he owns property that could be identified as a marital asset."

"What's that?"

"Something that the divorce court can divide. Usually, it's something acquired during the marriage, like a house. Did you and Phil ever buy any property or anything together?"

She squinted, trying to remember. "No," she said finally. "When I moved in, everything was already there. The only big thing he ever bought while we were married was my cello." Her eyes grew softer. "It was our third anniversary. I had the cello I'd been playing since I was fourteen. It's a good one, but it's a student cello. Hardly anything to write home about. Phil bought me a Lawrence Wilke. That's the one I have now. I couldn't believe he did that—I think it went for, like, twenty-five thousand even back then. It was all the money he had. This cello is so amazing, so expressive. You can play it as soft as silk, or you can push it and really make a statement. It makes me sound a hundred times better than I really am. Every time I pick it up, it's like—it's the love of my life. I could lose everything else I have in the world, and I'll be okay as long as I have that cello."

"You know that since Phil spent all that money on your cello, he might get it back in the divorce." I kept my voice even.

Her eyes widened in horror. "No! He can't have it! It's mine!"

"I'm just saying. It's a marital asset. The judge can do whatever he likes with it. Give it to you or give it to Phil. He can even order it to be sold and you two divide the proceeds."

"No!" She was more agitated than in the entire conversation about divorce and adultery. "I am not giving up my cello. It's not going to be sold. Nothing is going to happen to it. It's mine!"

"I'm just saying—"

"It's MINE!" She flung herself out of her chair and raced up the stairs. A second later, her door slammed. Then, I heard faint music that might have been Dvorak's cello concerto in B minor.

Forty-Six

Half an hour later, I was watching *Frasier* reruns when Ted and Holly returned. "Well?" said Ted.

"Well what?"

"Did you talk sense into her?" he demanded. Behind him, Holly mouthed *goodbye* and wiggled her fingers as she slipped out the door.

I muted the television. It wasn't the moment to admit I might have made things the teensiest bit worse. "You do understand that this isn't something that's going to happen quickly, right? It's not a one-and-done kind of conversation. I laid some groundwork, gave her things to think about."

"I'm going to give her some things to think about." Ted started for the stairs.

"I wouldn't," I said, following. "You're only going to make it worse. She has to reach her decision on her own. If you haul her back against her will, she's not going to stay."

"She will if I don't give her a ride out of there," said the brother in charge of the stables.

"Is that really what you think—that you can force her to stay married? Is that what Phil wants? A wife who doesn't want to be married to him?"

"Phil wants his wife back," said Ted.

"Even if she doesn't want to be back? Or would Phil rather have a wife who actually wants to be with him?"

"Look, you don't know my brother—"

"True, but I've had a lot more experience with divorcing couples than either of you. Let me handle this."

Just then, Isabella came down the stairs. Ignoring Ted, she said, "Well, that's done."

"What's done?"

"I just gave away my cello."

"What?" Ted and I chorused.

"Meg said that if I got divorced, the judge could order me to give my cello to Phil, or make me sell it and split the money with him. So, I gave it away instead. Now, it's not mine, and the judge can't do a thing about it." She tossed her head in a *so, there!* gesture.

Ted glared at me. "This is your idea of handling it?"

"Everybody hold on for a minute." I looked up at Isabella. "Who did you give it to?"

"None of your business." Her smile was smug.

Technically, she was right, but I'd deposed enough recalcitrant witnesses to have a few tricks left. "Actually, it is," I lied. "Because I expect it's your most valuable possession, isn't it? If you intentionally gave away your most valuable possession—didn't sell it for fair market value to a disinterested buyer, but just gifted it to someone you know—its value can still be attributed to you, which means that when the judge decides whether you should get alimony, he can factor in you having that twenty-five thousand dollar asset." She looked uncertain, and I pressed on. "It's still upstairs, isn't it? You say you gave it away, but it's still in your possession, which is strong evidence that you didn't really give it to someone with the intent of surrendering all control over it forever. So don't try to sell anybody on this idea that you don't own that instrument anymore, because we're not buying."

"Are you seriously thinking of getting divorced?" Ted's voice was calmer now. Just as I was using my professional skills, he was using his. I recognized the tone he used with stubborn reindeer. Where the other brothers tended to fight them, he eased the reindeer into doing what he wanted. I didn't doubt he still had the temper he'd been displaying ever since we left the Pole, but he was reining it in now. "Is that truly what you want? To leave your husband for good? Never go back to the Pole? Never see your family again?"

The smug smile slipped into trembling. "I don't know," she admitted. "I don't know what I want. I need to figure it out."

"With another man?" The edge was back in Ted's voice, just barely.

Isabella shot a glance at me. I shook my head slightly to let her know that I hadn't told Ted how many men she'd slept with. "You don't understand," she said. "I was a baby when I got married. I've never experienced the world. That's what I'm doing now."

"I thought your whole experiencing-the-world thing was supposed to be about pursuing your music career. If you just gave away your cello, it's clear that's not what you want to do anymore. So I'm asking you: do you want to stay married to my brother? Do you love him? Because right now, it sure doesn't look like it." His voice might have been calm, but his words were like red-hot pokers. He'd have been a sensational lawyer.

Her eyes glistened. "I don't know," she whispered. "I don't know what I want."

"Don't you think you owe it to Phil to figure it out?"

"That's what I'm trying to do!" The tears spilled down her cheeks.

"By sleeping with another guy?" The edge in his voice was more pronounced. I touched his arm lightly, a signal to pull back.

"My private life is my business! How I work out my life and what I want is up to me! It has nothing to do with you! If Phil's so hot to talk to me, why are you here instead of him? He knows where I am."

It was a fair question, but before I could frame an answer, Ted spoke. "You broke his heart."

His words were simple, but as effective as a bullet aimed directly at her heart. For a long moment, Isabella stood frozen, her hand at her throat. Only the tears rolling down her cheeks moved. Her lips parted. Her round blue eyes remained fixed on a spot only she could see. Then, ever so slowly, she shook her head. "No," she whispered.

"Seriously, Iz, what did you think was going to happen?" I said. "Did you really think he'd just nod and smile and go along with whatever you were doing? He's your husband. You cheated on him. What was he supposed to do?"

"Does he want a divorce?" The words barely squeaked out.

Ted seemed as if he was about to speak, but I laid my hand on his arm to stop him. "I don't know," I said. "He hasn't said. I know he loves you, but I don't know if he's going to get over all this." I paused, then delivered the zinger: "It may be too late."

Her face crumbled. She whirled and ran up the stairs, slamming her door. Ted turned to me. "Now what?" he asked wearily.

"Now we wait," I said. "They both have decisions to make. I think the whole giving away the cello bit might have been her way of calling his bluff. I don't think it had ever occurred to her that he might want to unload her."

"He doesn't," said Ted. "He'd take her back in a heartbeat."

"Something nobody had better tell her," I said. "If she thinks she has the upper hand, she'll use it." I glanced up the stairs. "It wouldn't shock me if she's up there calling Phil right now." I saw him stifling a yawn. "I don't know about you, but I'm ready to call it a night. I'll make up the sofa for you." With any luck, Isabella's paramours hadn't used up all the spare toothbrushes I'd stashed in the guest bathroom.

Forty-Seven

After the lengthy trip and the evening's stress, I thought I'd fall asleep instantly, but I found myself lying awake long after all other sounds in the house ceased. It might have been the fact that I was alone—no Ralph, no cats—but there was more. I couldn't help feeling as if I was missing a very important piece of the puzzle. Finally, I rolled over and dialed Ralph.

"Hey, babe," he said. "I miss you. What time is it there?"

I looked at the large red numbers on the bedside clock. "A little after two in the morning. What about there?"

"Just after six."

"I'm sorry. I didn't mean to wake you."

"I was awake. The cats miss you."

"Just the cats?"

A warm, rich chuckle. "Maybe not just the cats. How're things going?"

"Not good," I admitted. "I don't know what's going to happen."

"Anything I can tell Phil?"

"Nothing that's going to make him happy. That's one screwed-up little diva. She kept talking about divorce, and when I tried to scare her by telling her Phil could end up getting her cello, she called her idiot boyfriend, who apparently told her the answer was to get rid of it, so she gave it to him."

"That cello? I remember when Phil was trying to find it. We had half the workshop on the hunt. It had to be just right."

"I don't know who this idiotic boyfriend is—apparently, it's some-body new, not even that Simon guy—but for some reason, she thinks he knows all about this stuff. Sounds like a damned fool to me. He's trying like hell to get her to divorce Phil, but if he's like the rest of them, he'll dump her as soon as she's free."

"The rest of who?"

I couldn't help chuckling. "I keep forgetting you haven't dated much. One of the downsides of being a woman dating in your thirties and forties is that most of the men have gone through divorces. A lot of them don't want a commitment. They want a woman they can chase without getting trapped, so they're all into her until her divorce is final. Then, they suddenly have tons of reasons why they can't get involved. It's so sad—these women think they're leaving one guy for another, and they end up all alone, trying to figure out what happened."

"And you think that's what's going to happen to Isabella?"

"I'd put money on it. My gut is that it's not that this guy wants her as much as he doesn't want Phil to have her. He supposedly wants her to be free, but I'm betting that the second she is, he heads for the hills—with the cello he convinced her to give him."

"What do we do?" asked Ralph after a long minute.

"Try to keep her from making any decisions," I said. "And if I can manage it, I'm bringing that cello back to the Pole. She may have technically given it away, but she hasn't delivered it to him yet. Let Loser Boyfriend try to come and pick it up there."

"How can you do that? Doesn't she need it for her auditions or whatever she's doing?"

"I'll figure something out," I said with more confidence than I felt. Certainly it wouldn't have been the first time I'd bent a few rules for the greater good. The fact that my husband was making toys at the North Pole instead of making license plates in a Connecticut prison was proof enough of that.

"Just remember—we're all here if you need us."

I couldn't help smiling at the image of the Claus brothers standing shoulder to shoulder as some greasy boyfriend tried to abscond with Isabella's cello. "Counting on it," I said. I heard movement in the hallway. Likely Isabella heading to the bathroom for another box of tissues to blot her tears. "Got to go. Love you."

"Love you more," he said, and clicked off.

Forty-Eight

By the time I awoke, the morning light that normally streamed through my window had moved on. I squinted at the clock. Eleven-thirty. I pulled on my robe and stumbled to the kitchen to make tea. Two coffee mugs sat in the sink because apparently, it was too difficult for Ted and Isabella to open the dishwasher.

"Hey, Meg," Ted yawned as he came into the room. "Any coffee left? I slept like a rock."

"I don't know. How much did you make?"

He squinted at me. His hair stuck up exactly the way Ralph's did when he first woke up. "I didn't make any. I just woke up."

I looked again at the two cups in the sink, and my gut clenched. "Oh, no, she didn't," I muttered as I stormed past him and up the stairs.

The door to Isabella's room was open. The room was empty. No cello was in sight.

I went back to my room and grabbed my phone. *Where are you? Need to talk,* I tapped. No response. I went back to the kitchen and checked the calendar where she wrote all her rehearsals and auditions. Today's block was empty.

"What's going on?" asked Ted as he poured the last few drops out of the carafe.

"I have a feeling the boyfriend has been here."

His face darkened. "What makes you say that?"

"Isabella's not here, and neither is her cello. And look. Nothing on the calendar." I pointed to the empty space.

"You think he came and got it before she could change her mind?"

"Exactly." What a fool I was. What fools we all were.

Isabella never answered my text. We waited around all day, reluctant to leave the house in case she came home. My car was in the garage, which meant Mr. Silver Beamer was using his own. My old computer was still in my basement office, so I spent the afternoon running searches for sellers of used cellos as if I'd recognize hers. Truth was, all cellos looked pretty much alike to me. Even if hers was side by side with others, I'd never know the difference.

Around six o'clock, Isabella strolled in as if nothing were wrong. She carried only her purse.

"Where's the cello?" Ted demanded.

"Hello to you, too," she said.

"Hello," I said. "What did you do with the cello?"

"You mean the cello I used to own that I was free to give away if I wanted to because it was mine?"

"I mean the one that was so important to you that you left your husband and came down here to make a career out of playing it," I said.

"None of your business," she said archly.

"It most certainly is my business," I said even as I wondered whether she might be right. It was her cello. At least technically, she was free to do with it as she chose. Except that her choices were rocking the boat badly, and it was at least partly my fault for providing her with a home from which she could wreak such havoc, which meant that it was also at least partly my job to ensure she didn't cause any more trouble.

"Why?"

"Because—because—" But Ted couldn't come up with anything.

"Because the reason you're living in my house is so you can pursue your cello career," I said. "If you're not going to do that, we need to discuss your next move."

Her eyes narrowed. "Are you kicking me out?"

"Depends," I said. "I'm not running a Home for Wayward Wives. If you want to get divorced, that's your call and it's not my place to stop you, but the reason I agreed to put you up was because you were Ralph's sister-in-law and you were trying to be a musician. If that's over, you need to make up your mind about a lot of things. If you want to come home, you can talk to Phil about it. Otherwise, you need to start looking for a job, because the Pole isn't going to be paying your rent anymore." That, at least, was within my control.

She tossed her head. "It doesn't matter. I have a place to stay if I want."

"Your boyfriend's? Think again, honey. You said he's got kids? I guarantee you that if his ex-wife finds out he's got some little piece of fluff living with him while he's got the kids for weekends, she is going to haul him back to court so fast his head will spin. Plus, the judge will likely tell him he has to give up his overnights with the kids as long as you're there. Not to mention that the wife probably try to get more alimony, because he'll have someone sharing things like rent and utilities, which means he'll have more disposable income. Trust me—if he knows anything at all about divorces, he's not going to risk all this just for you." Granted, the chances of all this happening were probably fifty-fifty at best, but my gut told me that this guy would likely kick Isabella to the curb rather than pay an extra dime or lose the overnights.

Her eyes filled with tears. "Why are you being so horrible to me? All I want is a life like you had."

"No, you don't," said Ted. "You want a life where you can do whatever you want with no consequences. You don't care about anybody except yourself. Go ahead and get divorced. You'll be doing my brother a favor." He turned on his heel and marched out of the kitchen.

Forty-Nine

"Meg! Meg! Wake up!"

Dimly, I could hear a woman's voice. Someone was shaking my shoulder. I swatted their hand away, but the urgency increased: "Wake up! We've got trouble!"

"What?" I groped my way up from the fog of sleep. The trip back to the Pole had felt longer than ever, and I still hadn't gotten my bearings. I blinked several times, trying to focus. "What happened? Is somebody hurt?"

Anya stood by my bed, her face frantic. "It's Isabella."

"Is she okay?" I pushed my hair out of my face.

Instead of answering, she thrust her phone at me. I squinted, trying unsuccessfully to read. I held out my hand, beckoning, and she plunked my readers into my palm like a scrub nurse. Positioning them, I began to read—and my stomach flipped.

"I'm going to kill her," I muttered as Anya paced around the bed and back again. "How freaking stupid can one person be!" I snatched up my own phone and called Isabella's phone. After three rings, her chirpy voicemail invited me to leave a message. "Call me as soon as you get this. Day or night. You have no idea how much trouble you've just caused." Muttering curses the likes of which the Pole had probably never heard, I called my landline in Connecticut. This time, it was my own voice that instructed me to leave a message. "Call me!" I shouted.

I slumped back in my bed. Anya perched on the side. "I swear, that girl is getting stupider by the day," I said. "Does Phil know?"

"I don't know," said Anya. "I came to you first."

I rewarded her with a slight smile. "Good thinking." It was time for damage control.

"What can I do?" asked the Claus in charge of public relations.

"Keep it quiet. Phil will need to be told. I'll do that."

"What about Ralph?"

"He had to go to Chile." Talk about a time to be away from the Pole. "Whatever you do, don't let Julian know. That's the last thing he needs."

"Okay. I'll gather the news reports. When do you want to reconnect?"

"Give me two hours. I don't know how long it'll take with Phil." I handed Anya's phone back, and she left. I tapped Ralph's number to FaceTime. When he picked up, I said without preamble, "You need to come back."

"Is Pop okay?" He was instantly on alert.

I shook my head. "Isabella is filing for divorce."

"Shit," said my husband, who never used to swear before he met me. "How's Phil?"

"I'm going down now to tell him before he picks it up on his own. But there's one other thing. The case title is *Claus v. Claus*. Since she lives at my place and that's my address of record on everything—voter registration, DMV, my annual attorney tax return—they're resurrecting all the stories about you and your escape and suggesting that she and you and I—that we're all connected. I'm guessing somebody knows everything and is putting out just enough to get the media to connect the dots."

"Who? Why?"

"Her lawyer. To put pressure on Phil so he'll settle fast and give Isabella everything she wants." Divorce lawyers could be a nasty bunch.

"What do we do?"

"First, I'll tell Phil his wife is divorcing him." It was the most immediate thing—and likely to be the most devastating. "Anya is researching everything the media is saying."

"Why can't it just be a coincidence that their last name is the same as mine?" asked Ralph.

"Because that won't generate sales," I said. "At this point, they're only speculating, but all they need is one concrete piece of evidence that *that* Claus is *this* Claus—you—and the walls are going to come tumbling down."

"Is Isabella still at your place?"

"No idea. I tried calling her cell and the landline. No answer at either." For all I knew, she'd moved in with her new boyfriend.

"I hope she's okay," said my ever-generous husband.

Not being nearly as generous of spirit, I refrained from commenting. "When can you get back?" I asked instead.

"Tomorrow at the earliest. It's a long trip. I'm practically at the other end of the world."

"Come back as soon as you can, but be careful." We exchanged *I love yous*, and I clicked off. Then, I showered, dressed, made tea, and prepared to tell my brother-in-law that his world had just very publicly exploded.

*****

The email itself wasn't a shock. One simple line: *Will you accept service of process on behalf of Philip Claus?* The attached complaint wasn't a shock either. It was simple boilerplate, the kind every divorce lawyer has on their computer. The shock was the signature line.

Richard McGee, Attorney at Law, Nettis, Butler, & Gould.

Isabella was being represented by Rick. My former partner, Rick. And then the pieces fell into place.

Rick wasn't just her lawyer. He was the new boyfriend.

"Un-fucking-believable!" It was a word that had probably never been uttered at the Pole. I paced the room as I added to the list of firsts: "That slimy son of a bitch! I'll kill him!"

A tap at my door, and Owen poked his head in. "Um, are you all right?"

"Not even close," I snapped.

"Did you want these now?" He held printouts I'd requested half an hour earlier, after I'd broken the news to Phil who, understandably, wanted to be alone.

I took a deep breath. "Sure. Thanks." Owen came into the room and laid them gingerly on the corner of my desk. "Sorry. It's just—sorry." I knew Owen was the soul of discretion, but I needed to figure out what to tell my client. "Where's Phil?"

"In his office. Is everything okay?"

"I wish," I growled. Owen withdrew diplomatically. I FaceTimed Ralph again

"Hey, babe," he said as he shoved clothing into his duffle. "I'll be out of here in a couple hours. What's up?"

"I found out who the boyfriend is."

"And. . . ?"

"It's Rick."

Ralph squinted. "Your old partner? The one who got kicked out of the firm for sleeping with clients?"

"One and the same. Son of a bitch is screwing her and Phil at the same time."

"Unbelievable."

"That's almost exactly what I said." I sank into one of the wingback chairs. "I've got to tell Phil."

"Maybe I should do it." He zipped his duffle.

I shook my head. "It's my job."

"He's my brother."

"I know. But he's my client." He'd taken news of the divorce with the kind of stoicism I'd have expected from his mother, but this would be an especially low blow.

"Wait 'til I get back. We can talk to him together."

I shook my head. "I have to do it alone. Attorney-client privilege."

"Can you wait until I get home?"

I wished I could. "I'm so afraid he's going to hear this from some-body else."

"Like who?" Ralph asked, but we both knew. If she called, Phil would pick up. It was what any man in love would do. Resigned, he said, "Tell him I'm on my way back. He can call me."

"You're a good brother." Everything in me wanted to hug him. "See you tonight."

"I love you," my husband said.

"Love you more," I said, and we hung up.

*****

Phil took this latest news better than I expected. Certainly better than I had. "Can I still talk to her?"

"Legally, you two can always talk. Practically speaking, I don't recommend it. Rick is a dirtbag, to put it very, very nicely. Anything you say to her, he'll twist. Your best bet is not to communicate with her."

"What happens with the cello?"

"As I said, he's a dirtbag. I imagine he has it hidden somewhere."

"I hope she's able to get it back. She loves that thing so much."

I gritted my teeth. Isabella didn't deserve a man like Phil. "Let's leave that problem for her right now. Rick's going to want to take your deposition and find out what you own."

"Nothing."

"Really? Not even—" I waved my hand.

"Nothing. It all belongs to Santa. Actually, Kristofer set up something—I don't remember if it's a corporation or what—that owns everything. Santa is the head of it. But really, I don't actually own squat."

I contemplated this. "Where did you get the money for the cello?"

"When we got married, my parents gave us some money as a wedding gift. I invested it with a brokerage firm in the States. I knew even then what I wanted to use it for. Isabella didn't care what I did with it—she has absolutely no head for money matters. So I made some investments, and within a couple of years, there was enough to buy the cello."

"There's nothing left of that initial gift?"

"Not a cent." In other words, he'd converted a gift to both of them into a gift exclusively for her. I'd need to check into whether I could argue that this made the cello a jointly-owned asset. Probably not, but it was worth asking since as far as I could tell, that cello was the sum total of the marital estate.

My mind was racing. We would need to be very, very careful. If Rick thought we were hiding something, the entire Claus empire could be at risk. My stomach clutched at the question of what Isabella might already have told him. Where did she say she was from? Did she admit that her brother-in-law was Santa Claus? I had no doubt that in the context of pillow talk, Rick had charmed her into divulging a great deal of information. I also had no doubt that Rick was capable of blackmail and would happily use his knowledge about the Clauses and the Pole as a bargaining chip to get what he wanted in this divorce.

What if Isabella had disclosed Ralph's location? What if she had told Rick about our marriage? What if she had let on that I was now living at the Pole and running my practice from here?

I took a deep breath. First things first, and the thing that always came first was my client. I couldn't control what Isabella said to anyone, but I could manage the rest. "Here's where we're starting," I said. "We'll file a cross-complaint seeking dissolution of marriage on the grounds of adultery. That will put the focus on her rather than you. It may be worth trying to get her lawyer disqualified in light of their relationship, but I need to think about that some more. The point is to keep Rick off-guard so he doesn't have time to think about you." I rose to leave, and then I hesitated, laying a hand on his shoulder. "I'm really sorry about this. I hoped she'd get the music thing out of her system and come home. I never saw this coming."

"It's not your fault," he said.

I wished I could agree.

Fifty

I'd just opened an email from Kristofer when the phone rang. Not the desk phone, but my cell. I glanced at it. The number showed as "International – Origin Unknown," which meant it was coming from a Pole phone. As I answered, I flipped to the schedule to see who was home and who was abroad.

"Meg?" Isabella's voice trembled. I could hear the tears in her voice.

"I can't talk to you, Iz. You're represented." I tried to sound as businesslike as possible.

"Not anymore," she sniffled. "We broke up."

Certainly it was the smartest thing she'd done in a long while, but I knew enough to double-check. Ending a romantic relationship wasn't the same as firing a lawyer. I pulled up the judicial branch website and logged into e-services. Nettis, Butler, & Gould still showed as her attorney. "When did you break up?"

"This morning."

"Are you firing him, too? Because if you are, you need to appear in lieu of him so he's not on the case anymore. Right now, the case detail shows he's your lawyer, which means I can't talk to you directly. Call me after you've filed your appearance or hired new counsel." She was still Rick's client, which meant I couldn't even explain to her that an appearance was the filing that told the court whether she had a lawyer or was representing herself.

"Don't hang up!" she pleaded, clearly recognizing I was about to do just that.

"Iz, I can't talk to you. Your asshole lawyer would grieve me." If there was one thing Rick knew about, it was getting grieved for improper contact with the opposing party.

"He wouldn't." But her voice wobbled. She knew as well as I did that he'd do anything to gain an advantage, including filing a specious grievance. My own history with the grievance committee wasn't spotless. I couldn't afford another go-round.

"Talk to Ralph," I said. "Or Julian. Just not me."

"You're the only one who'll understand."

I sighed. "That may well be, but I can't talk to you as long as you have a lawyer, and right now, you still do. When you change that, we can talk. I'm sorry, Iz. That's how it has to be." I clicked off before she could protest.

Ten minutes later, my phone rang again. "Why did you tell Isabella to call me?" asked my husband.

"Sorry about that. She needed to talk to someone, and legally, I can't talk to her. She said she broke up with Rick."

"She did, and he's not happy. Now she's scared he's going to do something vindictive."

"He can't. Literally the only thing he can do right now is either file a motion to withdraw or advise her to appear in lieu of him." Except this was Rick, and we all knew ethical niceties were beyond his ken. "Let me call him. I'll see what's happening." I clicked off and dialed Rick. My call went to voicemail. "Hey, Rick, it's Meg Riley. I'm calling you on Claus. My client's wife says you're no longer representing her. Do you know if she's hired someone else or if she's going *pro se*?" *Pro se* litigants were the ones who represented themselves. "Please call me so we can sort this out. I need to know who I can talk to." I clicked off and followed up with an email that said the same thing. Then, I sent a text with the same message. If nothing else, there would be three communications on record that Isabella had fired Rick.

I texted Ralph to let him know what I'd done. He responded an instant later with a thumbs-up. Then he texted, *Have you told Phil?*

Not yet. Still trying to sort out what's happening. Not that this would stop Ralph from calling Phil. The Claus boys were as gossipy as any maiden aunts I'd ever met. So I added, *Please don't say anything to him yet.* I held my breath, waiting for a response like, *I already did,* but he just responded, *K.*

*****

Three hours later, Rick answered my email: "Have you been talking to my client?"

I typed, "Is she still your client? She called this morning and said you two broke up."

A second later, another email arrived: "She's my client, and if you talk to her again, I'll have you greived."

It was all I could do not to write back, "Do you mean 'grieved'? I figured you of all people would know how to spell it by now." But I exercised restraint because it wouldn't have done either Phil or Isabella any good. I merely typed, "Does this mean you intend to continue representing her? Because I need to depose her."

Unsurprisingly, he did not respond. I checked the case detail again. Still no new appearance for the plaintiff. Until that changed, my lawyer-hands were tied.

For the rest of the day, I periodically checked the case detail, but there were no updates. Finally, I went down to Phil's office to let him know about this latest development, but he wasn't there. He didn't answer his cell, so I left a voicemail. Then, I began to wander around the facility in search of my client.

I found Phil in the finishing room, painting a model car. He looked impossibly big, hunched over an elf-sized desk, but he had the same laser focus the elves did. I stood behind him and said quietly, "I need to talk with you."

He didn't look away from the car. "I'm busy."

"It's important."

He dipped his paintbrush in glossy red paint. A couple of the elves glanced up at me, then returned to their tasks. I waited as Phil completed his work. Finally, he rose to place the finished car on the shelf of items to go into the kiln. Then, he favored me with a look that combined annoyance and apprehension. I followed him out of the finishing room and through the labyrinth to his office, where he closed the door behind us.

"I already know," he said.

"Ralph?"

He shook his head. "She called me."

"She called me, too. I explained why I couldn't talk with her."

"She understands."

"What do you want to do?" He looked puzzled, and I elaborated: "We can push her—keep the case going—or we can sit back and wait. It's up to you."

Phil sat down and began fiddling with his keyboard. "I don't know."

"Does she still want a divorce?"

"I don't know."

"Do you?"

His hands stilled. "I never did."

When he didn't say anything more, I said, "Let's give her a day or two to sort things out. Then, we'll see where we are." He nodded, but he didn't turn to face me. I patted his shoulder. "See you later." I couldn't tell whether he made a responsive sound or whether it was his computer.

Fifty-One

Several days later, I approached the Claus table in the dining room and said to my husband, "I need to talk to you." I kept my voice low. Ralph glanced at the others who had already gathered for lunch.

"Can it wait until we eat?" He was taking the temperature of my tone.

"I don't think so."

"Okay." Raising his voice, he said, "We've got some stuff to take care of. You guys go ahead."

"Yeah, right," said Ted. "Newlyweds." The others chortled, and Ralph and I put our arms around each others' waists as we headed for the kitchen to get a tray for takeout.

Back in the apartment, he asked, "What's up?" He looked ready for anything from a complaint about his snoring to a delivery crisis.

"It's Isabella. She wants to come back." Her fervent plea was still ringing in my memory.

His face hardened. "What does Phil have to say?"

"I don't know."

"Has she talked to him?"

"I don't know."

"Is she still with that other guy?"

"She says they broke up," I reminded him. "She called again this morning. She wants to come home. Asked me to run it by you."

"She called it 'home'?"

"Yeah. You want some coffee?"

"Sure. Is this the first time she's talked about coming back?"

I filled the coffee maker and the tea kettle. "No," I admitted.

"Why didn't you say anything before?"

"I wasn't sure she was serious." I took two mugs from the cabinet.

His eyes widened slightly, but he gave no other sign of surprise. "You've never mentioned this."

"It was weird. I wanted to tell you, but I knew she was talking to me in confidence."

"You should have told me anyway."

"It wasn't my secret to tell." Even I heard the neutral lawyer tone in my voice.

"But I'm your husband." He sounded almost hurt.

"What's that got to do with it? Somebody tells me something and I'm automatically supposed to tell you?" Everything in me rebelled at the notion. Regardless of what certain politically-minded judges seemed to think, privacy was still a very real right.

"That's marriage. We don't keep secrets," said my husband, whose entire identity was based on secrecy.

"Are you saying that if you confide in somebody, they have an automatic right—or obligation—to tell their spouse? Even if you don't want them to?"

"That's how marriage works. In a marriage, you don't keep secrets," Ralph declared.

"That depends on the people. I've known plenty of married people over the years who haven't spilled my confidences to their spouses. Do you know how long it was before Michael told Ruby about you being Santa? Because I asked him not to, and he's my friend and he respected my request."

"That's different. You're lawyers. You have that whole attorney-client privilege thing."

"That has nothing to do with it. He did it because we're friends and I asked him not to tell her. Would have been the same if we were electricians. Holly's not a lawyer, but she's kept plenty of my secrets over the years."

"Were they secrets like this? I mean, this is pretty major."

"Yeah, there were some major ones." *Like kissing Scott.* Okay, Holly wasn't married anymore at that point, but I knew in my bones she'd never told a soul.

"How do you know they didn't tell?"

"Because I asked them not to, and they're my friends and I trust them. If you told one of your brothers something and asked him not to tell his wife, would he keep quiet?"

"That's different. We're brothers."

"Michael's my brother. Holly's my sister. Not legally, but in every way that counts. So it's the same thing."

"Have you kept any secrets from me?"

"You mean, since we've been married?" I asked carefully.

"Ever." Did he suspect something?

"What kind of secrets? Case-related ones? Of course."

"Personal ones. The kind that aren't lawyer-client stuff."

I almost asked, "About me or about anyone?" Not that it mattered. I hadn't told him about my drunken near-miss with Scott. Nor had I told him about Isabella's relationship with Tristan. What good could have come of telling Ralph how many guys she'd slept with?

"Yes," I said finally.

"Like what?"

I looked him in the eye. "Let me put it this way. If telling you would accomplish something, I've told you. If not, I haven't."

"So, you keep secrets from me." His voice was cool.

"As do you, my dear. For example, I don't expect you to tell me if Phil has confided things about his marriage that he's asked you not to tell me." It was a guess, but a good one: Ralph looked away. *Caught.*

"It's not the same," he said. "He's my brother."

"It's exactly the same," I countered. "If we're supposed to tell each other everything we know, then the source shouldn't matter. Maybe that's what some married people do. Thing is, I don't operate that way. If somebody tells me something in confidence, it stays in confidence unless they tell me differently. I don't want them to worry that whatever they tell me, I'll immediately run back to my husband and say, 'Guess what!' I never wanted it with my married friends, and I'm not doing it to anybody else."

"My parents never kept secrets." Ralph's voice was low.

"What makes you so sure?"

"I just know. It was how they were with each other."

"First of all, nobody knows what's going on in somebody else's marriage. Second, even if they did tell each other everything, think about where they lived. They had to talk to each other, because who else did they have? Especially when you guys were kids—it was just them." Something occurred to me. "If you know whether people are bad or good, you don't need me to tell you anything anyway."

"That's only for the kids," said Ralph. "Once they stop believing, I no longer know anything about their lives beyond the usual means— what I see in person, what they tell me, or what other people tell me."

"But Isabella believes," I said. "So, you must know everything about her."

"Once a child 'outgrows' Santa, I shut it off."

"Like an on-off switch? Can you turn it back on?"

"No. It's absolute. Trust me, it's better that way." His tone left no room for dispute.

"I can imagine." I reflected on the number of people who had sat in my office lying their fool heads off, even when they were under oath. While it would have been convenient to know what they'd really done, it would also have been one hell of a burden.

We settled in our usual spots with our lunch. "Back to the original point: Isabella wants to come home. Can she?"

"It's not my decision." Harry jumped onto the loveseat, snuggling next to Ralph's leg.

"It kind of is. You're Santa. If you say she can't come back, that's the ball game. That's why she asked me to talk to you."

"And if she hadn't asked, you wouldn't have said anything."

Back to this. "It wouldn't have been my place."

He shook his head. Clearly, the bigger subject wasn't over, but there was a more pressing matter. "It's up to Phil."

"Because you're leaving it up to Phil. You're making that choice."

"Yes." We ate in silence. David curled up in my lap.

"Are you going to talk to Phil?" I asked finally.

"He's my brother."

"So that's a *yes.*"

"Well, what do you think I should do? Keep it a secret?" he challenged.

"I think one of us should tell Isabella she has Santa's permission, but she and Phil are the ones who ultimately need to make this decision. And then, I think we should stay the hell out of it unless one of them asks us to get involved." He looked away, almost as though he didn't want to admit that this was a sound idea. I pressed on: "We don't know if they've already talked, or when she might want to do this, or even if she really intends to come back. All we know—at least, all I know—is that she's asking if it's an option. We tell her it is, and from there, it's up to them."

"I still think he should know." My beautiful, stubborn husband. "If our positions were switched, I'd want him to tell me."

"If our positions were switched, I'd trust Isabella to keep her mouth shut until I was ready to have a conversation directly with you. What if she's just floating a trial balloon? Do you want to get his hopes up for nothing?"

"You're assuming his hopes would be up," Ralph countered. "He may not want her back."

"Then it's up to him to tell her so, but I sure as hell don't want to be in the middle of that conversation." I took a bite of my sandwich as Ralph grunted his reluctant agreement.

After Ralph left to go back to the workshop, I called Isabella and got her voicemail. "I talked to Ralph," I said. "You can come home if you want. It's between you and Phil." I was tempted to remind her that Miko and the icebreaker were coming next week and I could really use her help. Instead, I disconnected and sat for a minute, phone in hand, wondering what Ralph was saying to his brother at that moment. Except maybe he wouldn't say anything, at least not yet. Maybe he'd wait until Phil called Isabella, or she called him.

And maybe we wouldn't know until she showed up in a sleigh.

Fifty-Two

Phil wasn't at dinner that night. Claire reported that she'd taken a tray to him in his office. I could tell that she and Anya were dying to find out all the juicy new gossip, but Ralph immediately started talking about the upcoming Season with all the details and deadlines that required attention. The other guys gratefully jumped into the discussion, steering it as far away from their brother's marital woes as possible. Moments like this reminded me of the differences between men and women.

After dinner, everyone assembled in the dining hall for our monthly Trivia Night. I'd have loved to bow out, but keeping up morale was now one of Mrs. Claus's jobs. I did my best to keep things rolling, making jokes and leading applause, but my heart wasn't in it. Homer, an elf who worked in the plastics shop, was the night's big winner, grinning proudly as Annaliese presented him with his prize, a huge platter of assorted cookies. As soon as everyone started to disperse, I grabbed my phone and checked for updates. No voicemails, no missed calls, not even any texts. I logged into the judicial branch website. According to the case detail, Rick was still Isabella's lawyer. Ten days out, and she still hadn't filed a *pro se* appearance in lieu of him. I had a sick feeling that he might have talked her into reconciling, if only to avoid losing the fee.

The halls were quiet at this hour. As I passed the library, I glanced in the open door. A young elf girl was curled up in one of the chairs, deep into her book. For an instant, I hesitated, reluctant to disturb her. Then, I entered the library and picked up the basket of returned materials. As I shelved the books, I tried to catch a glimpse of the title that had her so spellbound.

"*A Tree Grows in Brooklyn*," the girl offered, seeing my unsubtle effort.

I smiled, caught. "I love that book." It took a second for me to recall the girl's name. *Miranda*. Twelve years old. Eldest child of Faith, who worked in wrapping, and Glen, who worked in the finishing room. In addition to Miranda, Faith and Glen had three little boys, all under seven. No wonder the girl came to the library to read.

"I'm sorry, Miranda. I didn't mean to interrupt you." I restored the last volume to the shelf and replaced the basket on the corner of the checkout desk.

"It's okay, Mrs. Claus," Miranda said. I was about to leave when she asked, "Have you ever seen a tree? In person, I mean."

I nodded. "I love trees. There's a huge one in front of the library in the town where I used to live. I always wanted to climb it." My voice trailed off as a quick stab of homesickness hit me. There were no trees at the Pole.

Her eyes grew dreamy. "That must be so wonderful." I half-expected her to ask more, but she returned her attention to her book. I wished her a good night, but she was already deep in the story of the Nolan family in far-off Brooklyn.

Ralph wasn't in the apartment when I got there. Most likely, he was with Phil. Harry and David commandeered the loveseat, and Lulu was curled up in the center of the bed, leaving me only the armchair. I made tea and settled into the chair with David Handler's latest mystery about a writer and his basset hound, who was also named Lulu. "My Lulu's much prettier," I said to the book. Through the doorway, her triangular black ear flicked at the sound of her name.

Handler's writer-detective was busily running around Manhattan with his Lulu when Ralph finally came in. "How's he doing?" I asked.

Ralph grunted. "Phil? Last I saw, he was playing chess with Pop."

I frowned. "Then where have you been?"

"Walking. Trying to figure everything out." That was when I realized that his face was still slightly reddened from the cold, and the light dawned.

"By yourself?" I forgot about the writer and the basset. "Damn it, Ralph!"

"I know what I'm doing. I've been walking out there for a long time."

"But you're the one who said it's dangerous!" I remembered the time before we got married—it felt like a hundred years ago—when he took me out to see the wild reindeer. He'd warned me then never to go out alone, but here he was doing exactly that. "What if you got lost—"

"I don't get lost. Not here. I've lived here my entire life." He disappeared into the bedroom.

I dropped my book and followed him into the bedroom. "That's not the point! The point is, you know it's dangerous, and you know it worries me, and you promised not to go out there alone! What if you fell? What if you slipped on the ice and slid into the water and froze to death? What if you got mauled by a polar bear? What would happen to you? To all of us? To this entire place?"

"Do you mind? I've got a lot on my mind right now." He stripped off his sweater and shirt.

"And I don't? Do you understand what I'm juggling right now? I'm representing your brother in a lawsuit brought by my sister-in-law who your mother asked me to take in, and at the same time I'm trying to figure out how to do what your mother used to do to keep this place afloat when I haven't got the slightest idea what I'm doing! Plus, I have no idea how to be married, but somehow I'm supposed to understand that and be the sweet little helpmate for you even though we both know that's not how I roll, but I'm trying anyway. And then you go out walking across the tundra by yourself and for all I know, you're going to end up getting lost or hurt or drowned out there, and I'll end up a widow and Santa Claus will be gone, and I swear to God, if you die out there, I will never, ever forgive you for as long as I live!" I didn't realize I was crying until Ralph took me in his arms and I found myself sobbing against his smooth, warm chest. "Don't leave me," I wept. "Whatever you do, don't leave me."

"Never," he murmured. "I'm sorry. I didn't mean to upset you. I just needed some space."

"You could have gone to your office," I mumbled against his chest.

"That's what you do," he said. "Not me."

"Try it some time." I kissed his chest and moved out of his embrace.

"You like space in your head," he said as he finished stripping down. "I need real space." He headed into the bathroom and turned on the shower, and I sank down on the bed.

Fifty-Three

The ringing of the phone ripped me from sleep. This was getting to be a ritual. And since we'd just wrapped up the supply delivery from Miko and the icebreaker two days earlier, it was a ritual I'd happily have done without.

I rolled over and punched *talk*. "What?" I demanded. All I could hear on the other end was sobbing. "What's going on? Who is this?" More sobbing. I looked at the display. An "International—Origin Unknown" number, which meant Isabella. "Iz, what's going on?" She blubbered a response that was incomprehensible except for the word "soul." "What about your soul? Did you go to church?" Maybe she'd decided the way to deal with her behavior was to go to confession. Not the worst idea she could have had.

"Gone," she managed.

"Slow down. What are you talking about?" Beside me, Ralph stirred. I slipped from bed, pulled on my robe, and headed out to the living room, pulling the door closed behind me. "What's going on, Iz?"

"He sold it."

My gut clenched. "Your cello?" A renewed bout of sobs answered me. "Rick sold your cello?" That lowlife son of a bitch. There had to be some way I could kill him without getting caught. "To who?"

"I don't know," she moaned. "Just said . . . sold it."

"I'll finish him," I muttered. Louder I said, "Is he still your lawyer?" When I couldn't make out any words, I said, "Hold on." I took the phone from my ear and pulled up the judicial branch website. As of yesterday, Isabella Claus was self-represented. That stinking bastard. She fired his lying ass, and he retaliated by selling her cello. I'd have bet anything he was going to claim she gave him the cello as payment for legal fees.

"Okay, listen. You need to pull yourself together. I'm going to help you, but you've got to stop and take a breath. What time is it there?" I didn't want to call someone before sunrise. She sobbed something that sounded like "nine-thirty." "Okay, then. Settle down. I'll find somebody to represent you, and we can go from there."

"No! I don't want anybody to represent me! I want to come home!" She sounded like a child who was three blocks from her house when she realized she didn't really want to run away.

My mind raced. Phil didn't want a divorce, but that didn't necessarily mean he wanted her to come home to this insular community, at least not yet. What could she do if he said "no"? If she wasn't a Claus wife, who was she? Did she have a right to be at the Pole anyway? Ralph had said she could come home if she and Phil wanted that, but if Phil was cutting her loose, would Ralph override him?

"One thing at a time," I said in an effort to buy time. "First, you need a lawyer looking out for you."

"I want you!" she wailed.

"You can't have me. I represent Phil. I'm not an option." I could hear Ralph moving in the bedroom. "Just sit tight and don't do anything. I'll make some calls and see what I can do for you." A few more reassurances on my end and sobs on hers, and I finally clicked off.

The bedroom door opened. "Let me guess," my husband said.

"Rick got pissed when she fired him, so he sold the cello."

"Shit," said my husband. "Can he do that?"

"Depends. She gave it to him—"

"—that wasn't real!"

"Agreed, but it'll be hard to prove. He can claim she gave it to him as payment for her bill."

"Do people do that?"

"Some do, but most lawyers won't accept property as payment. We'd rather have money. Usually, we'll tell them to sell the item themselves and then pay us. But it's not unethical to accept it as long as the value of the thing is reasonably equivalent to the amount owed."

"Your profession is something else," he grumbled as he moved into the kitchen and filled the coffee carafe.

"So sorry we're not as noble as Santa Claus," I said. "Some of us have to worry about earning a living."

"You're defending what he did?" Ralph stared, pot in hand.

"Of course not," I snapped. "He's pond scum. He took unfair advantage of her. He knew perfectly well she wasn't really giving him the cello. But it'll be hard to prove." I pushed past him to put on the tea kettle.

"What can we do?"

"Right now, I'm going to call Michael and see if he can find her a lawyer."

"Would he take her case?"

"I don't want him to. Considering the way this thing is shaking out, I may need him to help get the cello back, and I don't want him conflicted out." I yawned as I headed into the bathroom. "I'm going to hop in the shower. When the water boils, make me a cup of Irish Breakfast, okay?" I turned on the water before I heard his answer.

*****

I didn't feel like sitting with the brothers at breakfast, so I got a tray and took it to Julian's apartment. Fingers mentally crossed, I tapped at his door.

"Come in," came his melodious voice. "Ah, Meg! Just the person I was hoping to see!" he said as I entered.

I set down the tray and kissed his cheek. "Nobody else here?" Finding him alone was a rare occurrence these days. Most mornings, at least one of the grandchildren could be found chattering or snuggling or seeking advice from Grandpa.

"We're on our own," Julian said. "Now, sit and talk to me. How are you doing?"

I poured his coffee, which he accepted with a smile. "I've had better days," I admitted.

Julian's regular breakfast was a thick-cut piece of Annaliese's bread, toasted and smeared with peanut butter and whatever jam happened to be handy. Today, she'd produced a jar of raspberry-peach, whispering, "I saved it for him." When I arranged the tray on his side table, his smile widened at the sight of the ruby-red topping. "My favorite!" he said. "Do have some."

"I have my own." I gestured to the second plate. "Annaliese said you wouldn't mind sharing, just this once."

His eyes twinkled. "I'll share with you any time, my dear." He bit into his toast, his eyes closed in pure bliss. "Isn't this wonderful." He munched, smiling contentedly.

I took a bite. He was right. For a minute, I allowed myself the luxury of tasting the clear sweet fruit against the salty-sweet peanut butter. Something about being in Julian's presence made it possible to believe that everything would indeed be all right.

He waited until we had finished our food and were sipping our beverages to inquire, "So what is making this not one of your better days?"

"Isabella called this morning. Things aren't good." I assumed he already knew all the dirt. I couldn't imagine how he must feel at the way his son's wife had behaved. If I'd been in his slippers, I'd want nothing more to do with the woman who abused my son's heart so horribly.

And yet— "How is she holding up?" Julian asked, his voice tender.

"Not well." I shouldn't have been surprised. The Clauses were cut from different cloth than the rest of us. "You know about the cello, right? How she gave it to her boyfriend to keep from losing it in the divorce?" He nodded. "Turns out, they broke up, she fired him as her lawyer, he sold the cello, and she's devastated."

"Do you know who bought it?" The man was completely unflapped.

I shook my head. "I need to get in touch with my friend, Michael, and see if he can help. Isabella needs a new lawyer. Then, I'll ask Michael to help me track down the cello. If we can find a way to hold Rick accountable, that'll be a plus."

"Do you have a plan? Please hand me the pot," he added. Instead, I picked up the small coffeepot and refilled his cup. The boys drank their coffee black, but Annaliese always premixed milk and a touch of sugar in Julian's coffeepot.

"Not yet," I said. "I suppose the first thing to do is to find out who bought the cello. The divorce can't move forward until we do. The cello is the only thing of value she owns." Since nothing at the Pole actually belonged to Phil beyond his clothes—and all Isabella owned was the cello—it should have been the quickest, easiest divorce on record.

"Have you talked to Philip?" Julian was the only person who called Phil by his full name. "What does he want to do?"

"I haven't spoken with him this morning," I admitted. "He was upset enough when she gave the cello away. I can't imagine how he'll feel now."

"Angry, I expect," said his father. "The girl was bamboozled. He would never want that." He eyed me as if debating what to say next, electing instead to take another sip of coffee.

"Does he want her back?" I asked. His thick eyebrows lifted just a bit. "He won't tell me. I don't know if it's because I'm his lawyer or because I'm not really family."

"Of course, you're family," said Julian.

"Not blood. I'm a married-in Claus, not a real Claus."

"Now you're being silly," Julian chided. "A married-in Claus is just as real as one who shares the Claus lineage."

I didn't want to argue with him, but I knew in my heart that I wasn't nearly as much a Claus as the rest of them. Besides, Isabella was a married-in Claus, and look how that was working out. So I pivoted: "I'm not you or Ralph or—" Too late, I broke off.

"Or his mother," Julian finished gently. "She knew Philip better than anyone. They were the proverbial peas in a pod. The other boys are much more like me."

"Even Mitch?" It was difficult to picture Julian bouncing around the way his youngest did, cracking jokes and flirting madly.

"Especially Mitch. Whenever I misbehaved as a boy, my father used to say, 'I hope someday you have a son just like you!' I'm quite certain that he's sitting in heaven right now having himself a good laugh. That boy has contributed to more of my white hair than the other four combined." He chuckled. "But Philip—he was his mother's son. Not like a mama's boy, mind you. But they understood each other. In some ways, her passing has been as hard on him as it has on me." I reached out and rested my hand on his knee. He smiled, patting my hand. "I appreciate what you're doing for him. You're doing what none of the rest of us can. Meredith would have been grateful to you."

"She'd have told me to get the cello back." I sat back and finished my tea.

"Indeed she would," Julian said. "She had great respect for you."

"She did?" This was truly news.

"Absolutely. She saw much of herself in you." I must have looked flabbergasted, because he said, "You're both hardheaded and practical.

You look at a problem, analyze it, and set out to solve it. And neither of you lets anything get in your way, even if it means rocking somebody else's boat a bit." He drained his cup. "Trust me, my dear. You assumed the role because you married Ralph, but even if things had been different and you were married to one of the others, you'd still be the best fit for the job. I have complete faith in your ability to serve as she did."

Tears prickled. I ducked my head. He reached out to take my hand, and I knew he'd seen everything. "I'll get the cello back," I promised, my voice cracking slightly. "And I'll bring Isabella back—if that's what Phil wants."

"If that's what they both want," he corrected gently. A tap sounded at the door. "Come in, Dulcie." A stout young elf entered with her cleaning supplies. We greeted each other, and I rose. "I should be getting to work," I said, leaning down to kiss Julian's cheek. "Thank you for—everything."

"Always, my dear." His eyes twinkled as I placed our dishes on the tray.

"You can leave that there," said Dulcie as I started to pick it up. "I'll take it back when I'm done."

"Not necessary, I'm heading down that way." I could feel Julian's approval as I bid them farewell and headed back down the hall, my mind whirling.

Fifty-Four

"That son of a bitch."

Michael was never one to mince words. He'd listened as I shared the latest developments. Then, after a pause, he made his pronouncement about our former partner.

"No argument here," I said. "But what can we do?"

"She could grieve him," he suggested. "But I'm sure Rick has the bill ready, and I'll bet you anything the amount due comes to just over what he got for the cello. And you know he's got a bill of sale to prove it."

"Which may or may not be legitimate. But regardless, how do we get our hands on it?"

"Easiest way would probably be to sue him, issue a notice for his deposition, and subpoena everything relating to the cello, but that's liable to take a long time."

"What about an injunction?" We'd both used injunctions through the years to keep a party from doing something while the lawsuit was proceeding. Except Rick wasn't a party, which meant we'd still have to sue him.

"What are you going to enjoin him from doing? The cello's gone. Most you can do now is freeze the funds—assuming they haven't already been spent."

"I'm sure he's squirreled the money away somewhere. Besides, it would let him know he's been caught speeding."

"I'm sure he already knows that," said Michael. "He's ready for a frontal attack. What we need to do is get him where he isn't expecting it."

"And that would be?"

"I'm wondering whether Trisha knows he's just come into a bunch of cash. Hang on." I heard him typing as he searched the judicial branch website. After a minute, he announced, "She's got a motion for contempt pending. My bet is that he's behind on his support payments." In family cases, parties routinely filed motions for contempt if the other party failed to pay alimony or child support.

"He's not smart enough to use this money to make up the arrearage." If he'd been my client, I'd have advised him to use the proceeds to pay Trisha whatever he owed for back support. At least then he wouldn't be fighting battles on two fronts.

"Not nearly. In fact, I'd like to know more about where he keeps the cash he's not using for his court-ordered obligations."

I smiled for the first time in this conversation. "I think we should find out, don't you? Call Russ Carsten. Tell him to send the bill to me." Russ Carsten was the best private investigator we knew. He was pricey, but he was worth it.

"Your client wants to pay for this?"

"Hell, no. This is personal. I'm paying for Russ. But don't let him know. I don't want him to get tangled up in Rick's crap. Because you know Rick's eventually going to come after me for something."

"For what? You haven't done anything."

"Except marry a fugitive," I reminded him. "If Rick finds out I'm Mrs. Claus, I guarantee all hell will break loose." I was convinced that he was behind the early attempts to stir up the media. Fortunately, the story had petered out. "Let's just hope he doesn't decide to tip off the police. I can't even imagine what they'd do." Memories of the harrowing months after Ralph's escape from prison reared up, when the state police and the feds used every weapon in their arsenal against me as they searched for Ralph. I forced the memories back into their little lockbox.

"You should probably transfer the condo out of your name," said Michael. "Right away, before he decides blackmail might be a nice source of income."

I was about to agree with him when something occurred to me. "Actually, I have a better idea."

"Do I want to know?"

"No worries. It's perfectly legal."

"So, do you want me to call Russ now, or do you want to wait a couple of days until you get your own stuff in order?"

"You might as well call him. He's discreet. Besides, no matter what I do, it's going to look like I'm doing exactly what I'm doing—getting everything out of reach of whatever goons Rick calls in."

"Still, the sooner you do it, the better." Michael was nothing if not philosophical.

The desk phone rang. "Hang on a second," I said to Michael, picking up the handset. It was Fred, calling to let me know they were running low on enamel paint and did I have an ETA on the shipment. "I'll check and get back to you," I said to him, hanging up. I picked up the cell and said, "Got to go. I have to track a shipment for the workshop."

"Before you go—who's representing Isabella now?"

"I meant to ask you if you knew anybody. She's self-represented now, and we can already see how well that's going."

Michael thought for a second. Then, he laughed. "I know just the guy. Used to do a ton of family. He's moving away from it now, but I'd bet for this one, he'd go back in."

The light bulb went on. There was only one person in the Connecticut bar who had even less use for Rick than we did. I joined in Michael's laughter, and we said the name together.

"Carter Fitzhugh."

****

The upside to hiring Carter was that he despised Rick even more than I did. The downside was that he would now be my opposing counsel, meaning that this relatively simple divorce was about to get a whole lot messier.

"I'll call Isabella," Michael had offered before we hung up. "You can't be part of that."

He was right. Not that Carter was any more noted for attention to ethics than Rick, but if he thought I was having improper contact with Isabella, his first act would be to move to disqualify me from representing Phil. I texted Isabella to let her know that a friend of mine would be contacting her with a recommendation for a new lawyer and to underscore that I couldn't represent her. "BUT I WANT YOU!!!" she texted back seconds later.

"As I said before, I cannot represent you," I texted back. "You need to hire a new lawyer." I typed, then deleted, "and the sooner, the better." I could not afford to appear to give her any kind of advice.

An hour later, as I was sorting through gift requests from southeast Asia, my phone rang. "Carter's in," said Michael. "Provided she's got the money."

I cringed inwardly. She didn't have a dime other than the pittance she'd earned when she performed with Ealaíonta, and that source of income had probably dried up since she didn't even own a cello anymore. Phil had already sent her money for her legal fees; I knew because Kristofer called to inquire, in the most delicate way possible, whether Ralph or I had authorized sending five thousand dollars to a Connecticut bank account. I had no idea where that money had gone, but if Rick was claiming he'd sold the cello so she could pay his bill, I suspected the five grand had been squandered on a romantic getaway. I could imagine Rick crooning in her ear, "Don't worry about my bill. We'll work something out. Let's just have fun."

"What does he want for a retainer?" I asked, bracing myself.

"Twenty-five." *Twenty-five thousand dollars.*

"Is he nuts? This is a no-asset, no-kid divorce. It should have been collaborative." It would have been, if Rick hadn't been involved. Actually, if it hadn't been for Rick, odds were Isabella would be home by now—with her cello. "Tell him she can come up with ten for the whole thing, but that's it. If he really wants to nail Rick, he'll take it."

Ultimately, after five minutes of haggling that was mainly for show, Carter agreed. "First things first," I said to Michael once the judicial branch website registered Carter's appearance. "We need to track down the cello. Anything from Russ?"

"Not yet. What are you going to do?"

"File a motion for contempt. It was a fraudulent conveyance." A fraudulent conveyance was when someone disposed of an asset in order to keep it away from people to whom they owed money. Giving away a valuable asset so that the divorce judge couldn't order it sold was a classic example of a fraudulent conveyance. "Besides, she gave it away before she even hired Rick. When Carter calls, I'll tell him I'm willing to mark the motion off if he produces the cello, and we'll go from there."

"Is she going to grieve Rick?"

"Don't know. He's pretty sneaky. He was screwing her before he filed the divorce, so technically, the rule about not having sex with clients doesn't apply." One of the rules of professional conduct precluded lawyers from engaging in sexual relationships with clients, but it made an exception if the personal relationship predated the attorney-client relationship. "On the other hand, I'm willing to bet he seduced her so she'd hire him for the divorce, which is doubly slimy."

"And not at all surprising," Michael concluded.

"Have Russ look into whether Rick's been sued or grieved by any other women he's slept with," I said. "I'm willing to bet he has a pattern of this kind of behavior."

"In which case the no-sex rule goes right out the window," said Michael.

"Exactly."

Fifty-Five

After we hung up, I made another call. Four hours later, after a flurry of calls and emails, I took a deep breath and signed a warranty deed conveying my condo to Rodrigo and Samson. An hour after I sent them the scanned deed, my bank account reflected a wire transfer of the higher purchase price they'd insisted on. "We're not taking advantage of you," Rodrigo declared when I named a lowball figure. "We know perfectly well what that property is worth. Besides, darling, you may have just saved our marriage!"

After dinner, when Ralph and I were alone in our apartment, I said, "Guess what I did today."

"You took out a sleigh and flew around the Circle," my husband guessed.

"In your dreams," I snorted. Trying to be casual, I placed the empty cat dishes in the sink and ran the water in them.

"I give up," said Ralph.

I squirted a bit of soap onto a sponge. As I scrubbed off the dried bits of cat food, I said casually, "I sold my place." I waited for a reaction as I rinsed the dishes.

"You did what?"

I turned to face him as I dried the cat dishes. "You heard me."

"I didn't—when did you—why didn't you tell me?"

"There wasn't time." I explained about Rick and the risk that he would rat me out to the police. "Rodrigo's been talking for ages about how they need more space, so it occurred to me that this was the perfect answer. They want to knock down the walls between the two units. This way, Samson can have his peace and quiet, and Rodrigo can have his parties and rehearsals, and they can be together when they want."

Ralph looked slightly dazed. "What about Isabella?"

"That's the best part!" I couldn't help but be proud of myself. "I put together a separate agreement so she can stay on at my place—what *was* my place—as long as she wants. Plus, Rodrigo says that whenever I need to come down, I'm welcome to stay there, too." I couldn't hold back my triumphant grin. "How perfect is that!"

"Pretty perfect," Ralph said, still not sounding enthusiastic.

"What's the matter?" His reaction to my brilliant plan made no sense.

"I just—I didn't think you were ready for a leap like this."

"What leap? We're married. What did you think? That I was going to keep my condo so I'd have someplace to run away to?" I tried not to feel insulted.

"No, of course not. But I guess I thought we'd talk about it first."

"Why? I'm the owner. Whether I keep it or sell it is my choice."

"I'm not saying it is. I just thought—it seems like a big decision for you to make without so much as mentioning it. How long have you been thinking about this?"

"Rodrigo brought it up when we were packing for the move." Was I supposed to tell my husband about every conversation I had with my friends?

"So—almost a year ago, and you never said a word. Why?"

"It never occurred to me he might be serious. Besides, what difference would it have made if I'd told you? I already knew what you wanted. I thought you'd be happy that I finally took the plunge. My mistake!" I marched past Ralph into the bedroom and slammed the door. At that moment, I understood why Rodrigo and Samson needed so much room.

A tentative knock on the door. I considered not saying anything, but of course he knew exactly where I was. Bedroom or bathroom, those were the choices. So I said, "What?"

Ralph opened the door. "Are you really sure this is what you want to do?"

"What do you mean?"

He sat on the foot of the bed. "I know how much your place means to you. Of course, I want you to be here forever—that's why I married you—but I don't want you to regret giving up your condo. There's no reason you can't keep it if you want."

"Of course, there is," I said. "Money. Not to mention the risk of Rick turning me in to the police. I don't know how it works when your assets get frozen, but I need to get everything out of Connecticut before we have to find out."

Ralph took my hand. "Is that really why you sold it? Just because of the money and police?"

I scooted down to be closer to him. "Huh-uh." I looked directly into his eyes. "I sold it because this is where I live now. I live here. With my husband. There's no reason for me to have the hassle and expense of keeping my condo when I have a home here."

He released his hand and wrapped his arms around me. "As long as you're sure."

"I am," I said, and that was the end of real estate talk for a good long while.

Much later, when I thought he was asleep, Ralph said suddenly, "I'm surprised Mom didn't think of dealing with your place and all your other accounts and stuff. Probably because none of the others had much when they got married."

"This is what comes of being an old bride," I said.

"A what?"

"That's what my friend Katie's mother-in-law said when she got married, that Katie was an old bride."

"How old was she?"

"Twenty-five."

"That's old?"

"According to her mother-in-law, but she was from a small town in Louisiana where girls get married young. When Katie and her husband went down to visit a few months after the wedding and the neighbors found out they'd just gotten married, several of them asked Katie if this was her second marriage."

"What do you think they'd say about us?" He moved my hair to kiss the back of my neck.

"They'd probably say you're a distinguished older gentleman who married some old crone." I bent my head forward as his lips moved slowly around to my ear.

"A crone bride," he murmured. His tongue played with my earlobe. "Come to me, my beautiful crone." I turned to kiss him, and that was the end of the day's update.

Fifty-Six

The next morning, Russ Carsten called. "Talked with Kimberly Austin. Nobody offered her the cello. Says if they had, she'd have pounced on it."

"Damn." I'd have sworn Rick would go to Isabella's teacher first out of sheer laziness. "What now?"

"I'll keep looking. She'll put out feelers, too. She said an instrument like that is a big deal. She gave me names of other cello teachers in the tri-state area to talk to. Plus, I've checked every store within fifty miles that buys and sells stringed instruments. Nothing."

"What about the other members of Ealaíonta? Would they know anything?"

"Maybe. Are there any distinguishing marks on it?"

"I have no idea. You'd have to ask Isabella—no, wait, you can't." A thought occurred to me. "Have you talked to Rick?"

"First thing. He told me to eff off." Russ would never swear in front of a client.

"Bastard." I knew no such delicacy. "What did you say?"

"I told him that seeing as he's her former lawyer, it's in his best interests to get the cello back."

"Did you tell him why?"

"Nope. But I'm keeping an eye on him. If he makes a move, I'll know." And he would. It wouldn't have surprised me if Russ had a surveillance camera trained on wherever Rick was living to catch him in case he came home with a large, bulky package that could contain a cello case.

"You're the best. Keep track of your time." It was the standard line to confirm that I would pay him for his work.

"I'll keep you posted," he said and clicked off.

I filed the motion for contempt and waited. I didn't have to wait long. The next morning, Carter had filed his objection, arguing that the gift was perfectly legal. I prepared a short reply arguing that she'd done it for an invalid reason. Then, I sent Carter an email:

Carter:

Does your client have the cello in her possession? If so, produce it and I'll mark off my motion.

Meg

I didn't expect a response, so it was a real surprise when my phone rang. "You know as well as I do that she doesn't have it," said Carter with uncharacteristic candor.

"Then she's got a problem, doesn't she?"

"Are you the one who hired Carsten to find it?"

I was tempted to ask how he knew I'd hired Russ, but I was tired of playing games. "Her husband wants it back. He gave it to her as an anniversary gift."

"Which means it was hers to give away."

"Ordinarily, you'd be right. But in this case, she intentionally gave it away to remove it from the marital estate. She can't do that."

"She's allowed to pay her legal bills. That's what she used it for."

"She didn't have any legal fees at that point. She hadn't even decided about the divorce. Ask her for the timeline about when she gave it away versus when she decided to file. Besides, I guarantee whatever fees Rick charged didn't come anywhere near the value of that instrument. It's early in the case, and he hadn't even done any discovery."

"She can pay a retainer if she wants to."

"Her husband gave her five grand for a lawyer. So if she paid a retainer—which I very much doubt—that's where it came from." I waited, but he was silent. "Look, it's a very valuable instrument. I guarantee that whatever Rick claims she owed, it didn't come anywhere near the value of that cello."

"You're doing a lot of guaranteeing, Meg. Have you been speaking to my client?"

Shit. "She lives in my former condo."

"You represent the husband while you're the landlord for the wife? Sounds as if you have a conflict."

"She was living there long before she filed. And she was *pro se* when I talked to her. Plus, I no longer own the place." *Don't ask me when I sold it.*

A long pause. It was clearly designed to make me uncomfortable. It worked. Finally, he said, "If you go forward with your motion, I'm going to need to disqualify you, because you're going to be a witness."

"You're missing the point. The point is that the cello was the only thing of value she owned. She gave it to Rick to get it out of the marital estate, and now he's sold it and won't say to who. The only way to recover it is to lean on Rick."

"And holding my client in contempt is going to accomplish that?"

"It's in her best interests to find out what that slimeball did with her cello."

I could almost hear Carter smiling at my descriptor. "I'll speak to my client."

"Thanks. I'll hold off on scheduling my motion for argument." It was my way of thanking him for joining the hunt for the cello.

"Fine." He wouldn't go so far as to thank me, but it was understood.

*****

The next morning, Russ called. "Making progress," he grunted when I asked. "Lawyer sold the cello to a dealer."

"Rick's doing drugs?" If he'd been in my office, I'd have strangled him with my bare hands.

"Not that kind," said Russ. "A guy who buys and sells musical instruments. Mainly violins and cellos. This one's in Cornwall. Preston Dixon." Cornwall was a little town in semi-rural Litchfield County. Out in the northwest corner of Connecticut, it was a stone's throw from the Massachusetts border and an easy drive to Tanglewood. It was also a favorite haven of wealthy New Yorkers who desired rustic yet lavish second homes in the country. Being an instrument dealer must have paid very well.

"Is Preston Dixon the name of the company?" It sounded like a law firm.

"That's his name. Second-generation dealer. All the best musicians bought their instruments from his father."

"Have you talked with this guy?"

"Our new buddy Pres has more on his mind than talking to me. Seems he's not as careful as dear old Dad was. Have you ever heard of something called provenance?"

"No."

"It's basically the history of the instrument. Who made it, who owns it now, who owned it in the past, and things like this. If you're trying to sell a cello or whatever to a good dealer—one who does his due diligence—the dealer won't take it until he establishes provenance. You'd have to give him what're called maker's papers—a certificate of authenticity, a certified appraisal, a bill of sale, photos of the instrument over the years—so he knows it's really your cello. The dealer might even call the person who made the instrument to confirm who originally bought it." One reason Russ was such an excellent investigator was that he did his homework.

"But you're saying that's only if they're a good dealer." I was scribbling furious notes.

"Which Pres isn't. He's what's kindly known as sloppy. He doesn't ask a lot of questions. So as far as I've been able to tell, Attorney McGee showed up at his door and told Preston he represented the owner who wanted to sell the cello because she needed some fast cash. Preston said okay and took it off his hands then and there."

"Did he pay Rick for it?"

"Claims he paid him thirty grand. Cash."

"As in dollar bills? Not even a check?

"He said that's what Rick wanted."

"And that didn't raise any red flags for this guy?" Pres was clearly not the brightest bulb on the tree. Unless. . . .

"Said he doesn't get involved in people's personal matters. As far as he was concerned, if the lady wanted cash, she could have cash."

"Which he just happened to have sitting around." Because after all, didn't everybody stash an enormous sack of dollar bills under the bed?

"He said he'd sold a violin for forty thousand the day before and he hadn't gotten to the bank yet." I could hear in Russ's voice that he didn't find this explanation any more plausible than I did.

"That's a whole lot of cash changing hands. It didn't bother him that 'the lady' wasn't even there to accept all this loot?"

"Nope. Her lawyer was, and that was good enough for Pres. Maybe he figures a lawyer would never lie."

"I suppose it's too much to hope this moron gave Rick a bill of sale." A bill of sale would contain the specifics about the instrument, including the manufacturer.

Russ snorted. "Just a receipt. Wrote it by hand on one of those pads that makes an automatic carbon copy. He showed me the copy. All it says is 'cello.' No identifying information. Just the date and the price."

Questions were swirling through my head, but I focused on the main one. "Does he still have the cello?" If so, I'd figure out how to get an order allowing Russ to seize it.

"Nope."

"Who did he sell it to?"

"Nobody. At least, not yet. He had a customer who's been looking for a Wilke, so when this came in, he called her and told her she could take it to try it out."

"He let somebody just walk out of there with that cello? How does he know she'll bring it back?"

"He says dealers do this all the time." I could hear the skepticism in Russ's voice.

"Where's the person who supposedly has it?" For all we knew, this purported customer could have taken the cello out of the state—or the country. She might have sold it to another unscrupulous dealer. Or she might simply have stolen it outright.

"He wouldn't tell me her name. Said it's confidential. I told him it was in his best interests to tell me. Didn't say more than that, but the guy turned white and threw me out of his shop. Turns out, he's got bigger problems than our cello. Look him up."

"He takes a valuable cello on some stranger's say-so, hands over a wad of cash, and then lets the cello walk out the door? I'd say he has problems." I typed "Preston Dixon Cornwall CT" into my search bar.

A second later, my screen was full of links to news stories about the cello dealer who had been arrested on larceny and a variety of other charges. Apparently, Preston Dixon had a nasty gambling habit. After he ran out of assets, he funded his habit by running a nice little racket where he accepted instruments on consignment, sold them, and didn't tell the consignors about the sales, keeping the money for himself. When too much time passed and the consignors demanded their instruments back, he'd tell them the instrument had sold that very day and he'd been just about to call them. Then, he'd take out a fast loan from an unscrupulous source to pay the seller whatever he figured they'd believe had been the real price. He might have kept this con up indefinitely, but one of his consignment sellers landed a gig as second cello in an orchestra in Seattle. When the consignment seller sat down at his music stand, he looked at the cellist next to him and realized that person was playing *his* cello—the selfsame cello Preston Dixon claimed he hadn't yet sold. The cello's new owner confirmed that he'd purchased it from Preston six months earlier, at which point the seller called the police and Preston's scheme unraveled.

"If this guy's such a thief, how is he still in business?" I asked as I continued reading about allegations that some of Preston's loans had come from shady figures, and possibly even the Mafia.

"It's not like you need a license to sell musical instruments," said Russ philosophically. "It's that due diligence thing again. A lot of people don't check him out—they just do a search for cello dealers, and his name pops up. Plus, he looks respectable. Tall, lean, gray hair, wire glasses—looks like classic old Yankee money. Comes off like a retired professor, complete with khakis and button-down collar. He's even got credentials—teaches at a fancy boarding school and plays in a chamber group somewhere in that corner of the state."

A very faint bell was ringing in the back of my mind, but I didn't have time now to try to address it. "This guy sounds like a con artist," I muttered. "Any idea how we get in touch with the person who has Isabella's cello?"

"Don't know. I'm going to keep looking."

"Thanks. Keep track of your time." I clicked off and continued reading articles, except this time, I was looking for specific information. When I found it, I dialed the office of the U.S. attorney in New Haven, introduced myself as a lawyer, and said, "I'd like to speak to the attorney handling the Preston Dixon case."

*****

As I listened to the government's hold music, I scanned more online headlines. Idly, I clicked one link in an article, then another and another, until this title popped up: "Married Physicists Win Nobel Prize."

It couldn't be. But it was.

Lucia McCormick and Anton Bruckweiller had won the Nobel Prize in physics. Both of them.

The article told how they'd been married young, divorced, and gone on with their lives, doing their research separately. Then, five years earlier, Lucia was diagnosed with amyotrophic lateral sclerosis. ALS, also known as Lou Gehrig's disease. A disease which was progressive and degenerative—and incurable. "It was my wake-up call," the article quoted Anton as saying. "Because no matter what I did, it wouldn't be the same without Lucia." Although they hadn't been in contact for years, he reached out. Her assistants were intelligent and hardworking, but her work had come nearly to a standstill because of her illness. "I couldn't stand for that," Anton said. "What she was doing was too important." And so Anton set aside his own work and joined her lab. "No one ever understood me the way Anton does," Lucia said. "I don't need to spell things out for him. We connect." And connect they did: the two pursued Lucia's work for the next three years.

I sat back, remembering them in my office. Lucia looked older in the photograph—no surprise, considering how many years had passed, and considering her illness. I found myself wanting to contact them, to see how they were doing, to ask whether they'd ever reconnected on a personal level or whether their connection was only about their profession. I wanted to know if it was possible for two brilliant, driven people to figure out a way to be together on every level.

Then, I noticed the date of the article. It was close to a year old. I searched further. My throat caught at another headline: "Nobel Winner Dies on Eve of Ceremony." Dr. Lucia McCormick died of ALS on December 3, a mere week before the ceremony at which they would receive their prize. I found Anton's acceptance speech on YouTube. His hair was nearly gone, his glasses were thicker, and his New York accent was still strong as he said, "Of all my regrets in this world, it is that Dr. McCormick and I spent so many years pursuing our work separately. Of all my joys in this world, it is that eventually, we resumed working together. No scientist—no one in any endeavor—could ever ask for a better partner than Dr. McCormick. She was my superior and my support in every way a person can be. More than anything, I wish she were present with us today." His voice cracked, but he continued, thanking everyone and talking about physics stuff I had no way of understanding. At the end, he came back around to Lucia, stating, "There may be some who can achieve greatness alone, but not I. May every one of you be granted a partner as superb as my Lucia. Without her, I would not be standing before you today." He kissed his fingertips and extended them to the heavens—heavens I didn't know if he believed in, but where I suspected Lucia waited for him, hands on hips, saying something like, "Seriously, Anton, would you just get back to work?"

Fifty-Seven

I walked into the tiny conference room on the lower level of the family courthouse, carefully expressionless. Rick was already there. He smirked as if he'd already won.

"Hello, Rick." I sat and took a pad from my briefcase. Then, we faced each other in silence, both knowing that whoever moved first lost the advantage.

Finally, Rick said, "So this is how it's going to go. You're going to tell Ruggiero to fire Carsten and lay off Pres Dixon. Then you're going to tell Carter to tell Izzie to stop bitching about my fee, and you're going to tell Trisha that you made the whole thing up about the cello and there never was any money." He sat back, his smirk broadening.

"Why would I do that?"

"Because I know everything."

I kept my expression as blank as possible. "Meaning?"

"You and the Santa guy. Izzie told me everything. I know you two got married. You know where he is. He's an escaped felon and you're harboring him, which makes you an accomplice. I'll bet the police would like to know about this. In fact, you and Izzie are both guilty, but you're an officer of the court, so that means it's not just your liberty that's at stake, but your license. You barely squeaked through the grievance proceedings last time—you really think the grievance committee is going to give you a second chance? Second time I was in front of them, I barely avoided getting disbarred, and unlike you, I hadn't even committed any crimes."

My heart was pounding, and I remained still only through the most valiant of efforts. Rick might be a dirtbag, but he was a smart dirtbag.

And every word he'd said was true.

When I felt comfortable that my voice wouldn't wobble, I said, "That's what you've got?"

"It's plenty."

"And if it were true, it would be blackmail and extortion. Last time I checked, that was illegal." Not that I'd checked recently. Nobody extorted anybody at the Pole.

"Just a little friendly persuasion. You take care of me, I'll take care of you." His voice was oily. "In fact, I should thank you. If you hadn't told Izzie she could lose the cello in the divorce, she'd probably never have given it to me."

"You knew she wasn't really giving it."

"She said she was."

"She'll say that wasn't what she meant to do."

He shrugged. "She's a competent adult. If she doesn't understand what it means to give something away, that's not my problem."

"It is when you're sleeping with her in order to take advantage of her."

"Consenting adults." A line he'd no doubt used many, many times to excuse his philandering.

"You were trying to coerce her into hiring you for her divorce—a divorce she wasn't even seriously contemplating until you filled her head with crap about how easy it would be. What was it, Rick? Were you that desperate for the fee?" His eyes darted around the room. "Were you behind in support? Maybe the judges weren't being so nice to you because of your reputation? Was Carter threatening to come after you for screwing his wife? Or was Scott getting on you about not bringing in more new clients?" *You owe me*, Scott had said to me. I knew in my gut he'd said the same to Rick, just as I knew Scott would have no compunctions about kicking Rick to the curb if he didn't generate enough business.

"You don't know what you're talking about!" Rick snapped.

He was on the defensive now. Good. "Believe me, I know," I lied. "That's why you're doing criminal now, isn't it? So you can represent your old buddy, Pres Dixon, and run up his bill the way you did with Izzie?" The U.S. attorney had been more than happy to tell me about her dealings with Dixon's lawyer, Attorney McGee of Nettis, Butler, & Gould. I lowered my voice to a menacing near-whisper. "Who do you owe money to, Rick? Somebody not so nice? Somebody who's been extending you some credit and wants you to pay up? One of your pal Pres's friends, maybe?" Maybe Preston Dixon wasn't the only one involved with unsavory characters. So I fired once more: "Does Scott know about all this?"

I was only guessing, but Rick's startled expression let me know my bullet had found its mark. "Stop it!" he shouted. "You're the one aiding and abetting an escaped felon! You and Izzie both! I could have you both arrested!"

"You're an idiot," I said unwisely. "My husband's name is Hank. Hank Riley. He works in a garage. And he's not even from down here, or didn't Scott ever tell you about my Mountie?"

"That's not what Izzie said—"

I assumed a relaxed air even though my blood pressure was likely reaching stratospheric heights. "Izzie likes attention—haven't you figured that out by now? She was afraid you might be moving on to the next skirt, so she made up a little white lie to keep you interested. She does that all the time. You know these musicians—they always have to have a little drama in their lives." I sat back in my chair as if I were totally chill. "Truth is, the similarity of the name was just a coincidence. My client, Izzie's husband—his last name is pronounced '*Klowss*,' not '*Klahz*.' It's German." I slipped my pad back into my briefcase and rose. "I can't believe you fell for her crap. Not that it matters, because you don't represent her anymore, which means we have nothing to talk about. See you around, Rick. Give Scott my best—and don't forget to tell him how you got conned by the woman you thought you were conning. He'll appreciate that information when the grievance committee sends you a nice little invitation to come and talk—which you know they're going to do as soon as Isabella files her grievance against you."

"Marshal!" he shouted.

His eyes were wild. I'd pushed too hard. Casually, as if my heart weren't racing, I said, "Nice chatting with you. Next time, let's do lunch." I picked up my briefcase and strolled out of the room and down the hall to the stairs next to the elevator. I dashed up to the main level, pausing for a moment to let my breathing settle so I would appear calm and professional as I strode through the courthouse. As soon as I was out the front door, though, I raced for my car and zoomed out of the parking lot, barely missing a pair of blue-suited men who yelled after me.

*****

I drove straight to Sandy's. As I drove, I called Ralph. "Send somebody down here. Now."

"Are you okay?"

"Just do it." My voice was trembling.

"What's—"

"I have to get out of here. Fast."

"I'm on my way." He clicked off before I could scream, "No! Not you!"

Then, I called Isabella. "Drop everything and get to Sandy's as fast as you can. Rick's threatening to turn us both in."

"But I don't have a car!"

"Call Holly or Rodrigo. If you can't get them, try Samson, or maybe one of your friends. Whatever. Just do it fast." I didn't want the record of an Uber if I could help it.

I made it to Sandy's in record time. With help from Sandy's husband Ron, I unscrewed my license plates, slipping the plates and my registration into my briefcase as he pulled a tarp over my car. We'd barely finished when Rodrigo pulled in, and Isabella hopped out. "Perfect timing, darling. I was just about to go shopping for window treatments," he said. "Nothing personal, but I'm redecorating the master bedroom." I kissed my friend and thanked him, and he didn't ask any questions although he rightfully could have. Then, Iz and I hunkered down in one of the horse stalls until my message app pinged to let us know our ride had arrived.

As always, the sleigh landed in the far pasture. As we hustled across the field, my heels sinking slightly in the soft ground, a lanky figure clothed head to foot in Claus-black climbed out of the sleigh. "Do we have time to water the reindeer?" Ralph called as we approached. I shook my head. We clambered into the sleigh, and I said, "Let's go!"

"Don't you want your jumpsuits?" Ralph asked.

"Go!"

As the sleigh rose, I maneuvered my way into the black flight garb, not even trying to avoid wrinkling my suit. Isabella did the same in the back seat. I kicked off my pumps and sat cross-legged, my feet tucked under my thighs in the hope that I could keep them warm enough.

Finally, Ralph asked, "What happened?"

"I met with Rick. He threatened to turn us in for harboring you." I'd explained everything to Isabella as we'd waited in the pungent horse stall.

"What about all the other stuff with the cello and the dealer?"

"I scared him. I think that's why he snapped. If we hadn't been in the courthouse, I'd have stayed, but there were marshals right there who could have taken me into custody before I had a chance to warn Iz." Except could they? Suddenly I couldn't recall whether a state marshal had authority to detain someone who wasn't under arrest. Not that it mattered. Rick would probably try to call both of us, and when he couldn't, he'd figure out that we'd gone back to the Pole—proof positive of my guilt and his power. *Shit.*

We landed outside a tiny town in Ontario to let the reindeer have a drink and a rest. I put my heels back on, not caring how absurd I looked. As Isabella filled the water buckets, I wrapped my arms around Ralph. "You shouldn't have come," I murmured. "It was Connecticut. You could have been caught."

He kissed the top of my head. "I'll always come for you." I lifted my face to his, and we kissed as Isabella discreetly tended to the reindeer.

Arms around each other, we walked a few feet away. "Does Phil know she's on board?" I asked in a low voice.

Ralph shook his head. "I didn't know she was coming. But we should tell him."

"Do you want me to call, or do you want to?" In other words, should he hear from his brother or his lawyer that his philandering soon-to-be-ex-wife would show up in his front yard?

"I'll call him," said Ralph. He pulled his phone from his pocket and called his brother while I pulled out mine and called Michael.

*****

"Unbelievable," Michael said when I'd told him everything. "Nothing personal against your sister-in-law, but is she a complete idiot? How could she have told him all this?"

"Pillow talk, I guess. Has he been in touch with you?"

"Not yet. What do you want to do?"

"For now, sit tight. I need to think this through." And figure out how to move all my accounts out of the U.S. so I didn't lose every dime I had.

"I recommend you do your thinking from up there. If Rick really is out to get you, things could get ugly down here."

"I'm sorry for dragging you into it—" I began.

"Stop that. You didn't drag me into anything. You referred a matter to me. That's all." Except it wasn't all, and we both knew it. If Rick couldn't get me, he might go after Michael to see what he knew.

As if reading my mind, Michael continued, "You're giving Rick way too much credit. Sure, he's a manipulative SOB who can't keep his pants on, but I don't think he's evil."

"I'm not sure about that. Besides, he'll do anything for a buck," I said.

"True enough," Michael said. "But I suspect you're right about the grievance committee. If Rick shows up in front of them one more time, I have a feeling that'll be it for his law license."

"I wish I believed that was as important to him as it is to you or me. I don't think Rick cares about it except as a way to make money, and if he can make money some other way, that'll be fine with him."

"Maybe he'll go into business with the cello dealer," Michael said.

"Or maybe he already has," I said slowly. "Maybe that's why one of his demands was that I lay off Preston Dixon. Maybe Scott already dumped him and that's his new partner. You know Rick—he's not a solo kind of guy. Always has to have a partner." My mind began to churn. "How much do I owe Russ Carsten?"

"Couple thousand, probably. He hasn't sent a bill lately. Do you want me to see if he can find anything out?"

"Ask him to see what's out there about Rick being involved with Dixon." Maybe it wasn't a coincidence that Rick had gone to the sleaziest instrument dealer in the state. Maybe they had more of a connection than a mere attorney-client relationship.

"Will do. Keep your head down and stay safe. I'll let you know when I hear anything." He clicked off just as Ralph approached me.

"Well?" I tried to read his face, but it was uncharacteristically blank.

"He says she can come back, but what else could he say? We're halfway there. It's not like he'd have me dump her in the wilds of Canada."

"And?" Clearly, there was more.

"I called Claire to have her make up the guest suite. He didn't say, but I'm figuring he's not ready for her to move back into his place."

"Makes sense." No reason Phil should suffer any more than he already had. "Have you told her?" I asked.

"I guess we should." The use of *we* didn't go unnoticed, but I didn't comment. We walked back to the sleigh where Isabella was dumping out the water buckets. She secured them in the back seat while we tightened the harnesses and the reindeer lifted their heads, refreshed and ready to go.

We waited until the sleigh was aloft before raising the subject of Phil. "Have you talked to him?" I asked Isabella.

"Not lately." Her voice was low. "I don't think he wants anything to do with me anymore."

"Can you blame him?" Ralph's voice was stern, but kind.

Isabella shook her head. "I can't believe I screwed up so badly. And the worst part is—I love him. I'm such an idiot. I can't believe I had the greatest guy in the world, and I threw everything away, and for what?" She began to cry. "I should call and tell him I'm coming so he can be—well, at the far end of the Arctic Circle if he wants."

"I've already spoken with him," said Ralph.

"What did he say?" Her voice was as teary as her eyes.

"Not much. I told him what happened and that you were coming, and was that okay. He said it was."

"What if he'd said no?" she half-whispered.

"We'd have found someplace for you to stay down here," Ralph said, carefully matter-of-fact.

I tried to be encouraging. "If he's willing to let you come, that's a good thing."

Isabella shook her head again. "That's just how he is. Kind. Caring. I feel so awful. I hurt him so badly. I wouldn't blame him if he never wanted to lay eyes on me again."

"He had that choice," I reminded her. "And he said it was okay for you to come back with us. So that's something." She snuffled, and I fished in my briefcase for a pack of tissues. I handed them to her as she began weeping in earnest. I faced forward to give her privacy. Ralph glanced at me out of the corner of his eye, and I shrugged slightly.

For once, my fear of flying didn't consume me, probably because it was outpaced by my fear of what would happen if Rick got anybody to listen to his stories of me marrying a fugitive. Or maybe it was because it was Ralph who was driving. The other Claus brothers were competent, but there was something about Ralph that made me feel protected.

"I love you," I said in a low voice, resting my hand on his arm.

He smiled, clearly appreciating the spontaneous statement. "Love you more," he said, his voice equally low. I wanted to kiss him, but it seemed insensitive with Isabella right behind us, weeping for her lost marriage.

Finally, it was time for our descent. "Home!" Ralph called, and the reindeer perked up, picking up speed. Even though Ralph was driving, I clutched the side of the sleigh and braced my feet against the front as we descended through the clouds. With only the slightest bump, we glided to a stop.

A crowd of somber-faced Clauses and elves stood before us. Certainly not the usual cheerful crowd. "What's this?" I murmured.

Ralph shrugged slightly. "Hey, everybody!" he called as if he was returning from a typical trip.

"Hi!" I said with a forced smile.

We climbed out of the sleigh. None of them moved. I could feel Isabella trembling beside me, and not with the cold. "Say something," I whispered.

She looked at the gathering. "Hi," she squeaked.

Then the crowd parted, and Phil stepped forward. He looked as serious as I'd ever seen. He walked across the snowy yard between his family and us. He stopped in front of Isabella. For a long minute, they looked at each other. Then, he placed his arm around her shoulders and turned to the group.

"This is my wife," he said. "I love her, and she loves me. She has come home. I don't want to hear a word against her. Ever."

Silence loomed. Then, Mitch said, "I don't know if I can agree to that." Phil's face darkened. Just as it appeared he might take a swing at his brother, Mitch said, "I mean, really—look at those boots. They're *purple!*"

Relieved laughter roared through the assembly. Over it all rang Phil's voice: "And she can wear them whenever she wants to!" He kissed her, and she clung to him, tears streaming down her face.

Fifty-Eight

In the days that followed, I watched the family's reactions to Isabella. Julian and Tillie treated her kindly, as if she'd simply been away on a trip. The brothers took their cues from Phil, meaning that if they harbored any resentment toward her, they kept it to themselves, at least for the most part.

Claire and Anya were less circumspect. It was like watching the new girl trying to join an established clique. When Isabella arrived at the Claus table for a meal, a minute later Claire and Anya would just happen to remember something they needed to do, hustling out of the dining hall as if to an emergency.

One part of me was seething. Phil had desperately wanted Isabella to come home, and she had. How could Claire and Anya be anything other than overjoyed for them? On the other hand, these women had had front-row seats to Phil's heartbreak. I could see how they might struggle to set aside their anger at how Isabella had mistreated their brother-in-law.

Or maybe their feelings were less about Phil and more about themselves. After all, somebody had to pick up the slack while Iz was gone. I was only good for so much; not only was I still learning Meredith's job—a full-time task in itself—but I was still practicing law, which further limited my time. Without complaining—at least, not within my hearing—they'd assumed more than their fair share of Pole chores. Considering that both Claire and Anya already had jobs of their own—not to mention children to raise—a little resentment would be justified. When I was a kid, our priest preached had about the prodigal son, and he reminded us that when the prodigal came home, his older brother who had stayed behind and done all the work was pissed as hell. Even at my young age, the brother's position made perfect sense to me. If my brother had left me behind with all the chores and responsibilities, I definitely wouldn't have welcomed him back from his gallivanting with open arms.

I could see that Ralph was torn, too, and I suspected his reasons tracked mine. As Santa, he was supposed to remain essentially neutral, but this was his family. It was his brother she'd cheated on. As hard as Santa might try to support Phil and Isabella in their reconciliation, it was unrealistic to expect everyone else to welcome her home with no reservations.

Isabella had been back for two weeks when Julian called the family together, ostensibly for cocoa and cookies, but we all knew it was his effort to clear the air. We gathered in Julian's apartment after dinner.

Phil and Isabella sat on the sofa nearest Julian. "Isabella doesn't owe anybody anything," Phil said, his arm around his wife.

"That's not true." Isabella's voice was barely audible. "I owe every person at the Pole an apology."

"No." Her husband was firm. "You had every right to follow your dream. Nobody can complain about this."

The silence spoke volumes. Even if they'd disapproved of Isabella leaving her husband to pursue her music career, I'd have bet anything that this was far from their biggest gripe now. Between her extramarital relationships and the divorce proceedings—well, the family could hardly be blamed for harboring some ill will, no matter how fervently Phil wanted to smooth everything over.

It occurred to me that for all his big words, Phil himself might still be struggling. Maybe that was why he was so adamant about everyone moving on. Maybe he figured that the sooner this chapter was behind us, the sooner he could forget. But it wasn't my place to ask. Their marriage was their own business. Whether they could make it work now, with this new dynamic, was up to them.

I half-expected Isabella to stand up and make a formal apology to the family for all the trouble she'd caused, but she wasn't moving. Her eyes were downcast. Sitting on her other side, I was tempted to kick her ankle to jolt her into action, but before I made up my mind, Claire said, "I need to put Ned to bed. 'Night, everybody." She kissed Julian's cheek and left without a backward glance.

Once Claire left, the gathering broke up, everybody talking over each other in their eagerness to dispel the uncomfortable atmosphere. Finally, only Ralph and I remained with Julian. When neither of them spoke, I said, "What do we do?

Ralph looked to his father. "What do you think?" he asked.

Julian's expression was mild. "You're Santa."

Irritation flared in me. "But what do you *think*?" I demanded.

Ralph's glance at me was unreadable: I couldn't tell whether he was telling me to pipe down or if he was grateful that I was pushing his father to speak. Assuming the latter, I continued, "Look, I'm not saying I know anything being married. I have socks older than our marriage. But you know. You were married for eons. Plus, these are your children. You know them better than anybody. If anyone knows what to do to get everybody happy again, it's you."

Julian's smile held a touch of sadness. "They're my sons, but they're not children. Neither are Claire and Anya—or Isabella, or you." I must have looked startled, because he said, "Don't think we don't know the load you've been carrying. You're trying so hard to do what Meredith would have done—not just in business matters, but everything at the Pole."

"That's my job," I said.

Julian reached over and patted my hand. "Your job is to be Mrs. Claus—in your own way. Whatever that might be." His gaze moved from me to his eldest son, then back to me. He started to rise, and we automatically moved to help. Ralph took his arm as I picked up his cane, and Julian smiled. "I have complete faith in both of you to sort this out," he said. "Now go on." He patted Ralph's shoulder, and he leaned over so I could kiss his cheek. "Shoo!" he said when we didn't move. Shaking his head as he chuckled, he headed into his bedroom, leaving my husband and me to watch the door close.

Fifty-Nine

Regardless of how everybody felt about Iz, the reality was that Christmas was barely two months away. In Santa's workshop, the kids came first. I tried to keep an eye on everybody anyway, and especially on Isabella. The girl was working her butt off to prove herself worthy. I encouraged her as much as possible. It was no more than Meredith would have done.

By December 23, we were all frazzled, exhausted, and exhilarated. The electronics team had produced a set of wireless headsets to enable me to maintain contact with Fred, Mitch, and all the workshop leaders; I wore mine unless I was showering or sleeping. My tablet, with its wealth of data about the status of gift production, finishing, wrapping, and storage, was my constant companion—even more so than Ralph, since he was overseeing the final touches on the more complicated gifts. Production and finishing were my bailiwick now, and sometimes it meant being in ten places at once. We'd moved as many elves as possible to the wrapping team, who now worked around the clock getting the gifts wrapped, tagged, and sorted.

The enormous warehouse Meredith had shown me so long ago, with shelves for so many different regions, was filled nearly to capacity. Two days before Christmas, I was bustling through the warehouse, barely looking up from my tablet, when I tripped and crashed to the frigid floor, my tablet skidding away. Muttering, I sat up, shaking my head and rubbing my knee—and then I looked up.

Loaded with gifts, the shelves reached toward the ceiling like trees in a forest reaching skyward. Oblivious to the chill permeating the seat of my pants, I gazed at the kaleidoscope of vibrant hues stretching so far above me. Slowly, I got to my feet, still looking up. All these months, I'd been so focused on managing, on minutiae, on scheduling logistics and juggling details, that I almost missed the best part. It was the spirit of loving, of giving—of Christmas—and it was here.

Heedless now of impending deadlines, I wandered the aisles, marveling at the sheer wonder of all that surrounded me. Literally millions of presents, each requested by a specific, special child who was personally known to none other than Santa himself, every gift wrapped in brightly-colored paper and decorated with bows and tags, piled higher than I could have imagined. Tangible evidence of love, created for children around the globe. Shelf tags proclaimed the destinations: *Vancouver, Lisbon, Kansas, Auckland, Johannesburg, Minsk*. And all of these wondrous gifts would end up in their proper places, because no child's home was too remote for Santa Claus.

Incredible. Fantastical. Magical. Christmas was right here, in a simple warehouse. Joy, waiting to be released into the world.

The child who tore off the colorful paper, squealing with delight at finding exactly the right baby doll or fire truck or whatever else they'd requested—that child would never know how much time and effort and love had gone into creating their particular gift. It was a miracle, pure and simple.

It was Santa magic.

*****

At midday on Christmas Eve, the gong sounded. Almost as one, everyone stopped what they were doing. The time had come.

Ralph stepped into the center of the workshop floor. My husband looked every bit as tired as everyone else at the Pole, but at the same time, he glowed with excitement. This was his moment. It was what he—what all of us—had worked toward all year.

He began by thanking everyone who had worked so hard, singling out elves by name, department, project. His memory was prodigious; he didn't miss a single person. He recounted funny moments and demanding ones. Then, as I knew he would, he moved on to the topic of Meredith.

"This year has been especially challenging since the loss of my mother." He paused, and a murmur ran through the crowd. Julian stood at the back of the room with his other sons; when Ralph mentioned Meredith, their smiles faded just a bit, tinged with sadness. "Most of us don't remember a Christmas when she wasn't at the helm. And as you all know, she had a tendency to store all the information in her head instead of writing it down, which could make things tricky at times." An appreciative chuckle. "Fortunately for us all, before she passed, Mom devoted several months to training her successor, my beautiful wife." He smiled at me and continued, "Our new Mrs. Claus has done a fantastic job getting us all ready for Christmas. In the space of just a few months, she's learned how to run this organization. And of course, tonight will be her biggest test as she and Phil manage the Control Center. So let's all show our appreciation and support for her in this new role."

The elves leapt to their feet, cheering and applauding as if I'd never screwed up, never made anybody's life more difficult because of my ineptitude or new ideas or general cluelessness. From the back, my brothers-in-law raised their hands as they clapped and whistled. Julian blew me a kiss, and Tillie smiled as proudly as if she were responsible for bringing me here. A lump formed in my throat, and tears prickled my nose as Ralph took my hand and kissed me. "You've done such an amazing job," he whispered.

"Not me," I whispered back. "Santa magic, baby." He laughed and wrapped his arms around me.

"Speech! Speech!" the elves were chanting. Ralph raised his eyebrows, and I nodded. He released me, holding up his hands for silence.

"I can't believe it's Christmas," I said. "This year has probably been the most challenging of my life—but I can't think of anybody I'd rather have done it with than the people in this room." I paused to look around, making eye contact with as many as I could. "Every single one of you—you're my gifts. You're Christmas. You're the reason that tomorrow morning, children around the world will wake up to beautiful presents that help them to remember that the spirit of love—the spirit of Santa—is alive and well, no matter what the world may tell them." Everyone applauded again. When the applause died down, I said, "To thank you for all your hard work, we've arranged for a special treat. Annaliese and her fantastic team have set up a feast in the dining hall. They'll keep it going all afternoon, so those of you who still have work to do won't miss out. It's our way of reminding you that we love and appreciate every single one of you. Merry Christmas!"

Everyone cheered. I caught Claire's eye; she was beaming. When I'd first approached her about a thank-you feast, she demurred, saying it would be too much. "Christmas dinner is coming," she said. "They can't do both."

"It depends what we do," I said, as if I hadn't already discussed the matter with Annaliese. "For the thank-you feast, we can do a buffet with a few hot dishes and a bunch of cold items—fancy stuff, like smoked salmon and fermented walrus." The thought of the latter still made me cringe, but Annaliese insisted that this particular delicacy was essential to creating a festive air. "Not to mention all the Christmas cookies with cocoa and mulled cider."

"Cider? Where are you getting cider?"

"You've obviously never been to New England in the fall. You can't turn around without tripping over a gallon of cider, so we laid in a supply back in October." The biggest challenge had been preventing it from turning hard, but Annaliese assured me that she could do it. I had no idea what trick she employed—or whether she called on Ralph for a bit of Santa magic—but now, the warm scent of mulling spices permeated the dining hall.

Shortly after everyone dispersed, Phil summoned me to the Control Center to meet with Ted about the flight plans. We were deep into the discussion when Ralph popped in with a tray. "Anybody want some walrus?" he asked brightly.

"Get that crap out of here!" I still couldn't watch anyone eat it.

"Oh, come on, it's good!" He set the tray on the desk and made a show of biting into a big piece of walrus. His brothers, sympathetic souls that they were, laughed as I squeezed my eyes closed and covered my nose.

"You have to eat it. It's a Claus family tradition," said Mitch, who had been passing by and stopped in to see what all the hilarity was about. "We all do it."

"You also grow beards and pee standing up," I retorted, and the brothers laughed harder.

"Not to mention, we have Santa magic," Ralph reminded me.

"Which you didn't get from fermented walrus," I said. "Now go and get your sleighs ready. We need to finish figuring out where you're going—and don't worry," I added, poking my husband. "You're not going to Connecticut."

"Why not? It worked out pretty well last time." He kissed me, snagged another piece of walrus, and slipped out the door.

"That man will be the death of me." But I couldn't help smiling as I said it.

*****

Finally, it was time. The sleighs were loaded. The reindeer were harnessed, prancing in place, eager to go. The Claus brothers were dressed all in black from head to foot. Charles was Ralph's second, and Ted's son, Justin, was his. Fred's second was Nigel from the plastics shop, and Mitch's was Kenda from the electronics team. Julian stood by the head of Ralph's lead reindeer, one hand on his cane and the other on her antlers. Claire held little Ned on her hip. Anya snapped photos that would one day grace my office. Tillie stood by a reindeer stall; Isabella stood slightly apart, but Tillie reached out her hand, drawing Iz to her side.

"Be careful," I whispered to Ralph as he prepared to board.

"Don't worry," he whispered back, kissing me. "I'll be back before you know it."

"You take care of him," I said to Charles.

"You know it," said the elf who had rescued Ralph from a Connecticut prison.

I watched, my heart in my throat, as the sleighs took off, one after the other. Once they were gone, the stable was almost unbearably quiet. Nobody seemed to know quite what to say. So, I said, "I'm off to the Control Center. You all have some time. Go get something to eat." I hustled out of the stable as if I were in a hurry to get to work when the truth was that I didn't want anybody to see me cry.

*****

Phil and I watched the multicolored travel lines tangling and untangling on the screen. Each stop took mere seconds, which meant that the lines never stopped moving as the sleighs traversed the globe. I could identify which color was which sleigh, but I kept having to consult notes to keep track of who was in Sleigh #2 versus #4. Phil, of course, knew the whole thing by heart, but he watched as if the fate of Christmas was in his hands.

"You know, I can watch this if you want to go and get something to eat," I said after a couple hours. I'd brought my electric tea kettle down from the office, but Phil hadn't shown interest in anything since his coffee ran out.

"I'm okay," he said, just as I knew he would. Nothing would have dissuaded Phil from his job. The devotion to Christmas that his brothers demonstrated on their respective sleighs was peanuts compared to their geeky brother's zeal for managing the Control Center.

"Do you want me to have something brought in for you?" I suggested. "We'll skip the walrus, though." Our attempt at a festive feast had gone a bit awry when it turned out that the fermented walrus was tainted. According to the last report, everyone who'd eaten it was puking their guts out.

"Nah, I'm good." He was peering at the screen. "Pull up the flight plans." His voice sounded . . . odd.

"Is everything okay?" I clicked on various buttons until the right-hand monitor displayed the flight plans for all the sleighs.

"Let me see Ralph's." His eyes were still on the monitor.

I clicked, closing the other plans until the only one that remained was the red strand of spaghetti that trailed down through Canada into the northeastern United States. "What the hell is Ralph doing in New England?" I demanded. I'd just seen those flight plans a few hours earlier. Fred was going to North America, and Ralph was covering the South Pacific, including Australia and New Zealand—as far away from the United States as he could get. Because of all the locations on the planet, there was no place more dangerous for Ralph Henry Claus, Department of Corrections Prisoner #16085478—make that *escaped prisoner*—than the state of Connecticut.

"He switched with Fred. Said he had something to take care of. Ted okayed it." Phil sounded as matter-of-fact as if Ralph had said he needed a new toothbrush, but his brow furrowed above his glasses.

I heaved an aggravated sigh. There was no reasoning with the Claus brothers. "I'm going to kill him," I muttered. He could have gone to Singapore or Ukraine or Peru. But no, my husband was heading straight back to the scene of the crime, the place where he was once incarcerated and where he broke out, guaranteeing that if they caught him again, they'd lock him up and throw away the key.

What the hell was wrong with Ralph? He knew better than to go anywhere near Connecticut. I'd even reminded him what Michael had reported to me a week earlier, namely, that Rick's disbarment proceedings were now under way after a predawn raid by the feds revealed that Rick had been stashing stolen instruments for Preston Dixon. If Ralph encountered a vindictive Rick while delivering presents to the McGee kids, it was anybody's guess whether Santa's Houdini powers would be enough to get him out of there before the prison doors clanged shut.

The other brothers checked in periodically. Mitch was in Düsseldorf, Ted was in Botswana, and Fred was in Christchurch. All places where Ralph could have been with complete safety, but no, not my husband. He had to go back to the one place on the globe where angry people still wanted to lock his ass up.

"I can't stand this," I snapped. "You want anything from the dining hall?"

But Phil was ignoring me. "Santa, Santa, this is Control. Come in, Santa." His voice bore the slightest twinge of concern, and I paused.

"What's going on?" I asked.

"Santa doesn't ignore a call."

And then, I understood. Ralph wasn't blowing us off. If he could have answered, he would have.

Something was wrong.

"Damn it!" I sat down next to Phil. "Where is he?"

Phil's eyes were riveted to the screen. "Marlborough, Connecticut. Butternut Hill Farm on Route 12. And he's been there for almost ten minutes."

Butternut Hill Farm was Sandy's place. Our safe haven. *Shit.* "He's in trouble. Keep trying to raise him." I stood up, my heart beginning to race.

"Where are you going?" Phil looked away from the screen just long enough to see me opening the door.

"I'm going to get my husband."

Sixty

I stormed into the stable. Phelan and the other elves were lounging around, munching goodies and drinking mulled cider. "Okay, boys, it's show time," I said. "Santa's in trouble."

Nothing I could have said would have gotten them on their feet faster. "What's going on, ma'am?" asked Phelan with more respect than he'd ever shown me.

"I need a sleigh and a team. Santa's down. He's in Connecticut, and I'm going to get him."

"You?" Phelan probably didn't mean to sound disrespectful, but I turned on him anyway.

"Yes, me. Set me up with a sleigh and a team. Now!" Elves scurried to do my bidding as I fought back panic.

"You can't go alone," came a voice from the doorway.

I whirled around. Isabella stood next to an empty stall. "What do you suggest?" I bit off the words.

Her voice was quavering, but firm. "You'll need a second sleigh. If something's wrong with Ralph and Charles or their sleigh, one person will need to deal with everything on the ground while the other delivers gifts."

She was right. Everything in me at that moment was focused on Ralph, but there were still gifts to deliver and the other brothers were in different parts of the world.

"Can you fly?" I asked. As if I had any skills to speak of.

A small smile broke over her face. "Like the wind."

I turned to face the open-mouthed elves. "You heard her! Hitch up a second sleigh! Now!"

"Um, Mrs. Claus—" One of the elves approached tentatively.

"What?" I tried not to yell.

"Just—are you sure?"

"Of course!" I didn't bother asking which part of the plan the elf was questioning. It didn't matter.

We needed to get down to Connecticut. Pronto.

*****

"Are you sure can you do this, Meg?" Isabella asked in a low voice as the elves hitched the sleighs.

"Of course," I snapped as if I had even the slightest reason to believe it was true. One of the elves was turning on the dashboard communications, and I heard Phil's voice come through: "Sleigh Five, Sleigh Five, can you read me?"

"Yes!" I shouted. The elf timidly pointed to the button labeled *talk*, and I pushed it. "Yes, I hear you!"

"You don't have to shout," said Phil even as Isabella said the same thing from behind me.

"Fine. I can hear you." I drew a deep breath.

"Okay. Your flight plan is ready. It's pretty straightforward. You shouldn't have any trouble." He sounded as if he was trying to calm me down.

"Great. So if I'm Sleigh Five, does this mean Iz is Sleigh Six?"

"Iz? What are you talking about?"

Isabella leaned near the intercom. "I'm going, too. Whatever's going on, somebody will need to deal with the gifts."

"But you can't—" her husband sputtered.

"Sure she can," I said. "And she's going to. I'm making an executive decision." After all, I was Mrs. Claus.

"Yes, ma'am," Phil muttered. The elves were wide-eyed. Isabella looked as if she would either curtsy or burst out laughing.

As the elves scurried to hitch up the sleighs, I said to Isabella, "How did you know about—" I waved my hand.

"There's a speaker from the Control Center in our apartment," she said. "Phil would never risk being anywhere without contact."

"Makes sense," I allowed.

Phil's voice came over the intercom. "Is everything ready?"

"You tell us," I said. "Are the flight plans in place?"

"They are. But Iz—honey, you haven't flown in a long time. Are you sure?" He sounded less like the head of the Control Center and more like a nervous husband.

"She is," I snapped. "Just clear us for takeoff." I climbed into my sleigh, and Isabella climbed into hers. We looked to each other and nodded.

Then it occurred to me: "Don't we need seconds?"

"Not for this," said Phelan. "The seconds are only needed for gifts." Which meant we were both flying solo.

Yikes.

"You'll go first, Meg," said Phil. "Iz will be a few minutes behind. We don't want the sleighs too close to each other."

I had no idea if this was logical, but it was too late to argue. I'd faked bravado in front of the Connecticut Supreme Court. I could fake it now. "Let's go!"

With that, the barn doors opened, and my sleigh took off into the night.

*****

"Hey, Control? Come in, Control?"

"Control here. What's going on, Sleigh Five?"

"Um, nothing special. Just wanted to make sure everything's okay on your end. How's everybody who ate the walrus?"

Phil didn't quite muffle his snort. "Pretty much as they were when you left fifteen minutes ago." In other words, still puking. I was willing to bet that was what had felled my husband, too.

"Fine. Just checking." I'd heard poor Annaliese sobbing in the kitchen as I'd raced past on my way to the stable. Clearly, she felt completely responsible for the debacle. As if it were possible to tell whether something that vile had gone bad. I'd reassure her when I got back.

"What about you? You okay?" Phil asked.

"Me? Oh, sure. I don't eat walrus."

"That's not what I meant." Phil wasn't the warm, fuzzy type, but he sounded marginally sympathetic.

"I'm fine." If I hadn't been clutching the reins, I might have crossed my fingers in the hope that I sounded as if I weren't lying.

"Okay. Sing out if there's a problem. I'll leave your mic open."

I'd flown at night before, but only as a passenger. Somehow, I never realized how quiet it was. With my night goggles, I could see the reindeer moving, but they weren't making any noise. Nothing was. It was like being in a dark vacuum, suspended in nothingness. I could feel my stomach lurching even though I hadn't consumed any tainted walrus.

"Oh, sweet Jesus," I murmured. "Don't let me die up here." Everything clenched—my hands, my jaw, my legs, my gut.

You're not going to die.

"What the—?" The voice startled me enough that I lifted my head. "Who said that?"

But there was no answer, only the quiet.

"Who are you? Who said that?"

"Meg? Everything okay?" came Phil's voice.

"Sure, fine. Everything's fine. I just thought—" But I couldn't tell him I thought I'd heard a voice. He'd make me land and have someone cart me off to the local nuthouse.

"You sure you're okay?" Phil appeared to be having the same thought.

"I'm sure. Just a weird—you know what, never mind. I'm fine." I was about to turn the intercom off when I had a thought. "Can you do me a favor? Can you play music?"

"Like what?"

"I don't know. Find something light. I need . . . something fun."

Silence. Just when I thought he'd written me off as a lunatic, the fabulously lavish prelude to *My Fair Lady* came through the speaker.

In the freezing night, flying through the darkness to who knew what kind of disaster, all I could do was laugh.

*****

God bless Phil forever.

Turned out, he dispatched Tillie to the library to find every soundtrack to every Broadway show and movie I'd brought, plus my old CD player. For the rest of my trip, he played songs from *My Fair Lady, A Chorus Line, Grease, Rent, Pippin, Camelot, Fiddler on the Roof,* and *The Sound of Music.* I wouldn't say I relaxed, but for the first time, I wasn't terrified out of my mind.

Then, without warning, Phil interrupted Julie Andrews singing about her favorite things. "They're right below you."

It took a second for me to come back to the enormity of my task. I was flying a sleigh on Christmas Eve. I was searching for Santa. I was trying to save Christmas. And I had to land this sleigh.

Oh. My. God.

I peeked over the edge of the sleigh. Darkness below, just as above. Pinpricks of light so scattered that I couldn't know if they were really there. "I can't see anything!"

Phil's voice was as calm and soothing as mine wasn't. "Tell the reindeer 'Santa'. They'll know."

"Are you sure?"

"Do it! Now!" Stress was sneaking through the cracks in his calm.

"Santa!" I squeaked.

The reindeer abruptly circled back and started a steep descent. I fought not to close my eyes or pull back on the reins. *Trust the reindeer. Trust the reindeer.*

With the slightest thump, we landed in our regular fenced pasture. It was my best landing ever, and I had nothing to do with it. Cautiously, I disembarked and made my way over the frozen ground to another sleigh. Sacks of gifts were heaped in the back seat.

But there was no sign of Ralph or Charles. Or the reindeer.

I flicked on the flashlight on my phone and shone it around, not caring whether I was seen. No Santa. No elf. But the light reflected off the sleigh. My gut clenched as it revealed a broken runner. *Oh, God, no.* They'd had a bad landing. I shone the light again, this time looking for evidence of where—or how—they might have moved away from the damaged sleigh. But I saw no blood, no sign of the frozen grass being smashed by someone crawling or being dragged.

Where the hell were they?

Screw secrecy. I called out, "Ralph! Charles! Where are you?"

We're in the barn, my husband texted.

I sprinted in the direction of the barn, stumbling over ruts in the dirt road outside the pasture fence. The relief of the familiar calmed me slightly. Thank God they'd made it to Sandy's.

Except it meant my husband was on the ground in Connecticut—the one place on earth where he was never, ever supposed to be. The place where he was most likely to be thrown in prison. Which meant that no matter what was happening, we needed to get the hell out of here before someone discovered him.

No sliver of light emanated from the barn, but my flashlight revealed the handle on the heavy door. I pulled it back, and light spilled out. "Where are you?"

"Over here!"

I closed the door and ran down the aisle between the stalls where horses dozed. In the last stall at the far end, I met a most remarkable sight: Ralph, clothed in Claus-black and with a greenish tinge to his complexion, crouched beside Charles, who was as pale as snow. The elf lay on what looked like a saddle pad on straw. In surrounding stalls, reindeer munched horse feed.

"Hey, babe," said my husband as if I'd come upon him in our kitchenette.

"Hey, babe," I echoed. "What's going on?"

"Hey, counselor." Charles's voice sounded weak.

"What's going on?" The question was directed to both of them now. Unsurprisingly, neither responded. "What are you doing?" My voice was firmer now. I was Mrs. Claus, and I wanted an answer.

"Trying to sort things out," said Ralph. Our eyes met. My first urge was to relent, but it was Christmas Eve. No matter what, there were gifts to deliver. We didn't have time for fluff.

I beckoned to Ralph to follow me. We left Charles in the stall and walked several feet away. "What's going on?" I asked for the third time, this time in a lower voice.

"I think it's his appendix." Trust Ralph to focus on the other guy first.

I nodded, my mind already clicking. "And you?"

"Food poisoning." I was about to tell him when he confessed: "I think it was the walrus."

I stifled a sudden urge to laugh. Ralph and his stupid fermented walrus. But there was no time for gloating. "We need to get Charles to the hospital. Does Sandy know you're here?"

"We tried not to wake her." Then his eyes grew round, and he turned to vomit into the hay of the nearest stall.

My mind was racing. Charles needed to go to the hospital, and the gifts needed to be delivered. Both were emergencies. I texted Iz to see how far out she was. She could get Charles to the hospital. I sent her Sandy's address and turned to Ralph. "Can you fly?"

"Of course," Ralph said heroically. I raised both eyebrows: the broken runner told its own story. "I'm sure I can," he said with somewhat less certainty.

I'd wait to lay him out later. His gift deliveries were dangerously behind schedule. My phone dinged. A text from Isabella: *ETA 5 min.* "Let's go," I said, hustling back over to where Charles lay grimacing. I knelt beside him and placed a hand on his shoulder. "Okay, here's the deal. Isabella's going to take you to the hospital to see if you need your appendix out."

"How do you think that's gonna happen?" Even in pain, Charles understood the risks.

"Santa magic, baby." I looked over at Ralph, who nodded. Santa magic couldn't heal, but it sure could do a lot of other stuff. "When you get there, all the info will be in the computer. Just tell them you're Hank Riley."

Charles looked as if he wasn't sure whether to laugh or puke. "Hank Riley? Who's that?"

"Me," said Ralph. "But tonight, you're me."

"So, I'm her husband?" Charles managed a lecherous grin.

"Don't get too excited, pal." I rested my hand on his glossy bald scalp. "Just be okay. No complications, no infections. And don't flirt with the nurses. I don't want to hear that my husband's a dirty old man." Charles did laugh that time, although he immediately grabbed his gut. "Take it easy," I said. "You're going to be fine."

"You two need to get going," Charles said. "There are a lot of gifts left."

"We know," said Ralph. "But we're going to wait until Isabella gets here to pick you up."

"You don't have to wait," said Charles.

"Actually, we do," I said. "So deal with it."

Charles looked at Ralph. "She's gotten to be a real hard-ass."

"Don't I know it," said Ralph, kissing the top of my head.

The few minutes before Iz arrived felt like hours. While I waited with Charles, Ralph headed out to the pasture to move the gifts from the broken sleigh to the one I'd brought.

Finally, Isabella hurried in, and I updated her on the situation. "How do you want to do this?" she asked.

"We'll deliver the gifts. You take care of Charles." I rested my hand on the elf's brow as if I'd actually have a clue what to do if he was feverish. "Call 911. I'll let Sandy know you're here so she doesn't freak out when the ambulance comes."

"What are you going to do about the extra sleighs?"

"Don't worry," came a familiar voice. "We'll get them moved."

We all looked up to see Sandy standing in the aisle. She was half-smiling. "Once you call, you've probably got ten minutes before the ambulance gets here. Move your livestock first. Ron and the kids will take care of the sleighs."

"Thank you," I breathed. I took hold of two reindeer halters and led them out while the other two followed obediently. With both hands full, I didn't have the benefit of my phone's flashlight, but the reindeer seemed to know exactly where they were going. Of course, they did. They were going to Santa, wherever he was.

By the time we reached the pasture, Ralph had finished moving the gifts from the disabled sleigh. He hitched up the team I'd brought out—the reindeer that had enjoyed a chance to rest and refresh—as I took the reindeer from my sleigh and from Isabella's and headed for the far pasture.

"Let us do it," said a middle-aged man in a plaid flannel shirt. "You need to get going. The ambulance will be here any minute." He and a teenage girl grabbed halters and hustled the reindeer around behind the barn while a pair of adolescent boys ran to the pasture and dragged the sleighs into the shadows of the trees at the far side.

It was as Ralph had said so long ago: believers are everywhere.

The reindeer who were now hitched to the sleigh lifted their heads as if hearing something. In the next instant, Ralph and I exchanged a look, acknowledging that we too heard the faint wail of the ambulance. "Let's go," he said, except he bent over to vomit again.

"That's it, Walrus Boy. I'm driving," I said as we climbed in.

"I can drive," he protested.

"You really think this is a time to argue?" I picked up the reins. "Let's go!" In a whoosh, we were airborne. Below us, the red lights of the ambulance cut through the darkness. "I hope he's okay," I muttered. To Ralph, I said, "Where are we going?"

He tapped the button on the dash. "We're airborne. What's the plan?" He listened intently as Phil laid out the flight plan. I glanced down at the new yellow line on the screen. "We're the red line this time," Ralph said. I nodded my acknowledgment, watching it from the corner of my eye as I steered.

"Let me know if you need to stop and puke," I said as we approached our first address.

He snorted. "How did I ever end up with such a sentimental wife?"

"Guess you drew the short straw. See how Iz and Charles are doing."

Obediently, he tapped his phone. "In the ambulance. She'll keep us updated." Before I could respond, he said, "Green house with pine tree out front. Slow the reindeer, and—now!"

The reindeer must have known what *now* meant, because the next thing I knew, we were balanced on the roof of the green house. Ralph hopped out, grabbed the sack, and disappeared down the chimney, as agile as if he were on flat, dry ground. I remained motionless, my heart pounding. What if he got caught? What if he got sick again? What if I did something to screw up this precarious balancing act and the sleigh fell off the roof?

Before I could conjure more disaster scenarios, Ralph was back in the sleigh. "Let's go!" he barked, and with another whoosh, we were airborne.

"That was fast," I observed.

"Have to be. We're behind schedule. Can you pick up the pace?"

"How do I do that?"

"Faster!" he called, and the reindeer obliged.

Even through my face mask, I could feel the biting winter wind. "Any reason you couldn't have had your little adventure in the Caribbean?"

My husband laughed. "You still think this is cold?"

"Compared to Aruba, yes."

"Wait 'til we get home. I'll warm you up." He rested his gloved hand on my thigh.

"Keep your mind on your job, Santa." But I couldn't help grinning as I piloted the reindeer through the frigid Christmas Eve darkness. I pressed the button on the console. "Hey, Phil, can we have my playlist?" Within moments, we were soaring through the night sky as the von Trapp children sang "Do-Re-Mi."

Sixty-One

Afterward, I couldn't have said how many stops we made. Single-family homes, duplexes, apartment buildings, even some cabins in various hinterlands. We did have to land a few times to allow Ralph to deal with the last of the fermented walrus, but for the most part, we operated like the quintessential well-oiled machine. In a remote part of western Virginia, we delivered a pony, although I had no idea where it came from before Ralph took hold of its halter and led it to the trough full of hay that I'd have sworn wasn't there when we landed. Ditto with the beagle puppy who went to a little girl in a farmhouse near Pittsburgh and a pair of kittens who went to a pair of twins in a suburban neighborhood outside Chicago. Santa magic, all over the place.

But the vast majority of the gifts were toys from the workshop. I blinked hard to hold back tears as Ralph took sack after sack of gifts down chimneys (some of which magically appeared as he approached). *We did this*, I thought. Ralph and me, all the Clauses, all the elves—we did this. We made Christmas for all these kids. Some of the homes were grand, but most were humbler. No matter. I knew from years of divorce practice that the fancy homes didn't necessarily house happy families. In some of these McMansions, the gift Santa delivered might be the only one the kid really wanted because their warring parents couldn't be bothered to care.

"You okay?" Ralph asked when he returned from one such delivery.

I rubbed my eyes. "Sure. Fine. How about you?"

"Doing okay." When we were in Manhattan, I'd insisted on stopping in Chinatown and getting a thermos of ginger tea which I then insisted he drink. He complained about the flavor, but we made fewer puke stops after he drank it. By the time we finished the southeastern seaboard of the United States, his food poisoning appeared to have abated.

We were racing the sunrise when Isabella texted to say that Charles was out of surgery and everything was fine. *They said it was lucky we came in when we did,* she added.

"Guess it's a good thing you got bad walrus," I observed. "Do we have any more stops?"

"Just one." He sounded as tense as I felt: the sun was coming up. We couldn't risk being seen. We exchanged brief glances. There was no way we wouldn't do it, but we had to get in and out fast.

"Now!" he said, and the reindeer descended. I'd barely landed when he leapt from the sleigh, grabbed the sack, and went down the chimney. I waited, ready to fly. The reindeer were poised for action.

But he didn't come right back.

Shit.

I listened. Noises were coming from the house. I waited. Still no Ralph.

"Damn him," I muttered. The house was a single story. I could get to the ground without breaking my neck. "Stay here," I said to the reindeer. I slipped out of the sleigh, slid down the roof, and landed in a shrub.

From ground level, I could hear the voices. I peered in a large picture window. Ralph stood by the fireplace, sack by his feet, hands in the air. A hefty man in a T-shirt and boxers shouted as he held a shotgun on Santa who, in all fairness, didn't look very Santa-like in Claus-black. Behind the man, a skinny blond woman and a skinnier blond boy cowered. The boy was crying. I could hear the wife pleading, but her words were indistinguishable.

No matter. It was time to roll.

I pounded on the door with all my strength. In the deepest, loudest voice I could muster, I shouted, "FBI! OPEN UP!"

The hefty man stopped bellowing. From the front step, I could see in the window just enough to catch his reflection in a mirror over the sofa. He still had his shotgun trained on my husband. "WE KNOW WHAT YOU'RE DOING! OPEN UP RIGHT NOW OR WE'LL BLAST THE DOOR DOWN!" I yelled as I kept pounding.

"What the—" The hefty man made a move toward the door, taking his eyes off Ralph for that one crucial second. An instant later, Ralph had disappeared up the chimney, and I raced to crouch behind the shrub.

The door flung open. "Who's out here?"

I remained as perfectly still as a cornered rabbit. Shotgun in hand, Hefty charged out of the house. "Who's here?" he demanded. I hovered behind his shrub as he ran around, demanding in more and more agitated tones to know who was here.

After several minutes of no answer, Hefty stomped back inside and slammed the door. Immediately, I ran from my hiding place as Ralph swooped the reindeer down. "Go! Go!" I hissed as I grabbed the side of the sleigh, and he took off with me still hanging on, my boots on the runner.

Breathing hard, I climbed into the sleigh, collapsing on the seat. Ralph was laughing so hard he was wheezing. "What was *that?*" he managed finally.

"I couldn't think of anything else," I managed.

"You were magnificent," he said, kissing my hand. "I can't imagine anybody else pulling that. . . ." He laughed and laughed, and I laughed with him.

"You okay?" came Phil's voice over the intercom.

"We're fine," Ralph wheezed. "All done. Everybody else okay?"

"All's well," said Phil. "Come on home."

"Roger that." My husband turned to me. "You want to drive?"

I gazed at this man I loved so much. "You take the reins."

*****

Our arms around each other, we followed the crowd to the dining hall for Christmas breakfast. Annaliese and her team had pulled out all the stops. Eggs, sausages, pancakes, muffins, urns of coffee and tea and cocoa—I hadn't realized how hungry I was until the aromas of her marvelous cooking reached me. I headed for my regular seat, but Ralph stopped me.

"Not today," he said. He indicated what looked like the head table at a wedding. "You've got to tell everybody what happened."

This, as it turned out, was a sacred part of Christmas at the Pole: those who had done deliveries regaled the others with stories of the night. Laughing and eating, we heard how Ted had delivered a bunny rabbit to a little girl in Johannesburg, how Fred narrowly avoided landing in a lake in Tasmania when a harness strap broke loose, how a little girl sleeping on the sofa in Munich woke and saw Mitch. "Lucky for me, she didn't scream," he said. "I shoved her new doll into her arms, and I put out all the other stuff while she was distracted, and I got out of there as fast as I could."

Our story of food poisoning and Shotgun Guy won cheers, but the real hero of the night was Isabella. Turned out, she gave a flawless performance as the wife of Hank Riley, appendicitis patient. As soon as he was discharged on Christmas morning, Isabella secured an Uber to Sandy's farm. Sandy invited them to stay for a day or two so Charles could rest up before traveling, but the patient was adamant that they had to go home right away to make sure everything had been handled properly. Reluctantly, Iz gave in, and as Charles dozed, sated with his post-op pain meds, Isabella commandeered their flight back to the Pole.

When they landed a few hours after our festive breakfast, we were all outside the barn to welcome them home. The applause from the entire Pole community echoed through the vast polar night. While Ted and Fred helped Charles out of the sleigh, Phil lifted his wife down, wrapping his arms around her. "I'm so proud of you," I heard him say.

"Iz, you're amazing," said Ralph, lifting his mug of mulled cider. "We all owe you a huge debt of thanks." And with that pronouncement from Santa, all was finally well.

Then, Ralph turned to the community. "Merry Christmas to all of you," he said, his voice trembling slightly. "You are all my family. Because of you, children around the world are celebrating this morning. Our heartfelt thanks to every one of you." Applause erupted again as he turned to Julian. "Merry Christmas, Pop," he said in a low voice.

"Merry Christmas, Santa," Julian said. He turned to me. "And merry Christmas to you, Mrs. Claus." He reached out to take my hand. "Meredith would have been so proud of you." Tears filled my eyes as he squeezed my hand.

"Thank you," I mouthed, because I couldn't make a sound. I looked up to see my husband smiling at me with so much love. The tears streamed down my cheeks, and he took me in his arms.

Still holding me, he announced, "And now, it's time to say good night!" Everyone laughed, and those of us who had been up all night retreated happily to our beds.

Sixty-Two

Gradually, I swam up from the depths of sleep to the conscious world. I could hear Ralph talking in the other room. Who was here at this ungodly hour?

I fumbled for my bathrobe and pulled the belt tight. As I opened the door, his words became clear: "You're going to have to make do with me, because your mother had a very long night, and she needs her sleep." I leaned against the door jamb, stifling my delight, as he continued, "I think I've got this. Harry, here's your food. David, here's yours, and Lulu, here's yours." He set the dishes on the floor. As usual, Harry scarfed down half his food and moved over to nudge David out of the way. "Cut that out, young man," said Ralph, moving Harry back to his own dish. "Let your brother eat his own food. What's the matter, Lulu? Don't you like it? Let's put some crunchies on it and see if that's better—all right, you two, you can have crunchies too. Everybody gets crunchies. Is that better? Good." He straightened and turned to see me lounging in the doorway, my grin wide.

"Hey, you're up! You want some tea? The water's hot." He placed my tea filter in a mug and reached for my jar of loose tea. "Irish breakfast okay?"

"Sure." As he scooped tea into the filter, I wandered over to where the cats were busily chowing down. "Hey, guys," I said, petting each in turn. They didn't look up from their dishes. "Did Papa give you some good breakfast?"

Ralph poured water through the filter into my mug. "'Papa'?"

"Would you prefer to be known as Daddy?"

His cheeks reddened under the stubble. "You're crazy," he muttered, and I laughed out loud as I wrapped my arms around him.

*****

"I thought I might find you here."

My head jerked up. My husband stood in the doorway of the office, a small smile on his face. "What are you doing?" he asked, seating himself in one of the wing chairs.

"What are you doing up?" I asked. He'd gone back to bed after feeding the cats.

"I had a nap. What's going on? We won't have any gift requests for at least a couple weeks."

"It's not that."

"Then . . . ?"

I took a deep breath. "I'm resigning from the bar."

"No! Why would you do that?" Ralph seemed genuinely dismayed.

I leaned back in my chair. "Because I'm not a lawyer anymore. This is my job now. I'm Mrs. Claus."

"You can be Mrs. Claus and still be a lawyer. Come on, Meg. You love being a lawyer. You can't give that up."

His earnest expression made me smile. "You're the last one I'd have expected to tell me I should stay a lawyer. I figured you'd want me to be a full-time Mrs. Claus."

"I want you to be happy," my loving husband said. "I don't think you're going to be happy if you quit being a lawyer."

"I think I can be."

We sat in silence on opposite sides of his mother's desk—my desk. Finally, Ralph said, "I'll make you a deal. Give it one year. If you still want to quit next Christmas, I won't say a thing. But give it time. There's no rush."

"But why wait? I've wrapped up all my cases." Kristofer had already moved all my accounts to Iceland. I'd transferred title to my car to Holly. My law license was the last tangible thing tethering me to Connecticut, to the life I once had.

"Then close your practice. It's just a business. You can always start another one. But being a lawyer—that's who you are."

"It's who I was," I corrected gently. "There was a time when it was all I wanted to be. But now—being here, being a part of all this—it's so much more than what I had down there. Sure, I knew what to do to represent Phil and deal with all that crap, and I'm glad I could help—but that's not who I am anymore." I rose and walked around the desk, sitting in the other wing chair, and I took his hand. "I've seen first-hand what's here, and this is what I want to do. There's nowhere else on earth that I'd rather be."

Ralph regarded me, and I knew he saw everything and more. "Obviously, it's up to you, but—are you absolutely sure? Do you really want to do this?"

"I do." His eyes grew misty. My heart swelled. He reached out, took my hand, and kissed it. I walked back around the desk and adjusted my glasses as I read my letter one more time. Then, under the watchful gaze of Santa Claus, I took a deep breath and clicked *send*.

Sixty-Three

On Boxing Day evening, after everyone had rested, the family gathered in Julian's apartment for our own private gift exchange. These gifts didn't come from the workshop; they were procured or created by the individual Clauses for one another. We drew names in October since we all knew how busy we'd be in November and December.

I'd drawn Claire's name. After much wracking my brain, I made up a gift basket containing a luxurious intensive hand cream, a lavender-scented candle, and as many other high-end items as I could come up with for a woman to enjoy an evening of pampering herself. Assisted by a couple of elves, I made the basket as beautiful as possible. After Claire and the other women had oohed and aahed over the basket, I handed her an envelope. "This goes with it," I said.

Claire opened it and squealed. "Oh my gosh! Seriously? Are you serious?"

"I'm serious," I said as firmly as I could.

"What is it?" Ted asked. She was waving it in his face, and he caught her arm so he could read it. Then he turned to me, slack-jawed. "Are you serious?"

"I'm serious," I said again.

"What is it?" Mitch demanded. He plucked it from Claire's hand and read it. Then, he burst into laughter. "Oh, I can't wait to see this!"

"Will somebody please tell us what that says?" asked Fred.

Mitch rose and held the card up as if making a state pronouncement. "'This card entitles the bearer and the companion of her choice'—hope that's you"—he added to Ted—"to an all-expenses-paid week at The Spa at Norwich Inn in Norwich, Connecticut.'"

"But what about the kids?" asked Anya, eying the card.

"Oh, that's the best part," chortled Mitch. "'All childcare services during the bearer's absence will be provided by one Megan Elizabeth Riley Claus.' Meg's gonna babysit!"

"It's not *that* funny!" I tried to sound indignant as everyone broke into laughter. Yes, I knew it would be a challenge. Luckily, I'd have Tillie and a coterie of elves to help me—just in case Claire decided to take Anya instead of Ted.

"It's Ralph's turn," said Tillie. "Ralph, who did you get?"

"I got Isabella." Isabella sat on the sofa, Phil's arm around her shoulders. She still looked a trifle uncomfortable in Claus gatherings, as if not everyone had fully accepted her even after her heroics on Christmas Eve. I wondered whether Ralph had used a touch of Santa magic to get her name, just to make sure her gift was as special as all the others.

Now, at Ralph's nod, Mitch went into Julian's bedroom, returning with a large rectangular package. I already suspected what it was: a new cello. For a new start.

Isabella knew it, too. Mitch set the package gently in front of her. Her eyes glistened as she tore off the paper. When she lifted the lid and saw a cello case, she pressed her hand against her mouth to stifle her cry.

"Good job, Santa," I murmured as she opened the case.

Her shriek was like nothing I'd ever heard from her. With trembling hands, she lifted the instrument. Tears poured down her face as she held it close.

"It's beautiful, Iz," I said. Everyone chimed in with their assent. Only Phil was silent, a stunned expression on his face. Then, he looked at his brother, who nodded, and Phil's eyes grew moist.

"What?" I asked, looking from one to the other. Then, it dawned on me. To Ralph, I whispered, "Did you—is that why you went to Connecticut?", and his smile told me everything.

"It's my cello!" Isabella sobbed.

"Well, sure," said Mitch, perplexed. "It's your present."

"No—this is *her* cello," said Phil. "The Wilke."

"The one that got stolen?" asked Fred.

"That's the one." Phil looked as if he might cry, too. "But how—?" Words failed him as he rested his hands on Isabella's shoulders, and she in turn caressed the cello as she wept.

Ralph's smile was gentle. "You of all people should know better than to ask Santa how he does what he does."

It took a while before Isabella stopped crying long enough to tighten the bow. Tears continued to slip down her cheeks as she tuned the instrument. Then, she drew the bow across the strings, and we all sat in awed silence as she played, "O Holy Night."

Finally, the rich, sonorous notes faded. Then, she turned to Ralph. "I can never thank you enough," she said, her voice trembling.

Ralph leaned over and kissed her cheek. "Merry Christmas, Iz." Phil mouthed, "Thanks," and his big brother winked. Later, when I asked him how he did it, all Ralph would say was, "Santa magic, baby."

Then, Julian said, "I drew Meg's name." No secret, since Julian was always the last to give his gift and everyone else had received theirs. He reached out, a small unwrapped box in hand. I thought Ralph would pass it to me since he was between us. When he didn't move, I rose to take it from Julian. My father-in-law held my hand as he said, "This is from both of us." Surprised, I looked at Ralph, but he seemed as puzzled as I was.

I opened the box and gasped. Inside was the antique emerald ring I'd seen on Meredith's hand every day. My mouth felt dry as I removed it from its box. Julian nodded to his eldest son, and Ralph reached over to take the ring. He slipped it onto the third finger of my right hand and kissed me.

"I—I can't. I'm not—I'm—" Now, it was my voice that trembled.

"Hush, my dear," said Julian. "You can. You are. You've proven it time and again—especially on Christmas Eve. If she were here, she would have put it on you herself—even though technically, that's Santa's job." A small smile played on his lips. He pulled me down and kissed my forehead. "You are a worthy successor. I have complete confidence in you." The others burst into applause as I sat down beside Ralph, my eyes glued to the ring.

Back in our apartment, I moved in a daze as I gave the cats their treats and got ready for bed. I came out of the bathroom to see my beloved husband setting his boots side by side in the closet. He turned around, and my heart swelled with joy. "I love you, Santa Claus," I said, embracing him.

"And I love you, Mrs. Claus." He kissed me, and I knew it was for real and forever.

I was home.

THE END

ACKNOWLEDGEMENTS

First of all, I'd like to thank everyone whose support for my first novel, *State v. Claus*, made writing this book seem like a good idea. Writing a second novel is very different from writing a first, and your enthusiasm for a sequel has been wonderfully encouraging.

Many thanks to my wonderful team of beta readers: Lois Lake Church, John B. Valeri, Kay Roseen, and Jonathan Grover. Your insights, comments, and suggestions were immensely valuable as I worked through draft after draft of this book. Thank you for your time, your expertise, and your beautiful friendship.

Special thanks to my editor, Sarah Hayes Gilligan of Cerebration. From catching the tiniest of typos to helping me to assess the overall work, your precision, insights, and recommendations were invaluable. Thank you, my friend!

Lawrence Wilke is indeed a real person. Not only does he make exquisite cellos in his Connecticut workshop, but he is delightful, enthusiastic, and generous in sharing his knowledge and expertise about cellos and cello dealers. Many thanks!

To Nicole Flores, Miko Golachowski, and everyone at Road Scholar, thank you for your wonderful seminars and materials about the Arctic Circle, including the North Pole. I wish I could have included everything you shared about that remarkable region. Thank you for sharing your knowledge and experience.

Thanks to my dear and supportive friends, including (but not limited to) Kathleen Morrison Grover, Karen Downey, Dawn Hoffman, Kiersten Schiffer, John B. Valeri, Donna Seely Ulloa, Mary E. Kelly, and Eliz Davoli, who encourage me and cheer me on with each new step in my writing and publishing journey, especially when my announcements include photos of cats.

Special thanks to my sister, Julie Marcus, for her enthusiasm and support. Julie was so excited about this book that she reread *State v. Claus*, just to tide her over until the sequel came out. At long last, here it is!

To my mother, Shirley Burgh, whose love and support for my writing has never failed over all these years.

Finally, to my beloveds, Olivia, Rosie, Danny, Charlotte, and especially my sweet Ned. Mama loves you all, for real and forever.

ABOUT THE AUTHOR

P. Jo Anne Burgh is an author, lawyer, entrepreneur, and cat lover. Her previous books are *State v. Claus: A Tale of Lawyers, Reindeer, Love, and Magic* (Tuxedo Cat Press, 2020), and *My Brother, Romeo* (Tuxedo Cat Press, 2021). In addition, her short fiction has been published in a variety of magazines and journals, and several of her stories have won or placed literary contests.

You can find Jo Anne at pjburgh.com; on Facebook at P. Jo Anne Burgh, Author; and on Instagram at @pjoanneburgh. Information about her books and upcoming events can be found at tuxedocatpress.com.